Chapter 1
Cameron

"AM I ALIVE?" I tug at the bow tie collaring my shirt as candlelight wanes in the private room of the restaurant.

"For many, deep in their hearts." From the seat beside me, Brooklyn nods through a saccharine smile. Despite the innocent glint in my older sister's eyes, I'm certain she's fucking with me.

Dante scoffs, running his lacquered pointer finger over his glass of wine. "A figment of imagination lacks physical matter and consciousness, so it cannot be considered alive…" My brother, only a year younger than me, lifts one of his sharp cheekbones with a ghostly smile. "Now, if we're to contemplate—"

"Let's not." I cut him off. Dante's musings are endless.

"Boys, this is a friendly game of Who Am I?, remember?" Dad raises his whiskey tumbler while Mom, glued to his shoulder, plays with the lapel of his tuxedo.

The pair are the ultimate picture of love. Even after so many of these anniversary dinners, they look like two lovestruck teenagers.

"Doesn't matter to Cameron." Alec swirls his glass of amber liquid before splitting the seam of his grin and tossing the drink back. "Even the friendlies are critical. Aren't they, little brother?"

"Can we focus?" I rap my fist against the tablecloth littered with eight place settings. My siblings groan.

Teasing, jabbing, and occasional competitive combat—minus the excessive bloodshed—is my family's love language.

That, and games like these.

For as long as I can remember, from when we were six boisterous children to now, as fully grown adults—well, most of us —our gatherings have always ended in a game of my parents' choice. Corralling six intense, hot-blooded kids must have been a Herculean task, yet they never seemed flustered.

We are all record-breaking champions in our respective sports, but tonight, we're those kids again. Teeth bared and laughter trembling the crystal chandeliers overhead.

I've never loved anything more than I love the people at this table.

Well, except for football.

Football is the love of my life.

"Am I a fictional character?" I fumble with my bow tie again, feeling the suffocating grip of my tuxedo.

"Yes, and you only have three guesses left," Francesca roars from the other end of the room. She props her heels on the restaurant table, adjusting her long chestnut hair over the straps of her beaded gown.

"Francesca, must you be so…" Dante begins.

"You really want to have a go at me tonight?" My baby sister shoots him a wicked glare.

"Right, because we all know how well that went last time, Frankie," Ezra chimes into the brigade. Our youngest brother is right. If I don't end this, the pair of them will turn their verbal sparring into a wrestling match.

Tonight's game is my least favorite. Who Am I? The name leaves much to the imagination. I scratch the paper stuck to my

CLOSE KNIT

CLOSE KNIT

KELS & DENISE STONE

BETWEEN THE SHEETS
PUBLISHING

Published by Between the Sheets Publishing

kelsdenisestone.com

Copyright © 2024 Between the Sheets Publishing LLC

All rights reserved.

Paperback ISBN: 978-1-964675-97-8

Ebook ISBN: 979-8-9864169-6-0

Close Knit

Editing & Proofreading:

Caroline Acebo at Brass House LLC

Caroline Knecht

Christine Yates

Cover Design: Chloe Friedlein

To anyone who has felt that their softness was a penalty.

forehead, wanting to tear it off. We've been at this for hours, and I'm starved for some quiet.

I rack my brain through all the previous plays. Indiana Jones for Alec. Anna Karenina for Brooklyn. Daenerys Targaryen for Dante. Captain America for Ezra. Mulan for Frankie. That can only mean I got stuck with the gag.

"Do I have any resemblance to this character?" I ask.

Dante quirks an eyebrow. "Everywhere but the looks."

"Come to think of it, you were this particular shade of green last time we were yachting." Brooklyn nudges her elbow into me. My dinner somersaults in my gut at the reminder of our last boat outing four years ago, which I spent retching over the side of a railing while everyone enjoyed the coast of Monaco.

"Not fair." Frankie swings her legs off the table and stands, pointing her finger at Brooklyn. "She gave it away."

So, I'm green? I roll my eyes. "Am I the Hulk?"

"Less destructive." Alec shrugs. "More isolated. Same grimace."

The sooner I can figure this out, the sooner I can retire to my hotel room.

An isolated, grimacing, green fictional character.

"I'm fucking Shrek, aren't I?" I rip the paper from my head, confirming my guess. A pandemonium of laughter and shrieks spills out of them. If we weren't tucked away from the bustle of the main restaurant, people would be gawking at us. "Care to clarify exactly how I resemble an ogre?" I glare at Dante.

"In spirit," he taunts. "There are layers to you. You have a big heart, but you only let the world see your hard exterior."

Ignoring him, I massage the strain on my brow. "Mom, Dad, happy anniversary again, but I'm capped. I have that early flight, remember?"

"Come on, why don't you stay for a few more days?" Mom frowns but untangles from my father and walks over to me.

Selene Hastings commands a room. What else can be

expected from an all-star WNBA player who is now one of the most renowned basketball coaches in the world? In her five-inch heels, she's got two inches on my six-foot-three frame as she envelops me in a hug. "We can have Carlyle arrange for you to take the jet."

The last thing our family's manager needs is to be bothered with my schedule.

"Thank you, but I want to start training before the rest of the team."

A new season, a new contract, a new club. Going for the Premier League title is the most important thing in the world.

No distractions.

No more scandals.

She nods with an understanding we've all been taught to have. Sports come first. They're our life. "I know," she says. "Let's give our layered boy a proper send-off."

Chairs scrape as my siblings rush us from every side. Arms drape over shoulders and squeeze.

"Good luck this season, son. We'll be watching every game." Dad places one of his palms on the side of my head and presses his lips to my temple. "Don't be hasty." He recites our family motto.

"Love you, guys."

I break away to leave, but Brooklyn is on my heels. "I'll walk you out."

Here comes the same old talk. My sister may only be a year older than me, but her nurturing and fussing over each of us is all too predictable.

"Please, spare me."

She chuckles, her heels clattering down the stairs beside me. "Only if you stop acting like a stranger and start responding to texts. You've been distant for months. I miss the old Cam. We all do."

The old Cam. I can't be that guy again—the one from before

the scandal three months ago, or, if I'm honest, before I moved to London two years ago. I used to turn to my family for comfort, but I can't let them see how broken I've become.

"I miss you too, but after everything that happened..." I hesitate. "It's best that I stay off my phone."

"Understandable. Just know that I'm here for when you're ready to finally talk about it."

My molars grind against each other. "I don't need to—"

"Blah, blah, blah," Brooklyn interrupts and places her hands on my shoulders, digging in her pointed fingernails. "We all know you're a big-time footballer. One who's taken too many balls to the head to have any feelings. If you won't talk to me, or any of us, that's fine. You do need to talk to someone, though. Maybe you can make some new friends on this team? Or a friend who has nothing to do with football? You just can't keep things in. Especially after the livestream—"

"Enough with the pity. It's mortifying knowing you all saw me that way." My throat feels tight, but I force the words out.

"None of us pity you. We all have baggage," Brooklyn says. "Just the other day, the *Stone Times* sports section threw out the headline, 'Brooklyn Hastings Too Aged for the Upcoming Winter Olympics.' I'm twenty-eight, and they treat me as if I'm geriatric."

My family has always been public property to be dissected and discussed by the most circulated newspaper in the world. I suppose that's the sacrifice we made when we became famous. But why should loving sports come with so much criticism? And it's only gotten worse since I moved to England.

The tabloids have exhausted me, their relentless chatter like a mosquito in my ear. I underestimated how feral football fans and the media would be across the ocean. But it's my fault for not keeping my guard up. That won't happen this season.

"Someone really needs to give those fuck faces at *Stone Times* a piece of their mind."

"Agreed," she sighs. "But you can't let it get to you anymore."

"My number one priority is winning. I may have a real shot this year. I won't waste time on feelings or talking or whatever woo-woo nonsense you suggest to get over what's already in the past."

She rolls her catlike eyes at me and groans. Big demands from a two-time Olympic gold medalist figure skater who considers excellence at any cost a triumph, however much it may hurt her. We all have our secrets and lengths we're willing to go to for success.

"Overton sure did a number on you." The mention of my old football club presses on a bruise that's taking too long to heal. Brooklyn must see that truth on my face. "Try to pick up the phone every once in a while. We're here for you."

"Loud and clear." I brush her off, and her grip on my shoulders softens.

We hug one last time before I bullet out of the restaurant. The warm early July air hangs thick across the San Francisco streets.

My moment of peace is shattered by a bright flash stinging my irises.

Fuck.

Not this. Not now.

"I see someone!" a voice shouts. The camera flashes multiply. Strangers on the street slow in their tracks to view the ensuing circus. Phones shoot up. The crowd of paparazzi doubles like an ocean swell. "That's Cameron Hastings."

How did they even track us down? We took all the precautions. A waiter must have tipped them off. Heat rises in my veins. Blood sloshes in my ears.

Never mind. I need to get out of here. *Fast.*

The reporters' voices echo as I set off in the opposite direction of my hotel to shake them off my tail.

"How did you feel about your time as a free agent?"

"What will this season look like at Lyndhurst FC?"

"Do you still keep in touch with the team at Overton?"

"Any comments on Mal Kelly's appearance on *Lust Island*? When was the last time you spoke?"

"Have you taken any good showers lately, Hastings?"

The last question forces me to walk faster.

Pick up the pace, Hastings. You're pathetic. Coach Rossi's voice echoes in my mind as the familiar burn of bile rises in my throat.

The street in front of me blurs, and I'm somehow back on the pitch at Overton Stadium.

Do you even belong here? Fucking act like it.

My feet propel me forward.

Go harder. Faster! No wonder you're a fucking keeper, Hastings. You run like a little girl.

My pulse races. I push forward.

Be better, Hastings. Be better if you want to be a winner.

I was born to be a winner, which is why I force myself to run faster. The shouting voices taper off with every slam of my leather soles on the pavement. A few more turns down alleyways, and I slow my pace outside of my hotel.

No one is in sight. I catch my breath, pull my phone out of my tuxedo jacket, and text the family group chat.

CAMERON

Take the back entrance when leaving.

Once I'm ushered inside by the doorman, I'm met with a mob of reporters. The St. Claridge staff attempt to corral them out. I escaped the prying eyes at the Hastings estate in Mill Valley this past week. The hotel was meant to be a one-night respite before facing the potential privacy invasion back in London.

There's no way I can get upstairs without being seen. I slip into the dimly lit piano lounge off the lobby. Ambient light casts shadows on the elderly patrons who are being lulled to sleep by the soft strum of keys.

Ideal.

Walking backward, I keep my gaze on the entrance, heading for a secluded booth. I slip in, peeking over the high velour back.

"Are you on the run?" A melodic voice startles me.

I turn to discover that the booth is occupied by the embodiment of technicolor.

"Uh, sorry." Instinctually, I clamber out of my seat. *Fuck.* The commotion from the lobby crescendos, and every booth is occupied. "Actually." I clear my throat. "Can I sit here for a second?"

"If you answer my question."

I slither back into my seat like an eel returning to its cave. "Question?"

"Are you on the run? Better yet, are you undercover?"

My focus homes in on the person in front of me.

Vivid blue-green, round, and expressive eyes framed by long, dark lashes stare back at me. High cheekbones and a pointed chin. A fair complexion that glows even in the lusterless light of the room. Her lips are full, with the upper lip slightly thinner than the lower one. They curve into a warm, infectious, slightly crooked smile. Then there's her wavy, long hair, the color of a lavender field.

She's striking.

I swallow around a dry throat. She raises one of her full and well-defined brows at me.

"Something like that," I manage.

"I figured with the tuxedo and the sweat on your brow, you must be fleeing from something interesting." Her eyes remain fixed on me as she works two wooden knitting needles together in a fury. A yellow ball of yarn rests on the table next to her.

I finger the strands of my hair, slicking them back. A reservation encases my body.

I shouldn't be entertaining anyone.

The plan is to get upstairs and catch a few hours of sleep. Yet intrigue simmers in my chest.

Who is she? A thick sweater hangs off her shoulder, revealing strong collarbones above the rainbow hugging her torso.

"Yes to the fleeing. No to the something interesting," I clarify.

"Hmm." Her eyes scan me. Has she figured out who I am yet? "Well, in that case, we'll need code names."

We. An ease settles into me instead of the immediate fight-or-flight response I expect.

"Do you not know who I am?" The words sound bigheaded, but I can't let my guard down. However much it's itching to collapse.

"Not if you don't tell me your code name."

I guess she really doesn't know me. Or she's a phenomenal actress. Wouldn't be the first time I fell for that.

I nudge my head toward her. "You first."

"Duck."

"Huh?" Her needles tap together like the gentle rain that falls against my window on nights when my nightmares keep me awake. It's unnervingly soothing.

"Your turn."

I scan the room again. Should I make a run for it? Flashes catch the corner of my eyes, and I look back at her. "Goose?" I respond.

"Are you asking or telling me?" The stranger stops knitting and reaches for the drink beside her, sliding it closer and wrapping her lips around the straw. Her gaze remains fixed on me as she sips.

A chuckle clips out of my chest. The release of warmth in my stomach feels foreign. Against every rationality, I'm compelled to indulge in this small game. I straighten and extend my hand out to her. "It's Goose. Goose Featherington."

"I like that." The grip of her small hand is firm yet gentle. We shake for longer than reasonable for two strangers on a no-name basis, and she's the first to pull away.

"Do you do this sort of thing often?" I ask.

"Attract handsome men on the run?"

The compliment forces a grin to my lips. "Handsome?"

"Please don't tell me you're one of those guys who lives in a parallel universe with no mirrors and pretends to be oblivious about what their face looks like." Another curled brow. Another spill of warmth into my gut.

"Well, thanks? I guess," I say because it's been so long since a stranger has complimented me. "I meant to ask if you frequently do whatever it is you're doing in…what looks like a place my grandparents would frequent?"

Dimples appear on her cheeks. "Your grandparents must have great taste. Mine only taught me how to give epic foot rubs."

My eyes narrow with curiosity. "Foot rubs?"

"Every time I'd visit my nana, she would crack open her rose lotion and sit by the television, putting these hands to work." She shakes her fingers at me. "Maybe that was TMI?"

"My grandparents used to take me to places just like this on Valentine's Day." I chuckle at the memory.

"That's adorable." Her hands cross over her chest.

"Pops always told me to treat a woman right. He taught me how to behave on dates: open car doors, use the right silverware, and always order dessert, even if I don't want it."

"Seems like a smart man." She laughs. "But tell me, are we on a date?"

"I wouldn't bring a first date to a place like this," I admit. Though I haven't brought a first date to anything recently. There haven't been any firsts for some time.

"Has anyone told you that you're a little judgmental?" She playfully kicks my shin. A tingling sensation spreads from my leg through the rest of my body.

The rush of escaping the paparazzi has left my defenses weak. "You're right. I'm sorry. I expected to spend the rest of my night alone, not befriending a beautiful companion."

"Well, now you don't have to be alone." A blush dances across her cheeks, and I let my guards stay down. Maybe the night doesn't have to end so soon. Especially since I'm speaking to someone who doesn't know who I am.

To this woman, I'm not tabloid fodder.

In her gorgeous eyes, I'm a man in a tuxedo named Goose. However ridiculous that sounds.

"You're not what I expected," I admit.

"Do you place a lot of expectations on invisible girls you interrupt in bars?" She takes another sip of her drink. I can't stop staring as she purses her plush lips together and sucks.

"You're hardly invisible." I lean forward. "That purple hair, your bright sweater, and those lips…if I were going to interrupt anyone's evening, you would be my first and only choice."

Her pupils dilate, and she bites her lip, sitting up and putting her knitting project to the side. She sets her elbows on the table, chin to her palms, and leans in close. "Are you flirting with me, Mr. Featherington?"

I am. For whatever careless reason.

Of course, I can't fully trust her, but maybe for one night I could try to let go. One night before buckling down and keeping my head in the game for the season. Besides, I can't get up and leave with the paparazzi still swarming.

"You really don't know who I am?"

Her laugh is as melodic as her voice. "Now you're making me nervous."

"Don't be. But you still haven't answered my question." I inch my hand closer to her arm, hesitating as my finger hovers near the bunched-up sleeve of her sweater. "Do you do this kind of thing often?"

"I come here because the music helps me unwind, and my sister works nearby." She pauses, shock splattering her face. "Oops, I'm not great at this whole 'no personal info' thing. Just forget I said 'sister' and pretend I said..." She thinks for a second before giving me a toothy smile. "My *handler*. You know, like an agent handler."

"My *handlers* are also in the vicinity," I say, playing into her game.

"Guess fate brought us together tonight." Fate, indeed. "Why don't you stay a little while?"

"Are you sure?"

"Yeah. And since we're in a place that calms my nerves, you can tell me what calms you."

I want to explain that a few months ago, through last year's season, an encounter like this would have been how I dealt with a loss. When Overton's hazing didn't let up and Coach Rossi would shred my every vulnerability to pieces, getting wrapped up in someone like her would have been the exact remedy I needed.

A distraction.

An impossibility this year. But right now...

The smell of vanilla lingers on her skin. Sweet and overpowering. I swallow and let my rough, scarred hands run over her colorful sweater before picking up the yarn on the table.

"You could say I like to play with balls," I tease, tossing the ball of yarn up a few times.

The sultry look in her eyes snaps, and she breaks out into a fit of giggles. "What about sticks?" She slowly strokes the wood of one of her knitting needles. The absurd motion causes my cock to twitch.

Fucking hell. Who on earth is this bundle of color and

smiles? Is she this bubbly and quick-witted when she's unraveled? What could that even look like?

"There's one I'm well acquainted with."

"Anyone else acquainted with your stick?"

"Nope. No yarn attached."

"You can't just throw out knitting jokes." She sighs emphatically.

"Why not? They make you all hot in that sweater?" I shoot her a wink.

Her tongue slides over the seam of her full lower lip. "Yes."

"Is it really doing it for you?"

"It's a good start," she teases.

"Good start? Never had someone turn me down so harshly."

"What a big ego. All you've brought to this table is a good code name and your love of playing with balls. Well, and that wink, which was so fucking hot. I'm sorry," she says, as if attempting to hold herself back. But she keeps going. "There's no point in pretending this brooding look of yours doesn't make the whole pond honk."

The warm rumble in my chest spills past my throat and into a hearty laugh. "You're very forward."

Her eyes widen, and her chest deflates. "Too forward? Am I making you uncomfortable?"

"No, not at all. I like it." She doesn't feel like a mystery I have to solve. No grand game to play. It's easy speaking with her, as if I'll always know where I stand with this lady named Duck. "I like you."

"To be fully transparent, I'm not normally this forward. I'm trying out something new in my life."

"What's that?" I itch to be closer to her.

"I'm doing a Yes Year. The name is self-explanatory, but the essence is to say the things I feel and open myself up to more adventure. Like we're having right now."

"I doubt you'd want anything to do with my kind of adventure."

Her eyes scan my face. She must see the brief dive in my mood, but she doesn't pry. "Why don't you order a drink and tell me about it? Or you can come up with some more knitting jokes, but I promise you, Goose, I've heard them all."

A no-expectations encounter with a beautiful stranger who is clueless about my identity. It's new. Intriguing. And it's the first time in months that my mind has been quiet.

"What are you having?"

She slides her drink over. "Try it. It's a vanilla shake."

I pause. "I don't really do sugar."

Those expressive brows shoot up on her face. "You don't *do* sugar? Who hurt you?"

"I'm strict with my diet."

"Right. Only stems, seeds, and leaves of grass for you."

Another laugh from me. Another dazzling smile from her. I skip the drink but take up her offer to stay.

Time slips around us as we continue our verbal foreplay. We share more funny stories about each other's grandparents. What music we like to listen to—every genre for her and high-BPM records for me. Our favorite parts of San Francisco—a spring day at the Conservatory of Flowers for her and a foggy morning at Point Bonita Lighthouse for me. When our laughter gets too loud, I slide into the seat on her side of the booth. We find reasons to touch—she playfully ruffles my hair when I admit that I have to make an effort to style it this way. I finger the collar of her sweater to inspect it, pretending to have any idea what she's talking about as she names each stitch. She runs the pad of her thumb over the small gold hoop in my ear. I hold my palms over hers when she attempts to show me how to use her knitting needles.

We're polar opposites.

Our worlds could never collide, but the spark between us could win a championship trophy.

A waiter interrupts our conspiratorial giddiness. "Hey, you two, we're closing."

For the first time in hours, I look up. We're the only people left in the bar. The musicians are gone, and the lobby is empty. Our night can't be over. Staying drunk on her is how I'd like to spend my last hours in San Francisco.

One last distraction.

"Why don't I walk you home?" she asks, gathering all of her things into her bag as I slide out of the booth and straighten the wrinkles out of my tux.

"I think that's my line."

She rolls her eyes playfully. "Don't be so antiquated."

"Sure, I'd love that." She reaches into her bag, revealing her yellow phone case. I stiffen. "Uh—what are you doing?"

"Texting my handler," she says, as if it's obvious. "Wouldn't want them to think I'm MIA."

"Right." I laugh. *Calm down, Cameron.* I'm acting like a spooked dog over a cell phone.

When she finishes her text, I help her out of the booth. Once she's standing in front of me, our height difference is obvious. She's about as tall as my baby sister. Five-six, five-seven? A whole head shorter than me. I scan her body and find her sweater swallowing her whole. No hint of her figure beneath the knit. But her legs, I linger on those for far too long. Elongated thighs that look soft to the touch. Jewelry hangs off one of her ankles and calls to the animalistic urge in me to run my teeth over the colorful chain.

"You're all sweater and legs."

"And you're ogling me."

"How could I not?"

When we enter the lobby, I loop her fingers into mine and tug her toward me. "Actually, I'm right upstairs."

"At the hotel?"

I nod. "I leave in the morning."

"Oh." A beat of hesitation passes over her face before she takes a step forward and follows me to the elevator bank.

I jab the call button, hoping the elevator takes its sweet time so I can steal a few more moments with her. Instead, the car right next to us opens immediately. Of course, it does. *It's too soon to say goodbye.* Holding onto her hand, I step into the elevator and press a bunch of random floor buttons before stepping out. It chimes and takes off. "I guess I'll have to get the next one."

She giggles, locking eyes with me. Neither of us dares to break this moment. We're teetering on the edge of a cliff. My thumb traces along the inside of her palm.

I should let her go, but then, without warning, she blurts out, "I'm going to kiss you."

"No one's ever announced it like that before."

"Too much?"

"Not at all."

Her eyelashes flutter closed as she tiptoes upward. I lean in, letting my hand anchor around her back. I memorize her hot breath trailing along my jaw. And then her lips are on mine. Sweetness explodes on my tongue, shattering my self-control.

I crave her, deeply, intensely. Even just for tonight. Her body presses into mine, and I groan. This is selfish, risky, and perhaps even wrong, but there's no time to mull over the consequences. I need to find out if her moans are as colorful and addictive as she's been tonight.

Just like our handshake, she's the first to pull away. Her pupils are hazy and dilated, like she's as drunk on me as I am on her.

"Maybe, instead of calling it a night, we could head upstairs," she says, a mischievous smirk playing on her lips. "And I can show you the seams of my sweater."

I raise an eyebrow, both amused and intrigued. "The seams of your sweater?"

"Absolutely." She leans in closer, her body pressing into mine. "You see, I'd need to take it off to properly demonstrate the craftsmanship," she says, her voice low and teasing.

"Your logic is flawless." My fingers find the hem of her sleeve, the fabric soft beneath my touch.

"I'm nothing if not thorough."

My throat tightens. One night. Nothing more, nothing less.

"Then let's not waste any time."

Chapter 2
Daphne

HOLY FREAKING BANANAS! What have I done?

Some people are yanked into this world with the confidence of gods. My older sister, Juniper, is one of those people. Dazzling, brilliant, and with so much self-esteem, you could use it to power a rocket ship.

The rest are like me, an extra-special brand of fake-it-till-you-make-it, whose every decision is thoroughly considered and digested until the cringe-inducing reel is on replay in my mind.

It was fun to pretend to be the former tonight, but now I'm in a hotel bathroom with a man whose name I don't even know.

Am I really about to have my first one-night stand?

It's only been two days since I committed to my Yes Year on my twenty-sixth birthday—an entire year dedicated to stepping out of my comfort zone. I wished for adventure, and now it's being served to me on a giant, hunky man platter, complete with an ear piercing.

Happy freaking birthday, Daphne!

I pinch my inner arm. Ouch.

Okay, not a dream.

Behind me, workout clothes hang off the door. I grab a tissue from the sink, wipe away remnants of mascara from under my eyes, and run my fingers through my hip-length lilac hair. The hotel lighting is harsh, making me look ghostly pale. Maybe dying my hair yesterday was a mistake.

Screw this! No more negative thoughts. I want this. I want him, and I can do this.

"You are a hot, charming, and delightful woman," I whisper into the mirror and throw up my arms. *Make yourself big for a boost of confidence!* My therapist's voice echoes in my head as I stretch onto my tiptoes. "You are going to go out there and have the best sex of your life!"

Or, at the very least, nice sex.

I slip out of my Mary Janes and miniskirt. Goose was right; I do look like a sweater with legs. But he didn't seem to mind. He spent the whole night staring at my lips, finding any excuse to touch me. I adjust the collar of my sweater off my shoulder, hoping to give it more of a boudoir-shoot vibe than a casual-frock look.

When I return to the room, he's staring out the window at the Golden Gate Bridge, San Francisco sprawling beautifully below from the fortieth floor of this one-bedroom suite. I hadn't realized how high we were, having spent the entire elevator ride up with our lips locked together. His tuxedo jacket is draped over a chair in the corner of the room. There are no personal belongings in sight besides the workout clothes in the bathroom and a small rollaway carry-on by the closet.

"Hi," I say, and he turns.

Even in the darkness, his stark features steal the breath from my lungs. A well-defined, square jawline hidden beneath unkempt scruff that hasn't fully filled in on his face. A sun-touched glow on his olive-toned skin. It seems he spends a lot of time outdoors. Thick and slightly arched brows sit above his deep-set eyes, which are an intense golden brown.

"Fuck." He splits the word in half before tugging off his bow tie and tossing it onto the bed.

"Did you mean Duck?" I giggle, attempting to cover up the blush stinging my cheeks with a smile.

"Look at you." The low light from the nightstand lamp covers his face in shadows as he strolls over to me. He props one arm against the wall behind me, and his muscles ripple beneath the white fabric of his shirt. Those arms could probably crush my skull in half, and I'd thank him for it.

I nervously wrap my finger into the hem of my sweater. "I have to be honest; I actually haven't done something like this before."

"Are you…is this your first—"

"Oh no," I clarify. "I've had sex plenty of times before. Many times. Lots of sex!" My voice roller coasters up. "Okay, maybe 'plenty' isn't so accurate, but I know what I'm doing. I just…"

He caresses my cheek and uses his thumb to lift my chin. My neck has to tilt all the way back to meet his gaze. He's tall and commanding. There's a skew in his strong nose that I hadn't noticed earlier, as though it's been broken before. I wonder how that came to be. Everything about his gruff appearance is endearing, albeit frightening.

"Are you nervous? We don't have to do anything you're not comfortable with."

"I am nervous," I admit. "But I want to do *this* very much. What I'm trying to say is that I don't want to be, um, *disappointed?* I mean, it would be great if we could both feel satisfied."

The escalating heat between my legs makes me certain that finishing isn't far off on the horizon, but my fluoxetine and self-sabotaging thoughts have been known to make intimate moments a struggle.

My college boyfriend, the first and only, always felt frustrated with how long it took to get me there. Which turned into a terrible cycle of faking it to cushion his ego.

Not tonight.

If I'm knocking on heaven's gate, I want the god in front of me to carry me there and thrust me over the threshold.

He throws on a nefarious smirk and leans closer, his breath on my lips. "Don't worry, all your feathers will be ruffled appropriately."

"Thank you," I whisper and rest my hand against his pecs. Pure muscle beneath his button-down. "You're very..." I swallow. "Firm."

He cocks a brow at me. "And you smell delicious."

We kiss again, but my kneecaps still turn to Silly Putty when he breaks the seam of my lips with his tongue and groans. He actually groans into my mouth.

My fingers rush through his slicked-back brown hair. I tug at his nape as our kiss deepens. The coarse scruff on his jaw scrapes against my skin as he travels down my neck. His lips clasp around the edge of my collarbone, and he sucks until releasing with a loud pop.

All right, if I was turned on before, this brought out a whole new level of euphoria.

"I really like that," I moan as he pulls my sweater aside and kisses along my sternum. "And that...oh, and that, very, very much."

He looks up at me, still crouched down. "Keep telling me what you're thinking," he says. "It's turning me on."

Yeah, I'm officially being hurled out of my comfort zone. Screw it.

He plucks me up as if I weigh nothing and sets me on the bed. I fall on my backside, keeping my upper half propped up on my forearms. He climbs above me like an animal playing with its food.

I arch my back and press my breasts toward him. "Kiss me

more, but here." I nudge my nose to my chest. He helps me out of my sweater, minding it with gentleness as he drapes it over the nightstand. The act is small and likely meaningless, but each of my vertebrae melts.

"The seams of your sweater were definitely worth seeing," he says, smirking. I'm left in my underwear, while he remains fully dressed.

"It's called a mattress stitch."

"*Mattress*, huh? Who knew knitting could be so sexual." Flames dance in his eyes as he clasps his mouth over the lace bralette covering my nipple. My skin pebbles.

"Oh gosh, you're exceptional at that."

He chuckles and continues to cup, tug, and massage every inch of my body until my nerves dissipate. Teeth against my jaw. Tongue tracing my pulse. Unmatched to anything I've ever felt before.

When he's had his fill, he navigates to the foot of the bed, moving with the litheness of a panther. He hovers above me. His golden-brown gaze consumes me. "Fucking look at you," he groans desperately.

I do as he says, running my own eyes over my long legs, which I always felt were too dimpled and plump, my soft belly, and my C-cup breasts, which are far fuller at the bottom than they are at the top unless I squeeze them into a push-up bra. But every part of me shines a little differently under his attention.

He bites his knuckle.

"Are you going to keep staring?" I attempt a seductive voice.

"All night." He winks again and gestures to my knees. "Open up."

I break into a laugh, and he does too, but it doesn't last long before his hands wrap around my ankles, tugging me down to the edge of the mattress.

"All right, Goose. Feathers are really starting to ruffle now."

"Oh, are they?" He lowers to his knees.

"Certainly." I shuffle closer and dig my heels into the mattress. He begins unbuttoning his shirt, but I clasp my hand over his. "Can you leave that on?" He kisses the back of my hand. The affectionate gesture makes me melt. "And roll up your sleeves?"

Another heavy laugh. "Anything the lady wants, she gets."

All right, this Yes Year is complete. There's no topping this.

He obliges me and extends his arm. Slowly, he unbuttons his cuffs, keeping his eyes on me as he deftly folds the fabric of each sleeve. My mouth waters at each deliberate motion. His corded forearms are robust and sinewy, hardened from what must be years of intense labor. His skin is taut, bearing marks—scratches and bruises that surely have their own stories.

"Close your mouth, sweet girl. You're drooling," he teases. He holsters his palms under my knees, tossing them over his shoulders. I whoop with surprise and fall flat onto my back. "Or don't. I do enjoy listening to you talk."

"You're bossy. I like it."

His scruff tickles my inner thighs. One of his hands slides beneath my ass. The other teases the waistband of my panties.

"These are cute," he says against my skin. "Can I rip them off of you and have a taste?"

Oh, fuck, that was so hot. "Rip them off?"

"It's a yes-or-no question."

"Yes, please." I seal my fate. He spins his finger through the lace. A quick sting and the sound of fabric tearing ripples through the room. "Okay, you didn't *actually* just do that. You ripped off my panties?! I could've sworn that was something people just did in the movies."

His smirk is cocky and irresistible. "You wanted an unforgettable experience."

"My god," I say, bemused. A drop-dead gorgeous man with an ear piercing is about to go down on me. I inhale deeply and nod at him, indicating for him to continue.

He doesn't hesitate; his tongue laps at the heat collecting at my center. It's like lightning strikes my chest, stealing my breath in a gasp.

"Fuck," he grunts against me. "You could drown a man between these thighs."

Between my shock and a crescendo of moans, he guides my hand into his hair. I grip the strands, drawing him nearer. My hips match his rhythm. Until the room shakes, or I do. Orange and red hues speckle the edges of my vision, and instead of resisting them, I follow them through a rainbow of spinning pleasure. My mind bursts like fireworks as an orgasm—an actual, man-made orgasm—releases from the base of my spine and corrupts me. I'm alive, so very alive.

He crawls toward me and collapses heavily by my side. He tips his nose to mine and plants a small kiss there. "How was that?"

"Mind-blowing." I half laugh, half sigh. I slither my hand between our bodies and begin undoing the buttons of his shirt, revealing his six-pack. When the last button slips off, he helps me push the shirt off his body before I undo his belt buckle and he stands, shucking off his trousers.

Adonis stands before me. Well-defined abs. Thighs the size of both of my legs combined. My gaze slides down his body, landing on his boxer briefs. My mouth drops open at the outline of his length.

"You ready?"

"Oh, no, I may have to tap out for the rest of the evening," I blurt. "Your penis is going to impale me."

He rubs his palm into the back of his head, looking down at the third leg taking up space between us, and says with a boyish grin, "I think we can make it fit."

"The word you were trying to use was 'hope,' mister. *Hope* we can make it fit."

"I'm going to grab a condom, and we can put all of that hope to good use."

He comes back sans boxers, and I rapidly blink, taking him in. It's huge. I mean, it's the biggest I've ever seen. "The penis has grown!"

"The flattery is appreciated, but maybe you can give my cock a nickname or something instead of calling it by the medical term?"

Heat flares beneath my skin at that term. "Is it killing the mood?"

"Surprisingly not." He drags the foil in his fingers to his teeth and rips open the condom wrapper. "Nothing could make me want you less right now."

"Wait," I say, reaching to brush his hand away. "I'm feeling lucky. I want to try and put your cock in my mouth." The words are foreign in my mouth, but I revel that his length seems to grow. "You know, if that's okay with you."

"Come again?"

"Your cock."

The corner of his lip lifts, and he steps closer. "Such a filthy word from such a pretty mouth."

"Cock." I say it again as if I'm learning a new language.

"So fucking sexy."

I'll take that as an invitation. I kneel on the mattress and brace one hand on his toned thigh, the other carefully holding on to him. Despite the fact that this sex god has obviously been in this position before, I go for it, no longer faking it till I make it, because he clearly likes everything I've done so far. I grasp him and lick from base to tip, savoring his warmth, the path of his veins against my tongue before I open my mouth as wide as it can go and lower myself onto him.

Tears pinch my eyes, but he doesn't move, doesn't grab at me or push himself further in. He brushes my hair out of my face and places the possessive weight of his hand on the back of my neck as I adjust to him.

"Fuck, sweet girl," he whispers. The praise ignites my will to keep going. "You can make it hurt too." I oblige, scraping my teeth against the length of him. His hand clasps around his cock, falling into a steady pattern that I match. "That's right. So right. You're doing so good."

We work into a rhythm together, with his cock hitting the back of my throat, until time whispers past us. I feel powerful and beautiful and sexy having this bit of control over him. Caring for him the way he cared for me. His eyes are rolled back as he doles out encouragement through labored breaths. My mind hums with pleasure when he finally releases his hold on me, withdrawing and kneeling in front of me to seal my lips with a kiss.

"I can't wait for you any longer."

"Me either," I gasp as he stands and lifts me up with him. The faint glow of stars glimmers across the window, casting a low light upon the bed.

He rolls down the condom with one hand before removing my bralette and positioning himself at the edge of the bed.

"Sit," he says.

"On you?"

"Now." His shadowy gaze begs beneath his thick lashes. I hold on to his shoulders and settle both of my knees on the bed, feet dangling off the mattress. He supports me by the waist as I lower myself onto him with an agonizing slowness. The piercing sting of pleasure burns through me as we both adjust to each other. My lungs forget to work with every inch of him. "Fuck," he groans into my jaw and then presses his brow to mine. "Breathe, sweet girl."

"I'm trying," I groan.

"Follow me." He locks our hands and inhales deeply. I mimic

him, falling into sync. The fullness of him inside me is bliss. My hips work slowly over his length. My lips at his forehead, his head in between my breasts, our arms bound around each other. It's so intimate. We find a rhythm that flows perfectly between us. I've only experienced such deep absorption when I'm hours into an audiobook that's tearing my heart apart, my hands immersed in an unbreakable project. It's consuming and overwhelming, yet what's happening to my body is entirely new. My senses sizzle as another wave of need builds. We're either fucking or making love, I have no idea. All I know is that it's perfect.

"Just like that, yeah? Just like that," he says against my lips and tugs me in closer. Our bodies are crushed together by his grip.

Sparks flicker behind my eyelids.

"You're making me see stars," I choke out.

"Is that what you want?"

"Yes, yes," I moan. "Yes."

"Then hold on." The gold of his eyes is swallowed whole by inky blackness.

Instinctually, I hold on to him. Gravity seems to fail, and I'm floating.

"Oh my," I gasp as he moves us to the other side of the room, still inside me. "What are you doing?"

"Bringing you to the stars," he says, as if it were obvious.

My back collides with the cold window as his hands grasp my ass and thighs. I stare at him, bewildered and even more turned on. He rocks himself into me. This time, he's not kind about it. This time, I'm certain we're fucking. And I'm certain that I love it.

"God, you're so good at this." At my words, he kisses up my neck, opens his teeth against my jaw, and captures each of my throaty breaths.

"Together, okay?" he demands. As if he knows I'm on the

brink and about to lose my every last shred of sanity. "Show me how good I make this pussy feel."

"Yeah." I bob my head. "Together."

And as if on his willing command, a few deep thrusts into my core, our release is simultaneous. His knees almost buckle beneath him as he roars with me, but he doesn't let me go until the pounding in my ears and the racing of my heart subside. As if he knows when I'm ready because he's there with me in a different realm.

He carries me to the bed, setting me down gently before his heavy body indents the mattress beside me. "Thank you for this," he whispers in my ear before placing his lips on the corner of my jaw. "I know it may be hard to believe, but I haven't let go and had this much fun in a while. My work—I don't get that many opportunities to relax with someone."

Our noses brush. The man who spent all night teasing me and laughing at my bad jokes reappears. His features soften.

I study the map of lines and wrinkles on his face. The crook in his handsome nose. A scar above his brow.

Who takes care of him in his real life? He mentioned his handlers, who could be friends or family, but if he's leaving, are they around that often?

"I'm the one who should be thanking you for making this the most special first one-night stand I've ever had."

With that, he dashes off to the bathroom and closes the door. The sound of a shower turning on seeps into the room. A tingling sparks up in my chest. Suddenly, the sober reality of being alone in a room after such a mind-blowing experience sets in. I yawn, checking the clock. Four o'clock in the morning.

When was his flight again? The details blur in my brain like a smudged chalkboard. Am I supposed to leave? I have no idea. I drag the duvet over myself, looking around the space. A twinge of longing pools in my heart, shattering the fantasy world I've lived in for the past few hours.

Go away. We were both clear about what we wanted. I orchestrated this whole escapade. It was a one-night stand, nothing more. Yet a sinking weight persists in my chest.

The bathroom door swings open, sending a flood of light into the room that hits me like a cold splash of water. He strides in, already dressed in black sweats and a matching tee, a towel extended in my direction. "Here," he says. "The shower is heating up for you, if you want it. I'll give you some space. But thanks again for tonight. It was...a pleasant surprise." His eyes are kind, but embarrassment creeps up my cheeks as I take the towel from him.

"Right." *Buck up. Two earth-shattering orgasms, and now you're considering getting "Goose" tattooed on your heart.* It wasn't fireworks and shooting stars for him like it was for me. And that's okay. I'm okay.

Stop being such a lover girl.

"The water should be warm by now." He smiles.

"Good," I reply, mentally face-palming at my lack of eloquence. "I mean, thank you. I had a nice time with you."

"Me too." He hesitates, as if considering how we should close out the night, but I collect my dignity and wrap myself in the towel before strutting off to the bathroom. A quick rinse, and I'll call myself a car home. One-night stand accomplished.

The bathroom door clicks closed, and I climb under the hot stream. An odd sense of emptiness creeps in—a lonely feeling of something unfulfilled.

Chapter 3
Daphne

"WHERE HAVE YOU BEEN?" Juniper answers on the first ring as I stare out the taxi window.

"Hellooooo," I sing. It's almost 5:00 a.m. My sister usually rolls in around this time. "I'm on my way home. Are you there already?"

"No, got tapped to work a double today," she says. I glance at the cab driver, who's focused on the road. "So, where are you?"

"I had a one-night stand!" I whisper into the phone.

"I figured from your *sleeping elsewhere, am safe, cucumber emoji* text message."

"Damn, I was sure I sent the eggplant!"

She giggles. "Spill. Did the geriatric pianist finally put the moves on you?"

My sister and I have been going to the St. Claridge Hotel piano bar since she started working the graveyard shift at UCSF Medical Center. It's our weekly tradition to get two shakes before she goes to work. I usually stay for an hour or two after she leaves, but no one has ever talked to me, except the occasional person asking me what I'm knitting.

"Thomas is a very polite gentleman, and he would never act indecently toward a lady," I tease.

"Oh, come on," she groans. "Give me more."

"You won't believe it, but I had two orgasms. One against a window! I thought I was going to have to call you to instruct my one-night stand on resuscitation." I clasp my hand over my mouth before relaxing. This cab driver has probably seen and heard worse.

Once I got out of the shower and was waiting for my ride, Goose was gone. My curious fingers snooped around the hotel room and found it scrubbed of any clues as to my mystery man's identity. Apart from his smell in my hair, it was as if he were a ghost.

"What was his name?"

"I have no idea, the whole thing felt so adventurous—"

"What do you mean?" she gasps, and I sigh, ready for her protector speech. "What if he was a murderer? A criminal? A white-collar crime is still a crime!"

Oh no. It would be just my luck to hook up with a crooked politician or oil billionaire's son.

"Okay, big sis, I need my friend right now. Not my bodyguard."

She's quiet, which means she's either screaming internally or she's fallen asleep. Neither would surprise me. "Fine." I practically hear her teeth clenching. "But did you use protection? Did you pee after?"

"Yes and no. Should I have? Am I going to die? I honestly don't think I could feel my vagina after what his *thing* did to me."

"No, you won't die, but we wouldn't want the high from your Yes Year to come crashing down because of a UTI. We'd hate for your groin to be screaming for help all the way from the UK."

That's right, the last thing my move to London in a month

needs is a UTI. I've been planning this adventure for months, and now it's just a matter of hopping on a plane. I've packed all my knitting and filming gear, mapped out a new schedule for my YouTube videos, and luckily I've been to London before—no tourist traps for me. Dual citizenship for the win! With my YouTube streaming revenue and pattern income saved up, I'm feeling pretty prepared. Especially since my apartment is rent-free.

My mom, Prim, bought the apartment back when she was a young artist in London. She was born there, and it was originally artist housing, but now most of the units have been gobbled up by some private company. No biggie, though! We kept it because Prim, being the stubborn woman she is, refused to sell and let go of all those memories. The other tenants are supposed to be really nice, though we have no idea who they are.

"Noted for next time, Dr. Quinn."

"So you really didn't get his name?"

"He called himself Goose all night, but it doesn't matter. I'll never see him again. He had a flight this morning, and I have no idea as to where."

His question rings in my ears. *Do you really not know who I am?* I thought it was all part of his persona, but maybe our evening of secrets gave him a privacy he hadn't had before.

"Who does he think you are?" Juni startles me out of my daydream.

"Duck."

"Goose and Duck?"

I shrug. "That's the only name I could think of."

"You know nothing about this stranger, and yet you gave up our family's nickname for you?"

"I didn't think it through, okay? I wanted to try and not let the little voices of doubt make me believe all the lies about how a girl like me would never have an adventure like I did," I admit, feeling small. "I'm trying something new, Juni. I want to figure it out myself."

"You're right. The only thing that matters is that you were safe and that you had fun."

When I was a kid, Juni appointed herself as my first line of defense. Middle and high school weren't easy for me, both socially and emotionally. Fitting in when you're born to stand out isn't a concept kids grasp while navigating puberty and pool party invitations.

My sister and our moms became vigilant protectors, driving me to therapy twice a week and ensuring I made the best of my teenage years. I'm forever in their debt for that. Now, as a functioning adult—who, yes, still lives with her sister and lacks dental insurance or a 401k—I hoped Juni would ease up on her big sister duties, but she never has.

It's another reason this Yes Year is the most important thing in my life. I need to prove to myself and to my family that I'm not afraid of the big world out there and that I want to carve out a bigger place for myself in it.

"If my one-night stand is any indication of how my Yes Year will go, then I'm looking forward to it."

"However potentially illegal that hookup was, I'm happy for you."

My phone buzzes with a notification.

10:00 a.m. Video Interview - Stone Times x Influencer Daphne Quinn (@wooly.duck)

"Crap! Juni, how could I forget? My interview is today." That leaves me only a few hours to catch a nap and prep for what might be one of the most exciting moments of my knitting influencer career.

"With the *Stone Times*?"

"I'm freaking out!"

"Don't. If you survived the impaling, this will be a piece of cake. Just be yourself, and they'll love you."

Just be yourself, and they'll love you. I repeat the words on a loop before exiting the taxi and rushing up the stairs to our apartment.

I can do this. I can do anything.

———

LIV PARKER: Hi, Daphne, or as some of our readers may know you, Wooly Duck. I am so excited to speak with you today about your charitable work for the UCSF Medical Center.

DAPHNE QUINN: Thank you for having me. I have to be honest, this is my first interview with a real newspaper, so I'm a little nervous.

LIV PARKER: Let's start with the basics. Tell me about yourself. Where does influencer Daphne Quinn come from?

DAPHNE QUINN: I grew up in Santa Cruz, in a cozy beach bungalow with my sister, Juniper, and my moms, Prim and Dani. Prim is a wedding portrait painter from London, and Dani is an accountant from San Francisco, making our household a mix of artistry and practicality. Some of my fondest childhood memories are of digging up outrageous eighties and nineties pieces from my parents' closets. I was the odd kid covered in glitter, trying to make bedazzled Uggs happen. Spoiler: they didn't, even when I tried again in college at the Academy of Arts in San Francisco.

LIV PARKER: Clearly, a lot of that influence has carried over into your knitting. But I'd love to know when the hobby began.

. . .

DAPHNE QUINN: I started knitting in middle school. Being a tween or a teenager wasn't easy for me. I was relentlessly bullied, and the way I coped with that led to my generalized anxiety disorder diagnosis. I tried various coping mechanisms, like painting, swimming, and juggling, but nothing clicked until I saw an older gentleman knitting on a bench at the Santa Cruz Boardwalk. That same day, I asked my mom to take me to the yarn store. The rest is history. I still visit that bench whenever I'm in town; the sunsets are gorgeous.

LIV PARKER: You speak about your mental health so openly, I can see how you've managed to gain over a hundred thousand followers and build such a tightly woven community online.

DAPHNE QUINN: Thank you. Knitting gives me a sense of control. In knitting, you can make all the mistakes you want, and you get to undo them. Where else can you do that in real life? Plus, I get to focus all of my energy on creating something beautiful that has a purpose. When I'm knitting, it's one of the few times my mind is free of any worries or concerns. Just me and my needles.

LIV PARKER: So, how did you start your page, Wooly Duck? What made you want to take a comforting hobby and turn it into a career?

DAPHNE QUINN: I started Wooly Duck in college, when one of my professors asked for the pattern of a midi dress I made out of upcycled yarn. She insisted that others would want to re-create my dress, and it all took off from there.

· · ·

Liv Parker: When did your charitable projects begin?

Daphne Quinn: My sister works at UCSF, and the hospital was looking for donations for the cancer center, to comfort patients and their families. Instantly, I knew that I had to get to work. The beanie pattern I used is beginner-friendly and available for free on my Instagram page. The pattern made it simple for me to get the project done rather quickly.

Liv Parker: You're telling me you knitted one thousand beanies all by yourself?

Daphne Quinn: Yes! Most of them I made during knitathons with my community online.

Liv Parker: Have you always used your knitting needles for good?

Daphne Quinn: No, but moving forward, I want to. The project was meaningful, and getting to make that kind of impact is something I want to pursue in the future. One day, I'd love to run a knitting retreat where people who have dealt with mental health struggles like me can find community through knitting.

Liv Parker: Sounds like you've got it all planned out.

Daphne Quinn: Totally.

.   .   .

LIV PARKER: So, what's next for Daphne Quinn?

DAPHNE QUINN: At the moment, I'm doing this thing called a Yes Year, which started on my twenty-sixth birthday two days ago, June twenty-ninth. My first order of business is moving to London at the beginning of August.

LIV PARKER: Yes Year? Say more.

DAPHNE QUINN: My work, as fulfilling as it is, requires that I spend a lot of time at home, or deeply homed in on what my fingers are doing. I want to break out of my comfort zone and say yes to anything that'll set me up for adventure. My family has an apartment in London, so it's not completely new, but it's exciting.

LIV PARKER: I think a lot of us could use a Yes Year. Do you have any inspiration for our readers?

DAPHNE QUINN: After the night of yeses I had yesterday, my biggest advice would be to just go for it when an opportunity presents itself.

LIV PARKER: Well, now I'm intrigued. But that's all the time we have for today. Thank you for speaking with me.

Chapter 4
Cameron

AUGUST 2ND

Lyndhurst's New Keeper, Cameron Hastings, Hastily Slips Up in His Embarrassing Debut

AUGUST 10TH

Mal Kelly Thrives on *Lust Island* While Not-Such-A-Keeper-After-All Hastings Is an On-Pitch Disaster

THE TEAM silently floods the locker room after our loss against Fairview.

Tamu Okafor, our captain and an impeccable striker from Nigeria, claps his hands together. "It's all right," he says with a confident grin. "We'll get them next time, team."

It's only the second match of the season, and we got pummeled again.

Premier League football is composed of England's top twenty teams, hosting the finest talent from around the world.

Each team plays each other twice during the season—a home and an away match. The team with the most points after thirty-eight matches wins the title and gets crowned champions.

A win is three points. A draw is one. A loss is unacceptable.

I ignore him and walk to my empty locker, passing the others filled with personal effects. At Overton, leaving valuable items behind meant they'd be destroyed or gone for good.

"Hastings, the save after halftime was ace." Okafor's voice roils in my ear. "Fairview's counterattack was impressive, but you had them pinned. Good stuff."

I grunt. *Is he being sarcastic?* We lost. I let a goal in. The sound of the ball hitting the net swooshes through my head.

Coach Robert Thompson attempts a motivational speech at the center of the room, near his office. He shares the space with my goalkeeping coach, Frank Murphy—the former England national team keeper known for his record number of clean sheets, which means he had no goals scored on him for over twenty matches.

Whether we lost or won, my previous coach, Mateo Rossi, would squeeze all twenty-five of his players into a windowless room with a flatscreen TV and break down how we could've done better through video analysis.

There were occasions when younger players would burst into tears, and he'd throw tissues at them, telling them to stop being babies. At one point, our lead defender set our striker's cleats on fire after he missed a penalty shot.

Military-level hazing.

Rossi condoned and encouraged it. It was how we became better footballers.

I learned to keep my guard up and avoid mistakes. I turned numb.

After my first friendly match with Lyndhurst, I expected the same routine. To my surprise, my new coach cheered for us in the locker room like we were on *Ted Lasso*. What a joke.

When the ridiculous pep talk is over, I hurry to the showers and take the farthest stall. Even though no one can see me through the fogged-up doors, my chest tightens under the stream.

I have nightmares about these exact shower stalls, including one where I drown in blood while my teammates laugh and record. I squeeze my eyes shut and picture her.

Duck.

I never think about hookups, but she keeps sprouting in my mind like a persistent weed.

Her scrunched-up nose, her lavender hair, and her laughter. Besides the Lyndhurst physiotherapists, she was the last human to touch me.

Addictive—that's what she was.

I change in the stall, soaking my socks and the hem of my jeans. A small price to pay for keeping myself safe from any further violation.

As I walk back to my locker, Coach nods me over.

"Hastings, swing by?"

"What's going on?" I say as I step into his office, leaning against the closed door.

"Take a seat."

I eye the two chairs across from Coach. Ivan Matos, Lyndhurst's former starting goalie and now my backup, sits in one of them.

"I'm good," I say. My fingers move automatically, peeling away the skin around my nails until I feel the familiar sting in my cuticles.

"Come on." Matos pats the seat. I don't budge. "You were solid out there today."

Matos and I have been training together for over a month, but I try to avoid him. Better we aren't friends. Especially since he'll take over if I lose my starting position.

"Could've been better."

Coach Thompson and Matos give me that unreadable look.

At least Coach Rossi was blunt about his cruelty.

I have nothing against Coach except his constant lurid smile. As a former Manchester captain, he had a respectable career, leading the team to a Premiership win before retiring and returning to the sport as a coach. After coaching at various clubs, he joined Lyndhurst a couple of years ago. Since taking over, he's been working to secure Lyndhurst their Premier League trophy—one they haven't held in ten years—while keeping them competitive among the top three ranked teams in the league. Many predict he has a good chance of success this year. It's an honor to train under him.

"Listen," Coach says, "I let you be during preseason, thinking you needed to adjust. But they're out there bonding, and you're sulking." I grunt. "Rossi's known for being tough." *More like a warlord.*

Everyone knows what happened at my old club last season; it was all over the news. Until my dad, who owns Viggle, the world's largest search engine, managed to scrub it from the internet. Still, I've seen my teammates whispering about it.

"Get to the point."

Coach sighs, rubbing his gray hair. "At our club, we celebrate every win and support each other through every loss."

Nerves churn in my gut as I recall my rocky start with Overton. They were my first break into the Premier League. They'd taken a gamble on me, an American keeper, and never let me forget it. The constant pressure and their strict methods wore me down.

When my contract finally ended, I was desperate for a change. As a free agent—meaning that I could join any club without a transfer fee—I had a chance to reshape my career. My sports agent worked tirelessly, negotiating with interested clubs. When Lyndhurst FC put forth an offer, it felt like a lifeline.

Now, with the ink barely dry on my new contract, I can't afford mistakes like today's goal. With three years until I'm thirty, time is running out to prove I belong in this league. The weight of expectation presses down on me, heavier than ever.

"Got it," I say.

Coach studies me. "I'll be straight with you. Ivan wanted you here. He saw something special in you."

Matos nods. "I did, Cameron. Those saves against Lakeside's penalty kicks last year were mind-blowing. Blocking three in a row set a record. But this team is a family. To recover, you need to work with the defensive line. See them as your brothers."

"I already have three brothers."

Coach sighs. "Cameron—"

"This team needs me to make saves," I say. "To command my box, stop shots, take crosses, and be unbeatable. That's why I'm here."

Coach frowns at me; it's the same look he had during preseason. "Why do you love being a keeper?"

There's no grand story. At six, I scored my first goal and fell in love with the sound of the ball hitting the net. Preventing that sound turned into an obsession. "Football makes me feel in control."

"But why do you love it?"

The question makes me uneasy. We're all here because we love football. But my passion hasn't been the same since I moved to the big leagues. Football here is tougher, with more at stake.

My pointer finger digs deeper into my thumb. "What are you getting at?"

"Three years ago, when you were playing for Los Angeles, you seemed to have a bond with your team. Or, at the very least, you had chemistry on the pitch," Coach says. "Bring some of that to Lyndhurst."

I shudder, remembering all the unanswered text messages from my old team. I was young and naive then. I thought I could treat my teammates the way I treated my siblings.

Annoyance pricks up my neck. "I am."

"Hastings, your team bonding skills make Roy Keane and Patrick Vieira look like best friends." I grunt. "Do you know why Ivan has stayed with Lyndhurst so long? The team relies on him. They know his presence is indispensable. He plays to each player's strengths. Sync with this team, or your starting position is at risk. Do you understand?"

Of course, I do. Despite our rocky start, Lyndhurst is a step up from Overton, who never won the Premier League title.

"Yes."

"Look, kid," Matos starts. "I've got a year left, and I chose to mentor you because I love this team. Lyndhurst deserves a good keeper. We don't want to bench someone we believe in."

Kid. A tic pierces my jaw.

I'm being lectured by a forty-year-old keeper who should've retired two years ago just because I don't want to make friendship bracelets with my teammates.

"What do you want me to do?" I bite. "Tuck each player in at night? Read them bedtime stories? I'm here to play football."

"You have everything you need to become one of the best keepers in England," Coach replies. "But you're playing small. You won't help bring Lyndhurst to victory if things keep going as they are."

I make one final plea. "The team and I barely practice together."

My training usually involves separate sessions to hone specialized skills. We're first on the pitch and last off, running drills for agility, reflexes, positioning, and distribution. I spend most of my time with Coach Murphy and Matos. In the afternoons, my teammates join me for trick shots and skill plays.

"Then I'll talk to Frank about that," Coach says.

I glance at the nearly empty locker room through the office window.

"Great. Is that all?"

Coach stands up. "One last thing." I raise an eyebrow. "We know your contract has clauses that are different from the rest of the players, but we'd like to make some adjustments."

Those clauses include no press conferences, no team housing, and no appearances on club social media. I'm sticking to a non-club nutritionist after Overton's strict diet made players pass out. NDAs for anyone handling my conditioning or physical therapy. "Talk to my agent."

"Nothing that serious we can't discuss here."

I nervously glance at Matos and back to Coach. "What is it?"

"I want you to move into the Lion's Lodge this week."

"You're kidding."

Mandatory team housing? My apartment in Knightsbridge is the one slice of home I have here, and he wants me to give it up to be *roomies* with my team?

"Do you want to stay in the starting lineup?"

There's the threat I was expecting. The truth behind his nice-guy façade.

If I don't fit in with the team, he'll hurt my chances at Lyndhurst.

"Yes." My arms drop to my sides.

"Well, there's your answer." He hands me a white envelope. "Your keys. Last flat in the house, top floor."

My molars feel like they may crack as I snatch the envelope.

Even though this buddy-buddy fake family of rainbows and pep talks drives me crazy, I can't risk everything I've worked for just because the coach won't let me keep the distance I need.

"Matos doesn't live there," I remind Coach. Neither does half the team.

"Because I have a wife and two sons," Matos chimes in. "You're here alone, and so are some of the younger guys. It'll be good for you to be among players your age."

Alone. *Thanks for the reminder, asshole.*

"Until the season ends," I agree.

Coach smiles. "Wonderful. And while you're being so agreeable, you also have to start riding the team bus."

In no universe would I choose the team bus over my SF90 Stradale, which Frankie spent weeks helping me personalize.

"You're pushing it."

Coach slaps a hand on my shoulder. "That's what family does. You'll get used to it."

I doubt it.

BROOKLYN

Carlyle said you're moving?

Send me your new address. Miss you!!!

I POCKET MY PHONE, ignoring my sister. The Lion's Lodge is just a fifteen-minute walk from Lyndhurst Stadium. A renovated brick building situated between an old arcade and a bakery that fills the streets with the scent of burnt sugar.

The aroma brings back memories of my mystery woman.

I shake them off.

Enough.

I need to get today's task over with quickly.

Fifteen of the team's twenty-five players live here, and I'm about to be the sixteenth. I'll move my stuff later this week. First, I need to figure out the essentials for the season.

Two hundred and eighty-five days left.

The lobby inside is musty and damp, a stark contrast to the high ceilings and ornate cornices above the concrete floor.

To the right, a propped-open door reveals a large room where members of my team are yelling at a game on TV. The room has sectional sofas and the Lyndhurst Lion emblem on the walls, along with jerseys of retired legends. To the left, a hallway leads to the apartments.

In LA, we had a common room like this. We'd hide beers in the cushions; whoever found one had to chug it. If someone dozed off, we'd stick a dirty sock on their face. Those were harmless pranks. Hilarious at the time. I wish I had appreciated them more.

When my teammates notice me in the hallway, they quiet down, whispering among themselves.

I grit my teeth and glance at my key fob. Apartment 3F. Third floor.

When I look up, Sven Gustafsson, one of the center-backs, is jammed into the tight staircase in front of me. He groans as he hauls the bottom of a bright pink sofa overhead.

I consider leaving, but Coach's words echo in my mind. *Do you want to stay in the starting lineup?*

Guess this is my shot to try and buddy up with my teammates.

"Did the movers forget this?" I ask.

Gustafsson glances over his shoulder, batting aside his long blond hair. "Who needs movers when you have friends? This is for the lady upstairs."

"Lady?" I clarify, pulling at my collar.

"Long story, but before the team moved in, this was artist housing. Her mom owned one of the apartments and refused to sell. Club decided to work around it."

"Around it? Does she have an NDA?"

"NDA? What are you doing in your free time that requires secrecy?" Gustafsson's mouth drops open. "Right," he says through a labored breath. "No need to worry. She seems sweet, and she doesn't know a thing about football. You'll see. Omar," he calls up the stairs. "Tell Daphne to come say hi to Hastings."

"Bit stuck up here," the familiar voice of Omar Mohamed, our right-back, shouts into the stairwell.

This was a mistake. "I'll come back later," I say, backing toward the door and wiping my damp palms on my jeans.

"Goose?" A voice. *That* voice. "Is that you?"

My blood freezes. A yellow phone case points straight at me, held by a girl with long lavender hair that cascades over an oversized knitted sweater. The same blue-green eyes, pink cheeks, and Bambi-like expression are caught between shock and confusion. She closes the distance.

Daphne. My duck?

What is she doing here, halfway across the world from where I last saw her? Is she even real?

This can't be a coincidence. She must've known who I was. What an actress. I'm a fucking idiot. I shouldn't have let my guard down. For what? One mind-blowing night that's infiltrated any waking moment not spent thinking about football?

Instead of asking her any of this, the words that tumble out are, "Are you stalking me?"

Her plush lips thin into a line, her forehead creasing. "Excuse me?"

"Stalking," I repeat.

Gustafsson and Mohamed are already up the stairs, while those in the common room gawk and listen to the disaster unfold.

"Why would I have any interest in stalking you?"

My mind short-circuits. "Oh, come on, you're filming. I saw you."

"Please don't flatter yourself. I'm vlogging, not creating some shrine to your ego."

Did Duck—Daphne—have this planned the whole time?

I will not have another Mal situation on my hands.

"Then why are you here, whatever your name is?" I whisper, trying to avoid a scene.

"Daphne Quinn," she corrects, hands on her hips and striking a bold pose. My eyes drop to her bare legs, my hands wanting to run over them again. *Focus, Cam.* "I live here. A better question is, why are you here? Why are *you* stalking *me*?"

Despite Gustafsson's explanation, I can't believe she's here, in my space. And worst of all, she's recording this.

Will she put it online? My fingers fidget with my already split cuticles.

This can't be happening.

"This is team housing." *State the obvious much?*

"And apartment 3E is my family's property."

"Since when?"

"Since I was born! What is your problem?" She looks even better in the daylight, nose wrinkled and nostrils flared.

My limbs are too heavy to move. I'm completely blowing this. We were never supposed to see each other again. *Fuck.* Has she seen the livestream leak? Is she another person who's gotten a rush from my own public humiliation?

Okafor exits the common room. "Hastings, you two know each other?"

"We don't," I bite out.

"He's right." She frowns. "At least, I have no idea who *that* is."

Her words cut deeper than I expected.

"Ma'am, I'll need a signature for the couch," a voice interrupts. The delivery guy walks past me to her.

And I do what I did at Overton last season—I run.

I slip out the door and past my car, sprinting without direction. Far from the Lion's Lodge, Daphne, and the team.

You're a fucking loser. Rossi's voice echoes in my head. My soles slam on the ground, my body burning from the inside out. *Look at Hastings, running like a little bitch.*

This is a cruel joke.

The night we shared, the freedom she gave me—it was all a lie. Now, nothing else matters.

Coach Thompson won't care about my issues. I have to go back.

I have to fix this, or I'll lose everything.

Chapter 5
Daphne

@BoundAndBoodUp: Will u b teachin us how2 make that sweater u wore in last video

"I will absolutely have a video tutorial for the Euphy Sweater on YouTube by the end of the month," I say, reading through the rest of the comments on tonight's regularly scheduled knitathon.

@StitchinKitten: Is this knitting retreat part of your Yes Year?

@KnitTheFUp: Can't wait for your knitting retreat!! Your struggles with anxiety are so relatable and I hope to give you a hug in person

My gaze narrows, trying to make sense of some of the comments. *Retreat?*

@KnitflixAndChill: Where is the retreat going to be? The article didn't say.

Oh, my goodness. Holy freaking moly.

The article!

THE ARTICLE. My eyes splatter with shock.

I forgot about my interview with the *Stone Times* almost two months ago. The reporter hasn't reached out since, so I figured they scrapped the piece.

I shake the confused expression off my face. *Just smile and wave like you know what's going on, Daphne. Smile and wave.*

"For sure, my wooly duckies, I am definitely considering hosting a knitting retreat." I say my biggest dream out loud to the twelve hundred people currently watching the stream.

I want to hide and tell them that the reporter made a mistake. But the comment section explodes.

@KnotSoCalmKnitter: there's no link in your bio, how much is this going to cost

@Yarnivore: can't make it this year will u be hosting next winter??????????

@MakingMemories: Will it be virtual or in person?

@WeavingWitch: COME TO PORTUGAL PLEASE

Maybe I can handle some of these questions tomorrow, after a good night's rest.

"Tonight's knitathon was a blast, friends. Remember, *knit happens*, so take it easy, and I'll see you on Saturday's live!" I sign off and end the livestream.

I take my phone off the tripod and sit in my boucle chair by the window with my knees to my chest. It's already seven o'clock. Since moving here almost a month ago and adjusting to the time zone, I've found it best to start my streams late in the evening to chat with followers back home and here.

Living alone hasn't been all bad. I miss my sister's hugs after her long shifts, sharing meals, and the little things you only notice about the people you love. My heart pangs with loneliness. Though it's been nice not being woken up at 3:00 a.m. by the blender, I do hate the silence. My TV is constantly cycling through reruns of *Gilmore Girls*, *New Girl*, and, if I want to cry, *This Is Us*.

I unmute my TV and open Instagram to find exactly what the article said that might have given my followers the impression I'd be hosting a retreat.

My inbox is flooded with over a hundred messages. My notifications are brimming with new followers. I catch a tag request from the *Stone Times*.

The post is a photo of me at UCSF Medical Center, surrounded by bags of beanies. The caption announces that I'll be starting a knitting retreat to help people with anxiety find coping mechanisms through knitting. All the plans are apparently in place, and I'll be making the announcement soon.

My heart stops. I must have misspoken in the interview. I could email Liv Parker to clarify, but my community seems excited.

Indecision washes over me. The usual intrusive thoughts take hold.

How much money would it take to run an event like this? I have some savings, but should I use all of it? How do I manage taxes or hire staff? Where would I get yarn? Could I reach out to the brands I've collaborated with in the past? What would the timeline look like?

A real businessperson would know these answers. Beyond logistics, can I meet my followers' high expectations in person without editing? There'd be no room for a retake, no magic filter. And, perhaps most importantly, am I qualified to help others with their mental health while managing my own?

Anxiety suffocates my chest. *Okay. Deep breaths.* A calming tactic since my first therapy session at twelve. Now's not the time to spiral and give in to the little voices in my head.

Isn't this the whole point of my Yes Year—to do things that scare me? This definitely scares me, but it's more like riding a roller coaster than running through a dark forest with a vampire on my heels.

"I'm a Yes Girl," I say to the empty living room, stretching my arms overhead. *Take up space, be confident, believe in yourself.*

I've moved to a new country alone—sure, one I've been to plenty of times before and into an apartment that was my mom's

—but I'm alone this time, ambling along the Thames, exploring bustling markets, and revisiting the museums of my childhood. My bravest move yet was stepping into a club alone, but anxiety crashed the party as soon as I got swept up in the crowd.

Still, this is feeling like an opportunity I need to say yes to.

I want to bring people together through knitting. To create a sanctuary for those struggling with their mental health. Share the joy of wearing your own creations, the magic of fixing your mistakes, and the tranquility of hands and minds in sync.

My streaming income from YouTube, pattern sales, and brand partnerships—in which I get paid to post content for different brands—have given me more than enough for a comfortable living. I don't have to pay rent in this apartment, and Juni always covered the bigger half back in San Francisco, so I've been careful with my savings. Would I spend money that I've worked hard for to make this happen? *Yes*, my heart answers instinctively. I can spare a couple of thousand dollars to start. Plus, the perk of having an accountant for a mom is that Dani can help me with any tax write-offs and a strict budget. She's done so in the past.

My nerves strum up again, and I grab my needles. Even when my thoughts calm, my anxiety manifests physically, begging for an escape. Tonight, I knit a Celestial Scarf for my online shop, a midnight blue piece flecked with tiny white stars. I've been weaving stars into more and more new designs.

Hosting a retreat has been my dream for years, and now that the article is out, it feels right. But my brain spins. There are so many moving parts. Where do I begin?

I need to start small, like I did knitting beanies for UCSF. Begin with a pattern, check my gauge, cast on stitches, and knit row by row. Break it down into manageable steps, make a list, and tackle the tasks one by one.

Once I have some answers, I can share them with my followers.

I need to get out of my apartment. If I stay here, I'll spiral and probably spend hours doomscrolling.

I wish I had a friend here. Just one. Yesterday, on the Tube, I complimented a girl on her crochet bag, but she just glared at me and put on her headphones. People here have been less chatty than in the States.

I could venture out into the cold rain and find a cafe to hang out at.

Or...I could go downstairs. Maybe the boys who helped me move my couch are home. I could invite them to hang out. Reality TV is always more entertaining with company.

Just go for it, Daph.

I spring into action and flick on the kettle. As the water does its bubbly dance, I shimmy into my glittery gold Gingersnap Sweater, the one that makes me feel like a warm, just-out-of-the-oven cookie. I pack up my scarf project, grab a throw blanket, and pour a steaming mug of hibiscus tea. Armed with all my comforts, I step out of my apartment, and the first thing I see is his door.

Cameron Hastings.

Stalking him? He wishes.

Of course, we'd end up as neighbors by some cruel twist of fate.

A single wall separates our apartments, with our front doors facing each other across a narrow hallway, while my bedroom shares a wall with his. His doors are so creaky that I've learned his schedule—he usually leaves around seven in the morning and gets home around nine at night. He won't be back for a couple more hours. But other than the noisy doors, his apartment is always silent. He must've lied about liking house and techno music when we first met. I bet he just sits in silence, muttering sarcastic remarks at dust bunnies.

My duck-printed slippers shuffle forward, and I press my ear to his door.

What does it look like in there? My only experience with boys' apartments was my college boyfriend's: laundry in the corner and Mötley Crüe posters held up by duct tape.

Cameron probably has a sports shrine or a lit-up cabinet for protein powder—two things equally devoid of personality. How much of the man I met in San Francisco would show through in his home? He was kind, tender, even funny. But the guy from last week? A completely different story.

I don't know what to expect from him. It's not as if he'll magically transform back into the guy who made knitting jokes and smiled about his grandparents' Valentine's Day dates.

I hear a creak from inside, and my breath catches as I bolt down the stairs.

When I reach the common room, it's disappointingly empty. But at least it's a new hangout spot, and there's a 90-inch television.

I carefully navigate around the sticky door. This house was built on a slope, and my moms warned me that getting out of the common room without a helper on the other side is like solving an escape room.

Before I settle onto the oversized sectional, I throw my blanket over the cushion to fend off the lingering boy stains etched into the upholstery. Despite the faint musk of sweat and cologne, it's manageable. Grabbing the remote, I nestle into my nook, untangle my yarn, and hit play on *Lust Island*—a reality TV show where single people come together in a villa to find love. As I cast on my first stitches, I can't help but wonder if my Yes Year might lead me to my own unexpected romance. But for now, I'm content with the drama unfolding on screen and the soft yarn sliding through my fingers.

BY THE TIME the front door creaks open, my scarf is nearly finished, my tea is empty, and I haven't had any panic attacks about my retreat. On-screen, Mal Kelly, this season's pot-stirrer, hurls a drink at some poor guy who chose the new bombshell over her.

The team floods into the lobby wearing white and purple uniforms, grass-stained jerseys, and workout gear. Some head upstairs, others to the common room.

Huh, Cameron isn't with them.

I grab the remote and start to gather my things as Omar flops down next to me. "Daphne! You finally came out!"

"Hey, guys." I smile. They remembered my name.

"Are you watching *Lust Island*? I've been trying to catch up but can't find the time," Omar says, rubbing the back of his neck.

Sven drops down on my other side. "Hey, neighbor." He says in a heavy Norwegian accent. "That Georgia Woods is…what do you call her, Ibrahim?" He looks around.

"Fit, Sven. Georgia Woods is fit."

"She's my absolute favorite. She is definitely going to win," I say.

Omar smirks. "I'm more into the bloke she stole from Cat."

They watch *Lust Island*?

Okay, this is the coolest thing in the world.

"You hungry?" Sven asks. "Ordering a couple pies for the team. You want in?"

This is a yes moment served on a silver platter. "I'd love that." I laugh. The common room is quickly starting to reek of sweaty boys. I politely tug my sweater over my nose, trying to mask the dude-stink.

Omar and Sven crack up. "Oi!" Omar calls out to the team. "We've got a girl here. If you're still in your kit, take a bloody bath, eh?"

The players groan but head to their apartments.

Sven, Omar, and the few who stay thankfully don't reek.

Universe, accept my overdue gratitude for letting me grow up in a house with minimal testosterone.

By my second slice of pizza, only Omar, Jung, Ibrahim, Sven, and Tamu remain, and we're all hollering at the TV as a recoupling ceremony unfolds. I've never had a friend group. I had my sister and some online friends scattered across Scandinavia, where there's a thriving knitting community, but hanging out with these guys is nice.

Tamu throws up a hand, loudly predicting Mal Kelly's imminent departure. Though he's only three years younger than me, he carries himself with the gravitas of someone ten years older—unless he's debating *Lust Island* with Omar Mohamed, who I learn is in a situationship with a guy from another prestigious league. Jung Tae-woo, a transplant from Korea, is possibly the most sartorially conscious guy I've ever met. We spend fifteen minutes bonding over brand sponsorships, though I doubt his Nike deal compares to the small yarn businesses that sponsor my Instagram posts. Ibrahim Kamara grew up nearby. His father is a legendary Somali player, and his mother is from East London. He has an impressive inability to modulate his volume, yelling with such gusto that it's endearing.

Turns out, a whole slew of other players live at home with their families. I feel like a fish out of water, but I'm flapping my little tail as best as I can.

Surprisingly, no one mentions Cameron. That sharp edge must be his default setting.

"I'm telling you, she's out of here!" Tamu yells.

"They can't possibly dump her tonight." I raise my voice over his, pointing at the screen. "Without her, there's no antagonist!"

"But Danny has a better connection with Nina than Mal," Tamu insists.

I snicker at the serious look on his face. "He does not!"

"Look at the way he sits closer to her. The look in his eyes, the banter."

"All right, we'll just have to wait and see."

"Would you ever go on the show?" Sven asks, his eyes twinkling with curiosity.

"We'd vote for you every time." Omar nods enthusiastically. "Especially if you got coupled up with a good-looking fella."

"Absolutely not," I say, shaking my head. "I don't think being in the public eye at that level is for me. I can barely wrap my mind around the community I built online." I pause, then add with a wistful smile, "But if I'm being honest, I would love to help make outfits for the show, like the ones Georgia is always making and wearing." She's my favorite this season, and not just because she's a crocheting queen. She seems so genuine.

"Well, that makes one of us," Omar says with a grin.

"He's always falling for the part-time footballers who go on the show," Jung says, his high cheekbones lifting with a smile. All of the Lyndhurst players are tragically good-looking, of course.

I decide to drop a bombshell of my own. "I have to be honest with all of you." I pause dramatically, ensuring I have their full attention. "I don't know a thing about soccer."

The room erupts into laughter, and I join in, feeling lighter than I have in ages.

Sven catapults out of his seat, nearly knocking me over. "Soccer?!"

"You can't use that word here, Daph." Tamu spins a platinum-bleached curl in his pointer.

I turn to Omar in hopes of finding sympathy, but he's shaking his head at me.

I widen my eyes at him. "What did I say?"

"We play football here," he titters.

I'm confused. "Isn't it the same thing?"

"More or less." Jung shrugs, and Tamu tosses a stale pizza

crust at him. Jung leans in close, bumping me with a firm shoulder. "If you ever want to get them riled up, just keep insisting that there's no difference."

"But is there? I genuinely have no idea. I tried watching a YouTube video on the rules, but it was hard to follow," I admit and recross my legs, being mindful of the stitches on my needles.

"No, there's absolutely no difference," Sven chimes in. "If you ever want to find out for yourself, you're more than welcome to come to a game."

A Yes Year opportunity in the making. "You know what? After my knitathon this weekend, I'll crack open a book and learn the rules. Then I'll take you up on that offer."

"A knitathon?" Jung asks, his eyebrows lifting in surprise.

"Yeah, it's where me and a few other knitting influencers make items to donate to local charities. It lasts all weekend," I explain, feeling a warm glow of pride. "I've been looking up community shelters that may be in need of beanies and mittens before winter. Making an impact was important to me in San Francisco, so I figured I could do it here too."

"Really? That's so cool." Sven beams, his eyes lighting up. "I used to knit; I need a refresher."

"You'd want me to teach you?" I ask, taken aback by his enthusiasm.

"Why not?" His eyes grow wide, and his hands land on my shoulder. "Actually, this is perfect." Sven turns to his teammates. "Maybe we can do something like a knitathon to help Femi?"

"Solid idea," Omar agrees, nodding thoughtfully.

"I can't even twirl pasta around my fork, and you expect me to knit?" Ibrahim protests, a hint of uncertainty in his tone.

"Femi?" I ask, curiosity piqued.

"He's the head groundskeeper. He's been maintaining the pitch at Lyndhurst Stadium for nearly forty years," Omar begins, his voice tinged with admiration. "A few years ago, he began using a prosthetic leg, and we all want to chip in for a new bionic one."

"It's really high-tech, we've done a ton of research!" Jung exclaims, his excitement palpable. "It's better on damp surfaces, like the grass on the field. The NHS won't cover it, and he's mentioned how helpful it would be."

"The current one's been causing him issues, but he's too proud to accept direct assistance from us," Omar explains, his voice tinged with concern. "We've been brainstorming ways to raise money that he'd be more likely to accept. A fundraiser feels less like charity and more like community support. What if we knit match day scarves and auction them off? It'd be like a knitathon, but spread out over several days to fit our work schedules. We can handle the logistics, but if you could teach us to knit them, that'd really help us make a difference for our friend."

"Of course," I say. "I can help. When do you need them by?"

"His work anniversary is in mid-November, so probably around then."

"That gives us a little over two months. I think I can make that work." A smile cracks across my face at the idea of having my own little community here and helping out with a good cause. "I would love to teach you guys. It would be a perfect opportunity to practice for my knitting retreat, and I have a ton of excess yarn."

"We could work on the scarves on Wednesday? We'll provide the grub?"

"Sounds good to me. We can even start tonight," I offer.

"Let's do it!"

As the guys start arguing over what food to get next week, the front door opens. I glance at the clock beneath the television. 8:59 on the dot.

My eyes dart to the lobby, where a familiar figure in black clothing glides in like he owns the place.

His hair is slicked back, and there's a grimace on his face as raindrops trace a path down his neck. How can a man be so annoyingly handsome? My body tenses. I can almost feel his ghostly fingers grazing my cheek, my neck, my chest. I want to lick the water from his skin.

Good grief, what am I thinking?

I'd never admit it out loud, but I sort of wish he'd come over here, poke his head in, say hello, and maybe even apologize for being a Grouch-a-saurus rex to me last week. I straighten my back, but Cameron doesn't look my way. My gut knots up like it does when I realize I've been knitting the wrong stitch for an hour—only this feels worse.

"Hastings, wait up," Sven calls out to him, waving his arm out for attention. Cameron stops at the edge of the doorway, not offering a response. A chill spreads through the room. "We're going to karaoke after the Oakwood United match this Saturday," Sven says. "You're coming, right?"

"It's Sven's birthday," Omar adds.

"See you then," the familiar, deep voice says quietly.

Even that small sound causes unrest in my chest. As he's about to leave, his eyes catch mine. There's something in them. Anger? Nerves? Regret? I can't read his expression, and given how badly I misread the situation that unfurled between us back in San Francisco, there's no point in trying to figure it out now.

We learn from our mistakes, Daphne. Unlike knitting, there's no undoing his behavior.

"Oh, weren't you guys together?" Jung points at the TV, and lo and behold, there's Mal Kelly, laughing away like she's the star of her own sitcom.

He dated Mal? As in, reality TV queen Mal?

"I guess," is all he says before he's out of view, leaving a trail of stunned silence in his wake. The echo of his slamming footsteps reverberates through the building, and I'm left staring at Mal Kelly on screen, yammering on about something I've lost all interest in.

Is she Cam's type? A woman who's as stunning as she is confident, who's made a name for herself by breaking hearts? She did mention once that she had a soft spot for famous footballers, but she never dropped any names.

Was Cam heartbroken over her? Was I just a clumsy rebound?

My pizza turns over in my tummy.

The show started filming in May, so they couldn't have been together then. At least he didn't lie about being free of any entanglements.

Damn knitting jokes!

I hope he gets tied up in a net and, *argh*, I don't know, can't unwind himself for an hour.

"Is he always like that?" I ask the team.

The question seems pointless. The less I know about him, the better.

Honestly, the two minutes I spent looking him up online after I found out his name only resulted in a jumble of soccer news I couldn't understand and the revelation that he's from California, born into a wealthy sports family.

"Standoffish?" Sven lifts a brow at me.

Omar sighs. "He's new to the club, so we don't really know him yet."

"But we're trying." Tamu shrugs a shoulder. "We've had a rough start to the season. He probably needs some time to come around."

Maybe the losing streak is what's causing him to be a different person since the last time we saw each other? A drop of sympathy forms in the back of my throat, but I swallow it away.

"I heard his last team really turned him inside out," Ibrahim says with a frown. "Overton's known for making players run until they pass out. The coach carries a roll of duct tape to slap over players' mouths if they make a bad call. And that whole livestream—"

"Let's not fuel any rumors, yeah?" Tamu ends the conversation, reaching for the remote and turning up the volume.

We finish up the episode, which left the guys severely disappointed that I was, in fact, right in my recoupling predictions.

"All right, hit pause," I say, rising from the couch with a newfound resolve. "I'm going to grab some knitting supplies, and then we can get to work."

Chapter 6
Cameron

Overton Coach Endangers Players' Lives with
Illegal Heatwave Practices! Fines to Rossi.

WHAT WAS I thinking watching Daphne Quinn bond with my teammates? Her smile and curious eyes were pure torture.

I should have gone inside my apartment by now, but I lingered, listening to their laughter from the top of the stairs. Each laugh sharpened the ache in my chest.

To make things worse, they're watching *Lust Island*. Did they tell her about Mal Kelly and me? Whatever they said would be tabloid drama anyway.

Mal and I lasted five months. I met her at a club. Back then, I went out a lot, trying to escape how bad things had gotten after I replaced Charlie. Anonymity felt like intimacy. My rule was one-night stands only, but Mal kept showing up. It was convenient, and there were no strings attached.

It wasn't love, but it didn't matter—not to anyone. Once the livestream hit the tabloids, Mal made our fleeting connection seem like more than it was. Turned me into her "damaged goods" footballer she was only trying to save. All she cared about was fame, and my name in the tabloids gave her that. Now, I've learned my lesson.

That's why I need to avoid Daphne Quinn at all costs.

I'm so lost in thought that I don't notice the sound of stairs creaking until it's too late.

"Oh, you're here." Her voice startles me. I shoot up from my seat, retreating toward my apartment. She can't see me like this.

"Wait, Goose—uh, Cameron, can we clear the air? I think we got off on the wrong foot last week." I fumble with my keys. "Hellooooo?" A tap on my shoulder freezes me.

"I'm busy," I mutter, avoiding eye contact.

"Kinda looked like you were just sitting. Alone. In the dark."

"I wasn't."

"Sure…" She draws out the word with disbelief. "Well, isn't this a bizarre situation?"

I need to get away from her.

"You're an influencer," I say uselessly.

"And you play soccer." A sassy tone clips her voice. "Glad we got our professions out of the way."

"Premier League footballer," I clarify for no reason. *That's helping, Cameron.*

She groans. "Okay…Look, I'm not going anywhere, and it doesn't seem like you are either. So let's just start over and try to be neighborly."

I release a long, low sigh and face her. *Big fucking mistake.* Those blue-green eyes blink up at me. She stands there with her arms crossed over her baggy sweater.

She's so close.

Too close.

"I can't afford any distractions," I say into the four feet of space between us.

"And I'm distracting you?"

Yes. Very much so. More than I care to admit, frankly. "This *coincidence* has been distracting."

I'm an asshole, letting my gaze get stuck on the slopes of her neck, on the little spot behind her ear that made her giggle when I kissed it. On the thicker bottom lip that hangs slightly open. She's expecting me to say something, but all I can do is stare at this gorgeous woman who's obviously upset with me.

Because I was a fucking dick to her.

That's all I can be—what I need to be—to keep both of us safe.

"I had no idea who you were or that you'd be living here when I moved to London. Not that I owe you an explanation," she says with sarcasm, sparking a fire in me like she did in San Francisco.

"Are you sure?"

"Yes," she snaps. "How crazy would that be? My mom mentioned the building had been sold to a private group, but I had no clue it was a sports team. If I'd known, I might have nudged her to sell. My neighbor has been acting like a total jerk!"

"It's not that crazy in my world." People do things for personal gain all the time, especially influencers.

"I don't know anything about *your world*. Sports? Not my thing. Unless you count pickleball, which I only tried once because my mom insisted. Spoiler alert: I was terrible. I couldn't even serve properly. And can I just say, the biggest letdown was discovering there are no actual pickles in pickleball." She wrinkles her nose in that adorable way and laughs. Despite myself, I can't help but smile. "See? The guy I met is still in there somewhere," she says, playfully poking my pecs.

The shock is immediate, and I step back, hitting the door.

"No," I say harshly. "He isn't."

"I'm literally looking at you right now." She scowls.

"You don't understand. Here, I'm Cameron Hastings, a

keeper for Lyndhurst. The only thing that matters to me is winning the Premier League."

"But can't you be both? Are you really going to ignore me and pretend like the night we shared—one that I'm pretty sure was special for both of us because you thanked me for it—never happened?"

I have to leave, but I can't move. This whirlwind of a girl, full of energy and sweetness, has no right to think she understands the man she spent just a few hours with. She doesn't truly know me.

Yet with her, I was more myself than I'd been with any other woman.

I lean in, lowering my voice. "Yes, Daphne, that's exactly what I need to do."

"Why?"

"Because the night we spent together *did* happen, and I haven't been able to stop thinking about it. About you."

Why did I just say that out loud?

Surprise paints her face. "Then why are you avoiding me?"

Because what I showed her was vulnerability. Here, there's no room for weakness. My life is about survival and becoming a better competitor. I need to focus and stop my breath from hitching every time I catch her scent.

"Because the only thing I'm allowed to think about is winning."

"Says who?"

"Do you always ask this many questions?"

"You didn't seem to mind it before!"

"Well, I do now," I say.

Why do I care if she's upset with me? It's what I wanted.

She stares at me, and just as I'm ready to lock myself in my apartment, she scrunches her nose. "Then fine. If the only way you know how to act is like Cameron Hastings, the keeper— however ironic that sounds because you are clearly *not* a keeper

—then I take back my 'you're welcome.' Yeah, I retract my pleasantries." She huffs in a way that pulls at something unnatural in me. How does she manage to look this adorable when she's angry?

"What?"

"The night we were together, the night I thought was special for us both, you thanked me for the fun we had. Well, I'm taking back saying you're welcome for it."

She can't be serious. "You never said you're welcome."

"How do you know?" She taps her foot against the floor, and the whole disappointed-in-me glare on her sweet face is driving me up the wall.

I know because I remember.

I remember every single thing from that night. The way she wanted to see stars, the way I wanted to oblige and impress her. Our familiarity with each other. The slope of her stomach against my lips. The way it rose and fell with every breath I coaxed out of her.

Does she want me to burst into her apartment and recount to her every detail? Relive the sounds and groans she made because of me?

Enough. Enough of this fucking shit.

I grunt and slot my key into the lock.

As I swing open the door, the oddest noise, between a trill and a scream, comes from behind me. I glance over my shoulder to see her standing there, red in the face. "What on earth was that?"

"I don't know." She throws her hands in the air in exasperation. "If you're grunting to express your feelings, then I may as well make a noise for how I feel. That seems to be the only way you want to communicate, so let's grunt and groan until we figure us out."

I stare at her, stunned. She's too emotional. Too honest. Too risky. Too much. Too pretty. So fucking pretty.

"The last thing either of us should be doing is grunting or groaning at each other."

"That's not what I meant!"

"Good, because there's no *us* to figure out." I drop the words between us like a final match whistle and turn away from the disappointment written on her face. This is for the best.

"Real mature!" she says mockingly.

I don't bother to defend myself as I enter my place, slamming the door behind me and heading straight for the shower. I let the water cascade over me, hoping to wash the day away. But my thoughts won't settle.

Images of her invade my mind—the lavender hue of her hair, the intoxicating scent of vanilla that clings to her like a secret. For a moment, I imagine her here, her fingers up my arms, her breath on my neck. A stubborn echo.

Focus on winning the Premier League.

Reality snaps back. I make the water colder, but the heat she left lingers.

Chapter 7
Cameron

"CAMERON! How's your first two months at Lyndhurst?" An interviewer shoves a mic in my face.

"No comment." I swat it away, rushing onto the team bus. Fucking vultures.

The team doesn't seem to mind the press as they belt out, "Because mayyybeeee, you're gonna be the one that saves meeeeee," as they stumble out of the karaoke bar in downtown Oakwood.

I hustle to the back seat as they all scream "Wonderwall" off-key.

It's been screeching renditions of "We Are the Champions" by Queen, "Super Bass" by Nicki Minaj, and "Water Under the Bridge" by Adele all fucking night.

Despite our win today, I let Lyndhurst down with a missed save. Oakwood's striker faked a shot, and I dove the wrong way. The sound of the ball hitting the net still echoes in my mind.

I should've read his body language better.

As the driver readies the bus, I put on my noise-cancelling headphones. I miss my Ferrari's Italian leather seats. A notification comes through on the text chain from my LA club.

#11 MAGIC MARCUS AXEL

cameron hammer hastings, you killed it out
there today

#4 OCTO OLLIE BENNETT

Black & gold will always look better on you but
the purple is growing on us

#8 DYNAMO DIEGO RIVERA

FUCK YEAH!!!!

I see the old contact names and the silly nicknames we made up one night at our old stadium. I haven't been on a team bus since my Los Angeles Football Club days. After games, we'd huddle and howl like wolves—a brotherhood.

I hesitate over the notifications, then swipe them away. I can't open that door to the past—the memory of how close we used to be hurts too much.

In six years, we won two MLS championships, and I earned three Goalie of the Year Awards. Back then, I was the youngest player to win both Rookie of the Year and Goalie of the Year. I was on top of the world.

Isn't this supposed to be my prime? Or has it already passed me by?

I didn't even enjoy our win today; my heart wasn't in it. Maybe too much has changed for me to ever feel the same way about football.

Before I know it, I'm on my anonymous Instagram account, scrolling through Daphne's profile. I haven't been on social media in months, but after our encounter on the stairs three days ago, my curiosity got the better of me.

Initially, the occasional monitoring was to make sure she hadn't posted anything about me or any member of the Lyndhurst team, but clicking on her page has turned into a daily occurrence.

A compulsion.

The girl who manages to disarm me with just a look. The girl who made me want to do whatever it took to make her smile, laugh, and moan.

The one I need to keep away from, no matter how alone I feel here.

Daphne has another post today—there's been a new one every day.

She's sitting by a window, holding her knitting needles in both hands, and what might be a starry cardigan with the caption: **@wooly.duck** *is yarning for more London adventures, one stitch at a time!*

Stars?

I scroll through her story. Two new slides. The first shows a cup of tea beside her project. The second—a selfie—stops me cold.

I bring my phone closer, studying her face. Her slightly uneven lips curl into a smile. Braids cascade down her shoulders, framing her face in a way that makes my pulse race.

Being an asshole is my way of keeping distance.

Still, her voice rouses me through the bedroom wall we share. She's in my mind when I fail to work her out of my system.

The bus begins to move, and I put my phone away before my motion sickness takes over.

Gustafsson slides in next to me, interrupting my solitude. "What are you listening to?"

I hesitate before answering, "Just some music. Helps block out the noise."

"Maybe you've got 'Bring Me to Life' by Evanescence playing in there?"

I remove an earbud and force a small smile. *Try to be a little friendly.* "Not quite."

"Oh, come on, there's nothing like screaming a good song at the top of your lungs for some emotional release."

Not sure how that could ever be helpful. "Sure."

"You remind me of a moody teenager in one of those American high school movies." He nudges me and calls out, "Hastings here is waking up inside. Let's set the mood for him."

"Great song choice, Cameron!" Kamara shouts, lifting his speaker. Wallowing piano creeps into the bus. The team belts out the first verse.

"Can you not?" I snap. "I just want some peace and quiet after tonight's howling."

"All right, sorry, man, just some friendly teasing." Gustafsson grins awkwardly. "Thanks for coming to my birthday celebration, by the way, even though you hate karaoke."

"I don't hate it," I say, stretching out my legs. My stomach turns woozier with each bump in the road. "I'm just a football player, not a singer."

Gustafsson laughs, taking my lightheartedness at face value. "Man, this guy's hilarious."

Mohamed pokes his head over the seat in front of me. "You've got humor and talent, Hastings. That save in the second half was ace."

"Should've anticipated the striker's crosses in the first," I admit, trying to contribute to the conversation.

"We will next time." Mohamed bumps my shoulder. "Clearly, your move to Lion's Lodge helped us win. Coach always knows best."

I nod more warmly, hoping they see that I'm trying to be friendly.

They don't quite seem to notice my effort. "You know, we could've worked as a team to prevent that," Gustafsson says. "I'm the backbone of your line of defense. You got hawk eyes; just shout what you see back at me." I don't need a breakdown of each player's role in the game I've been playing since I was a child. "Maybe you can come hang out with us in the common room some more? We can get to know each other better. Make the defense line stronger."

"I'll keep my eye on the ball, and you do the same."

From behind Mohamed's head, Coach watches our exchange. He throws up a thumbs-up and a smile.

"Did we get off on the wrong foot with you?" Mohamed frowns, folding his arms over the seat and dropping his chin to his hands.

"Is it 'cause we're hanging out with your girl?" Gustafsson asks.

My breathing escalates. "What?"

"Daphne!" he says, as if it were obvious.

There's nothing mine about Daphne. "Like she said, we don't know each other."

"You sure?" Mohamed asks. "Seemed like there was some history between you two."

Exactly the kind of gossip I hoped to avoid.

"She's pretty too," Tae-woo says from the row beside us. I may as well get a megaphone and announce this entire conversation to the rest of the bus. "And friendly."

Of course, they all love her. I glance down at my hands and notice I'm white-knuckling my earphones.

"Best we all steer clear of her." The words come out as more of a threat than I intended.

"That'll be hard since she's helping with the auction for Femi." Gustafsson shrugs.

"Auction?"

"Yeah, she's teaching us how to knit scarves so we can auction them off the Sunday after the Sutton FC game in November. We're planning to surprise him with a new bionic prosthetic."

My mouth tightens into a thin line. She's helping them fundraise for our groundskeeper, someone she hasn't even met?

Everyone around me is a do-gooder, while I'm constantly waiting for the other shoe to drop.

"You should join us next week," Gustafsson offers.

I glare at him. "I'm busy."

"Don't be like that."

"Hastings's just got that Overton skin of steel, Sven." Okafor's voice comes from beside Mohamed, though I don't see what eye roll he's surely tagging onto the remark.

"Coach Rossi is a fucking tyrant," Gustafsson says pitifully.

"Not at Lyndhurst. Here, we care. Genuinely. There are about thirty pairs of ears ready to listen if you ever want to talk." He nudges my shoulder with his again. A pain splinters my head.

"And we're excited to start practicing with you next week," Mohamed says. "Those new team bonding drills will be fun!"

"Until then," I grunt, tossing my headphones back into my ear.

I don't believe them. I can't.

There's no room for letting people in when you're trying to be at the top.

Charlie, my best friend at Overton, initially seemed to genuinely care. I was his backup keeper, and when he was injured, I stepped up. After he recovered, Rossi made him my backup. He was the only teammate I trusted. But everything changed when I became the starting goalie.

He grew distant before betraying me in the worst way possible by livestreaming me in the shower after a game. Just a harmless prank, he said, but by morning, the footage had gone viral, and the tabloids had sunk in their claws. My teammates saw my dick. Everyone did. My sisters. My entire family.

The American athletic brands that once cheered on my every move coldly turned away. My other sponsorship deals vanished. The harassment was relentless, forcing me to abandon social media altogether. I couldn't bear to read the comments. My agent took over my Instagram.

Somehow the whole thing got spun into me doing it for attention. *The new American keeper making a splashing name for himself.*

If this had happened to a female athlete, everyone would've recognized it for what it was: a blatant violation. But instead, I got offhand compliments about my body, like someone exposing me was some kind of twisted favor. *Nice abs. Would tap that. Whoever's riding that pole is lucky.* It's as if my privacy didn't mean as much because I'm a man. The double standard was maddening, but all I could do was brush it off.

I miss the days of being celebrated for my talent on the pitch, of hearing my name spoken with admiration.

Of not being accused of orchestrating a stunt to get my name into the Premier League news cycle.

All that remains is the pain of betrayal, lost friendships, and a damaged reputation.

Rossi hated the media attention, and he took out his frustration on me. I remember those tough solo training sessions in the cold, with rain soaking my gear and my hands stiff as the machine kept launching balls at me. It felt like he wanted to break my spirit. It was a nightmare.

Everyone else stayed at Overton, but it was time for me to move on. My two-year contract ended, and when the summer transfer window opened, I left Overton.

They saw me as weak. But I'm not weak. Not anymore.

Chapter 8
Cameron

September 13
Lyndhurst Stumbles Again with Another Draw
Against Alderly

AFTER TODAY'S PRACTICE, I needed some relief. That's how I ended up with over £632 worth of candles from Beacon & Bramble Company, all in a futile attempt to capture her scent. And then there was the sugar cookie I bought last Friday—temptation in a neat little package. It went straight in the trash, though; I couldn't bring myself to eat it.

I shrug my wet leather jacket over my shoulder and linger at the entrance to the common room. Daphne's been decorating again—she's added these mismatched throw pillows and two blankets, one orange and the other navy blue. My fingers itch as I wander to the sofa and touch the fuzzy yarn.

It's soft and warm, like she was. A shiver runs down my neck. I feel like a fucking creep as I pick up the blue throw. But here I am, standing mesmerized like a kid holding his first football.

Keeping my distance has been pointless. I find myself pressing my ear against our shared bedroom wall, waiting to catch any sound of what she's up to, or squinting at the labels on her packages just to see where they're from. It's absurd, especially since *I've* accused *her* of stalking. And here I am, stroking a blanket just for a fleeting connection.

"*Help!*" A piercing shout echoes through the Lodge, snapping me out of my daze. *Daphne?*

I drop the blanket, grab my bag, and rush upstairs toward the commotion.

Daphne's door is propped open with a giant cardboard box. She stands on her bright pink couch. Her tiny pajama shorts are both a blessing and a curse because, damn, those legs are heavenly. Her baggy sweatshirt has two yarn balls strategically placed on her breasts with the words *Show Me Your Knits* in bold letters. I snort. She's a walking contradiction—annoyingly adorable and infuriatingly sexy all at once. It's like the universe decided to create my own personal brand of torture by thrusting her into my life.

"Help!" she cries again, oblivious to my presence.

"What the hell is going on?" I bark, scanning the room for any sign of trouble. Two mugs sit on the coffee table, and yarn is scattered everywhere. Is someone else here?

"What are you doing?" Her brows shoot up in shock, eyes narrowing with suspicion.

I state the obvious. "You screamed."

"Not for you!" she snaps back, crossing her arms defensively. "You don't need to barge in here like some knight in tarnished armor."

"Right." I turn to leave, but not before saying, "I'll remember that for the next time you scream for help."

"Good, because I don't need saving," she fires back. "Especially not by someone who thinks the world revolves around them." I grunt in response. "Oh my god, it's flying!" Daphne shouts, pressing herself into the corner of the couch, climbing onto the armrests, and grabbing the wall for balance.

Let it go, Cameron.

She doesn't need me.

"Daphne?" Gustafsson barrels down the hall toward us. "What happened? I was only gone a second!"

A twinge of jealousy blooms in my chest. They're hanging out at her place together?

She points a trembling finger toward the floor, shifting her feet on her couch like she's walking on hot coals. "There's a s-spider, Sven! A big one." A throaty scream hums through her mouth. "It has wings!"

Gustafsson lets out a high-pitched scream that doesn't match his physique. He shoves me aside and leaps onto a kitchen chair, arms flailing as he yells, "Ahhh! It's going to eat us!"

They're acting like a rabid dog has invaded the Lodge.

"Seriously?" I say, standing at the entryway. "It's just a spider."

"I have." He gulps, growing paler by the second. "How do you say it? *Araknofobi.*"

"Arachnophobia?" Daphne clarifies.

Then why would he run into her apartment instead of back to his own? I hide my begrudging eye roll.

"It's a huge one! Please, get rid of it!" Gustafsson yelps.

"It'll go away on its own," I grumble, spinning on my heels to leave.

Gustafsson bursts with another scream.

"Wait—please." Daphne's trembling whisper stops me in my tracks.

This is ridiculous. Fine. Whatever. If I help my teammate, then maybe it'll get back to Coach Thompson that I'm being a team player. That's all this is. I'm helping prevent any harm this spider could cause one of my center-backs.

Nothing more.

This isn't about helping Daphne at all.

"Where do you keep your glasses?" I ask.

"Don't kill it!" Daphne frowns, pointing to a cupboard beside her stovetop vent.

I hate that she thinks I'd hurt the poor thing—he was probably just seeking some warmth in the cold spells of autumn swooping over the UK. I sigh, opening her cabinet.

"Do," Gustafsson pleads. "Crush it, Hastings. Stomp on it!"

I pluck a glass from the cabinet and snatch a stray envelope from the counter. In a smooth, confident motion, I trap the spider under the glass and slide the paper beneath it.

"There," I say, holding up my prize. "Spider conquered." I look at the tiny, helpless creature distorted by the glass. *I know exactly how you feel, buddy.*

Rising to my feet, I steal a generous glance around her apartment. Photos hover above her couch, showcasing Daphne and her family. Some frames have illustrations—watercolors of a duck and yarn with needles. The largest one is a painting of the Santa Cruz Boardwalk. Her place is vibrant and cozy, with fresh flowers on the kitchen table, a mountain of pillows on the couch, and knitted items everywhere. The opposite of my minimalist space, which has only the basics—a bed, a table, and a chair.

That sweet smell again. I panic, checking the hallway to ensure my bag of candles is still there. I can't let her see them.

"You're officially anointed the spider wrangler of the building," my teammate says. He's frozen on the kitchen chair, eyeing me as if I'm moments from releasing a demonic spirit into the room.

"Don't mention it," I reply, trying to keep my tone gruff. "Seriously. Never mention it again."

"Thank you," Daphne whispers. Her eyes are glued to me, her expression a mix of relief and something else I can't quite place. Gratitude, maybe? Admiration? I hope so.

I can't remember the last time someone saw good in me.

"I—I just did what needed to be done," I stammer, downplaying my actions. "To help Gustafsson."

The burst of heat beneath my skin from her gaze returns, just as it did the night we were together. It's despicable that she has this much power over my emotions.

I commit her rosy cheeks, beautiful legs, and wary smile to memory. A smile I didn't think I'd see after our run-in two weeks ago. I beeline out the door, kicking my bag down the hallway and making sure the spider doesn't escape.

"*God natt*," Gustafsson calls out as my door clicks closed.

Once inside, I crack open the living room window and release the small spider onto the brick windowsill.

"There you go, little guy."

The creature skitters off.

After shutting the window, I grab my bag and line up the candles on my nightstand with ritualistic precision. I light *Vanilla Bean Dream* and *Custard Cream*, their scents curling into the room. But it's not quite right—her scent was sweeter, fresher, like a hot sun in the middle of winter. I light more candles. The potent smell is suffocating, but it envelops me in a blanket of calm.

Daphne briefly needed me to be the knight in tarnished armor or whatever the fuck she called it. The way her lips parted in a soft gasp when I trapped the spider. The way she begged *please*, like it was a lifeline.

It felt good to be needed.

———————

THE GRASS beneath my cleats feels heavier than usual as I tap both ends of the goalpost and recheck the Velcro on my gloves. The warm-up session for our new team drills is well underway.

I feel on top of the world when I'm in my box. It's the one place I've always felt powerful and in control. But when I started playing in the Premier League, that power started to slip. "How's it going at the Lodge?" Matos asks, swapping spots with me in the box as I prepare for Murphy's throws.

"Fine." I squat, readying for my catches.

"Rough start to the season, but that win against Oakwood United at least got us moved up in the table."

The twelfth spot out of twenty. That's pitiful.

"We need another three points against Brookfield City."

"Tamu's feeling good about the match." Matos claps his hands together. "Scoring goals isn't Lyndhurst's problem."

No, *I* am, apparently.

I catch Murphy's throw without losing my grip and toss it back to him before swapping with Matos. "Our defense line needs to stay focused."

"Our defense line is afraid of you," Matos says. Murphy fires shots at him, and he blocks each one with ease. Nerves burst open in my chest at his skill level. Sure, his reflexes are slowing down, but Matos is good. "You know, I trained under Rossi in my youth league, way back when."

"Really?"

"He was a legendary player, but as a coach, he didn't just apply pressure—he splintered kids."

"Making diamonds." I repeat one of Rossi's famous lines. Usually followed by, *But fucking failing!*

"There's a reason Rossi's never won the league. People aren't diamonds; they can erode or crack. That kind of coaching changes the way you think about this game."

Has it?

Is that why my voice always falters when I give directions to teammates? Why my heart isn't fully in it during my pregame rituals?

Beyond the walls of my old club's locker room, few truly grasped Rossi's methods. I wonder if Matos ever saw the same coach I did. The man in front of me is warm and encouraging with players. There is no way he endured the grueling drills, verbal assaults, and crushing weight of impossible expectations. Or maybe Matos is just better at hiding his scars.

A part of me wants to know the truth.

"Last season, I called out the wrong direction to my right-back, asking him to pass the ball back to me," I begin, my voice wavering. "It was a misjudgment, leading to a turnover and an easy goal for the opposing team. I cost us the game."

"Against Rosewood?" Matos interjects, his brow furrowing. "I was surprised they let you guys go on. Looked like no one could see their teammates."

It's true. The rain was relentless, turning the field into a muddy swamp. My sight was hazy, with sheets of water blurring the pitch. We were sliding around the field like kids at a water-park. The ball skidded unpredictably, and every step felt like wading through setting cement.

"You watched it?" I attempt to mask the surprise in my voice.

"Wasn't kidding when I said I had my eye on you, kid," he replies, a hint of a smile playing on his lips.

This time, the term doesn't boil under my skin and make me feel belittled. This time, it feels like I'm talking to a teammate.

"It was some of the worst rain I ever played in," I admit.

"But you were strong."

The compliment unbuckles the strain of tightness in my chest.

"Rossi..." I swallow the dryness in my throat. "He—for two weeks after that game, he'd have me pull out a roll of duct tape in the locker room and tape my mouth shut before every practice."

That'll teach you to think before you speak. His words drip through my skull.

"Cameron." Matos's voice is shrouded with pity. Regret sets in. Why did I say that? I panic, wanting to run off the field. *Do you even belong here, Hastings? You don't act like it.* "That's fucking disgusting."

"It's fine."

Enough. What am I doing talking about this? You're pathetic, Hastings. Be better, be stronger. Suck it up.

"No, it's not," he says. "That's never fine. That's not how you play football. That's abuse. I mean, surely it's against the federation's rules. A coach like Rossi should be suspended, not just fined, for skirting the lines of dangerous drills. You have to report—"

"Forget it," I bark.

No suspensions. No fines. The last thing I need is more attention. The last thing I need is a news cycle about how Cameron Hastings couldn't handle it…couldn't cut it.

"All right, okay, man." He takes a surprised step back, his eyes wide with confusion.

It wasn't until I came to the Premier League that I started to doubt my abilities, that I became afraid of making mistakes. Sure, Rossi wasn't a walk in the park, but we're all here playing at the highest level this game can be played. We all need to handle our stress ourselves.

I replace him in the box as Murphy speeds up our warm-up drill. "We all want to win."

"But at what cost?" Matos shakes his head at me, and our conversation dies there.

After the warm-up, Coach Thompson calls for a new drill: a two-on-two scrimmage designed to hone our defensive skills. Our first opponents, striker Okafor, midfielder James, and number 12, are already at the center of the pitch, ready for the whistle. I position myself between the goalposts, knees slightly bent, ready to spring into action. My central defender, Gustafsson, dons the 17 jersey and stands at the edge of the penalty box, ready to intervene in the impending attack.

Easy.

The whistle sounds, and the attacking duo springs into action.

I stay focused on Okafor, tracking his movements, while Gustafsson positions himself to intercept any passes. Okafor is known for his deceptive shots, so I brace myself, hands out in front, prepared for any eventuality.

Before I know it, Gustafsson breaks from his position and tries to intercept the ball, leaving his defensive area exposed. A pang of frustration hits me. What is he doing? He should be keeping an eye on 12, who's already skirting toward the far post. *Watch for the switch!* I want to yell, but my voice is lost. Gustafsson is an experienced center-back; he should be able to read the game. I know what it's like to have your every move criticized. The last thing anyone needs is micromanagement.

No. Say something. The words catch in my throat. I open my mouth, but nothing comes out. Doubt creeps in. What if I mess up? The pressure builds as I stand frozen. The silence suffocates me. *Come on, Cameron. Get it together.* Still, the words don't come. *Say fucking anything.* And while I'm stuck, it happens.

Tamu executes a swift pivot and sends a through ball to James, who's now unmarked on the opposite side of the goal area. And now I see exactly how they're going to take a shot, but now I need to get into position to block it, and I can't afford the split second it would take to tell Gustafsson what I'm seeing. I'm too late to help him do his job. I'm just too late.

Number 12 shoots.

I jump, outstretching my hands, and I know even before I hit the ground that 12 has scored on me. The sound of the ball hitting the net bites through me like a bullet.

I fucking loathe it.

"What the fuck was that, Gustafsson?" I yell, ripping my body off the grass.

"I was waiting for you to call it," he shouts back.

Coach Thompson, with Murphy close behind, trots over.

"Let's run it again," he says, clapping his hands. "Hastings, you need to communicate with Sven if you want him to stay back. Make sure to do that next time."

The rest of the scrimmage proceeds similarly—I miss twelve out of eighty-four saves. Meanwhile, on the other side of the pitch, Matos and Mohamed don't concede a single goal.

Chapter 9
Daphne

TEACHING football players how to knit is like herding preschoolers who argue over who's the best student like there's a trophy at stake. It's hilarious and, honestly, kind of adorable. Sure, they're eager to get Femi's scarves right, but my patience is starting to stretch thinner than the yarn we're using.

If this is any indication of how my retreat will go, I'll need to build up my hand stamina.

Okay, that sounds positively filthy.

The guys sit around me as I demonstrate how to cast off a scarf for the third time this evening. *Lust Island* booms in the background.

Omar looks like a grizzly bear trying to delicately assemble a house of cards. His massive fingers fumble with the delicate yarn, ensnaring it in a never-ending loop of frustration.

"This has got to be harder than bench-pressing a small car," he grumbles.

"It isn't." Sven shakes his head.

He, on the other hand, is a knitting prodigy. His needles click away, effortlessly creating a perfect stockinette stitch. Sure, he asked for a private lesson last week, but that was cut short after the spider fiasco. Sven simply could not sit in my apartment. His arachnophobia had him swinging his head around my living room, looking for any sudden movement.

My gaze keeps abandoning my project and jumping up to the entrance of the common room. Cameron's late today. It's already a quarter past nine.

Where is he? More importantly, why do I care?

"Sven, you're such a teacher's pet." Ibrahim nudges his friend's elbow, attempting to mess him up.

"No need to be jealous, big boy," he laughs. "My sister's taught me to knit." He shrugs nonchalantly, as if he isn't turning the macho stereotype on its head. "I used to make sweaters for my pet iguana."

When Sven showed me pictures of the tiny iguana in a white sweater, I nearly peed myself. Cozy, adorable animals are my weakness, apparently—right up there with gruff footballers who rescue spiders.

Ibrahim side-eyes Sven. "They have iguanas in Oslo? Isn't it too cold for them?"

"Hence the sweater." He laughs. "Daphne, do you sell the pattern to this scarf on your website?"

"I do! It's one of my bestsellers. I have over a hundred patterns on my site, and I'm always adding new ones."

"I'll have to check out the others and buy some," Sven says.

"Thanks, Sven."

Omar, Jung, and Tamu have their tongues stuck out in deep concentration.

"While Sven's picking up a new side hustle, I doubt we'll have an easy time auctioning these off when they look like this," Tamu muses, glancing at the tangled mess in his lap.

"Everyone gets better with practice, I promise," I say, hoping I don't come off as some cheesy motivational poster. "These scarves will be made with love, and that's all that matters."

"I guess," Tamu says. He doesn't look convinced.

"We'll get it right, just like we'll get that play right with Hastings on the pitch," Omar assures him.

I want to find out more but before I can pry, Jung says, "You're announcing your knitting camp tonight, right?"

My nerves wriggle with excitement. Since the *Stone Times* article came out a month ago, I've been flooded with support and patience from my knitting community. My mom and I sat down to go over an estimated budget for the event. I've organized a list of sponsors, from yarn suppliers to mental health providers, that could all pitch in and lower costs. Despite my nerves, things seem to be working out.

"Yes, tonight is the big announcement." I glance at the clock. "I actually have to get going soon to set up."

"If you can manage to teach us poor saps how to knit, your followers will be positively stoked," Ibrahim says in the only volume he knows—loud.

They all cheer.

After so many years of keeping my social circle to my sister, moms, and online community, being here with them has made me realize how lonely I truly was. Three months into my Yes Year, and taking risks is paying off tremendously. I like this feeling of belonging. My knitting retreat is only going to multiply it.

"Thanks, guys." I pack up my tote bag and loop it over my shoulder. "Same time next week."

"Night, Daph!" they say in unison.

Next to the mailboxes in the lobby, there's a stack of packages with my name on them. I crack my neck, ready for the only form of exercise I actually enjoy: lugging PR boxes up and down three flights of stairs.

At least at the end of this cardio, I'll have a whole new slew of yarn to play with.

The best part of my job is how lucky I am to be sponsored by brands I love. My streaming income is consistent enough to keep me comfortable, but the sporadic brand sponsorships give me a boost here and there.

Definitely a big enough boost for me to be able to invest in the retreat!

I grab the biggest box, struggling with its unwieldy size, and ascend the stairs. Halfway up the last flight, my arms strain with the effort. You'd think yarn wouldn't be this heavy, but my thighs are burning. My foot catches on a step, and I stumble, the box almost slipping from my grasp.

"Need a hand?" A voice startles me from behind.

Not just any voice. Cameron's voice.

Of course, it's him.

I turn. He's standing with the rest of my boxes stacked like a Jenga tower in his strong, hefty arms. The soft hallway light illuminates his chiseled, brooding features. His dark hair is tousled in a perfect just-rolled-out-of-bed look.

My cheeks burn, the same way they did when he burst into my apartment like a sexy, heroic exterminator. Must my body betray me so cruelly? He's just a man! A handsome, grunting man with a voice that raises the hairs on the back of my neck.

And he's wearing that gold hoop in his ear again.

Must he do that when I'm fuming at him?

Are his deep brown eyes swirling with that familiar mix of mischief and sadness? I can't tell, and it doesn't matter. The last thing I need to be doing is trying to figure out what any of his looks or actions or sexy half-smiles mean.

"Shouldn't you already be hiding out in your apartment? It's after nine," I blurt out before realizing my mistake.

"Keeping tabs on me?"

"No. Of course not. Just surprised to see you lurking at this hour," I retort, trying to regain some composure. I fail. Miserably. "What are you doing with my stuff?" I attempt to change the subject as I climb up to our floor.

"I'm only trying to get up the stairs."

"So you decided to steal my boxes and follow me up here?"

"Don't know if you forgot, but we are neighbors. If you don't want me to help you carry these, then I'll walk them downstairs, and you can bring them back up yourself." His tone is annoyingly calm, but the way his brows lift tells me he's enjoying this.

"Fine, but don't think for a second this means you're off the hook. You still owe me an apology for being a complete jerk the other day." He climbs another stair, gets closer, and cocks his head before letting out one of his signature grunts. That rumbling sound makes my blood boil with vexation. "Seriously?"

He tilts his head, still silent. Immature and ridiculous. I want to crack him open and see the guy I was with in San Francisco, not this statue. *No, Daphne.* He's not a flawed stitch I can mend. *I haven't been able to stop thinking about it. About you.* Why did he have to tell me that? Why turn everything between us into such a confusing mess?

"You know what? Take my boxes. Throw them down the stairs, or take them to your apartment and burn them! You can add Package Thief to your résumé, right below Spider Exterminator, Stalker Accuser, Premier League Soccer Jerkface, and Man with That Sexy Gold Hoop Earring," I babble out in frustration.

Ugh. I know how to manage my emotions, but with Cameron Hastings, I feel so out of control.

"Sexy?" His mouth quirks to the side.

He gives me *that* look again. The smoldering, I'm-too-cool-for-this look. My body instantly melts like a popsicle in July. Traitor! Why does this meathead act totally work on me? What primal cavewoman switch gets flipped in my brain when he does this?

"The hoop is doing all the heavy lifting."

"That so?" He steps closer. A familiar, sexy wickedness flashes into his eyes. "Want to try it on?"

"Oh, please. If I wanted to accessorize, I'd wear something that doesn't scream pirate wannabe."

"Pirate wannabe?" He chuckles, shaking his head. "You've got quite the comebacks, Daphne." The way he says my name makes the tendrils in my stomach tighten.

"And you've got quite the ego, Cameron." I try to look unimpressed.

"Look, I'm—"

"Don't *look* me. You're hot and cold, up and down, and it's exhausting. One minute you're helping me, the next you're accusing me of stalking you."

He takes a deep breath, gaze softening. "Maybe I'm just trying to figure things out."

The words snap some sense into me. I don't want to be collateral for some gorgeous man who can't vocalize his feelings.

"I thought there was no *us* to figure out." I sigh. "Please just leave my boxes here. I'll get them later."

I whirl around to storm up to my apartment, but my slipper slides along the tile, causing me to lose my balance. The large box in my arms collapses to the floor. In one swift motion, Cameron drops my packages onto the landing and tries to steady me, placing his hands on my shoulders. We end up losing our balance, stumbling backward as we struggle on the staircase. We slide down four stairs before coming to a stop on the landing, my back pressed against the wall. He steadies me, his six-foot-plus frame towering over me.

His hot breath fans across my face. A mix of fresh grass and earthy musk fills my senses. My traitorous mind spins with the memory of being with him.

The way his scruff brushed against my knuckles, the tenderness of his lips when he kissed my palms.

His presence is dominating and overwhelming. Oxygen

drains out of my lungs. We stare at each other for a long time, his gaze scanning my eyes before it dips to my lips.

I want to kiss him again. Against every rational instinct in my body, I want to rise up onto my tiptoes and get a small taste.

"You smell nice," he says with an icy drawl.

My knees wobble. Warmth pools in my belly. I want to tell him to whisk me into my apartment so we can finally get rid of all this ridiculous pent-up tension between us. But I can't. Not when I risk being brushed off by his cold shoulder again.

It takes all my might to push him away. "Thanks," I snap, my voice slicing through the tension like a knife. I scramble to pick up my large box. "Good night." I scurry up the stairs, unlock my apartment, and toss the cardboard barrier onto the floor.

The entire living room spins as I attempt to calm my racing heartbeat, but his inescapable image flashes in my mind.

That strong jawline. His not-so-perfect nose. His hands clenched into fists while he avoided my gaze. What gives guys like him the license to be such jerkfaces? The patriarchy, that's what. His first red flag was bright and clear—what kind of person doesn't eat sugar? There has to be some sort of grumpy-dude manual out there, one that lays out all the qualifications for being a certified grouch.

One: never smile

Two: avoid sweets

Three: grunt instead of using words

Four: don't pet puppies

Okay, I don't know about that last one. But my point stands.

I have my knitting retreat to announce, scarves to knit for Femi, and a whole nine more months of my Yes Year. I don't have time for guys who don't know what they want. The last thing I need is someone messing with my composure.

Stop it, Daphne.

"I am a strong, confident, charming woman who doesn't

need to second-guess herself," I say out loud. And it's not my problem if he doesn't want anything to do with me because, frankly, it's his loss.

I'm a Yes Girl!

Except maybe when it comes to Cameron Hastings.

Chapter 10

Cameron

Lyndhurst's Defense Fails to Catch Up in the Third Loss of the Season

PATHETIC.

I hit rewind again. Kamara's image fades, leaving my box exposed. Rosemont's striker fakes left; I'm too slow. The whistle haunts me, then the stadium erupts with cheers.

One goal. That's all it took.

We've lost three out of six games. Lyndhurst's—*my*—chances of winning the championship slip farther away each week. I can't help but wrestle with regret for not staying with my old club. Overton has eleven points; we're stuck with five. The thought has been sprouting up more often than not.

Parkside City, the top team for the past two years, is struggling due to injuries and club drama. If there was any year to win, it's now.

I refocus on the screen. My teammates rely on each other, but not on me. I'm a liability. I need to find that old fire before it's too late. I rewind the tape over and over, wincing as the ball hits the net repeatedly. I don't deserve to rest until I learn from my mistakes.

Rossi's voice echoes in my head. *You call that a defense? You're pathetic*, he'd sneer, making me rewatch every miniscule error.

Exhaustion clings to me as I slump on the sectional in the common room. I grab one of Daphne's soft blankets, draping it over my head. The warmth provides a momentary solace.

Footsteps on the stairs send a panic through me. I fling the blanket and pillow aside, trying to appear nonchalant.

"*Lust Island* on Wednesday and Sunday nights, bum, bum, bap, boo, bap!" Daphne's singing sprinkles into the common room like a burst of confetti. She freezes. Her eyes flit to the discarded blanket and pillow before they meet mine. Does she know what I was doing? "Oops." She stumbles. "Forget I was here!"

No matter how many boxes I lift or spiders I banish, it doesn't negate the fact that I was an ass.

"Wait!" I call after her.

She spins around frantically in the doorway, and her knitting project snags on the door handle. Stepping back into the common room, she tries to free it, but in the midst of the struggle, the door swings shut.

"No, no, no, please, this can't be happening." She sighs, wrestling with the knob. I pause the television and stroll to the end of the sofa.

"What's wrong?"

She taps her forehead on the door three times before spinning toward me. "The house is built on an incline, so if this old door shuts, it gets jammed, which means we're stuck." This must be the universe's way of nudging an *I'm sorry* out of me. "Can you call one of your teammates to let us out?" She throws her hands on her hips.

"I don't have my phone. Don't you always need to have yours for influencing?"

She scowls. "You know what? It's fine. Everything is going to be okay. How about I stay on this side of the room?" She passes me, tossing the soft orange blanket onto the couch and sitting down to work on her knitting. "And you can have that side. Someone will get us out of here soon."

She grabs the remote and switches to *Lust Island*. My jaw ticks. *Fuck.* She hates me. I've actually made a woman who looks like she would skip down a sidewalk to avoid stepping on an ant hate me.

Guilt claws at my throat. It's easier if she hates me, if I continue pushing her away like I have with everyone else. Keeping people at arm's length is safer. But I miss how alive I feel around her—a glimpse of who I was before signing my first Premier League contract.

Daphne's like a vibrant lifeline in my dull world. When I'm around her, a door cracks open, just a bit, and I want to step through it without fear.

No.

Being around her is bad news. Dangerous. Exhilarating.

You can't be him again, Cameron.

Selfishly, I long to feel alive with her again. Loneliness urges me to connect with her, with my teammates. But my fear is like an overrun field of weeds.

I pace behind the couch.

Regardless of how I feel, she's owed an apology. But where would I even start?

Sorry that my influencer ex decided to use my lowest moment as a stepping stone for some cheap reality TV fame.

That because of Mal's shifty moves, the mere thought of being around a woman sets me on edge?

Or, *sorry for my sharp edge and trust issues.*

None of these apologies cover the most important point.

Forgive me for feeling drawn to you even though I don't fully understand why. For the heat that flares inside my blood every time I see you. You've got me tangled up, and I'm scared of what it might mean for both of us. Sorry that your constant presence consumes my every waking thought, and I'm pissed because the only thing that's ever taken up that much fucking real estate in my mind is football.

Yeah, dumbass, tell her that.

Reluctantly, I drag myself to the opposite end of the sofa. She's stubbornly glued to the TV, refusing to acknowledge my existence. "Hey, look, I'm—" My words choke off as she tears her gaze from the screen, blinking at me in anticipation. "Sorry about what happened."

"*And?*" Her eyebrow arches at me, challenging.

"And?" I echo back, baffled.

"You don't need me to tell you that that was a terrible apology," she retorts, her eyes glinting with a fire that does that annoying, fucking funny thing to my insides.

A lump forms in my throat, and I swallow hard. I want to make this right. "I'm sorry that I accused you of stalking me." I tip my head to one side, flexing my jaw. "Not a lot of people call me out on my behavior. That sounds bigheaded, but it's true."

And damn it, she's attractive when she's putting me in my place.

She studies me, probably trying to figure out if I'm playing games. I'm not. But getting her to believe that? A long shot.

"That's a start," she says.

I roll my shoulders, my hands finding refuge in my jeans pockets. "I've been dealing with stuff."

"Not very well," she snaps back, and I smirk.

My sisters would get a kick out of her sass. "No. Not very well."

"Doesn't give you the right to be a jerk to someone who's making a genuine effort to be nice to you," she says.

"I was an asshole," I admit. "But I've been trying. The boxes? The spider?"

"Words hurt, Cameron."

I know how true that is. "Sorry again."

She doesn't seem convinced. What more can I do? Beg for her forgiveness? Ask her to come upstairs and let me show her how sorry I am? It's ridiculous to feel this way about a fling. "Can I make it up to you?" The words slip out.

"Perhaps."

"What do I have to do?"

She thinks for a moment before saying, "One hundred push-ups."

"Not the response I was expecting."

"Maybe stop making assumptions about me," she scolds me, highlighting the adorable wrinkle in her nose.

"I—uh, I lost a match today."

My legs are on fire from all the sprinting. My core feels like it's been through a blender. And let's not even talk about my shoulders and arms. *Am I actually considering this?*

"You asked me what you could do. Now all I'm hearing are excuses."

Is her forgiveness even worth it? What am I trying to get out of this? Being just neighbors doesn't feel right, but I have no time for another situationship. My sister's advice echoes in my head: *Maybe you could make some new friends?*

Could Daphne, of all people, be a friend?

It seems absurd to hang out with an influencer while also dodging the media, but Daphne isn't like Mal. Online, she paints herself as kind and charitable. She advocates for mental health. The *Stone Times* described her as genuinely good-hearted.

Maybe I need someone like Daphne, who sees through me without trying to fix me.

"Okay," I manage, shrugging off my leather jacket, feeling

every ache in my lats. "One hundred push-ups, and we can be friends?"

"*Friends?*" Her forehead wrinkles in surprise. "You don't even want to be neighbors with me."

God, she has no idea.

"I do, I—" I can't articulate what I want.

"Right, sorry, you don't want to be thinking about me at all."

"I shouldn't have said that." I palm the back of my neck. "I shouldn't have acted the way I did. You trip me up, and—fuck, I don't know what the right move is around you."

"I'm a person, not a game. There's no right move."

She's got a point. I've become so used to walking on eggshells during every interaction I have. There used to be consequences if I said the wrong thing or didn't act right. *Used to be.* Guess I haven't shaken the habit of treating my relationships like they were a play on the pitch.

"The real reason that I've been so hot and cold is because you're a reminder that I let my guard down when I should've been focused on football." There it is, the truth laid bare. "I should be keeping my mind on the most important thing in my life instead of thinking about what happened between us. My head's scrambled."

"Football, foosball, or ultimate frisbee, I have no idea why it matters that much. Or why I, someone who hasn't a clue about sports, am causing you to act like a stereotypical meathead when you were nothing like this when we first met."

"I had a rough year. How I've been toward you—it isn't me." I collect my breath. It wasn't the old Cam at all. "I'm sorry again, Daphne. I want to be better."

"That's a much better apology." She stares at me, eyebrows raised. "But I still want my hundred push-ups."

No woman I've slept with has ever spoken to me the way she does. And some misbehaved part of me wants to prove myself to her. The same part that strived harder, gave more, and paid closer attention when she praised me during our night together.

I want that praise.

I crave her approval.

If a woman like her could see something in me, then maybe I'm not the complete disaster I fear I am.

"Fine," I grumble, dropping to the worn-out carpet.

"Count them out loud," she orders. "I'm not the best with numbers, and we wouldn't want you to lose track and have to start over, would we?"

The corners of my lips curl up. She's amused by this. The competitor in me is too.

"Yes, ma'am." I inhale a sharp breath and begin. "One, two, three…" I fall into an easy rhythm. Before I know it, I exhale, "Fifty." I toss the hair out of my face. "If you wanted to make this a challenge, you'd sit on top of me."

"I tried that once and got accused of stalking."

"I deserve that," I say, counting down the remaining fifty. By the hundredth push-up, my biceps and back scream, and sweat drips from my brow. I stand up, brushing my hands off on my jeans. "So, friends?"

"*Trial* friends." She nods approvingly. "But I'm not having sex with you again."

That was to be expected, but disappointment still floods my chest. She'll be the first woman I fucked first and friended later. Probably for the best. Sleeping with friends sounds messy.

"Understood."

"After what happened between us, I've sworn off soccer boys for the rest of my life."

Relief coats my disappointment. Despite having no right to get possessive over her, I'm not exactly thrilled by the idea of my new…friend fooling around with my teammates.

"Smart girl." Silence lingers between us. How do I stop this conversation from falling apart? The first time we spoke, it felt effortless. *Think, Cameron. Think.* A memory flashes to mind. "How's your Yes Year going?"

Her eyes light up. "You remember that?"

"Hard to forget." *Hard to forget anything about you.*

"It's actually going really well. To think that on my birthday I committed to a completely new lifestyle, and then two days later, we met. Life is so strange."

"We hooked up two days after your birthday?" June twenty-ninth. Why hadn't she mentioned it?

"Yes, and because of my Yes Year, I'm living across the world and planning a knitting retreat."

I vaguely remember a mention of a retreat in the *Stone Times* article. "Do you normally do events like that?"

She shrugs. "No. Usually, I create knitting patterns and share them with my followers. I do livestreams on Thursdays and Saturdays and a bunch of other knitting things." Well, that explains who she's always talking to behind the shared bedroom wall of our apartments.

"And you get famous off of that?" I awkwardly kick my feet around.

She frowns. "There you go again with the judgment and assumptions. Stop it. I have no interest in being famous. Knitting is a way for me to connect with people."

"I guess I haven't met many people who do what you do and don't want fame out of it."

"Is that why you have something against people in my profession?"

On the television, Mal Kelly and a group of women sit around a firepit. I wince. Daphne seems to notice, flipping the channel. I expect her to ask for more details, but she doesn't.

"Not *against*," I say. "You just continue to surprise me."

"It's quite fun doing that." She smiles. "Who knows, if you're not a bad friend, I might even reserve a spot for you at my retreat. You can see what it's like to be around people who share their feelings."

"Don't think so."

"You say that now, but if I managed to get you to open up tonight, then you might learn to talk about all the stuff you're mysteriously figuring out."

The comment makes me want to nudge her shoulder, but maybe we're not quite that friendly yet. "To be fair, I had no choice. We're locked in here."

"Watch it, you're on thin ice." She laughs.

I laugh too, the foreign feeling warming my bones. I glance at the sofa again. It's big enough to seat a group of eight, and I consider the spot farthest from where she's sitting the most appropriate place I could choose without disrupting our trial friendship. I settle opposite her, and one of my fingers brushes over the orange blanket I've become very well acquainted with. "This is really impressive."

"Thanks." Her cheeks dimple. "You can use it if you want. It doesn't bite."

"That's all right." I pull my hand away.

"Come on, what are you afraid of? That you'll like it?" *You have no idea just how much I like it, Duck.* She stands, grabbing the throw and shaking it out. I freeze as she drapes it over my shoulders, the familiar softness and warmth encasing me. "There. Much better."

Sure is.

The silence dares me to reach out and feel the smooth skin of her cheek and the silky texture of her lavender hair. *How can someone so unfamiliar feel so safe?*

A noise from the television grabs Daphne's attention, and she returns to her seat.

An urgency erupts inside of me. I need to cement this friendship. Who knows how much longer we have in this room alone. I can't lose this feeling of ease now that I've got a real taste for it.

"Can I propose something?" I ask.

"Proposing already? We just became friends."

Smartass. "What if I can help make your Yes Year more exciting? To make up for how much of a jerk I was to you."

She raises a brow at me. "Tell me more about this being-a-jerk-to-me part."

I shoot her a glare. "*Enough.*"

"Then just the making-it-up-to-me part."

I lean my forearms on my thighs. The next words feel like a gamble. "What if I give you some more opportunities to say yes?"

"I already said this is platonic."

I suck air through my teeth, shaking my head at her. "What a filthy mind. But I'll take it as a compliment."

"Oh, hush!" She drops her knitting project and tosses a pillow at me, but I block it, tucking it into my chest and holding it close. "Guess that was never going to work." She rolls her eyes. "You're literally a professional."

"I'm sure you'll get past my defenses eventually." The easy flirting spills into our conversation. "I only meant that I can show you a different side to London, one you haven't seen before. I've lived here for a few years."

She considers me. "Maybe. As long as I don't have to make any acquaintances with the grumpy storm cloud that follows you around." Frankly, I'm growing tired of it too. This could be good for me. A way to get my mind off of this terrible season and how much I'm fucking up my communication on the field. "What do you even like to do for fun? Ignore puppies?"

How is it that every single thing that comes out of her mouth shocks me? "What?"

"Never mind."

"Okay." I reluctantly don't probe. "Honestly, it's been a while since I had any kind of fun."

"You're doing a terrible job at selling me on this tour."

"Between games and practice, I don't have that much time."

"Your team does."

She's right. I could sacrifice a night of game replays and studying our competitor's stats for a break. Last season, rest wasn't an option, but if keeping my mind off of football for even one night would feel as good as this does, then it may be worth it. It may make me a better player. "Well, on Mondays and Wednesdays, our practice ends at one o'clock."

"Then why do you get home so late?"

My pulse rises. "You tracking my schedule?"

"Gotta be sure I avoid those hallway run-ins."

She's really going to make me work for it, isn't she? "I stay back to extend my training. But I could be better about rest days like my teammates. We could hang out then."

"Restful adventure? Sounds right up my alley." She nods. "Wednesdays I'm committed to the guys, so Mondays work for me. But no funny business."

"No funny business," I promise.

She stares at me for a while. "We're really going to hang out…as friends? In the real world?"

The gravity of the question sets the hairs on the backs of my arms on edge.

Am I really going to risk getting seen out in public? And put her in danger of the tabloids? It's only been six months since the back-to-back scandals broke.

Surely enough time has passed, but maybe not?

A scared part of me wants to flee, but another part buried deep inside of me—the old Cam—refuses to give in.

"We are." I'll just need to figure out where I could take a girl like her without getting harassed by the paparazzi. "But…can I ask you to not post about whatever we do online? I like my privacy."

She softens. "I won't. I like my privacy too. Besides, my

followers don't know a single thing about sports. The last thing they want to see is content about soc—*football* players."

I believe her. "Then expect to hear from me."

"Okay," she says speculatively.

I readjust her blanket on my shoulders. I love its comforting weight and wish I could keep it on my bed, just to hold on to that feeling. "So, where in California are you from?"

"Santa Cruz, born and raised. And you?"

"Marin County."

"*Oh, bougie.*" Her fingers return to working yarn onto her knitting needles. She's like a machine with that thing.

"What about your parents? You mentioned your mom owns this apartment?"

She gives me a half smile. "My mom, Prim, paints wedding portraits. She was born in London. Before your team bought out the entire building, this used to be housing for young artists. This city is where she met my other mom, Dani, who's an accountant from San Francisco. An opposites-attract story."

"My parents are the same." It's strange to reveal morsels of information about myself so easily.

"A painter and an accountant?"

"No." I chuckle. "An opposites-attract story. My dad's in tech, and my mom's a three-time WNBA champion."

"Yeah, I learned that in my *stalking* of you." My pulse escalates, and I freeze. She immediately notices the discomfort. "I'm joking. Well, only a bit. I looked you up. *After* I found out who you were."

My pointer digs into my cuticle as my nerves take over. "Don't believe everything you read online."

"I only skimmed the top half of your Wikipedia page. Had to make sure you weren't a criminal moonlighting as a sports person. You do live right next to me."

There's no point in being a hypocrite. I've perused her account almost daily. "Fair enough."

She continues clicking her needles together. "The night we met, you said you had handlers in the area. Want to tell me about them, Goose?"

The silly code name tugs at the corners of my lips. "I was celebrating my parents' anniversary at Benu with all five of my siblings. "

"Let me guess, you're the middle child."

I shrug. "Yes. Two sisters and three brothers."

"That explains everything."

She stirs another fraction of laughter out of me. "And you're the youngest?"

"My oldest sister, Juni, never lets me forget it."

"Explains everything," I mock in return.

"You don't act like you come from a big family. But I guess you do have the whole holing-up-in-your-room-and-not-talking-to-anyone thing down."

"I talk to people," I say defensively.

"People who don't live in this apartment building?" she deadpans.

"My family." Though it's been weeks since I've properly checked in with them. Before every game, the group chat explodes with good luck messages. Yet I haven't mustered up the nerve to explain that the Lyndhurst season so far hasn't been a success, and I'm the root of the problem.

"You miss them?" Her voice softens. "I miss my family a lot."

She's so open about her feelings. I stop my nervous picking and clutch the pillow harder into my chest. "I do."

"At least you have your teammates here. They're really nice."

"After today's loss, I doubt any of them want to be on the same team as me."

"Isn't that the whole point of a team? To be together when you lose?"

Now she sounds like Coach.

Before I have a chance to answer, a ruckus blares from behind the door of the common room. Daphne's ears perk up. I yank the orange blanket off of my shoulders and toss the pillow onto the sofa, quickly sliding back into my leather jacket.

A muffled shout seeps into the common room. "Who closed the door?"

"Yay! The rescue crew has arrived." She stands. "We're in here!"

"Daphne? Is that you?" A large bang slams against the door. "We'll get you out."

I sober at the realization that our moment together is over. As she walks past me, I reach out and gently lock my fingers around her wrist. Those blue-green eyes glance over her shoulder at me. What a fucking sight for sore eyes.

"I'll slip my number under your door," I say. "Plan on next Monday at three?"

"Sounds like a plan." She lifts the corner of her lip at me, and I let go of her.

The door slams open, and half of my teammates rush in.

"Hastings?" Okafor's voice snaps me to attention.

"What were you two doing in here?" Mohamed's eyes scan the pinball machine, the blankets on the couch, and the television.

"Cameron asked for a knitting lesson," she teases.

"Are you going to help with the auction for Femi?" Okafor chimes in. A pang of jealousy hits me—not the romantic kind, but the kind that comes from seeing the ease with which she's bonded with my teammates. I feel like a kid in a sandbox, wanting to be part of their friendship.

"She meant spiders." I clear my throat. "I was helping Daphne prepare for another spider emergency."

"Another spider?" Gustafsson cries, his voice an octave higher than usual. I grin at the hulking footballer, who could probably bench-press a car, quivering at the thought of a tiny arachnid. "I can't handle those things, man. They're like tiny, creepy ninjas."

I nod at Daphne before pushing past them. "Don't worry, Gustafsson, you can leave the spider battles to me."

The guys stare at me in disbelief. I slip upstairs, listening to the chatter and laughter pouring out of the common room. For the first time in months, their liveliness doesn't sting. When I step inside my apartment, I catch my faint smile in the window reflection. Ideas for things to do with my new friends start tumbling around in my mind.

My heart races, and my palms sweat. I might have a chance, after all this time, to not just exist, but to try and live again.

———

CAMERON

Need a nice London spot for a Monday afternoon.

Where should I go?

No press. No phones.

BROOKLYN

Cam has finally entered the chat!

After a long hiatus...............

CAMERON

Been busy.

MOM

Are you going on a date?

Give me a call this week. Dad and I miss your face!

DANTE

Let's not jump to conclusions, perhaps Cameron's simply attempting to take himself out.

CAMERON

Nvm.

BROOKLYN

We're kidding

But how nice are we talking? Dinner? Cocktails? An activity? A show?

I have so many questions

DANTE

You're in luck, brother. An old friend of mine owns a private botanical garden on the outskirts of London. I can overnight you the key.

CAMERON

A key?

Who's the friend?

BROOKLYN

Fancyyyyy

DANTE

Klaus is a good guy, don't worry. He and his wife bought it from a minor lord last year. The place is very exclusive and private.

FRANKIE

sry was on the track. don't take her to rise, got food poisoning there. not sexy for first date

if taking the ferrari, DO NOT bring food in it.

ALEC

how are you handling this recent loss?

CAMERON

Fine.

EZRA

Nice save in the last 10 mins of the game :)

BROOKLYN

Season going better than Overton?

Made any new friends?

CAMERON

Mail the key, Dante. Thx. Gtg.

BROOKLYN

Don't ghost again!!!!!

Chapter 11
Daphne

A SERIES of *tap-tap-tap*s comes from my front door. I pause, not wanting Cameron to think I've been pacing by the door waiting for him like a lovelorn heroine in a cheesy rom-com.

Because I haven't—at least, not for more than fifteen minutes.

The day whirled by as I penned a rough agenda for my knitting retreat, created a shiny new page on my website for sign-ups, and planned out my content for the month.

I know better than to believe the grumpy, brooding man haunting our apartment complex is gone for good, but everyone deserves a second chance. Being friends with someone I've seen naked…that'll be a feat in itself. Sure, this might be one of those mistakes I told Juni I needed to make, but maybe that's okay. I'll learn, grow, and clean up any mess that comes my way.

Another knock comes. *Be cool, Daphne. Be cool.*

I open the door. Cameron occupies the entire frame. His black leather jacket conceals a dark sweater that matches the rest of his grim outfit. The small golden hoop dangles from his left ear. Despite his solemn appearance, he's dreamy.

I swallow. *Be fucking chill, girl.*

"Oh, it's you," I say in a breathy voice, casually leaning against the door. My socks slide across the floor as my body slowly slithers toward the floor. I readjust.

"Like I promised."

"Cool, I just finished shooting."

He glances into my apartment, which is a carefully curated chaotic display of outfits tossed everywhere, surrounded by props and lightboxes. In the corner, my tripod stands ready, my phone still clinging to it, capturing the aftermath of the day.

"Good."

"Are we making a stop at a funeral?" I tease. "Or is the all-black outfit for an emo concert you're taking me to?"

"This is *charcoal*." He shoots me a playfully disappointed look.

"My sincerest apologies."

"Did you make your outfit?" He gestures to my striped, cable-knit sweater woven in hues of pink, yellow, and orange yarn with a matching skirt.

"I did. It's the second skirt I ever had fit me properly after blocking it."

"Blocking?"

"It's like giving your finished piece a spa day. You soak it until it's sopping wet, or, you know, steam it. Then you use your hands to stretch it nice and taut, and then you let it dry!"

"That's—uh," he stutters, palming the back of his neck in that cute, boyish way. His pupils swallow the brown of his eyes. His Adam's apple bobs as he gulps. *Did I say something?* "Guess you could say we both block balls."

"Was that an actual joke?" I snort, playfully nudging his shoulder. "We must really be friends."

"Well, give it a spin," he says.

"A spin?"

"So I can see your skirt. I have a very sudden interest in knitting."

"Oh!" I blush.

"Come on." He tips his head at me. "The full three-sixty."

I swallow and twirl. He makes a noncommittal sound. Has the hallway suddenly gotten warmer? I never feel particularly sexy, but as his gaze trails over my legs, the confidence he roused in me returns full force.

"Since you're suddenly interested in knitting, I'll have to give you a real lesson soon." I smirk, and he nods. "So, can you tell me where we're going? I hate surprises."

"I wouldn't have taken you for someone who hates surprises."

"There you go again with the assumptions," I say, needling.

"I'll need to cut it out or you'll have me on the ground doing push-ups again."

I let out a noise between a gasp and a laugh. "I'm glad you're finally understanding how this relationship is going to work."

"We're going to a garden. Just wear comfortable shoes." The gentle firmness in his voice shoots a shiver up my spine.

"Yes, sir."

A little harmless flirting is okay between friends, right? I slip on the boots beside my "Knit Happens" welcome mat.

"Did you get the apology gift I left for you?" Cameron asks from above me.

The day after we were trapped together, a soft-serve ice cream maker showed up at my door. At first, I didn't know if I should accept it, but who am I kidding? I like nice things, and if Mr. Grumpy Pants wants to max out his credit card trying to make up for how he acted, I won't stop him.

"I did, but you can't buy your way into an apology."

"That's not what—"

"Also, I like milkshakes, not soft serve," I deadpan.

He frowns. "I—"

"I'm messing with you, Goose. It was one of the *sweetest* gifts I've ever received, thank you. If today goes well, I may even invite you over for a special treat."

That look blooms over his features again, but it extinguishes when I finally stand. "I don't do sugar, remember?"

"You didn't *do* friends either, but look at us!" He cocks his head, and I piece together the insinuation. "I didn't mean it like that. I only meant that you may change your mind. If you don't, then you can do your push-ups, and I'll be horizontal on the couch, enjoying my dessert."

"Sounds like you'd enjoy that."

"I might!" I chirp, shrugging on my coat. "Lead the way."

We make like birds and swoop down the stairs, bypassing the ghost town that is the common room. Only a couple more episodes of *Lust Island* are left this season, but the guys and I are set on maintaining our Wednesday night knitting circle and reality TV tradition. Next up on the docket is *The Great British Bake Off*. There's still a month and a half until the auction for Femi, and with only Sven having an auction-worthy scarf ready, the rest of the guys need to catch up.

Maybe Cameron will cave and join us eventually. He'd probably see a kindred spirit in Paul Hollywood's stern and serious demeanor. Actually, he and Paul are two peas in a pod. Both are equipped with a hard exterior and a soft, warm center.

Like an éclair.

Aw! Cameron is just a grumpy éclair.

The early October air bites at my skin as I step outside. The scent of fallen leaves, damp earth, and smoke hangs heavy in the air. I trail after him down the sidewalk until Cameron circles around a car, one that could more accurately be described as a metallic panther, and gallantly opens the passenger door for me.

"Get in." He tosses his head toward the seat.

"This is your car?" I stand frozen with shock.

The shiny black exterior gleams even beneath the overcast sky. It's low to the ground and has headlights that resemble a predator's eyeballs. In so many ways, it's the only car a brooding guy like him could have.

"I don't do the Tube," he says.

"This thing must've cost a fortune."

"My baby sister, Frankie, designed it. She's a junior driver this year."

"Huh?"

"F1. Motorsport."

"That's so cool." I bet everyone in the Hastings family is as impressive as Cameron. "Growing up, my sister and I shared a Prius, but I haven't driven much since moving to San Francisco eight years ago."

"Want to take it for a ride?" He shoots me an unfairly charming smirk.

My mind, traitorous thing that it is, screams, *YES PLEASE!*

"Not even an hour into our little rendezvous, and already you're giving me the chance to say yes. Kudos to you, sir. Kudos."

With a grace that's utterly infuriating in its elegance, he slides into the passenger seat, leaning over to pop open the driver's door for me. "Get in the car, Daphne."

The car's interior exudes luxury, with plush black leather seats and gleaming surfaces. The driver's seat is set too far back for my small frame, and he reaches over to adjust it. His earthy scent overwhelms me. I have to resist the urge to lean in for another sniff.

"All right, this is nothing like a Prius," I admit.

"You're going to start the engine." He points to the button on the steering wheel, and I press it. I wrap my hand around the black leather steering wheel. Between us, there are switches with lettering on them, and he toggles a few. "Now, you're going to want to—"

"I got this." I cut him off, swatting his hand away. I can handle this. I buckle up, check my mirrors, and awkwardly crane my neck to scope out the road from my left. *This can't be that hard.* I press my foot on the gas, and the car roars to life. A deep growl morphs into a high-pitched scream. The steering wheel shudders under my hands. The scent of gasoline fills the air. *"Ahhh!"* I yell, startled by the explosion of noise and movement. I snap my gaze over to Cameron, who's biting back a grin. "What was that?"

"You didn't take it out of park," he says and flips another switch.

"I knew that."

"Sure."

I do a final sweep behind me, making sure I won't run over a squirrel, and then gently hit the gas. The car lurches forward, and I jolt back. Adrenaline floods my veins like an overflowing river. I try tapping the pedal again, but again, my head slams onto the headrest, causing me to shriek.

"Okay!" I hit the brake, put it in park, and burst out of the car. "I've driven a sports car. It's all yours now."

Cameron slips past me by the hood. "You'll get it next time," he says, and an image of his rough hands pushing me up against this beast of a car flashes in my mind. I cough, attempting to tame my filthy thoughts.

He slinks into the driver's seat, adjusting the seat to accommodate his long legs. A vein twitches at the top of his tanned hand as he clutches the steering wheel. My mouth dries at the sight of his thumb digging into the leather, the rest of his rough knuckles turning white as he adjusts the mirrors.

"We'll go to the countryside next time," he says, "so you can edge more than a couple of inches off the road."

Trust me, I've been edged plenty from this entire interaction. "Yep, we'll save that for another day."

"Counting on it," he murmurs in that tantalizing growl that sends shivers down my spine. Before I can react, he leans over me, and in one smooth, deliberate motion, he buckles me in. His fingers graze my hip just enough to send my pulse into applause. "Safety first." He winks, lips curling into that infuriating and belly-warming smirk.

My heart pounds so loudly I'm certain he can hear it.

"Those grandparent dates sure did make you an honorable gentleman." I laugh awkwardly. This is starting to feel dangerous. It's only outing number one, and I'm already wishing he'd thrust himself right into me like one of those steamy vampire TV show stars Juni is obsessed with. Maybe without the bloodsucking.

Or, I don't know, he might like that. Maybe I would as well.

Where is my mind?

We're supposed to be just friends, but the incidental touches and lingering looks remind me that we started as more. His brooding charm makes it hard to remember why we chose to stay platonic.

As he rolls out into the street, he flashes me a look that tells me he's wondering the same thing.

———

HALF AN HOUR LATER, we're strolling through opulent hedges toward an expansive conservatory fit for royalty. Cameron may have made me feel like a princess when he asked me to twirl, but I'm definitely underdressed for a place like this.

"Is this yours?" I stammer as he retrieves a wrought-iron key from his pocket. There's no denying that Cameron is extra wealthy. But the idea of him casually owning an estate-sized garden is beyond my understanding.

"No." He unlocks the gate and holds it open for me. "I've never been here before. My very-well-connected brother recommended it."

"You're going to need to give me a full family debrief." I laugh.

We step inside, and my mouth falls open. Despite the dreary sky, the garden is vibrant and alive. The breeze makes the greenery dance, and the air is thick with sweet perfume. In the distance, an archway is illuminated by twinkling fairy lights, casting a magical glow over everything. This is Narnia-level transportation to a different world.

"My parents named us in alphabetical order, so that usually helps people keep track," he explains, walking ahead of me. "Alec, Brooklyn, me, Dante, who's responsible for all of this, Ezra, and Francesca. We're each a year apart from one another."

I crane my neck, taking in this magical place. "Must've been great having so many built-in best friends growing up."

"Yeah," he says apathetically. "Do you hear that?"

In the distance, the low hum of bass reverberates.

"Music?"

We follow the noise through a bend deep in the garden until we're met with a crowd of people dressed in glitter and glam. They're dancing around a grand marble gazebo, which serves as a DJ booth. The loud music pulsates through the very heart of the garden, making the plants sway in rhythm and the flowers bloom in time with the beat.

"I'm going to kill Dante."

"A secret garden party?" we say at the same time.

"I didn't realize this would be a full-on rave." He rubs his temples. "My brother likes to pull stunts like this. Unlike you, he doesn't hate surprises. We can leave."

"Are you out of your mind? *This* is exactly the sort of

surprise I can rally behind." I squeal, bouncing on the balls of my feet. "I tried to go clubbing when I first got here, but it just didn't work out. There are certain Yes Year moments that don't work solo."

"You went to a club alone?"

I arch a curious brow at him. "Yes." My body instantly shimmies to the music. "Come on, let's go dance." He hesitates. "You told me you like house and techno music; don't pretend you don't like dancing to it!" I ensnare his hand in mine. A warm shock flies through me. The deep caramel of his eyes lights up. There's something there, but neither of us spends too long investigating it before we break into the crowd.

Electronic vibrations wrap around me, sinking into my bones. I surrender to them, my body swaying however feels right. Time turns liquid. Cameron sways his shoulders alongside mine, bouncing on his feet. He doesn't invade the friendly distance between us, but he also makes no effort to drop his gaze from me the entire time. The little wrinkle that usually camps between his brows has vanished, replaced by tiny beads of sweat. It's tragically unfair how good-looking he is when he lets loose a little.

My head buzzes like I've been dusted with fairy powder and I am floating in a sky of cotton candy, my feet kicking up fluffs of sugary sweetness.

I didn't plan on bringing out my inner child today, especially not around Cameron, but here she is. She's the girl I usually keep under wraps—the one from before the bullying, before I had to relearn how to love myself. She's loud, laughs obnoxiously, and moves however she wants without worrying about who's watching. And when she looks at Cameron, she sees the boy he may have once been. A boy who makes it okay to be my kid self. She wants to grab his hand, spin him around, and shake all the brooding right out of him.

The beat drops.

The crowd erupts before a human wave crashes back to earth and makes the ground tremble. Suddenly, a girl dressed like a glittering fairy tumbles into me, sending my entire body straight into Cameron's chest.

The heady scent of fresh grass clings to his skin, more potent than the actual garden we're in.

"Woah," I gasp, feeling the firmness of his muscles under my fingertips as I cling to him for balance. Our breaths mingle, his warm and slightly ragged, mine caught between a gasp and a sigh.

"I'm finding it hard to believe that you don't like it when I catch you." His laugh is low. Maybe I do like it when he's there to catch me. Just a little. But I'm certainly not doing it on purpose. Unless my subconscious is sabotaging me.

I steal a glance upward, craning my neck to meet his gaze head-on. A hushed conversation flits between us. Goose bumps march across my skin. His hand moves from my waist to the small of my back, tugging me flush against him.

My palm slides up his chest, feeling the hard planes of his body. The contact is dizzying, making my head spin and my pulse quicken. Our bodies move together to the rhythm of the music, each beat drawing us closer, each sway making the world around us fade into the background. My mind flies in and out of the present and back to the night we spent together.

Gosh, I want to kiss him again, taste his sweat on my tongue. Instead of showing me the stars, maybe he can show me the sky above us, the vines of ivy trailing up the walls.

But I can't. I know I can't. If we share even a fraction of what we did the night we were together, I'll turn into a mushy, feelings-infused mess.

Why must I be such a softie? Women with dazzling brilliance and bucketloads of self-esteem don't fall for their one-night stands. Or do they?

He leans down, whispering in my ear, "Having fun?"

"Yes!" I shout back, reluctantly removing myself from him. I think he's having fun, too. He just needs a little fun foreplay. A slow burner, as they'd say on *Lust Island.* "Let's get some water. It's hot!"

He laces his fingers into mine and leads me to a colorful, flower-adorned bar, pulling out an empty stool for me.

"Stay here, I'll be right back."

"Okay!"

Cameron approaches a bartender adorned with giant blue butterfly wings.

A gorgeous merman appears at my side, his bare chest glittering beneath the lights. "Is this Missoni?" He tugs at my sweater.

"No. I made it." I smile.

"Can I buy one?" His head bobs with the music.

"Only the pattern."

He retrieves his phone from his glistening tail pocket, opens Instagram, and hands it to me. I enter my username, and he clicks follow, leaning in close. "What do I have to do to get you to make me one?"

I laugh. "Show me how you did your hair." I run a finger over his blue seashell braid.

He scrolls through his account. He's a hairdresser, a very prominent one at that.

"Stop by the salon, and we'll trade!" he shouts back.

I beam. "Deal."

My new friend dives back into the crowd, and I look up at Cameron watching the exchange. I wave him over. He sets a colorful cup brimming with ice in front of me, and I down the liquid.

"Thank you! This has been the best afternoon."

"You make a new friend?"

"Yes! I love people!" I say loudly, leaning into his shoulder.

"In a world with social media, I think all of us are starved for human connection."

He doesn't respond or lean away. I stretch my neck to see his face, his eyes boring into mine. The garden melts away.

A monarch butterfly floats above us, perching itself on top of Cameron's head before it flits off in a different direction. Animals always have good instincts about people.

Without thinking, I brush my thumb over the hoop dangling in his ear. "I like this."

"Brooklyn got her ears pierced a few years back," he says. "She wouldn't stop complaining about how bad it hurt. I joked that it couldn't be that bad."

"Never underestimate a woman's pain!"

He throws up his hands in defense. "Learned my lesson. She dared me to do it, and Dante grabbed a lighter, ice, a sewing needle, and an apple before he impaled me."

"I know a thing or two about getting impaled by a Hastings," I blurt out with a laugh. That was so inappropriate, but my sense of humor comes out naturally with him. "Regret it?"

"Helped me get girls. Though some say it makes me look like a pirate wannabe."

"Guess I owe you an apology for that." I giggle.

"You really don't." He brushes me off with another knee-weakening wink. It makes me thankful I'm sitting down, or my swooning would give him another reason to catch me.

Play it cool, Daph. Be friends! "So, does Dante live in London?" I ask, taking another sip.

"No. He does fencing in the States, but he's a socialite. Loves expensive art, exclusive clubs, anything highbrow."

"He's got good taste. It's dreamy here." I'm thankful for the little spot of privacy at our corner of the bar. "What about everyone else?"

"We move around a lot because of our careers. Ezra is an Olympic swimmer." I try my best to keep track of each sibling and their profession, wanting to memorize the little details. "You know about Frankie and Dante, but Alec ice climbs and Brooklyn figure skates."

"That's so cool. You must be good at a lot of sports, then! Did they ever play football with you?"

He scans my face as if he's contemplating the information he's handing over. I want him to continue.

"When we were kids, my dad would bet that if I could block all of my family's free kicks, then he would do one of my chores. If I missed one, I was stuck with his. So one night I was feeling lucky, and we went out to our field—"

"You have a field at your house?" I fail to hide the shock in my voice.

He nods. "Along with a karting track for Frankie, a bouldering wall for Alec, and an ice rink for Brooklyn." There goes my jaw onto the floor again. He laughs at my expression. "I promise, it's not all that."

"Sure." I roll my eyes, softly kicking his shin. "Go on, one night you were feeling lucky."

"My siblings were easy saves. Mom kicked a curveball that nearly cost me the bet, but I managed it well. Then it was Dad's turn. He's never been a professional player, but he's really into sports. That's how he met my mom—well, more accurately, he bought her basketball team to get her attention."

"That's the most romantic thing I've ever heard!"

"They're like two lovestruck teenagers," he says with a soft expression.

My foot continues bouncing through the space between his legs. I want to touch him—touch the softness inside of him. "Ugh, I'm sorry, I keep interrupting you."

"It's fine." He bumps his knee against mine. "It was Dad's turn. He always favored left, so I dove, and for the first time, I saved one of his shots. To this day, it was one of the best one-on-ones I've ever had."

His glistening smile melts me into an actual puddle in my seat. Okay, this whole don't-catch-feelings-for-your-one-night-stand thing is off to a terrible start. Why does he have to be so adorable after all the gruffness these past couple of months? It's spinning my head right off my shoulders.

"That's sweet, Goose." I tap my knuckles against his firm stomach.

Mistake—big mistake. Oh man, is that the opposite of soft.

"What's with the nickname?" He leans another inch closer. *Don't breathe too deeply, Daph, or you will literally pass out.* I brush off the tingling in my body and shoot him a quizzical look. "Yours, not mine."

"Duck?" He nods. "My family gave it to me. When I was a kid, it went through a ton of variations. Daphne to Daffy to Daffy Duck to just Duck. Well, as my moms and sister would say, Duckie."

"It suits you."

"Are you saying I look like a duck?"

"No, though you're friendly and obviously like to migrate."

"Don't go whipping out duck jokes now." Another kick that closes the inches between us. "You're goose-like also. Strong family, protective, and you mate for life—though in your case, it's with your balls."

He cracks into a laugh. I do, too.

Behind him, a man appears like a shadow. "You Cameron Hastings?"

Cameron's softness shatters. His body goes stiff again. "No," he says over his shoulder with a cold note in his voice before he glances back at me and stretches out his hand. "Let's get out of here."

I hesitate. Does Cameron know this guy?

"Wait, it fucking *is* you, Hastings," the man barks like a bulldog. "Tosser. Watch what you're doing to Lyndhurst this season."

I slip off my seat and step in front of Cameron. "What's your problem?"

"Get back, Daph."

"This why you can't keep your head in the game? Got yourself another distraction?" the guy shouts, puffing out his chest.

A few heads turn as his loud voice breaks over the music. My stomach tightens.

Suddenly, the guy lunges around me, grabbing Cameron by the collar of his charcoal sweater and ripping it. Cameron's eyes widen with shock. The stranger's face twists in anger, his knuckles white.

"Hey, leave him alone!" I shout, but the guy just scoffs.

Despite being taller than the stranger, Cameron seems frozen. The crowd around us closes in, their faces a blur of concern and curiosity. My pulse pounds in my ears.

"Enough," Cameron growls, snapping out of his daze and shaking the man off of him. "Daphne, let's go." He wraps his fingers around my wrist. I trail behind him, barely able to keep up with the speed of his long legs. We weave through the dancing bodies until we're outside the iron gate in total darkness.

"What was that about?" I pant, but Cameron keeps walking toward the car. "Cameron."

"I don't want to talk about it." I yank my arm back, planting myself on the mossy ground below my feet.

"I do," I declare. "Who was that? Did you know him?"

"No."

"If there was anyone who should've gotten a piece of grumpy Cameron, it's that guy."

He sighs, looking wearier than I've ever seen him. "Football fans are…they're passionate about their teams. We had a rough start to the season. I didn't want to stick around and hear about it."

"Okay, but—"

"People like that," he says, gesturing at the conservatory

behind us, "are starved for a scandal. They'd call reporters, snap pictures, and feed the tabloids a buffet of steaming shit about me, you, or us."

I blink, still not fully grasping the severity. "So he was shouting at you for no reason?"

"There's an aggressive subculture among some football fans. Some don't just hurl verbal abuse; they thrive on it. They get a kick out of putting people like me on the front page of a gossip column."

"Oh. It's not just about the game?" I ask, my naivety evident.

"No," he says softly. "It's about everything else too. And while that guy might not have tried to assault me, well, apart from ruining one of my fucking sweaters, he'd definitely yell at me just to get a reaction."

"That sounds…exhausting."

"It is," he admits, his shoulders slumping. "It's why I don't want to be seen out in public with you."

The words hurt more than I expected. I get that we're not dating, and I don't exactly want to be on the front page of a gossip column because I went to one botanical garden with my new friend, but the way he says it makes it seem like being seen with me is the worst thing in the world. He's a regular feature in the news, surely he's used to the spotlight.

After all, he dated Mal Kelly.

A flurry of questions whirls around my mind. Why else does he not want to be seen out in public? What else is he afraid of? But I've never been one for excavating secrets people don't want to share. That's a one-way ticket to Codependencyville.

"Are you embarrassed of me?" I let slip, the words propelled by a sudden, irrational fear that's taken root in my mind.

"No," he asserts. "It's not like that. I—" He shakes his head as if he's trying to properly arrange his thoughts. "Last season, the tabloids were all over me. They spread lies, they twisted stories, they took a painful moment and made sure it hurt me." There's pain in his voice.

"What happened?"

Cameron's gaze drops to the ground. "It's in the past now. But I don't want that to happen again. More importantly, I don't want *you* to be their next target." His behavior confounds me, shifting from puzzling to forthright in a matter of seconds. As if he can read my thoughts, he steps closer and says, his voice faltering, "I'm not hiding anything from you. There's just stuff that isn't real, stuff that felt humiliating, stuff that—I don't want you to get the wrong impression of me."

Part of me can't resist this man with sad eyes and a kind heart. "I'm not swayed by gossip, Cameron. I wouldn't believe something someone twisted and posted for clicks. I do trust you. But is this why you haven't done anything for fun lately? Because you don't want to be recognized?"

"Yes," he confesses.

Well, that can easily be resolved. "Then let me plan our next da—" I pause. "Outing."

"No. I made a promise. I won't take my brother's recommendations next time."

"Compromise is the key to friendship, right?" I remind him. "I'll pick the least public place you could imagine. And," I say, reaching for the collar of his sweater, "let me mend this when we get back home."

"You don't have to do that. I have plenty of charcoal sweaters." He tries to brush me off but doesn't step back. In fact, his chest presses firmly into my hand, as if he wants to be touched by me.

"Well, I want to," I say.

"Okay," he softly utters, his voice nearly a whisper amid our mutual silence. "Now, let's get you home."

Yet he stays still, and so do I.

DAPHNE

Do you know who this is...

@ch1kl100?

THE HANDLE BELONGS to a private Instagram account that's been hovering at the top of my story views. It's only been two days since we last saw each other, but I've been looking for an excuse to talk to Cameron again. And sure, it's a longshot that this faceless, no-posts account is him—likely impossible. But the random profile has been appearing in my notifications more often than not, hearting posts and lurking in my story views.

The chat bubble groundhogs in and out of the screen.

CAMERON

Yes.

DAPHNE

A friend of yours?

CAMERON.

It's me.

I knew it wasn't another bot! Considering *he* once called *me* a stalker, it's a little hypocritical on his part to creep on my social media page. But maybe he's as curious about me as I am about him.

I suddenly feel shy. He's seen every story, he knows I had two bowls of rainbow cereal for breakfast today.

DAPHNE

I'll have to alert the authorities.

CAMERON

?

DAPHNE

You're stalking me lol!

CAMERON

Research.

DAPHNE

Trying to come up with some more of those knitting jokes?

CAMERON

Planning activities for your Yes Year.

DAPHNE

By keeping an eye on me?

CAMERON

You have a nice page.

DAPHNE

Nice enough for you to use your Finsta to spy on me.

I'm never letting you live this down.

I click back into Instagram and request to follow him. The next message comes instantly.

CAMERON

You want to follow me back?

DAPHNE

That's what friends do, Cameron.

:)

CAMERON

I don't have any posts.

DAPHNE

We'll have to fix that on my next Yes Year activity!!!

CAMERON

We have away games the next two weekends.

I'll be free the 26th.

DAPHNE

See you then buddy.

"Buddy?" I cringe, locking my phone and tossing it onto the couch. Seriously? Could I have picked a worse word? *Pal? Bestie? Hottie with a rocking body?*

He makes me nervous, calm, and excited, all rolled up into one.

My phone pings, and I leap for it, heart racing as I open the message.

CAMERON

Looking forward to it.

I let out an excited squeal, then immediately clap my hand over my mouth. Okay, so maybe I like him. How could I not? He's unlike anyone I've ever met—a walking contradiction of gruff exterior and hidden softness that makes my heart do somersaults.

Now I have a date to plan. For once, the butterflies in my stomach feel less like anxiety and more like…possibility.

Chapter 12
Cameron

DAPHNE QUINN

We'll be meeting here today: Whispering Wool
Farms

See you at 2pm!!!!

I STARE at her message from this morning, wondering if I've
arrived at the right place. It took me forty minutes to drive into
the middle of nowhere for Daphne's Yes Year activity. My car is
parked in an uneven, muddy lot facing a blue house with a
matching barn beside it. Rain pelts my windshield as I periodi-
cally glance in the rearview mirror, looking for her.

CAMERON

Where are you?

DAPHNE QUINN

Be there in ten minutes. :)

CAMERON

Ok.

I tap my feet incessantly against the floor of my car, cycling through house music playlists, attempting to calm my restless nerves.

Finally, a taxi approaches. Someone gets out, swinging a bag in their hand as they walk down the gravel driveway. They have pitch-black short hair and are dressed in a black sweater and skirt combo, sporting a handlebar mustache that looks like it was stolen off a cowboy in a Western.

What in the hell?

That can't be Daphne.

I exit my car, stepping straight into a muddy puddle. There go my brand-new sneakers.

"Hey, big dog!" they call out. I recognize the voice immediately.

"Daphne?"

"Ready for an adventure?" When she reaches me, she loses her composure, keeling forward as a burst of laughter tumbles out of her.

"What is all of this?"

"You don't want to get recognized. So, I've come up with a solution."

"Your solution is to drive into the middle of nowhere and dress up like Mia Wallace with a mustache?"

"Honestly, I'll take that as a compliment. I thought the wig and mustache combo was giving a Velma meets Hulk Hogan vibe." She snickers. If she thinks that look is attractive, then sure. "Do you like it?" She spins, her skirt flaring out slightly, and for a moment, the absurdity of her getup vanishes, leaving only the heat coiling around my spine. I hope she keeps up this spinning routine each time we hang out.

"You look ridiculous," I mutter, trying to suppress a grin.

She stops twirling and places a hand on her hip. "Ridiculously *good*, right?"

"Sure, Duck."

"Come on, what do you think?" she asks again, softer this time.

"The outfit and wig can stay, but the 'stache has to go."

"Oh, come on!" She hands me the gift bag she's holding. "Open it." I pull out a baseball cap, aviator shades, a long blonde wig, another mustache, and a raspberry-red sweater. "I got you a disguise too," she says with a triumphant grin as she leans on the hood of my car.

"No."

She groans loudly, flapping her arms. "What is with this constant *no*? Is that your favorite word? Yes, Cameron. Come on, say it with me. We're saying yes." I stare at her blankly. "All right, we'll try that again later. Now, throw on your costume. We're on a schedule!"

"I've never had a woman boss me around this much," I admit.

"Well, if we're going to continue hanging out, you better get used to it." Her lips curl into an irresistible pout. "In fact, you should be grateful for my guidance."

I chuckle. "Guidance, huh? More like unsolicited commands."

"Tomato, tomahto," she says with a dismissive wave of her hand.

My heart races. It's getting harder to say no to her, and I'm not sure I want to.

"Fine. I'll do it, but lose the mustache. And I'm not wearing the wig."

"Killjoy," she teases.

"Brat."

"Ugh!" She rips off the handlebar mustache and pockets it.

I open the driver's door, shrugging off my jacket and tossing it on the seat before replacing it with the retina-burning, bright-colored sweater. A vanilla scent surrounds me. The fabric is soft, like one of Daphne's blankets. "Did you make this?"

"Yeah."

"You knitted an entire sweater in two weeks?"

"You're making it into a big deal." She circles me and sits behind the wheel on top of my jacket, her legs dangling out of my car. "I do this for a living. It's just a stockinette stitch. Literally took me half a season of *Gilmore Girls* to throw together. It's nothing." But to me, it's everything. No one has ever made me anything before. The thought that her hands touched every inch, every stitch, fills me with a warmth I can't quite name. "Now come on, put on the rest of the outfit," she insists.

"Thank you, Daphne."

"It's honestly nothing."

I need this distraction today. My mind's been tumbling all week after Lyndhurst's last two games ended in a draw. At this rate, winning the trophy seems impossible. At the botanical garden two weeks ago, I found a rare moment of peace. With Daphne, I don't feel like a goalkeeper burdened with unmet expectations; I'm just a man enjoying the company of a beautiful girl with an addictive laugh. She makes me forget everything. Her infectious sunshine is finally starting to claw its way through my clouds.

"So, what are we doing here?"

"I thought it would be fun to visit a few locations I had in mind for my knitting retreat, you know, since I have you to drive me around for the rest of the day." Daphne peers out at the expansive pastures, which are speckled with hundreds of sheep.

"Why a farm?"

"Not just any farm. A sheep farm!" I stare at her, head cocked. "Wool comes from sheep, silly."

"Naturally." I've never thought about where my clothes come from, but she makes me want to learn.

Daphne checks her phone. "Miranda Lambright, the owner, is meant to be our tour guide."

"Do you think that's her legal name or a code name? Lamb...right?"

A bubbly laugh escapes her. "Maybe there's a shady black market for wool."

"Then it's a good thing we're undercover."

Daphne kicks out one of her feet and bumps my shin. She looks up at me with mirth in her eyes. "For a footballer, you don't seem too keen on getting dirty."

With a husky chuckle, I rest my forearm on the car roof and lean closer, my voice dropping to a low whisper near her ear. "I love getting dirty when the game gets interesting. I can get you dirty too."

She bites her lip, struggling to maintain her composure. "W-what?"

In one quick motion, I grab her hands and tug her out of the car. She pops up, her boots squelching into the thick, sticky mud. Some splatters across my jeans. "See, now we're both a mess."

"Does all of this come naturally to you?" Her cheeks flush, and she makes no effort to let go of my hands.

"You bring it out of me." I flash her a smirk that I know drives her wild.

She swallows hard. "You're impossible."

"You'll get used to it," I say before we are interrupted by a cough.

"You must be Daphne," a stout woman with curly orange hair calls out in a thick British accent from the porch.

"Miranda, nice to meet you!" Daphne calls as we approach.

"The one and only. Who's this boy dressed like a beet?"

Usually, an insult from a stranger would irritate me, but Daphne made me this sweater. Frankly, I'm the best-looking beet on this farm.

"Oh, him?" Daphne tilts her head toward me. "This is Goose, my assistant for the day."

First, I'm begging for an apology, then I'm her chauffeur, and now I'm her assistant. Next thing you know, I'll be like a dog at her doorway, waiting for my next command.

"Nice to meet you both! Come in." Miranda welcomes us. "Tell me about your event. I've heard of knitting circles, but never a whole retreat!"

Daphne lights up. "I want to raise mental health awareness through the therapeutic art of knitting."

"Sounds lovely!"

"Are there any hotels nearby? Some guests will be coming from out of town."

"Nothing for at least twenty minutes."

Daphne gives me a disappointed look, a silent *Ugh*. It hits me that she wants to share this with me—to invite me into her world. I'm honored and a bit surprised. Perhaps I didn't forget how to have friends after all.

"Gotcha." She nods. "How many people does the barn fit?"

"Give or take a hundred. I know you're looking at a March date, and I have to warn you, it'll be as muddy out here as it is today."

"That's good to know!"

For the next hour, we tour the property while Daphne describes her retreat to Miranda. She outlines plans for breakout sessions, silent knitting, guest speakers, social hours, and even a yoga session—called "body knitting." By the end of the weekend, she hopes to donate most of the projects to hospitals or shelters. Her genuine desire to help others leaves me speechless.

At the end of our tour, Miranda agrees to lower the rate for the barn and give a talk about wool production.

"Let me grab a few yarn samples for you." Miranda smiles. "Feel free to pet those little guys. They were born last month." She gestures toward a small pen inside the barn, where baby sheep are huddled together.

"Thank you so much, Miranda, truly." After the owner leaves, Daphne turns to me and squeals, "How freaking adorable is this?" She rushes into the pen, sitting cross-legged on a pile of hay. The little animals swarm her—who could blame them? "Cameron, aren't you going to join me?"

"Not my thing."

She scowls. "I let the no-sugar incident slide, but not petting a fuzzy baby animal is unforgivable."

Fucking hell. I already put on a disguise and let the mud ruin my shoes. I guess I can pet a goddamn sheep. "Fine."

"Yay!" she sings in a melodic voice, making me feel far more than I should for a friend who has sworn off footballers forever.

Standing awkwardly, I spot a small, lone lamb at the back of the pen and approach it, gently stroking its head. It lets out a soft bleat. *Okay, this thing isn't horrible.* I pick him up, and Daphne watches me.

"What?" I ask.

"Just something about a big, tough man holding a baby sheep." She sighs dreamily.

"Doing it for you?"

"Oh yeah. But in a very platonic way." There goes that ego boost. "I think the guys would love these fluffy babies. Maybe I can convince them to do a field trip out here once we finish our projects for Femi's auction."

She fits in so seamlessly with my squad that it stirs a pang of jealousy.

"How's that going?"

"Really well. Moving to London was terrifying. That first month, I felt so invisible, and my nerves were all over the place. I kept pushing myself to try new things, but it was hard." She was lonely, like me. "Now, it's starting to feel like I've found my people. I never imagined, even in my wildest dreams, that I'd befriend a bunch of professional athletes, but the guys treat me like a little sister, and they've given me this amazing opportunity to put my knitting needles to good use."

"It's nice that you're helping Femi." I've rarely talked to the groundskeeper, but he cares deeply about his work, and I appreciate that.

"I'd do it for anyone." It's hard not to feel like one of her charity cases, but I shove the thought aside.

"Everything you're planning for your retreat sounds impressive," I say, eager to steer the conversation away from my insecurities.

"Thanks. I've checked out places in London, but they're not quite right. I want something that feels like the treehouse my moms built back home. Juniper and I would spend hours there, sometimes falling asleep and waking up to find that our moms had joined us with cozy blankets and late-night snacks. This place has a similar rugged charm."

"Minus the lack of nearby hotels, right?"

Her eyes widen, as if she's surprised that I've been listening. "Someone's been a very good assistant today."

The praise hits me like a well-timed save in the top corner. It's funny how a few kind words can make me feel worthy again.

Three sheep gently nudge their wet noses against her leg, begging for her affection. *Get in line, buddies.*

"I'm certain that whatever you do, it'll be exactly how you imagine it," I say.

She gives me a crooked smile and tilts her head to one side. "Can I be honest with you?"

"Shoot."

"I'm worried about pulling this off. I know I can, but occasionally these voices in my head tell me I'm just an influencer, and where did I get the audacity to run a whole retreat focused on mental health?"

I feel a twinge of empathy. "You're more than an influencer," I assure her. "You're Daphne fucking Quinn."

She laughs. "Well, Daphne fucking Quinn struggles with anxiety. I was bullied as a kid, so being inside my brain can be exhausting."

I grit my teeth. How could anyone bully this girl?

"I guess I didn't picture you as someone who struggles with anxiety."

"What did you picture?"

My body stiffens. "I didn't mean to assume."

"No, Goose," she says softly. "I'm genuinely curious about your assumptions this time, for retreat research purposes."

When I think of mental health struggles, my mind goes to my oldest sister. The pressures of being an Olympic figure skater led Brooklyn into some tough situations, but we supported her as a family.

"I guess when I picture someone with anxiety, they avoid things that feel threatening, prioritize safety over new experiences." *Someone like me.* I block that thought. "It's the opposite of what you're doing this year."

"I'm good at faking it. Fluoxetine helps too."

"Anxiety meds?"

"Yep. Been on them since I was a teenager," she confirms.

Her admission catches me off guard. Vulnerability like that, just offered up so easily, is foreign to me. My throat tightens, and I struggle to find the right words. How can she be so open, so unguarded, when I can barely scratch the surface of my own feelings?

"I'm still having a hard time understanding how anyone would ever bully you."

"It's easy to get bullied when you're too much." The light in her eyes fades.

"Maybe those bullies were too fucking little."

"I guess." She pauses, kissing a lamb on its head before sighing. "The worst of it started after my eleventh birthday."

"What happened?"

"I planned a huge party—fairy-themed, obviously."

"Obviously."

"Prim and I spent hours designing decorations, and Dani took me shopping for the best outfit my allowance could buy. I picked out a vintage frock covered in coral glitter. When the big day came, I expected my entire class to show up, but only the popular girls came." My stomach tightens. "They spent the whole month before that getting close to me, but when my moms left us alone, they huddled in a corner, giggling behind their phones. They left before we even cut the cake. The next day, I found out they had posted pictures of me and my party online, mocking me."

Anger rises in my throat. "Fuck those girls."

"It's in the past now. I always say that some people survive bullying, and others become bullies. The rest are like me, they take up knitting and make it their entire personality," she jokes. The lightness in her voice doesn't quite land.

"I'm sorry you had to deal with that."

"It sucked, but it made me a better and more empathic person. Unfortunately, most people have to deal with bullies in their lives. I guess you know something about that." She kicks my foot with her boot. "After that encounter with the fan."

You have no idea, Daph.

My chest tightens, and I pick at my cuticles, tearing the skin to relieve the pressure. Each sharp sting is a reminder of my failures.

Knowing Daphne's story, I'm ashamed of how I treated her when I first arrived two months ago. Letting my fears take control and keep me safe was how I survived my bullying.

Unlike me, she became more resilient. She started helping others. Perhaps I could try that. Opening up to Matos at practice a few weeks ago wasn't the worst thing. It felt validating to know that the last two years weren't just a nightmare I'd concocted.

The silence stretches like a bridge between me and her. I want to cross it.

Don't be so fucking weak, Hastings. Rossi's voice barrels

into my mind. I retreat inward. My mind races, replaying every criticism, every failure.

"Cameron?" Daphne's voice anchors me back into the present.

"Huh?"

"Where'd you go?" she asks gently.

"What do you mean?" I tense, clutching the little lamb tighter into my chest.

"You just sort of disappeared behind your eyes. Are you okay?"

"Fine. Yeah." I brush her off, but she stares at me, unconvinced. Maybe I can take one step forward. "When I first got to Lyndhurst, I didn't know how to be open," I begin shakily. "Honestly, I'm still struggling to get on with my teammates. My old coach, he was tough, led with fear and discipline. Nothing was ever good enough, but his methods got us to fifth in the league." Her eyebrows furrow, so I add, "That's a good place to be if you're the only American keeper in the Premier League."

Her foot gently grazes against mine, and the subtle touch is enough to calm me. She's beautiful, truly listening as if every word matters.

"I had no idea. What about your old team? You must've had someone you could lean on."

"They were tough too, except for my backup goalie, Charlie. He was my best friend there. In my first year, he helped me get through the club's hazing. We did everything together, not just practice. He showed me a different world in London. Funny enough, I was his backup first, and after he got injured, I stepped up. But then—" I pause, the weight of the memory pressing down on me. "Things changed." I trusted him the most, and he invaded my privacy. The one person who was supposed to have my back. It shattered me. I lost my confidence and my best friend in one fell swoop.

I expect to find that dreaded pity written across her face, but instead I find an emotion I can't read.

"Is that why you never hang out with your teammates?"

She really sees right through me. Even when I'm scared—scared of making mistakes, of getting yelled at, of not being enough.

"Sort of."

"Thank you for sharing that with me," she says softly. "You don't have to carry all of that alone anymore, Cameron. I'll be a good friend to you, and you have the rest of the guys too, right? What about your coach now?"

"My new coach believes that friendship is the solution to all our problems."

"Well, that's not the wildest idea, especially since it's been working so well for us."

"It's different."

"How so?"

Because you're not my teammate and because you knock me off my feet effortlessly, asking for nothing in return—apart from making me cuddle sheep and wear a bright red sweater. "It just is."

We sit there for a while, and the feeling of safety and weightlessness returns.

"Cameron?" Daphne's voice cuts through the thick silence. My heart stutters, expecting the usual lecture on resilience.

"Daphne?"

"The sheep is eating your sweater." She laughs, the sound light and infectious.

The tiny lamb in my lap gnaws on the hem of the sweater, mistaking me for its mother.

"Hey little guy, this is mine." I gently tug the baby off.

Daphne is right. Saying yes to more of life's ridiculous adventures might be the first step to finding myself again.

Today was just the beginning.

Chapter 13
Daphne

"I'm in love," I declare, taking in the high ceilings at Petal & Plate, a cafe in Knightsbridge right beside Hyde Park. The place is bathed in natural light, and trailing plants drape over the exposed brick walls. The floors feature beautiful mosaic tiles, and there's a cozy couch area by a wood-burning fireplace. It's like a Pinterest board came to life.

"I thought you might like it." Cameron nods.

It's Saturday, and he spontaneously showed up at my door an hour ago, asking if I was hungry. I didn't have the heart to admit I'd just polished off three waffles—I was too curious about his plans. When I joked about grabbing our disguises, he smirked, saying it would be private where we were going. And god, that smirk is irresistible.

"So, are you finally going to tell me why we're here outside of our regularly scheduled Yes Year shenanigans?" I keep my tone light. But when his eyes drop to the ground, I regret asking. "You know I hate surprises."

"No, it's just—we had a draw today, and I didn't want to sit alone in my apartment watching reruns of what went wrong on the pitch." His voice is uncharacteristically soft. "I needed to get out of my head for a bit."

A hot blush creeps up my neck. "And I help you get out of your head?"

He meets my gaze with a mixture of surprise and another emotion I can't quite pinpoint. "Yeah, you do. I wanted to be around someone who gets it...gets me."

What does that mean?

The thought sends a thrill through me, a thrill that mingles with confusion. He must mean that in a friendly way.

Over the last week, I sent him a good luck text before his last game and teased him endlessly about hearting my Instagram story. Our DMs are filled with bird memes and private places around London that he wants to take me to.

Isn't this what friends do? Send weird messages, help each other escape their minds, and make each other feel like they've had one too many shots of espresso whenever they're together?

Totally normal.

"How do you know about this place?" I ask, putting a stop to my nonsensical thoughts. We shuffle forward; a few people are still ahead of us in line. I eye the pastries lit up in the display case. Half of them are sold out since it's late afternoon, but the remaining ones glisten under the glass, practically begging to be devoured.

"My apartment is right across the street."

I whip around, staring at him like he just told me he's secretly a superhero. "You have a second apartment in Knightsbridge?"

He lifts a shoulder at me, a bit sheepish. "The Lodge is temporary. Coach insisted that it would help me bond with the team."

That makes sense. "Must be tough giving up your home."

"It's okay." His smile is soft, almost like he's trying to convince himself. "Hasn't been all bad."

I flush, thinking of the few glimpses I've gotten of the apartment across the hall from me. "Now I get why your current place looks like a serial killer's hideout." Seriously, it's so bare. My fingers itch to add a splash of color. "No decoration, a lone couch, one sad chair."

He chuckles, running a hand over the back of his neck. "Says the person who looks like they live in a bowl of Fruity Pebbles."

"You could call me a *cereal* aliver." I snicker.

"You're ridiculous. But really, I didn't see the point in moving my stuff over if I'll only be there until the end of the season."

Obviously, I knew he wouldn't be my neighbor forever, but the reality of his leaving makes my chest deflate. If we both move away, could we still be friends? I mean, who else will ask me to twirl in my outfits and laugh at my terrible puns?

"Meanwhile, I dragged my entire life across an ocean, knowing I'd only be here until next summer," I say. "But I can't imagine living without all my stuff."

"You're not planning on staying in London?"

He studies my face as if he's learning how to knit in the round for the first time. There's no point in talking about *our* future—because, let's be real, there isn't one. Just his and mine, separately.

"I'm taking it one month at a time. Originally, I thought I'd move back home after my Yes Year was over, but who knows? Maybe if my retreat goes well, I'll stick around," I offer. "You'll have to show me your actual apartment sometime. I'm going to place my bets that everything in there is fifty shades of charcoal."

His mouth quirks up in a smirk. "You'd be surprised. Though the hardest thing to give up were my heated floors and view of Hyde Park."

"Heated floors? The best my apartment has to offer is a leaky faucet. Although I kind of like the ambient sound. Is that weird?"

"Not at all. Whenever I take a bath, I like to sit in the tub while it's filling up. Reminds me of a waterfall."

I blink at him. "Wait. Did you just admit to being a bath person? And here I thought you were all about cold showers and grit."

He laughs, a warm sound that makes my heart flutter. "I contain multitudes."

"Cameron, is that you?" A woman with hair like a shimmering silver waterfall rambles toward us, her eyes twinkling with recognition.

My heart skips a beat. Oh no, is this another crazed fan? I instinctively grab Cameron's arm, ready to shield him. My pulse quickens, but then his face softens.

"Nice to see you, Rosie." He doesn't pull away from my grasp. "Daphne, this is Rosie. She owns this place."

"Oh! It's so nice to meet you," I say, surprised. "I'm head over heels for your design. It feels like a little bit of me."

"Thanks, sweetheart." Rosie beams. "Thought you moved or something, Cam. Vanished without a word. I had a Don't Kale My Vibe smoothie waiting for my favorite American every morning for a whole week before I gave up."

The realization hits me—he brought me to his cafe, where he knows the owner and has a usual order. I glance at him, finding a softness that makes everything else fade. This is one of those moments where being a class-A lover girl is failing me miserably.

"I promise, it's temporary," he reassures Rosie as she moves behind the counter and taps the current worker on the shoulder to let them know she's taking over.

Rosie looks between us with a knowing grin. "You two ready to order?"

"Uh—" I stammer, too stunned to speak.

"Give us a minute," he says, and Rosie nods, whirring the espresso machine to life. "Got a burning question, Duck?"

"About a thousand."

"I'd come here for a smoothie before driving to Overton for practice last season. Rosie hates football and cares very little about what I do. Her place doesn't attract a big football crowd."

"That about covers it. Except...what exactly does one put in a Don't Kale My Vibe smoothie?"

"Lots of greens."

My nose scrunches. "Yuck. Like I said when we first met, you're all about stems and sticks. I, on the other hand, am in the mood for something sweet."

"Are you ever not?"

"You should try indulging sometime; it might make you less grumpy." I laugh, but he just gives me that classic stare. *Aw, my grumpy éclair is back.* "All these pastries look amazing, I can't choose! Almond croissants are my favorite, but those Danishes are calling my name."

"Why not get both? Or get everything. Whatever you don't eat, you can take home." He leans in, his voice dropping to a conspiratorial whisper. "To indulge yourself."

I arch an eyebrow. "Are we still talking about pastries, or—"

"Enough," he says in that tone that sends shivers down my spine. "Pick whatever you want, my treat."

"You sure know how to spoil a girl."

We order and find ourselves at a table on the top floor. Plates of pastries litter the table as Cameron sips on his green smoothie. Over the speakers, a soft jazz tune plays on the piano. The first night we met floats into my mind.

"This feels like our first date," he says, watching me.

How is he always thinking what I'm thinking?

I'd trade the rest of these pastries to end this day like that one. My back against another window, the soft glow of Hyde Park's city lights casting a romantic spotlight on us.

"So you admit it was a date?"

"I—"

"I'm just teasing."

He smiles. "I didn't tell you this earlier, but I like this sweater, especially the stars."

Is my subconscious out here knitting star-shaped love letters while my brain is just trying to cry over a Netflix show?

"Thanks, yeah, trying something new." I laugh. "Always gotta keep my patterns fresh."

"Do you sell this one on your website?"

I nod. "I do! I uploaded it a few days ago."

"How impressed I am with the fact that you make things with your hands—real, tangible things—is never going to wear off." The butterflies in my belly return tenfold. I like it when he talks to me about my knitting. It makes me feel like he cares. I've been trying to do the same with his football stuff—I bought *Soccer for Dummies* at the bookstore. "Apart from knitting, do you do anything else with your hands?"

I touch you pretty well. The reminder of his firm body against my palms makes me choke on a sliver of almond.

"Wouldn't you like to know?" I tease through a loud cough. His eyes darken just a tad. *Stop flirting with the man, Daphne! Get a handle on yourself.* "Okay, I'll be serious. I can sew, but you already know that after I fixed your sweater." I leave out the part where I pretended to need more time locating the correct shade of charcoal thread just so I could huff his sweater for a few more nights. And the fact that I embroidered a very small heart into the hem of it in secret. "I also crochet and embroider. I picked up a lot of textile skills in college. But knitting is repetitive. Like your practice drills, I guess." His eyebrows raise. "What, a girl can't study football in her free time?"

"My kind of girl." He winks, and I'm certain my panties just combusted.

I need to change the topic fast, otherwise I'll end up vaulting over these pastries and taking a big ol' chomp out of his lip.

"You know, high school me would've laughed at the thought

of hanging around a cafe with a big-time jock like you," I say, grabbing a strawberry Danish to shove into my mouth because, let's be real, it's safer than devouring the man sitting in front of me.

"I would've been too focused on the balls flying at me to approach a pretty girl like you."

Pretty girl. My cheeks burn.

Okay, clearly, my methods of distraction are terrible. *Come on, Daphne. Talk about something unsexy. Think. Think!*

"So, football…is that it for you? Your endgame?"

Cameron slings one of his muscular arms onto the table, his leather jacket pulling taut. "Yes."

"Won't you have to retire at some point?"

A beat of disappointment flickers across his face. "Eventually. But I try not to think about that. Most players retire between thirty-four and thirty-six, but some keepers play longer. The goalkeepers who avoid injuries can continue playing into their late thirties or early forties. Ivan Matos was the starting goalie at Lyndhurst before I joined this season. He's in his forties."

"That still seems so early. What do they all do after?"

"Become coaches, managers, or scouts to develop new talent. Others move into sports broadcasting or become pundits. Some start businesses, get involved in charity, or start new careers outside of football."

"Have you thought about what you'd like to do?"

"No. Football has been my life since I could walk," he admits. "For those ninety minutes on the field, I become the most powerful version of myself."

"Did you ever play another position?"

His fingers skim my side of the table, nearly grazing my elbow. "Never. Being a keeper is indescribable."

"Try to describe it."

"Most football fans write off the position. But without a good goalie, you can't win trophies. When I'm in my box, it feels like destiny. It's about having the courage to make the right call and trusting my gut. Plus, I hate hearing the ball hitting the net. That fucking *shwooo*." He imitates the sound. "Stopping that sound is a compulsion."

"Wow." I exhale, trying to ignore the rapid beat of my heart. "I know it's not the same, but when I'm knitting, I also feel a compulsion. Like I can't rest until the project is done."

"Sounds a lot safer than a ball flying at you at eighty miles an hour."

I chuckle. "That kind of intensity must be exhausting."

"At times. The real stress comes from contracts, club politics, managing all the relationships…" He breathes out heavily. "My future isn't guaranteed. There's a chance that I might not be with Lyndhurst next year, or anywhere in the Premier League. It's hard not to think about that."

There are so many layers to Cameron, layers I hadn't even begun to peel back. And he's letting me in so easily. It feels monumental, like when I finally finished knitting the Posey Lace Sweater after months of work.

"When are things like that decided?"

"May."

Relief settles over my shoulders. "That's ages away. Maybe you can just focus on the here and now?" I suggest.

He looks like he wants to say no yet again, but he settles for, "Not bad advice."

The cafe hums around us, couples chatting, a woman sketching, someone smiling into their mug of tea. We've been lingering, talking about nothing, for who knows how long. A cozy bubble of calm. Cameron's vibe seems to have improved because of his kale smoothie. My mountain of pastries has a similar effect on me.

"Should we head out? Wouldn't want a waiter telling us they're about to close the place up like last time," Cameron asks reluctantly.

"Yeah, I need to get ready for my livestream anyway," I reply, packing all the extra pastries into a box, feeling content but not quite ready to leave. "Wouldn't want to disappoint my biggest fan, Mr. ch1kl100," I tease. Cameron grimaces and lets out a quiet grunt. This one doesn't set my nerves on edge. I'm certain this particular grunt comes right from his gooey center. "Thanks for bringing me here. It's really lovely; it reminds me of my cozy childhood treehouse."

"Then why don't you host your retreat here?" he suggests as we descend the stairs.

"You wouldn't mind if I invaded your personal haven?" I ask, trying to hide my excitement.

"I'll send you Rosie's email. I'm sure she'll be able to give you a good deal on the rental."

This could be my big break! If Rosie can give me a sweet deal, I could pull off this retreat with just a smidgen of my income and a sprinkle of my savings.

"I'd like that so much," I say, practically bouncing into the air and missing a step.

He chuckles, but a serious look crosses his handsome face. "And Daphne?"

"Yeah?" I swallow.

"Have a good night, lovebirds! Don't be strangers!" Rosie calls from behind the counter, breaking the moment.

"See you around, Rosie," he says.

We laugh off her interruption, and the tension dissolves. But as we head out into the night, I sense that whatever Cameron was about to say, whatever comes next—I'm ready for it. More than ready.

———

DAPHNE@WOOLYDUCK.COM

Venue Booking Inquiry for a Knitting Retreat

Hi Rosie,

Hope you are well! It was so lovely meeting you yesterday with Cameron. I wanted to inquire about renting out Petal & Plate for a knitting retreat I'm hosting. The retreat is intended to bring awareness to mental health through the cozy act of knitting.

I'd love to book the venue for March 6th and 7th of next year. It will be the five-year anniversary of my knitting channel, @wooly.-duck. I'm expecting about 50 guests, along with a few volunteers and speakers. Please let me know if you have an event brochure and if you're able to answer a few of the questions below!

Could you provide information on the rental rates for a full-space buyout? The retreat will require breakout rooms for small group activities. Is there a specific catering menu? Do you have any AV equipment and Wi-Fi available?

Could you please outline the payment terms, including any deposit requirements and cancellation policies?

I look forward to hearing from you soon!

Knit Regards,

Daphne Quinn

@wooly.duck

EVENTS@PETALPLATE.COM

Re: Venue Booking Inquiry for a Knitting Retreat

Hi Daphne,

Pleasure meeting you with Cam! Send him my love. He's lucky to have someone looking out for him.

Would be delighted to host your event. Please find attached our rental brochure, which should answer all your questions. Feel free to stop by, or you can email me here if you need more information.

Best,

Rosie

Owner, Petal & Plate

Chapter 14
Cameron

OCTOBER 31ST

Mal Kelly and Brody Kayl Split Two Weeks After *Lust Island* Finale.

November 3rd

Former *Lust Island* Queen Mal Kelly Spotted with Everton FC's Jose Dias: Will This New Footballer Be a Keeper?

I STAGGER up to my apartment after practice, exhausted. My nightmares have been relentless. I'm haunted by the same recurring dream of running on a pitch, paparazzi screaming, and spiked balls raining down on me.

Each time I hang out with Daphne, it feels like a break for my frayed nerves. But when I'm not with her, the unease creeps back in. Twice this week I've watched her livestream, Daphne's voice lulling me into sleep. She joked about me being her biggest fan, and honestly, she's not wrong.

I linger in the hallway in front of her door but stop myself from knocking. I don't want to burden her with another unscripted adventure or the weight that's crushing me.

Sighing, I retrieve my keys from my bag and turn toward my door.

"You're finally home!" Daphne says, surprising me from behind. She's in her doorway in an oversized T-shirt that drops to her mid-thigh. This one says *Knotty Girl* above a pile of tangled balls of yarn.

"I am," I say, my gaze running over her little ankle bracelet. That fucking chain drives me wilder than I want to admit.

"I've been waiting. Stay here." She disappears into her apartment, returning with her hands tucked behind her back. *Waiting for me?* My palms sweat. "A couple of the guys mentioned that it was your birthday, but that you didn't want to celebrate it—"

"I'm not one for birthdays." It's just another date on the calendar.

Yet I'd be lying if I said I wasn't touched by what the team did today. No grand gestures or fuss, just a simple, heartfelt surprise.

When I walked into the locker room this morning, my locker was covered in purple, gold, and black confetti, small balloons, and a photo of me winning my second championship with Los Angeles FC. A card signed by each player sat there too. Not a single word was uttered about it, but the faint smile on Coach's face said it all—they planned it together. At Overton, my teammates hid my lucky keeper gloves under a mower on maintenance day.

"I know." She sighs, twisting her duck slippers into the carpet below. "But you made the time after my birthday special, and I wanted to give you a small gift in return. I promise I won't sing or ever bring it up again, and next year we can pretend that your birthday doesn't even exist. But until then…" She sheepishly extends one of her hands to me. "Since you don't eat sweets, I figured I could make you a birthday cake."

In her palm sits a knitted chocolate cupcake with pastel frosting, a mere a few inches tall. In the middle, a small candle stands among colorful sprinkles. A small yellow flame-shaped stitch is right on top.

I reach out to collect the small gift, my fingertips grazing over her knuckles. Her Bambi eyes widen, gauging my reaction.

When I turn the stuffed cupcake over in my fingers, the soft yarn brushes against my rough calluses. It's delicate and carefully made—much like the woman standing before me.

Sunshine in human form.

Each stitch is tiny. The attention to detail is meticulous. The hours she must have spent on this. For me. A heat labors up my spine.

I am so fucked.

My throat dries. I'm speechless. Daphne blinks at me expectantly as she whispers, "Do you not like it?"

"Uh—" I want to thank her, but all I manage is a gruff, "Would you like to come to my game next week?"

Her frown vanishes. "When is it?" she asks excitedly.

It's too late to take it back. But the regret-fueled panic I expect doesn't come. *Fuck that.* I don't want to take it back.

I want her there. I want Daphne Quinn to watch me play.

"Next Saturday. Kickoff is at eleven."

"I'll be there. And now I can finally put all the facts I've learned in *Soccer for Dummies* to the test."

"You bought a book?" I like the idea of her on her couch in one of her ridiculous pun shirts, trying to understand my world.

"Couldn't have you making football jokes I didn't get." She takes two small steps toward me, the space between us shrinking. I take a step forward, challenging her. The harsh hallway lighting flickers above. "But there's one thing I couldn't find the answer to." I narrow my eyes. "Is there some kind of rule where I have to pick a player's jersey to wear?"

"That's not a rule." My teammates must've mentioned something to her. My molars grind together. The idea of her in another player's jersey awakens a darkness in me. "I'll leave the tickets at the call box under Duck Featherington," I say, changing the subject.

She rises onto her tiptoes, the hem of her shirt rising. I wonder if she's wearing any panties. She's so close, I could reach out my hand and check. "Are you saying I'm picking up the tickets as *Mrs*. Featherington?"

She knows exactly what she's doing to me. I'm nervous—actually, fucking nervous. It's fun. My tongue rolls over my lips.

"Don't get your feathers all ruffled up." I keep my tone hushed.

"I thought you knew I liked my feathers ruffled?"

Fuck. It's late. I need to get to bed, but I stay cemented to the floor, clenching the cupcake in my fist. She stretches her shoulders back; her hardened nipples peek through her shirt. My brain short-circuits at the realization she's not wearing a bra.

Her lips are slightly parted. An image of her on her knees in front of me flashes in my mind. She's so damn beautiful, so damn perfect. There's a haziness to her blue-green eyes that I want to get lost in.

One movement, and I could be touching her.

"Should I bring a disguise?" she offers sweetly.

"Come as yourself," I whisper, my patience hanging on by a measly thread. I don't trust myself to be around her.

"I can't wait, Goose." Her crooked smile does it, as does the curve of her lower lip and those fucking dimples.

Without thinking, I curve my pointer finger below her chin, leaning closer and closer until my mind goes blank with the smell of her skin. Daphne's eyelashes flutter closed, and she stretches her neck, her veins pumping lazily.

I know exactly what she would feel like. How her body would mold perfectly to mine. How she'd whimper and the corners of her lips would lift into a smile. How this beautiful long hair would feel when my fingers rake through it.

Pressure builds at the base of my spine.

I could kiss her. Maybe I should.

This friend thing we have isn't going to work for much longer. I want—no, I *need*—more than that with her.

I take my time, running the knuckles of the hand that holds her gift along her upper thigh, up her waist. Her shirt hem draws upward, revealing more and more of her legs. I want to sink my teeth into her, kiss her along her collarbones. Forget all my problems and just focus on her pleasure. Get her to moan those compliments that come so easily to her.

Her breath hitches—a soft, barely audible sound that sends another shockwave through my system. My pulse rockets like it's working overtime.

Kiss her. Just one taste.

I lean in, pivoting at the last second to kiss her cheek, so close to her mouth. I know that the shortest measure matters. A hairbreadth could decide the difference between a triumphant save and an utter defeat. A few centimeters to the left could mean carrying the taste of her home with me.

The faintest gasp escapes her as she presses her body into me. My dick pushes against my jeans.

Control yourself.

Her fingers twitch against my thigh, a small, involuntary movement that nearly undoes me. Every rational thought is drowned out by the overwhelming need to claim her in a way that leaves no room for ambiguity about what's happening between us.

I can't risk ruining our friendship. But for one more second, I selfishly linger against her burning cheek.

"Good night." I break away, my throat hoarse. "Thank you for the gift."

"Huh? Oh, n-night," she stammers, her fingers brushing against the place my lips just were.

Closing the door behind me, I lean against it, the world quiet. In my hand, the crochet birthday cake feels heavier than it should. I bring it up to my nose and inhale deeply.

Daphne's unraveling me. With one fucking knitted cupcake.

I should put a stop to this. To everything. No more Yes Year activities. No more dropping by unannounced. She's affecting me without even trying. She's seeped into all the cracked and crooked parts of me, filling spaces I didn't realize were empty.

I'm fucked. More than I've ever been.

And the scariest part? I don't really want to run away this time.

Chapter 15
Daphne

DAPHNE

Hope practice went well! Can't wait to see your footwork in person. ;)

Hope I got that right or I'll have to return Soccer for Dummies and give it a two-star rating.

GOOSE

That's right.

Now put your feet to work and check your door.

DAPHNE

Again?

I RUSH to my front door, swinging it open eagerly. Cameron's been busy preparing for the match this weekend, but every day he's left small gifts outside my door—slices of cake from a top-rated bakery, a pothos plant, a bag of gummy worms, and today, a little teacup with a yellow duck painted on the bottom. I press the cold porcelain to my cheek, right where he kissed it a week ago.

DAPHNE

!!!!!!!!!!

I love it.

GOOSE

Talk later. Gtg.

I'm completely ducking smitten.

Chapter 16
Cameron

DAPHNE QUINN

You got me a jersey?

#1? Cute!

I have the perfect outfit to wear with this. :)

CAMERON

Looking forward to it.

DAPHNE QUINN

Good luck today. I'll look for you on the pitch.

You'll be the hunky one at the goal right? ;)

Is pitch right?

CAMERON

That's right.

Good job.

DID she mean to call me hunky? My mind races through alternatives—chunky, funky, junky? I scan the message again, and a smile crests my lips. Then I glance at my response. *Good job?* That's the best I could come up with?

Focus, Cameron. You have a game to win.

I roll my shoulders, crack my neck, and toss my stuff in my locker.

"All right, team, let's go out there and put our best foot forward," Coach Thompson says, positioning himself just outside his office, looking every bit like a general preparing his troops for battle. "Jung, keep an eye on that knee. We can't afford any injuries today—not with twenty-six games left. Hastings, pay attention to Sutton's striker. The kid's got a hell of a diagonal run. If you see him moving before your defense does, alert them."

"I've studied the tapes," I assure him, my voice steady but my heart racing. "He likes to fake, and he favors the right side of the box. Gustafsson, that means we've got to keep our communication line open today."

"You got it!" Gustafsson says, giving me a thumbs-up.

We've been grinding through drills all week. Each one helps me with my assertiveness on the field. Little by little, it's finding its way back.

Matos catches my attention and nods. He stayed after practice on Thursday to watch tapes with me, silently calling out notes on Sutton I hadn't picked up on.

Coach continues his speech, breaking into tactics for the game.

When he's done, I dive into my pregame ritual, wrapping each knuckle carefully—left hand first, then the right—before I'm ready for my gloves.

Around me, my teammates are lost in their own routines. Gustafsson mutters under his breath, clutching a picture of his family like a talisman. Kamara blasts the same track on repeat, the sound leaking out through his over-ear headphones. Our captain is engrossed in a tome that changes titles with each game —from *The Renaissance: When Art Got Real* to *The Past Is a Foreign Country: They Do Things Differently There.*

There's an odd solace in these routines, watching each man absorbed in his rituals. A quiet rhythm of readiness. The sensation of belonging swells within me. Being around Daphne has made me realize how much I've missed feeling like part of a team.

Some of them chatter about next weekend's team gathering at Matos's house, and for the first time since starting this season, I wish they'd invite me. But I understand—after I said no too many times, they've stopped asking.

But then Matos catches me staring and says, "Hastings, you in?"

"Uh, sure."

"Glad to hear it."

"Damn it, anyone got some extra tape?" Tae-woo asks, wincing as he rubs his knee. His injury from the friendlies still lingers like a shadow.

"Here," I say, tossing him a fresh roll from my locker.

"Thanks, man." He catches it with a grateful smile. I hope all my effort pays off on the pitch today.

I return to my locker, running my thumb over the tiny flame on the cupcake Daphne made me. It's the last thing I do before slipping on my gloves and smearing them with Vaseline.

"Guys, our neighbor finally came to a game!" Gustafsson exclaims, holding up his phone to show @wooly.duck's Instagram story—Daphne's selfie outside the stadium.

"I didn't put her name down at the call box." Mohamed nudges Gustafsson's arm. "Did you?"

"No," Gustafsson replies, confused.

"Huh?" Mohamed turns to Tae-woo, who merely shakes his head in response. Okafor shrugs.

They're going to find out sooner or later.

"I did," I say.

They all stare at me. You could hear a pin drop. I just admitted to inviting the girl I'm secretly having way-too-complicated feelings for to our football game. Will they see her as my weakness, one they can exploit? No, I can't think like that. I've been at Lyndhurst for almost five months, and they haven't fucked me over yet. If anything, despite their efforts, I've been... what does Daphne call me? A grumpy storm cloud to all of them.

A lone whistle sounds from the back, and that's the extent of their shock. They're all too scared of me to ask any more questions, which makes the silence even more awkward. Fantastic. Just what I needed—a roomful of grown men acting like I announced that I'm switching out my team colors mid-season.

"Lions, gather up!" Okafor shouts. The team huddles, arms draped over each other's shoulders. Instead of keeping my hands to myself, I throw them over Gustafsson and Kamara's shoulders. There's a warmth in the huddle—a sense of belonging I've missed. "Who's sending us out today?"

"Let me," I offer for the first time this season before I can second-guess myself.

"All right, Hastings," they cheer.

I clear my throat. "Lyndhurst Lions, hear our roar!" There's more to the chant, but it's entirely cheesy. Everyone looks around, expecting more. Instead, I just growl, "Let's fucking win today."

They burst into the signature lion roar, a rallying cry. My jaw loosens, and I join them. The sound grumbles from deep within my chest. Fuck, this is a great cure for pregame jitters. I should've been doing this all season.

Our huddle disperses, players whooping, slapping each other's shoulders and butts, amping each other up. Nobody touches me, though, and I kind of wish they did.

We jog to the tunnel and line up. Sutton is on our left. My senses are alight. The weight of my kit, the familiar feel of my gloves, the cool kiss of my cleats against the floor.

I'm ready to win today.

My heart thumps fiercely as I stand among my teammates,

the crowd's impatience crashing around me, seeping into my bones. *Be big.* I chant my mantra silently, a prayer I've whispered since I was a kid with a football. *Don't be hasty. Be enormous. Own your box. Be big.*

My shaky nerves settle as we all step forward, crossing the threshold from the musty confines of the tunnel into the open expanse of the pitch. The smell of dewy grass fills my lungs. The stadium roars to life—a cacophony of cheers and jeers. The vibrant green of the field stretches out endlessly, the goalposts at either end standing like sentinels. Above it all, a sea of purple jerseys swells and ripples in the stands, moving as one. A living, breathing entity.

The world seems to slow down as my team disperses into their positions. I step between the sticks. The sounds fade into the background, replaced by the rhythmic thump of my heartbeat.

I tap each side of the goalpost—left, then right—grounding myself.

Goalkeepers don't win games; they save them. The weight of that responsibility is like a mountain on my shoulders. People will only remember the ones I miss. But I can bear it. I have what it takes.

You should try using your hands instead of just standing there! Rossi's voice echoes in my head. *The only thing you're good at blocking is Overton's chances of winning!* Not today. *Is your uniform too heavy? Why aren't you diving?* The nerves crawl up my arms, shoulders, and neck, tightening around my airway like a noose. *Be better, Hastings.*

Fuck this. *Enough.* I've had enough.

My gaze sweeps across the blur of the crowd.

Then, like a spotlight cutting through fog, I spot her in the directors box. Daphne is impossible to miss. Her lavender hair catches the sunlight, shimmering like a halo. She spins around, showing me the number on her back. 1. She's wearing it, my jersey.

We cannot lose today with Daphne here, wearing my number.

Keeper's jerseys are rarely seen in the stands, yet she wears mine with pride. A calm breaks into my chest, silencing the shouts in my mind.

This is my sanctuary. My box. I'm the last line of defense. *Be big*, I tell myself, making sure the only person in my mind is me. *Just focus on the here and now.* Daphne's singsong voice somehow weaves its way through the chaos.

My very own good luck charm.

Be big. Be impenetrable.

The referee's whistle cuts through the air, a sharp sound signaling the start of the game. I square my shoulders, cast one final look at my defenders, and steel myself for what's to come.

This is it.

The game begins.

Win.

Chapter 17
Daphne

WHAT A GAME WE HAVE HERE! Lyndhurst versus Sutton, with the Lions in the lead. Thanks in large part to their goalie. Hastings is putting on a masterclass of goalkeeping, denying the Sutton Strikers time and time again.

YOU'RE RIGHT, Marty. He has been the linchpin of Lyndhurst's defense today. It's safe to say his move from Overton has seen him develop into a formidable force between the posts.

"LYN, Lyn, Lyndhurst, Lyndhurst! Go, go, go, Lyndhurst!" I chant with the crowd.

Seated in the directors box, I basked in the warmth, munched on snacks, and sipped drinks all day. Famous faces surround me, with kids in Lyndhurst jerseys zipping around. Everyone's laughing and chatting.

On the field, Cameron stands in a vibrant uniform that hugs his broad shoulders. He looks commanding, powerful, and attractive with a capital A. His muscles bulge under his tight shorts as he bends low, guarding the goal. If I wasn't in public, I'm sure I'd be drooling.

My other friends sprint along the field, but none of them shine the way Cameron does.

Who knew sports could be this fun? I'm even able to follow the game a little, although I still don't understand how anyone can run for ninety minutes straight.

I run my hands through my newly dyed hair—my merman connection from the botanical garden squeezed me in for a lilac root touch-up yesterday.

"Are you Daphne?" a stunning woman with large eyes and brown curls asks, sitting down in the empty seat beside me. She wears a Lyndhurst jersey that matches mine, tucked into leather pants. Confidence radiates off of her, her shoulders square with impeccable posture.

I smile brightly. "I am! Nice to meet you…"

"Bea." She extends her hand; there's a martini glass in the other. "Bea Matos. Ivan's wife. The backup on the bench for the new guy. Same jersey."

"Oh, Cameron?" I clarify, spotting a purple scarf wrapped around her neck. I'm pretty certain Sven made it, given the beautiful stitching and his signature braided rib bind-off.

"Yes." She winks at me.

"We're neighbors!" I laugh nervously. "I live in the same complex as half the team."

"I heard. Have to say, you're such a sweet thing, helping with Femi's auction tomorrow." She tugs at the scarf. "Snagged one of these the moment I saw it. Going to be wearing mine all season."

"It looks stunning on you. And it was nothing," I say. "Just glad they got finished in time."

"I'm so glad to finally meet you. The lads couldn't stop raving about you at the barbecue last weekend. Ivan and I host the whole team often, and I do watch parties when they play away. You should come. All the partners do."

"Oh, no, I'm not anyone's partner."

"I just thought since you're wearing—" she says expectantly.

"Well, smart girl." She pats my thigh. "I was going to warn you about dating footballers, but, truthfully, I was also hoping for some boy drama. Living with all those hot mates under one roof?" She fans herself.

So the jersey *does* mean something. Butterflies flutter in my belly, just like they did the night Cameron kissed my cheek. The things my poor rose-shaped vibrator had to witness after he left me breathless—well, you could say I was so thorny, I wilted with excitement.

Gosh, I'm so thankful no one can hear inside my brain.

"They remind me more of hanging out with my sister." I laugh. "We watch reality TV and knit together. We just finished *Lust Island.*"

"Oh my goodness, Georgia Woods so deserved that win!"

I beam. Bea and I seem like we're going to be very good friends. "Yes. I thought the same, she's an absolute queen. And she makes her own outfits too? I'm obsessed with her."

"You're right, she's always got her ball of yarn and crochet hooks."

"If I wanted just a hookup, I'd have stayed home with my wool!" We mimic Georgia's famous catchphrase together and burst into laughter.

"You know, I've been wondering what I'll do after Ivan retires this year," she says with a cheeky smile. "Maybe I'll take up knitting scarves like you to fill up all my free time."

"You totally should." I almost burst out of my seat. "I'm hosting a knitting retreat next year; I'll send you an invite."

"No way!" she shouts. "Nanny taught me when I was younger, but it's been years. Here's my number." She takes my phone out of my hand and punches in her contact info. "If you're at the next home game, let me know. You can bring your tools, and I'll bring mine." She returns her focus to the game before standing and pulling me up by my arm. "Look, Tamu is going for it."

The ball flies across the field to Tamu's feet. He runs at lightning speed, kicks the ball, and the opposing team's goalie dives, but it's no use. Tamu scores as the keeper skids along the grass. *Ouch.*

The stadium erupts. Bea tosses back her martini, sets down the glass, and wraps her hands around my shoulders, jumping.

"*Olé, olé, olé, Tamu, Tamu, all the way!*" Bea and the rest of the box chant. I sing along, my heart bursting with excitement.

After things calm down, my mind returns to Bea's friendly advice. Wouldn't it be interesting to get insider tips on dating a footballer? Not that I'm planning to break my rule anytime soon.

"So." I attempt to be nonchalant. "What you were saying earlier…about dating a footballer. Would love to know more, just to understand the boys better." There goes that plan. I'm very much chalant.

Bea's face lights up with mischief. "Well, let's start with the perks: romantic getaways, gifts, VIP access, and exclusive events."

Cameron has been doing that stuff for me, minus the romantic getaways. We do friendly activities instead. I'm sure he provides the same treatment to all his friends, or, well, when he had a bigger friend circle.

"Doesn't hurt to be spoiled," I say.

"True, but that stuff gets old quickly—and this is coming from someone who really likes stuff." She laughs, showing off the rings on her hands. "Then there's the other side of things. When Ivan signed with Lyndhurst, it was overwhelming. The constant spotlight, the tabloids, the pressure, the travel. Lucky for me, I love seeing the world."

"The idea of traveling does sound exciting!" I can knit

anywhere—on a cozy couch in England or in a bustling cafe in Italy. And what about all the wonderful yarn stores I'd discover worldwide?

"It is, but I've been fortunate that Ivan hasn't been moved around much. That's not the case for many partners. It's tough on them, packing up and relocating when a better offer comes along." She sighs. "Even harder when the offer is worse."

"I had no idea."

"Yep, they can be called away at any time. Once, we were celebrating our fifteenth wedding anniversary when Ivan got a call for an unexpected training session. I ended up alone in the restaurant."

"On your wedding anniversary?" I frown.

"Thankfully, Ivan hasn't missed the birth of our two boys." She rolls her eyes. "But the tabloids camped out all night for a picture of our firstborn."

"Seriously?"

"They're ruthless, but that's just how it is in this world. I've come to terms with being second to football. It's his first love, and that's okay. He's still my best friend, and I'm his. They live and breathe this game. Honestly, sometimes I love it just as much. I wouldn't trade it for anything."

A tightness clings to my heart. "How long has Ivan been playing?"

"He was the starting keeper for ten years. I've spent a lot of time in this box. But let me tell you, if you don't have your own life, it's easy to get lost in theirs."

"I can't even fathom how tricky it must be, especially with a family. But isn't compromise and understanding the bedrock of any great relationship?" I ask.

She blinks rapidly at me. "Wow, you are wiser than your years."

"Thanks. I have therapy to thank for that." I laugh, but

there's still a heaviness in my chest at her confessions. "I appreciate you sharing all of this with me, Bea."

"Of course, sweetheart. If you ever fall for one of them and think he's worth it, trust me, make sure he's a man who can navigate all of life's challenges with you. Because there will be plenty." She squeezes my hand. "It's why all of us partners stick together."

"I'm glad to be a part of it."

Her attention is pulled back to the match, but my mind spins.

If Cameron and I were to ever be something, it wouldn't be like dating a normal person. It means media exposure, impromptu moves, and spending some weekends alone.

But those things don't sound too bad.

My individuality matters. I have my retreat, and I wouldn't mind moving around a bit, especially with how much I've enjoyed London. And finally, I love my own company, as long as I have a pair of knitting needles in hand.

Maybe I could amend my no-soccer-boys rule. I've gotten familiar with Cameron's schedule over the last few months. The dedication, time, and energy he pours into his career are sexy—I wouldn't ever want him to give that up.

My brain is turning into a tangled mess. But then again, every good knitting project has its knots and tangles, right? They always turn out beautifully in the end.

Could Cameron and I be something beautiful too?

Bea sits back down from cheering and turns toward me. "Even if you are just a friend, it's nice for Hastings to have you here. Nobody ever cheers for the keeper."

A wave of sadness washes over me. Why wouldn't he get the support he deserves? It's clear that goalies are crucial.

"Why not?"

"It's not a sexy position, but it's the most important one on the pitch," she explains, keeping her attention on the field. A whistle blares, and Bea slams her hand against her chair. "Are you fucking kidding me?" she shouts. "That wasn't a foul!" I struggle to catch up with what's happening. It looks like the referee called a foul in the penalty area. "Here comes your friend! No, get back, Omar!"

The other team has the ball, and Cameron stretches his arms out in front of the goal. His eyes are like laser beams on the target, his body coiled and ready.

The stadium goes silent, watching the opposing striker. The ball rockets toward the goal like a wild cannonball, and I barely have time to gasp.

Then, there's Cameron.

He launches himself across the goal, hands stretched out, fingers splayed, his body twisting midair. Every muscle in his body is perfectly tuned, like a warrior on a battlefield. With unbelievable fluidity, he catches it. The ball snaps into his hands, and for a moment he hovers there, suspended in midair like he's defying gravity.

I'm left staring, completely awestruck.

Forget charming.

Forget kind.

Forget all the sweet little things he's done.

Right now, Cameron Hastings is a freaking god.

The stadium erupts in cheers, but they're only half as loud as they were for Tamu.

"Thank fuck." Bea sighs with relief. "They do not need any more losses this year."

My attention is caught on the lazy crowd, despite the miracle Cameron just performed in front of me. "There's no chant for when the keeper blocks a goal?"

Bea shrugs. "Never."

Well, that won't do.

AFTER LYNDHURST'S WIN, everyone from the box lingers awhile. Bea eventually convinces me to meet Ivan and the rest of the team, who don't live at the apartment complex. They're all thrilled about me helping with the auction for Femi tomorrow. By the time Cameron appears in the doorway, I feel like my friend group has doubled.

I sidle over to him. When he spots me, his head lifts, and he gives me this adorable, soft look. I'm half a second away from melting.

Seriously, with that look—full of intentions and unspoken words—how is a girl supposed to keep her cool?

"I should get going," I say. "Thanks for inviting me. Another perfect Yes Day in the books."

"Need a ride?"

"It's a fifteen-minute walk."

He frowns, his eyes searching mine. "Need a ride?" he repeats. His voice is low and intimate.

My heart does a jitterbug. "I'd love one."

I follow him out into the private player's parking lot. The air between us buzzes with a new kind of static, like pulling a fuzzy blanket out of the dryer without a dryer sheet, making every hair on your arm stand up.

Is this real or just postgame adrenaline? Whatever it is, when we reach his car, I awkwardly hover by the hood, not quite ready to hop in.

"So, are you going home to binge-watch the game rerun?" I ask.

"Think so," he says. He looks utterly wiped out, with dark circles under his eyes, his shoulders slumped, and his usually bright gaze dull and distant. By his face, you'd think his team had lost.

"Not going to celebrate with the team?"

He shakes his head. "No. Gave it my all today. Didn't want to lose and make your first football match a letdown." His thumbs are raw and bleeding, like he's been picking at them again. I hate the pressure he's under.

Football has been my life since I could walk. Cameron's words echo in my mind.

I wonder when he ever takes time to recharge.

"You could never disappoint me. Even if you lost." He scans my face before his lips tug into a half-smirk. "But isn't watching replays work too? You deserve a nap after that game. I broke a sweat, and all I did was cheer."

"It's better to watch them when the match is fresh."

"I used to feel the same way about my knitting patterns," I share with him. "I'd push through for hours, even with all the mistakes. But then I'd switch to an easy project, come back to the tough one, and feel refreshed." He makes a noncommittal grunt. "So, Cameron, when do you get to have a real break?"

He looks across the parking lot before his golden eyes bore into mine. "With you, mostly."

And just like that, he dropped a bombshell. He finds his peace with *me*. My heart flutters like fabric in the wind.

"I feel the same." And without overthinking, I grab his hand. He stares at our interlocked fingers. I wish I could read his mind, or swaddle it in a nice, comfy sweater. "You looked so good out there. I-I mean, you played really well," I stammer.

"Thank you."

The cold November air whips through his hair, tousling his perfectly unkempt locks. "Cameron, are you sure me wearing your jersey doesn't mean anything?" I ask, needing to know. I want to hear him admit that he is beginning to like me as more than a friend. I need to make sure my feelings are reciprocated.

"It doesn't have to." He avoids my gaze.

"Would you care if I wore someone else's jersey?"

"If that's what you want." His foot taps incessantly on the pavement.

"I don't," I say.

"Good, because I'd rather you didn't." His eyes fix on me, his fingers tightening in my hand.

"Glad we're on the same page." I nibble on my lower lip. "I wish I had come to a match earlier. I learned so much today by hanging out with the WAGs. They're a blast!"

"Like what?" He strokes his thumb over the inside of my palm.

"Ivan's wife said no one cheers for the keeper."

Cameron shrugs, running his free hand over his neck. That adorable tic makes me want to pin his arms to his sides and kiss him senseless. "Not often," he admits.

I pause, trying to find the perfect words. "There's no way I'm letting you miss out on the best part of the game—at least, it was for me." I reassuringly rub his strong forearm. "I'm making you a promise. I'll wear your jersey and cheer obnoxiously loud, so you always know you have a friend in the stands."

A tiny smile tugs at the corners of his lips, a rare crack in his tough-guy façade. "You're coming to another game?"

"I'll even make you a chant." His head tilts skeptically. "What, you don't believe me, Goose?"

Finally, he lets out a full laugh. "Do I get to hear this chant?"

"You can't laugh at it. Promise?"

He makes an X across his heart. My hand feels cold in his absence. "But just remember, there's a reason I never made the cheerleading squad."

"Why? Because you look too irresistible in a skirt?" He motions to the mini I'm wearing, and I gulp.

"Goal or bust, in Hastings we trust!" I declare, repeating it for emphasis. "I know, it's a bit last minute, but what do you think?"

Cameron's stare is a blend of blankness and tension, like when I gave him that crocheted birthday cake. I'm like a science project under his scrutiny.

"I love it, Duck."

"Good."

Time beats slowly. My body hums with the ache to touch him.

Screw this. No more waiting. I fling my arms around his waist and hurl myself into his rustic, salty musk. The muscles of his back flex before softening. He crooks his arms around my neck, urging us closer, making me feel small and safe in his embrace.

His fingers tangle in my hair as he cups my head. His chest expands with each breath, as if he's inhaling not just air, but me too.

I shuffle my feet forward, burrowing myself deeper into his torso. I close my eyes and memorize every sensation—the way his fingers feel, the soft hum of his breath, the heat radiating off of him. Our hearts batter against our rib cages in sync.

Rain starts to fall, but we don't move. Our embrace feels more intimate than any kiss. I get lost in the sensation of him against me. Hard and soft. Something tenses under my stomach —oh my, that is most definitely hard.

Fire floods my core. Without breaking our contact, I settle on the edge of his car hood. His body is heavy over me. He grips me tighter until we're practically dry-humping in this parking lot. Without a doubt, this is the sexiest hug of my life.

The rain is like a baptism, washing away the silly idea that we could ever be just friends.

He gives me a look he's given me a dozen times before, but this time I finally understand. It's like I'm the center of his universe. In his gaze, I sense everything: hope, fear, desire, and something that feels dangerously irresistible.

He's a victorious lion, relaxed yet brimming with energy.

Cameron is *all* man.

"God, Daphne." He sighs against the top of my head. "You —" He chokes on the next words. I wait for him to say it. *Come on, Cameron, take the lead.*

I want Cameron Hastings. His hands roam along the top of my back, running across his last name, each touch sparking a fire inside me. *Say it, Cameron. Say you want me like I want you.*

"You're a really good friend."

Friend.

He unhooks from me, and suddenly I'm so cold. My heart drops. "Yeah." I force a smile. "You too, Cameron."

He reaches into his jeans pocket and pulls out his keys. "Want to drive?"

"Drive?" I blink. He jingles the keys. "Right, the car!" Disappointment is probably apparent in my voice. "Yeah. Heck yeah."

He tosses me the keys, and they spin in slow motion under the stadium lights. With a quick move, I snag them midair and dash toward the driver's seat, adrenaline fizzing out of my veins.

Before he gets in, he shakes his head, rubbing the sides of his temples. He looks absolutely tormented.

And I'm certain that I did that.

I think Cameron Hastings definitely loved my chant.

And the sight of me in his jersey.

And our not-so-*friendly* hug.

But most of all, I'm now certain he wants me as more than a friend.

Chapter 18
Daphne

November 16

Influencer @wooly.duck Teams up with Lyndhurst Lions to Raise £80K for Groundskeeper's
New Prosthetic on 40th Anniversary

SVEN

Auction went fantastisk yesterday!

Tusen takk, daph! <3

c u wed for british bake off!

DAPHNE

I'm so glad! Can't wait.

AFTER TWO MONTHS of hanging out with Cameron, I decided it
was time to come clean. So when she texts me…

JUNI

Big sister mode activated

I wince. Things have been uneasy with her since I moved four months ago; she's been keeping a very close eye on me.

It's tough when people have a fixed view of you. She still sees me as her anxious, hermit little sister, avoiding risks and people.

But people change.

DAPHNE
No thank you!!!

JUNI
I looked up Cameron. Have you seen these articles?

DAPHNE
Don't want to.

JUNI
Don't be naive. Look at this article.

Cameron Hastings bares it all...

I delete her message. I promised Cameron that I wouldn't look him up or peruse tabloid drama. And I don't want to. He hasn't done anything to break my trust.

DAPHNE
There are always two sides to every story.

Unless he did something illegal, I don't care about rumors.

JUNI
Be serious.

DAPHNE
Thank you for caring, but please respect my wishes.

I have this under control.

JUNI

But you are not a casual relationship type of girl.

If you catch feelings, he'll just hurt you.

Then I'll have to fly over there and hurt him.

She's saying it as if I'm intending to make a lifelong commitment to this man, and I'm not. All in all, I've known Cameron for such a short time, and in that time, I've really liked who he is. I want to keep getting to know him...and maybe kiss him, damn it!

DAPHNE

Juni, I'm not a kid anymore.

You can cut the bodyguard act.

JUNI

You're right. I'm sorry.

I am still really excited to see you for Christmas next month.

DAPHNE

Me too.

I love you.

JUNI

I love you too.

I close the chat with my sister and open my thread with Cameron. Tonight, he organized a low-key helicopter flight around the Thames after I mentioned how cool it would be to see the skyline in my stories last week. Hopefully something like that isn't too difficult to cancel because tonight, I'm ready to stop playing it safe.

I want him.

DAPHNE

Can we cancel the helicopter plans tonight and stay in?

GOOSE

Good with me.

What do you have in mind?

DAPHNE

Movie night at my place?

GOOSE

See you soon.

Chapter 19
Daphne

TONIGHT'S THE NIGHT. I'm making a move on Cameron Hastings.

I'm nervous and giddy, but so freakin' ready. I shift on the couch beside him, his leg resting against mine. He's sprawled out under a purple blanket, limbs everywhere, like he's perfectly at home.

"Heading back to San Francisco for the holidays?" I lean in, hoping the highlighter on my cheekbones entices him. When he kissed me on his birthday, I swore it was because of this shimmering powder. Tonight, I've gone extra radiant, aiming to draw his attention to exactly where I want his kisses—all over me.

"Maybe for a few days," he says, running a hand through his hair. "My parents go all out with this giant tree. We always decorate together, have a huge luncheon and dinner, watch movies, and play games like Who Am I? and Never Have I Ever."

"That sounds so fun." Cameron's family seems so normal. I wonder what he's like around them. Does he laugh like he laughs with me? Is that furrowed brow finally relaxed? "I'm visiting my family too before my moms go on their holiday trip. Maybe we'll bump into each other at the St. Claridge," I say, trying to sound casual.

"I'll be counting down the days."

Heart, meet somersault.

"Me too." I grab the remote from the coffee table, which is littered with my movie snacks—gummy bears, popcorn, Maltesers—and Cameron's healthier options—crudités, fruit, and hummus. Perhaps tonight is the night he finally caves and indulges in some real treats. I scroll through the movie options. "What are you in the mood for? I'm a sucker for a good tearjerker."

"Why would you want to make yourself cry?"

"It's cathartic. Crying is almost as good as an orgasm." He glances at me, eyes lingering on my face before settling on my lips. I blush, turning away. "And don't get me started on those animated shorts where people do kind things—like adopting a stray dog or sharing a cookie with a stranger. I've got a whole collection bookmarked for emotional release. I could show you sometime if you've got pent-up feelings."

He chuckles deeply. "I have a way to work those out on my own."

It's like we're playing a sexy game of cards, but I'm already ready to fold. He's so close. Just a few inches away. I click into a random movie, trying to hide my burning cheeks. "What about this one?"

"You're kidding."

I look at him, puzzled. "What?"

"*Shrek*?" He grimaces.

I gasp dramatically. "Do you have something against a classic that challenges fairytale stereotypes and celebrates being true to oneself?"

"You won't believe this, but the night we met, my family gave me Shrek in a game of Who Am I? because they think I resemble him." He shakes his head, but there's a hint of a smile.

He really is an ogre. My ogre.

"Oh my gosh, they're right! I always thought of you as an éclair—hard outside, soft and gooey center—but Shrek is even better."

"Seriously?" He grabs my hand and places it over his rock-hard abs. The muscles ripple below his shirt. We both freeze, our breaths catching. "Anything soft and gooey about that?"

Nope. Just me. My whole body feels like a marshmallow Peep in the microwave, puffing up and getting ready to burst.

"Nope, that's hard. Really hard."

He releases me, but I let my hand linger. In one swift movement, I could be kissing him again. But I chicken out. I want him to make the first move. I need to know that he can be vulnerable.

"If I'm Shrek, does that make you my ass?" he asks.

"Mine's not nearly as scrumptious as yours," I let slip pulling my hand back. *Ugh, I'm blowing this.*

"Scrumptious?"

"You know, it's nice and juicy because of all those squats you do during drills," I say, rolling my eyes casually.

"You've become quite the expert on my drills lately."

"I need to understand the game so I'm not lost when I go to the next one."

"And my glute workouts are a part of that?"

I shrug. "It's in the book."

It totally isn't.

"Sure."

I gulp, hitting play.

After two bags of popcorn and half a bowl of gummy candies —all devoured by yours truly—we're at the part where Fiona reveals her ogre self to Shrek. Cameron's head rests on my shoulder. His steady breaths rise and fall. He's like a giant, sleepy house cat, and I'm the lucky one he's chosen. I've been trying to stay statue still, except for the occasional gentle scratch up his arm or a lingering whiff of his hair.

Gentle tears catch in my tear ducts—Fiona's confession always gets me. I sniffle and glance at Cameron. He's biting his lip, and—wait, is he…crying?

My mouth drops open.

It's disarmingly intimate. His stoic façade is cracked, softened by the glow of the TV. He scrunches his nose, trying to hold back tears, but it's too late—a single drop escapes and hides in his scruff. Warmth blooms in my chest and settles in a decidedly inappropriate place.

Am I actually getting worked up over this man crying?

The heat between my thighs multiplies. My heart beats wildly and loud enough that I'm sure he can hear it.

I trace the tear's path on his skin. Cameron straightens beside me. He swipes at the wetness on his cheeks. "For fuck's sake," he groans, his voice low and sleepy.

I let out an awkward laugh.

"Hey," I say, trying to keep things light. "At least now you can admit this is almost as good as an orgasm. Or, you know, if anyone asks if you've cried during a movie, you can say yes."

"Yeah, that'll definitely help during my family's game of Never Have I Ever. Though I doubt it'll make me the winner."

"How does someone even win at Never Have I Ever?"

"I can show you now," he says, swinging a leg onto the couch and stretching his arm across the back. It's muscular and strong.

My insides flutter. "You want to play?" I pause the movie.

"Yes. The rules are that for everything you've done, you eat one of my movie snacks."

I cringe at the plate of veggies. "That's devious." He smirks in a challenge. "Fine. But if I have to eat rabbit food, you have to eat one of my gummy bears."

"I haven't had something sweet in my mouth in months."

My insides turn to lava. "Worried you'll like it?"

He flexes his beautifully scarred fingers and swollen knuckles over his black jeans. "You have no idea."

This is pure torture. Every interaction with him lately has been mind-blowing. When we agreed to be friends, I thought I could handle it. His frosty greeting when we met again made me believe I could resist temptation. But getting to know him has done the one thing I feared most—it's made me really like him. A lot.

Maybe my sister is right, and I'm just a hopeless romantic with zero ability to keep things casual.

But Cameron Hastings has ignited my life in ways I never imagined. All those adventure-less years seem like ancient history when we're on a Yes Year spree, whether I'm racing his car down the coast, playing undercover laser tag, or biking through Hyde Park wrapped in sweaters and coats.

Everything about him makes me want to say *Yes, Yes, Yes.* My body is screaming *Please, Please, Please.*

"Well, you first," I whisper.

"Never have I ever…" He scans the room. "Made someone a gift."

I pick the least offensive of his snacks: an apple slice. "You're just trying to make me eat this, aren't you?"

"No idea what you mean." He grins, watching me as I crunch on the apple while biting into my Cadbury bar, so it's like I'm eating a chocolate-covered apple.

"Never have I ever kissed someone in the rain." I bite my lip, thinking about his body pressing over me on his car hood. Is that too obvious? Who cares.

He pops a gummy bear into his mouth, chewing slowly. "This thing tastes like rubber."

"Douse anything in sugar, and I'll put it in my mouth." His pupils widen. "I mean, I like sugar. Tell me about this rain kiss of yours," I say awkwardly, hoping he'll change the subject.

"My first kiss was in the rain," Cameron says.

"Really?"

"I was sixteen. She played on the girls' football team," he says, a nostalgic smile playing on his lips. "We were finishing practice, and it started raining. Everyone ran for cover except her. She was laughing, spinning in the rain."

A pang of jealousy mixed with longing strikes me. "And then?"

"I had no clue how to talk to girls back then," he admits. "Told her she'd ruin her cleats. She called me a smartass and punched my arm. Then, I kissed her."

So what he's saying is that if I punch him, he'll be more likely to kiss me.

"That's so Cameron of you." I gently slug him in the shoulder. He laughs but makes no effort to put his lips on mine. There goes that theory. "Have you ever dated another athlete?"

"No," he murmurs. "It'd be hard. Balancing a relationship and my career seems impossible. It'd take someone special for me to make time for them."

"That makes sense."

My heart skips like a scratched record. He always makes time for me.

I wish I had a neon sign over my head that said, *Pucker this girl up, Hastings.* If he doesn't have time for a girlfriend, maybe we could just be a friends-with-benefits situation. That would definitely check off a Yes Year activity.

"What about you? What was your first kiss like?" he asks.

"Nothing that romantic," I sigh, cringing. "My first kiss was at a freshman orientation party. I was so nervous I bumped noses with the guy. He laughed, but I was mortified. His friends called it the Clumsy Kiss for weeks. It was so embarrassing." I remember wishing the ground would swallow me whole.

Cameron's expression intensifies, his jaw tightening.

"That guy didn't know what he had," Cameron says. "If it

had been me, I'd have considered myself the luckiest guy on earth."

I blink. "Really?"

My heartstrings turn into a honeycomb stitch. "Anyone would be lucky to share a moment like that with you. And if anyone ever teases you again about how you kiss, they'll have to answer to me."

I sink into the couch, ready to give up on my plan. If he wanted to kiss me, he would've already.

"Thanks, Cameron."

He leans in closer, tucking a stray strand of hair behind my ear and grazing the top of my cheek. *Wait, maybe my shimmering highlighter is working!* "I mean it, Daphne. You deserve someone who appreciates all of you, clumsy kisses and all."

You.

I want you.

I want that to be you.

"Maybe I'll get a second chance at a first kiss."

"I hope you do." The air thickens with tension, a charge neither of us can seem to defuse. He clears his throat and laughs awkwardly. "All right, my turn. Never have I ever stayed up all night talking to someone."

My mouth drops open. "That's a low blow; you know my knitathons go all night!"

"Rules are rules." He shrugs, handing me a carrot, letting his fingers brush against my knuckles. I chew and think of my next question.

"Never have I ever seen the northern lights."

Neither of us chomps on a movie snack. "Want to add that to your Yes Year adventures?"

"I wish! Maybe after my retreat, we could take a trip. You know, if you can pencil me in."

He inches closer, like a slow-motion wade through a pool. "I don't see why not."

It'd take someone special for me to make time for them. His voice rings in my ears. I'm special.

"Yeah," I say breathlessly, draping my legs over his. Our faces are so close, I'd settle for an Eskimo kiss at this point.

His fingers rub along my thighs, his eyes scanning my body until a spark lights up behind them.

"Never have I ever been...tied up," he says, voice low and teasing.

"Excuse me?" I cough. My mouth goes dry.

"All tied up." He tilts his chin downward to my shirt that reads, *All Tied Up*, with yarn threading through the letters.

I brush him off. "It's just a knitting pun."

"Knitting pun, huh?"

"Yes!" I laugh, nudging his firm shoulder hard enough that his golden hoop shakes.

It's getting unbearably hot. His eyes seem darker, more intense. Cameron leans in, his breath warm on my skin. "I don't believe you," he whispers, sending a shiver down my spine. "I think you like the idea of being tied up, just a bit."

Do I? Maybe with the right person. "Sounds like you're more into that idea."

"Never tried it. Maybe with the right person."

Oh gosh. He can see right into my brain, can't he? "All right, uh, never have I ever...broken a bone," I say. He eats another gummy. His jaw moves, and his scruff is doing things to me that should be illegal. "So, does this mean I get the story of how you broke your nose?"

"The first time?"

"How many times were there?" I squint, leaning in to inspect his nose. It bends slightly in the center, the bridge fitting perfectly between his brows like it was designed to be there.

"Three," he admits. "And then there are the finger fractures. Most were minor, but this one..." He holds out his left hand, showing off a rather crooked pinky. "This one never quite recovered."

I trace over his rough skin before interlocking our fingers. "I love your hands," I whisper. "I mean, like, they're so strong. You can see your work in them. All of that saving and stuff." Heat floods up my spine "I like your nose too."

He watches me as I lift my free hand to his face, running it along the bridge of his nose and stopping at the tip.

"You do?" he breathes heavily, looking at me from under dark lashes. He grasps my hand tighter, massaging my palm with his thumb.

"Yeah. It gives you character. And I'm really into characters."

I continue my exploratory touches along his face, traipsing up to his brow, tracing the strong lines of his jaw. My pulse is frenzied as I run along the fade on the back of his neck.

Cameron leans into me. Our game has shifted to How Much Can You Take? He tugs me closer, his lips hovering teasingly over mine.

"So, what else do you like about me?" His voice is a tantalizing purr.

The pad of my thumb traces over his pierced ear. My nerves thunderbolt as if I've touched a live wire. I map a path to his jaw, savoring the delicious roughness of his stubble.

"The things I'm discovering through this Never Have I Ever game," I admit. "Your turn."

"Never have I ever…" His gaze roams over me with a slow intensity. "Had an ankle chain between my teeth."

Neither of us grabs a snack. I raise an eyebrow and remove my hands from him. "You're sure you didn't do that the night we were together?"

"I'd remember that."

On my ankle, my little seashell chain dangles innocently. Cameron stares at it like gears are turning in his head.

"Well, I have an easy fix," I casually suggest, uncurling my leg.

In one swift move, he grips my calf, warmly and confidently. His touch is hot. I fall back into the couch corner as he plants a slow path of kisses along my calf. His scruff grazes my skin, each bristle a tantalizing spark.

When he reaches the chain, my brain turns to mush. The moment stretches like taffy. His tongue glides over the metal in a deliberate, lazy motion. His eyes bore into me, promising everything we've been and could be.

Call a doctor, because I've officially flatlined.

"I—I guess you have to eat a gummy for that one." My voice trembles.

"Totally worth it." He drops my leg, giving it one last lingering glance. Then he grabs a gummy and bites it in half. *Please sink those teeth into me!* my brain screams.

"About that night..." I hesitate. *Be confident, Daphne!* I've kissed him once. I can do it again. "When you said you hadn't stopped thinking about it, what did you mean?"

Instead of *Soccer for Dummies*, I should've grabbed *Flirting with Gorgeous Men for the Clueless.*

That familiar crease above his nose reappears. "It felt easy being with you."

"In what way?"

"I've never been with someone who—" His focus zeros in on me. "Complimented me so much. It was a huge turn-on. I loved how vocal you were about what you liked. You were sexy."

Cute, adorable, sweet—those are my usual labels. Sexy? Only with Cameron. My insides melt.

"Oh, good," I croak. "You used your mouth well too." *Did I just say that?* "I mean, your words were nice." My senses spin.

"Have you been thinking about it?" he asks.

Pfft, have I thought about it? Only in my bed, in the shower, anytime I'm in his car. When he looks at me or flirts.

Or when he laughs, like he's still getting used to the idea of joy.

"Sometimes," I say. Our bodies sway closer, like magnets with a mind of their own. "Never have I ever…fantasized about a friend of mine in a very unfriendly way."

Cameron hesitates, eyes darting to the gummy bowl. Slowly, deliberately, he picks one up and pops it into his mouth. My heart somersaults. I reach for a carrot and take a bite.

"Never have I ever wanted to ditch my no-soccer-players rule," he says, his tone dead serious.

"Don't you know by now, Goose? In our world, it's called football."

I reach for the coffee table, but Cameron's hand intercepts mine. He grips my jaw, bringing his mouth close, hovering over the spot he kissed on his birthday but not making contact.

"You have no idea how long I've waited to hear you say that." His lips brush against mine, tentative and teasing. A jolt of heat shoots through me.

More. I need more. My eyelashes flutter closed, and it's like Cameron really can read my mind because he kisses me.

The world stops.

It's slow at first, almost as if we're both afraid to break the spell. But then he's climbing over me, his warm, solid body pressing into mine as his hand moves to the back of my neck, pulling me closer, deepening the kiss. It's like a dam has burst, and all the pent-up desire and tension between us floods out, drowning us both.

I gasp against his mouth, and he takes advantage, slipping his tongue past my lips, exploring, tasting. I melt into him, my hands sliding up his chest, feeling the hard muscles beneath his shirt. My absolute favorite. He groans, a deep, primal sound that sends heat pooling low in my belly.

His breath is hot against my lips. "You're so perfect, so beautiful."

"And you," I breathe. "You make me feel so alive."

Our kisses become urgent and desperate, like we can't get enough of each other. His hands slide under my shirt, brushing my skin, and I shiver. I tug at his shirt, pulling it over his head, and he does the same to mine.

"I've never stopped thinking about you." His voice is raw with emotion. "Every time I'm around you, I lose my goddamn mind."

"Cameron."

"Your sweaters and your punny shirts make me fucking crazy," he says as he peppers hot kisses along my neck and collarbone, down to the swell of my breasts. "I've thought about you in ways I can't even begin to explain. Every laugh, every sigh, every little sound you make—it's been living rent-free in my mind since that first night. I've thought about you in ways that would make you blush." He nibbles on my earlobe and licks down my throat. I gasp, my nails digging into his shoulders. "I've dreamed about you, Daphne. About us. About what it would be like to finally have you again."

He says the words I've kept locked up for months. His athletic body is a marvel under my hands—every muscle is taut and defined. Around him, I'm safe, beautiful, and sexy.

"Tell me. Tell me everything," I plead.

The undeniable stiffness in his jeans grows. "Late at night, when it's just me and the sound of you through the wall, I let my mind wander. I've pictured you in my arms, imagined your skin against mine, and tasted your lips. I think about you in the shower, imagine you there with me, your purple waves drenched. I watch your livestreams just to hear your voice. I've even—" He pauses, his voice husky. "I've even touched myself thinking about you."

No more waiting. I need him. I unzip his jeans. "You have no idea what you do to me," I groan while he devours my neck again. "I've thought about you too, Cameron. Every day, every night. I've wanted to kiss you since your birthday. Maybe even before that."

His hands are everywhere, but it's not enough. I need more. I arch against him.

"Then let's stop thinking and start doing."

I let out a breathy plea. "Yes, yes, yes." I nod eagerly as Cameron tugs off my shorts. He kisses me again, more demanding.

Then, a buzzing noise slices through the sirens wailing in my head.

I'm lost in the sensation, in the heat and the passion and the overwhelming desire, but the pinging and vibrating continue incessantly, and I stiffen.

The last time my phone blew up like this was when the *Stone Times* posted about my knitting retreat. The heat between my legs tangos with anxiety, cold dread seeping into my bones.

"Ignore it," Cameron mutters, breathless and desperate. I try, but the notifications triple until my phone tumbles off the coffee table. I pull away, trembling with unspoken terror. "No, Daphne. Stay."

"Sorry, I should…it could be my sister or my moms," I stammer, reaching for my phone. I silence it and try to make sense of the blur of notifications, my mind spinning, panic setting in.

An image pops up. Not just any image—it's me and Cameron. In the parking lot of Lyndhurst Stadium on Saturday. My breath hitches, fear knotting in my chest.

November 16

Cameron Hastings: More Successful in Scoring with Yet Another Influencer than Saving Goals for Lyndhurst.

. . .

I'M IN A TABLOID. We're in a tabloid. This cannot be happening. The photographs turned our smiles, and a deeply personal moment, into a spectacle.

"Is everything all right?" Cameron asks, his voice tinged with worry.

I have to tell him. My fingers tremble as I scroll through the rest of the article. My heart races as I read the comment section, even though I know I shouldn't.

another uggo for hastings lol

Just another PR stunt, if you ask me.

She's obsessed!!! DESPERATE MUCH

totally just helped w/ auction 2 get 2gether w/ him

wtf is a knitting influencer?

LOL AS IF HE'D EVER GO FOR SOMEONE LIKE THAT

WAG wannabe

My chest tightens like the air's been sucked out of the room. The flush creeping up my neck isn't from Cameron anymore, but from the raw feeling of being scrutinized by hundreds and hundreds of strangers online.

In this panic, memories of my eleventh birthday flood back. The fairy-themed party. The popular girls. The pictures they posted of me and my party online, mocking me. Calling me names like loser, weirdo, and freak.

I keep scrolling, each comment sharper than the last. I blink rapidly, trying to erase the article burned into my retinas.

"Duck?" Cameron's face falls. He knows exactly what happened because it's happened to him too. I shakily turn my screen toward him. His face is calm, but his jaw clenches and his brows furrow. "Fuck." He's trying to hide it—the panic? The fear? He takes a few shaky breaths, his face solemn. It's the same expression he had when that fan attacked him. Then he grabs his clothes. "I'm going to take care of it."

"Cameron." I reach for his hand, but he won't meet my eyes.

"It's okay. It's just a rumor. We aren't dating, so it's a lie anyway, right? It's fine."

"I'll have this taken down." His growl displays none of the tenderness he whispered a moment ago.

"Okay."

"I promise." He tilts my chin up. "We're okay. I'll fix this. I'll make it right."

But his face betrays him, flickering with anger and something else—regret, maybe. My stomach knots, twisting sharply. Did I make a huge mistake? Did we just complicate everything?

"Okay," I say, my voice quavering. I search for reassurance, but all I see is the widening gap between us.

Cameron picks up the blanket and wraps it around me, his touch gentle but distant. He pulls me onto the couch next to him, but now there's a space between us that feels like a chasm. Unspoken truths and hidden fears press down.

"I'm not going anywhere. I'll take care of it."

His words spin in my mind, tangling with Bea's comments about the relentless media attention. The reality crashes down: what we have is no longer just ours. It's out there, exposed to the world.

I try to grasp what he's saying, but the realization hits me: this isn't okay.

Chapter 20
Cameron

November 17
Has Influencer Daphne Quinn Slipped Past Lyndhurst's Defense Line?

BETWEEN THE GRUELING practice and my guilt over the photo plastered everywhere, I'm a walking time bomb. No one said anything to me all day, but those familiar whispers from when I first joined the team seem to be back. Or maybe it's all in my head.

The locker room is empty except for those of us who stayed late for extra training. Coach and the offensive line are in the media room, reviewing plays for Saturday's game. I pull out my phone from my duffel and text Daphne.

CAMERON

Hey. Thinking about you.

How are you?

DAPHNE

:/

CAMERON

Be home soon.

I barely reach my locker before my defensive squad rushes over. Gustafsson throws an arm around my shoulder, Tae-woo right behind him.

"Congratulations, Hastings," Tae-woo says, holding up his phone, which displays the article about Daphne and me.

"About time you made it official." Gustafsson grins, running over to see the picture for himself.

"We haven't." I sigh. Last night ignited something between us. I let my feelings show, almost claimed her, but of fucking course the paparazzi had to ruin it.

Gustafsson's brow furrows. "Didn't know you were keeping it under wraps."

"There's nothing to keep," I say, the words tasting like gravel. "We're just friends. She gave me a hug after the game, and you know how tabloids can twist things."

"The *Stone Times*? They're full of it," Tae-woo chimes in. "Last year, they claimed my sister was my new girlfriend."

"Your sister?" I grimace. At least my teammates understand what it's like to have lies printed about them. "That's revolting."

"Hope Daphne is taking it okay," Gustafsson says.

"She's fine," I say, finding it hard to believe my own words.

After the initial shock wore off, we settled into the silent comfort of another movie. She drifted off to sleep, her head resting on the couch. I slipped out quietly, not wanting to wake her, but I couldn't sleep. My mind raced with thoughts of where the night would've led if we hadn't been interrupted and how the gossip would affect us.

This morning, when I checked in on her, she assured me she was okay.

Deep down, even after I get the article taken down, I know the damage is already done. The damn tabloids have sunk their claws in, hurting someone I care about. The girl with the bright smile and laughter that somehow brings a part of me back to life. The girl whose mere memory keeps the nightmares at bay, the girl who's always alive in my mind, the girl who knows all of this now.

My girl.

And admitting that, even to myself, feels like the first breath of air after almost drowning. It's not just about me; it's about protecting her. It's about us. That realization hits me hard.

The locker room door creaks open, and Femi, moving with ease and confidence thanks to his new bionic prosthetic, bursts in, breathless and wide-eyed. "You got company outside, Hastings. Swarming the entire parking lot."

Not this again. My chest tightens, my vision narrows. The air thickens. I can't breathe, can't think.

Why won't they leave me alone? My mind fills with the roar of flashing lights. I'm pulled, prodded, microphones shoved in my face, cameras smacking into me.

Every flash of the camera feels like a punch. My knees buckle, and I slump onto a bench, feeling their intrusion pressing in on me. I want to scream, to push them all away, but I'm trapped under their relentless gaze.

The room spins. My vision darkens at the edges.

"Cameron." A voice echoes. "Hey, Hastings!" I focus my vision. Okafor stands over me, face blanched with concern. "You all right?"

My pulse screeches in my ears. "Fine." I bat him away and try to force the weight of my mind's intrusion off my shoulders. Maybe I can outrun them again. "Fuck. I just—I don't want to deal with them."

"Let us help?" Gustafsson settles down next to me, his presence a surprising comfort.

"Help?" A part of me wants to believe them, but another part screams that this is just pity. "You don't have to do that," I say, the words thick with the remnants of mistrust. The tabloids are ruining my life, threatening to take everything away again. Cost me my dignity. Cost me another season. Cost me someone who means something.

"We want to." Tae-woo joins us, falling to the other side of me, his voice steady and sincere. They both smile at me. There's no pity on their faces, just genuine kindness. They consider me a friend despite the walls I built around myself at the beginning of the season.

Still.

"I don't need your pity," I snap, feeling defensive. "I can handle this on my own."

Okafor shakes his head. "It's not pity, Hastings. We're your teammates. We've got your back."

"Yeah," Tae-woo adds, his tone gentle but firm. "We've all been there, man. We know what it's like to have the media breathing down your neck. You don't have to go through this alone."

I glance between them, my defenses crumbling like ruins. "Why are you doing this? Why do you care?"

"Because you're one of us," Okafor says simply. "And we don't turn our back on a lion."

"All right," I finally say, the words heavy with relief. "I appreciate it."

For a moment, the mistrust I've held onto loosens. In the locker room, the metallic clang of lockers, the sharp smell of sweat, and the loud laughter had always been harsh reminders of the camaraderie I couldn't touch, the brotherhood from which I felt a thousand miles away. But now, surrounded by my teammates, their support makes me realize I'm not alone.

"GO FOR LEO."

"It's me." I can't hide the panic in my voice. I shift in the driver's seat, relieved to have returned to the Lodge without the paparazzi swarming me. My teammates escorted me to my car and past the reporters. I felt pathetic.

"Cameron?" Dad asks. "Are you all right, son?"

Regret washes over me. I feel like a kid who can't fix his own mess. Dad helped me with the livestream March by using his connections to silence the tabloids. It's good to have a father with influence.

"I assume you saw the news already."

"Carlyle forwarded it this morning. Who's the girl?" Dad asks.

"She's a…" I pause. To call her a friend feels too simple, too inadequate for what Daphne has come to mean to me. "Her name is Daphne."

"The one from the auction on Sunday?"

"Yes," I admit, smiling at the thought of her.

"What's she after? Another Mal Kelly situation?" Dad wonders.

"No, she's nothing like that. She's…" I struggle for the right words. "It's different."

"There hasn't been a girl in a long time," Dad notes. Even over the phone, he reads me well. "Can't say I'm not happy for you." His words are warm and comforting.

"Can you fix this? I don't want the media focusing on my personal life instead of the matches."

"I don't know, Cameron." He sighs. "If this were like the situation at Overton, I'd understand, but this is minor. A headline about a fling won't affect you."

"She's not a fling, and it's—it's affecting her." My frustration seeps into my tone. The comments were ruthless toward her.

"I hear you. And I'm sorry this is hurting your girl, but you're in the public eye. From what I understand, she is too, isn't she? This is what your life will be like if you keep playing at this level. I can't protect you from everything."

"I'm not asking you to," I insist. "I just want these tabloids to stop spreading lies."

"You think the media will ease up if you win the Premier League? What about when you go to the World Cup? Players' lives become headlines when they're not on the pitch. It sells copies. Maybe this isn't what you want to hear, but if there's no real story here, maybe you can just let it go instead of running from it?"

The memory of the last scandal still haunts me. Headlines ran for over a month after he scrubbed the internet. Sure, the Overton locker room livestream still lurks in certain corners of the internet, but no big papers would touch it for fear of losing shareholders.

I can't let this gossip train cost me Daphne or the Premiership.

"Let it go?" No. I didn't want advice, I wanted a solution.

"The things your mother and I dealt with in the media back in our day. When she found out she was pregnant with Alec during her playoff season and had to miss the championship game, people said awful things about us. But you know what, Cameron? None of that mattered. We stopped reading them."

"But you were married to Mom. It's not the same," I say, frustration in my voice.

"The only opinions that matter are those of the people you care about and trust, Cam. Sounds like you have someone to weather this with."

"Dad, I can't have what happened at the end of last season happen again."

"All right." He sighs. "I'll get Carlyle on it. Lay low for now. How about coming home for the holidays? The rest of the family will be here. If you're worried about your girl, bring her along.

UK tabloid gossip doesn't have quite the same impact over here."

Christmas is only a month away, but with the big match against Overton on December nineteenth looming, I can't even think that far ahead. Charlie is probably loving every minute of me getting dragged into the media.

I hesitate. "I'll think about it." *Would Daphne be ready to meet my family?*

Dad continues, "Carlyle will arrange for the jet for Sunday the twentieth. You can fly the morning after your Overton game." His voice softens. "Come home, son."

"Okay," I reply, my voice barely audible.

Relief washes over me, and we end the call. I check my messages. Still nothing from Daphne. Worry churns in my chest.

We had something special, our own world. Last night was a turning point. I showed her what she meant to me, and I know she felt it too. But now the media vultures are circling. I can't stand losing her to this chaos.

Chapter 21
Cameron

"IF YOU DON'T RESPOND, I'll have no choice but to assume you're in danger and break down the door," I declare, my voice losing its humorous tone. I knock again, my ears straining to decode the troubled shuffling from behind the door. "Daphne?"

The door swings open, but instead of the usual burst of vibrant color and sunshine, her place is shrouded in unsettling darkness. The radiant smile I look forward to is absent, replaced by a quivering pout.

Red, swollen eyes meet mine, their usual sparkle dimmed.

Her hair is in a messy bun—a far cry from her usual styles—and she's wearing an oversized tee with a salacious old lady knitting in a rocking chair above the words "I'm a Hooker" and a pair of sweats.

"Hey." My voice cracks. I bend down to her eye level.

"Hi," she murmurs, a shadow of her usual self. She moves further into her apartment, putting a distance between us that feels more final than it should.

"Duck, are you okay?"

"I'm not," she says with a quaver in her voice.

"Can I come in?"

She scans my face as if deciding whether to let me in—not just into her apartment, but into whatever weight is crushing her mind right now. She steps aside. Her coffee table, typically a testament to her organized chaos, is now overrun with candy wrappers and half-eaten bags of chips. Empty glasses and mugs are scattered around the living room. Crumpled tissues litter her fuzzy rug.

"I'm handling the article," I assure her.

She curls into a ball on the couch, her phone lighting up her face. "It's not the article. It's..." Her voice trails off, and my heart aches at her struggle. I've felt defeat on the field, but this feels different. "Just see for yourself." She hands me her phone, showing her latest YouTube video. "It's the comments."

I scroll through the first few of thousands.

Lol. Never bring me back to this side of the internet again.

Why would Hastings be with someone like that

Mal Kelly did it better

THIS is the reason Lyndhurst's keeper cost us the early matches????

Attention seeker

What is this therapy knitting nonsense

Are you signing up for Lust Island Season 9?

Sorry, you knit for a living? How is that even a thing?

Cameron obv likes them dumb

WHY DOES SHE USE SO MANY EXCLAMATION MARKS

Hear earlobes look like saucers

She looks like and talks like a child

Purple hair attention much

An insidious anger pulses in my temples.

I clutch her phone, memorizing the names and profile pictures behind the cruel abuse aimed at Daphne. I should have kept an eye on the situation. When Mal spewed lies about me, she was praised in the media. But when it's Daphne, the sweetest soul I know, the world turns against her?

She knits for charity, for fuck's sake.

My jaw clenches, and my fists ball up. Then realization crashes over me. I did this. I brought these vultures into her safe space. Guilt claws at my throat.

"I'm sorry," I manage.

"It's not like you wrote them." She sighs. "You can't believe any of this nonsense. They're all lies, you must know that."

She grabs the phone from me, and her bloodshot eyes fall back on the screen. "I—hundreds of comments are pouring in on all my videos and posts. I've gained over ten thousand followers, and I don't want any of them. I don't want a single one of these strangers in my life. They crashed my website."

My mind spins. When this happened to me, my agent turned off all the comments on my public pages. We cut off posting, apart from the contracted brand deals that were already lined up. That helped cut out so much of the noise. "Why don't you turn off the comments or private your page until we get the article taken down?" I ask, desperate for a solution.

Her face scrunches up in disbelief. "Why don't you stop playing football?"

"What?" I've obviously said the wrong thing, but I don't know what to do in this situation. My instinct is to run, to numb, to block.

"This is my job, my life. Turn off the comments? Make my account private? Do you not understand that this is how I keep my community? It's how I connect with people. I respond to every comment, every question about yarn and stitches and recommendations. But these comments, they're all about me," she breathes out, the words cutting through me like a knife. "They're all about who I am…and who I'm not."

I remember her telling me about being bullied online as a kid; this situation is probably bringing back all those painful memories.

People are ruthless.

I can't really promise her that tomorrow this will blow over or that there won't be more pictures.

"You're right. I shouldn't have even suggested that." I reach for her, but she flinches. "These comments are fucking ridiculous. And they aren't true. You are the sweetest, kindest, most wonderful person to ever exist." *Fix this, Cameron. Fix it.* "What if you delete the app for a day? Or stay off your phone?"

Daphne shakes her head in a panic. "I don't need a solution right now. I know I can delete the app. I can sit here and delete each and every comment before ten more sprout up. Do you not understand what's hurting me? This is my safe space. Every time I opened my socials, I felt excited, I felt connected. Now I want to throw up. Even my emails are full of reporters asking me to confirm the relationship."

"Look, I get that, I've been there. The best thing for us to do is lay low," I tell her, trying to soothe her. "Until the article gets taken down."

"My retreat is in four months! I can't lay low." She sighs. "The worst part is that I don't even care about the article. When I saw it last night, I thought, *Oh well, this rumor sucks*, but I thought the comments would stay on the article, not filter to my personal pages. When I helped with the auction, no one even paid attention to my channels, but now this?"

"You didn't do anything. This is my fault," I confess.

"It's so stupid, Cam. I feel like that eleven-year-old girl again, reliving everything that was said to me now multiplied through a megaphone," she whispers. "I thought football was about community, about love and support."

This game is my life, but its darker aspects are undeniable. Despite the fact that these hostile people are the minority, they always seem to make their voices heard. Now they're screaming at Daphne.

"This will all blow over," I say.

"What if I can't do my retreat? What if a sponsor sees the hate and decides to pull the funding? My followers aren't going to want anything to do with this, with me. I already put down the deposit and made the plans," she stammers. "I—I worked so hard to put myself out there, to take a risk, and now…I knew this Yes Year was going to get me in trouble. I should've listened to my sister. I should've played things safe, not decided to leave my comfort zone."

I need to make everything okay. I feel helpless—until my eyes catch on a pair of loose knitting needles on the coffee table.

I grab the needles and a spare ball of yarn next to them.

"Hey, hey, hey." I drop to my knees. "Daphne," I say, trying to get her attention as she looks past me.

"What is this?" She glances at the supplies in my hand.

"I need you to teach me how to knit," I say.

"What?"

"It's now or never." I force a smile. She doesn't seem to register it. "You said knitting is a good distraction. We can use a distraction, can't we?"

"I can't even think straight and—"

I close my palms over both of her hands, pulling her phone away. "If I don't learn how to knit, I won't know what to do with myself."

She inhales, her face softening. "Okay."

Over the next ten minutes, I struggle to grasp the basics of knitting. She's patiently explained the long-tail cast-on method multiple times, but it feels like solving a Rubik's Cube in the dark. Watching her knit with practiced ease is mesmerizing.

"Now you try." Daphne hands it over to me. I attempt to mimic her, but my fingers are as useless as two pool noodles on land. "No, Cameron, you have to stab it, strangle it, and throw it off a cliff."

I laugh at her serious tone. "I never knew knitting was so

violent." A half-smile flickers across her face, but it's fleeting, a ghost of her usual warmth. "Can you just show me again?"

She wraps her small hands around mine, guiding me through the motions. I should be focused on learning, but all I can think about is the crease in her nose, the intensity in her eyes. Our faces hover dangerously close. I want to go back to last night, to finish what we started, to make her feel better in a way my words are failing to. But we can't. Not now.

Just as her breath graces my jaw, she pulls away. "You're doing good," she says.

"It's sweet of you to lie."

"Thank you for knowing exactly how to help," she says. "As for everything else, I'm going to contact my therapist and try to work through it."

Surely there's more I can do. "I'm heading back to California for Christmas. Do you want to fly back with me and get away from all this?"

"You think this bullying will last that long?"

I can't promise her anything. "I really don't know."

"I already booked a flight home to spend time with my family."

"I'm taking the family jet after my last game of the year. There's always room for one more if you want to cancel your flight." Her eyes don't shine with adventure the way they have during her Yes Year activities.

"Oh no. Your games!" She winces. "I—I didn't even think about those. The last thing I want is to end up in more tabloids."

"That's okay. You don't need to come to them." My voice is solid. I'm trying to maintain control, but inside, I'm crumbling. Of course, I want her there. Seeing her in the crowd on Saturday was the highlight of my game. But I know I can't worry about her in the stands while trying to keep my head on the pitch.

Her lip quivers. "Maybe no more Yes Year stuff around London for a while? You know, to avoid being caught out in public again." The finality of her statement cuts through me like a blade. "We can still be friends, though, right?"

Her words hurt. The thought of losing her, of her not being in my life, is unbearable. She's been my anchor in the chaos of London. And the idea of us being just friends, after everything I've shared with her, after everything we've been through, is unthinkable.

"Whatever you want to call us, Daphne, is fine with me," I say, my voice thick with restrained emotion.

She studies me for a moment. Her eyes flicker with an unspoken question, as if she's considering reopening the door that led us to this couch last night.

A huge yawn overtakes her, and she looks so vulnerable, so heartbreakingly beautiful, that my chest tightens. "Do you—do you mind staying for a while? I really don't want to be alone."

"Of course, Duck. I'm right here," I promise her, my voice low and gravelly with suppressed emotion. I don't think she understands the gravity of what I'm saying.

I sit beside her on the couch, the space between us a chasm I desperately want to bridge. She leans her head on my shoulder, and I wrap my arm around her, pulling her close.

I'll keep her safe.

Chapter 22
Daphne

"I FEEL SO GUILTY," I admit to Erin over the Zoom call. "Yesterday was one of the worst days I've had in a long time. I just rotted, doomscrolling and letting myself spiral."

"Daphne, there's no right way to handle extreme stress."

"I know, but I ate so much junk food trying to fill the hole inside of me. Eventually, I was as physically sick as I felt mentally," I stammer, my words tripping over each other.

The best thing about virtual therapy is taking sessions from the comfort of your pj's. Normally, I have one session a month, but Erin had an opening today. This hour for myself was very much needed.

"I'm sorry to hear yesterday was tough, but it's understandable given the article, the comments, and Cameron. It's okay to have days when usual coping strategies don't work. Reaching out for support is a good step."

"I know, but how do I move forward? I'm worried sponsors will pull out of my retreat or people will crash the site when I post tickets in the middle of January. I don't want to put anyone at risk."

"Those are valid fears, but that's two months away. You have time to figure things out."

"But what do I do right now? I hate that I feel like that preteen girl getting bullied online again. I hate that I can't fix this myself."

The thing that no one warns you about is that no matter how much time passes, no matter what story you tell yourself, whether you turn the bullying into an act of revenge or live with a heart full of love, there will always be a voice in your brain. One that visits you in the best moments of your life and in the worst. One that appears, often or occasionally, and lies to you.

Mine says that I'm too much. That I'm trying to get attention. That I'm weird. That I'm not capable of helping anybody. That I'm a freak. That because I'm still in therapy after so many years, I'm not equipped to talk about anxiety.

However radically I show myself love, no matter how much acceptance I get from the people who matter most to me, the idea of being misunderstood still makes my stomach queasy. And those comments yesterday did all of that and more.

"You're not that girl anymore, Daphne. You have choices in front of you."

"Cameron suggested that I take down my socials," I say. My palms grow sweaty. "But I can't do that."

Erin gives me a sympathetic glance. "When was the last time you took a break from posting?"

"When I got the flu two winters ago." I bite my lip, trying to calm my nerves.

"Okay, that's a long time. You use your account to spread awareness about mental health, but your mental health is just as important to your community. You're allowed to take some time away to care for yourself."

I blink at her. Of course. "I'm a hypocrite."

"You're hardly a hypocrite. You're being dealt a difficult situation that few of us know how to handle."

"I tell people to care about their mental health, but I'm not even taking care of mine. How am I supposed to run a retreat when I can't even manage my anxiety?"

"You *can* manage your anxiety," Erin reminds me, and I feel embarrassed that my fatalist thinking is getting ahold of my tongue. "You've been doing it for fifteen years. Sometimes the way we take care of ourselves evolves and changes. What used to work may need an adjustment given your current circumstances."

"You're right. I have the power to step away from this temporarily. Maybe just for a week?" Then I'll see how I feel. I'll make an announcement and go offline. Even though that terrifies me and I love making content and talking to people, it's for the best. This whole thing made me feel like giving up on my retreat, and that's not okay. I hate that this is making me doubt myself.

"One day at a time. Can I ask, how is Cameron handling this? You've expressed feelings for him in our last session. Could this perhaps bring you closer?"

"He's dealt with this kind of thing before." I fidget with the sleeve of my sweater.

Cameron seemed to know how to handle it. How to fix it. How to calm me down. He had the right idea: get away from it all. Maybe running *is* the best way to get through this.

"That's useful."

I shrug. "I like who he is as a person and how he makes me feel. The version of myself that I am when I'm with him. But now, I don't know if our worlds make sense together." I don't want to be in the tabloids ever again, and that doesn't seem to be something Cameron can avoid.

"Maybe if you take him up on his offer to go to California next month, you can spend some time together outside of the routine you've made in London?"

"Maybe. But now that we've kissed, everything feels so

complicated." My mind races with questions. What are we? How do we move forward? Are we still just friends, or are we more? What do I even want?

"It doesn't have to be complicated, Daphne. You both clearly care for each other. Sometimes stressful situations bring people closer together."

"Are we trauma bonding?"

"I wouldn't go that far." Erin chuckles. "Look, you don't have to define your relationship. Sure, your bubble has burst, but the feelings you have for each other haven't just vanished."

"That's true. I want to be around him, and I've never casually kissed someone before. How do I make sense of that? Isn't this the part of every relationship where people decide if it's make-or-break?"

Erin shakes her head. "Did you like kissing him?"

"So much."

"Do you want to do it again?"

I hesitate, scared to admit it out loud. "Yes."

"So, why not just do that?"

"But what does it mean—"

"That you two are good friends. That you care for each other, and you like kissing. And that can be it for now, until everything blows over and you're ready to have a conversation about both of your feelings. You've only been spending time together for two months. From what I understand of modern dating, you don't need to rush and label your relationship."

It has been such a short time, even though my feelings for him are big. "You're right. The last thing I want to do is lose my friend over a shitty tabloid story," I say. I don't need to complicate the situation even more. "But am I being too soft about this? Should I just go online and tell everyone to fuck off? Is that what a Yes Girl would do? I'm worried that me running away is running away from my Yes Year."

"A Yes Girl is whoever you want her to be. Boundaries are healthy. There's no manual for this."

"You're right, Erin." I sigh. "I'm going to make a post and take a break until I'm ready to log back on. Maybe after the holidays."

I already have the next two weeks of content planned out. I'll schedule those sporadically and make sure my sponsored posts are up. Then I can delete the apps and stay offline.

People take breaks for the holidays all the time. My community won't just disappear.

"Good." She smiles, glancing at the corner of her screen, likely checking our time. "Talk soon, Daphne. If you need anything, I'm a call away."

"Thank you."

Closing my laptop, I take a deep breath. I feel so much better than yesterday. Sometimes all I need is a good cry, binging on all my favorite snacks, a debrief with a therapist, and some grace to allow myself to feel shitty. It's a deep cut, and it's impractical to think it will heal overnight.

I wish I had asked Cameron to stay the night. I didn't want him to think I couldn't take care of myself. But he was there for me when I needed it most, and I can trust him.

It takes me an hour to craft the perfect caption and schedule my posts, but once it's done, I hit publish and delete the apps from my phone. My nerves are still a bit fried, but there's a sense of relief washing over me. Tomorrow is a new day.

Just one more thing to do.

DAPHNE

Thank you for being there for me last night.

GOOSE

Anytime.

I mean it. I'm only a door away.

Now more than ever, I don't want to be alone or out in public. The weather outside matches my dreary mood. Maybe Cameron and I can lean on each other for the next month. Surely, after the New Year, no one will be talking about that article. Like he said, it will blow over.

GOOSE

DAPHNE

Want to come over for dinner?

Shrek 2?

GOOSE

I'll grab some salads for us on the way home.

DAPHNE

You mean turkey club sandwiches from Petal & Plate right?

Extra cranberry sauce. :)

GOOSE

Be there at 8.

My anxiety dances around my body. I walk over to the bathroom and glance in my full-sized mirror. I make myself big. I stand up on my tiptoes and reach my arms overhead. *Take up space.* I swallow a deep breath and shoot it out of me, pulling funny faces until I manage to get myself to smile a little. But I still need to get my hands busy.

I can survive forty-six days offline. I've been wanting to knit my first rug for my bedroom. That should take a month, and I can make beanies for the local hospitals too. I probably have the yarn I ordered downstairs. I slip on my slippers and open my door to a huge bouquet of...lettuce? Flowers and lettuce and pods of peas.

I grab the card.

STICKS & STEMS & SEEDS

For Duck - From Goose

I take it in—Cameron's messy handwriting on the card, the inside joke behind the bouquet. Something so small, a shared bit of our humor, makes me feel seen, cherished, and understood.

Who knew a bunch of lettuce and peas could do that?

A halfhearted chuckle falls out of me. And it's exactly what I needed.

Chapter 23
Daphne

KNOCK. Knock. Knock.

I glance at the clock. It's ten. I've heard the same sound a dozen times over the past three weeks.

Cameron.

My heart somersaults. I drop my knitting and hit pause on *Little Women,* before walking to the front door.

Staying offline for three weeks has been tough, but necessary. Those first few days, my hands instinctively reached for my phone, a rhythm of a habit too ingrained to break. But ever since I stepped back, I've found myself more present, more in the now. My therapist hit the nail on the head. How could I champion mental health for others without first tending to my own?

I even put a child lock on sites like the *Stone Times* to stop doomscrolling. Cameron got ridiculous the piece taken down. He said there's still stuff lingering but the rumors will fade. The little bubble we've created has been a godsend.

Bea has stopped by a few times to drop off pastries and check in on me, which is an incredibly sweet thing to do for someone she just met.

Therapy has helped too, even if it rattled me at first. Understanding the root of my triggers and making peace with the fact that the bullying from years ago can still affect me deeply was not something I planned to do. Some mean comments online and all the negative self-talk I've ever heard in my head came rolling back. One day at a time, I remind myself. I can handle it.

Cameron's solution to escape from everything was valid. Sometimes, withdrawing from the world isn't the worst option. Not being online means that I've been holed up at home, planning my retreat and posting patterns to my shop, but otherwise, the content break has been helping me gain perspective.

I swing open the door. Cameron stands there, his usually bright eyes dull and heavy. "Can I—?" He hesitates, glancing into my apartment. His right pointer finger digs into his thumb like it's a stress ball. "Am I interrupting?"

"You're not. I'm just watching a movie."

He looks at me for a long, hard moment. "Would it be all right if I sit with you for a while?"

For nearly a month, Cameron's been doing this adorable thing where he migrates to my place—never quite staying the night, but definitely playing house.

"Of course," I say. Untangling our kiss has been like sorting out mangled yarn. It wasn't just a heat-of-the-moment thing; we said things we can't unsay. But diving into the what-are-we chat? Not happening. At least, not until the media storm is over for good and I can go online without hyperventilating. For now, we're in that awkward limbo between friends and something more.

"Hungry? I've got churros, and you look like you need some sugar." I head to the kitchen. Food fixes everything, right?

"No, thanks, though," he mumbles, setting down his training bag before collapsing onto my couch. I grab a bowl with two churros, hit play, and sink into the couch, my body settling into the groove his weight has carved over the last few weeks. We sit in silence, him looking like a moody statue.

When his fingers start their usual self-torture routine, I decide to break the ice.

"All right, what's on your mind?" I turn to face him with my best, encouraging smile.

"We've been working on this new play all week." He swaps his nail-picking for twirling my hair around his fingers.

"Are you planning on using it at your next game?" I ask, my voice soft and coaxing.

"Yeah, against Overton." He sighs. "I have to lead the play, so there's a ton of pressure to get it right."

Last Wednesday, the guys were as thrilled about *The Great British Bake Off* as a cat in water. Usually, they're drenched with excitement, but the upcoming match has everyone in a funk. They haven't lost a game since September, but they drew last week's game, which is no different in Cameron's eyes.

This Overton game is a dark cloud hanging over his head. His old team didn't exactly throw him a farewell party, and now he's up against his ex-coach and that dreadful ex-best friend. I can't shake the feeling that there's more to the story, but I'll wait until he's ready to share it.

I wish I could be there to cheer him on, but we agreed it's best I stay in the no-match zone until the new year. A girl's gotta keep her boundaries, even if it stings not being there for him.

"How are you feeling about playing your old team?" I ask.

"Fine," he mutters. I want to tease the truth out of him, unravel his thoughts like a ball of yarn, but I know better. Cameron's the kind of guy who needs to unsnarl himself. "It's just another game—I want to win," he says, but there's a hollow ring to it, like a bell that's lost its chime.

I want to tell him it's okay to be scared, that it's okay to not have all the answers, but the words get stuck in my throat like a too-big bite of cheesecake. Instead, I lean into his touch, offering silent comfort. Sometimes, just being there is the best way to say you care.

"So, in my *Soccer for Dummies* book, I read that a lot of players have these kooky pregame rituals. What if we do yours together?"

"You want to wake up at 4:45 a.m. with me and tape up your hands?"

"Sure!" I say, forcing a smile. He knows I'm a zombie before nine o'clock in the morning. "Come on, what else? There's gotta be something I don't know about."

He looks at me and hesitates, his face twisting into an awkward scowl. Uncomfortable, he rubs the back of his neck and finally confesses, "In the States, I used to sleep in my uniform the night before a game. It was a superstition from my LA team days. We all slept in our uniforms one year. Never lost a single game that season and even won the MLS Cup. For big matches, I still do it, though it hasn't worked for years."

His confession puts my brain to work.

"Hold on a sec," I say, darting out of the living room like a woman on a mission. My heart races as I make a beeline for my closet. I fling open the door and begin rummaging through my sweaters, tossing them aside until I finally uncover his jersey. A grin spreads across my face as I throw it on over my pajamas and sprint back to the living room.

I drop to my knees beside his duffel bag, my fingers trembling with anticipation. Half expecting the musty scent of a locker room, I unzip the bag and am greeted by the surprisingly fresh aroma of clean clothes. Everything is neatly folded, just like my Cameron. Of course it is. My heart swells with affection as I fish out what I'm looking for.

"What are you doing?" he asks, eyeing me suspiciously.

"Put it on," I command, tossing his uniform at him.

"I trained in this earlier," he protests.

I roll my eyes dramatically. "This kit is cleaner than the socks I threw on this morning. Put it on, Cameron."

He pauses, the moment heavy with anticipation, before whipping off his shirt in one swift move, unveiling his chiseled-by-the-gods abs. The spark in me that had dimmed after the tabloid drama suddenly flares up, setting my insides on fire. Sure, anxiety and my fluoxetine don't exactly fuel the flames, but Cameron's body could single-handedly power a space mission with its sheer hotness. He wriggles out of his jeans, down to his black boxer briefs that cling to all the right places, and then slides on the purple shorts.

"Happy now?" he asks, with a smirk that's more adorable than annoyed.

If only he knew. "Yes! Now we've got half of your old ritual down."

"Are you planning to take me to bed next?" He arches a brow, and despite the playful tease, I can't help but notice that the dark circles under his eyes seem lighter—or maybe it's just my hopeful imagination playing tricks on me.

"Let's save that for after we do one of *my* rituals." He nods, clearly intrigued. "You're going to think this is nuts," I admit, feeling a tingle of excitement. "But I like to give myself a pep talk." I spread my legs wide like a superhero. "Something like, *I've got this. I am a strong, confident, and charming woman. Take up space!*"

I glance at him, expecting him to bolt at any second. Instead, he just stares at me with this blank look. *Oh great, he definitely thinks I'm bonkers.* But then his expression changes, a mix of surprise and amusement lighting up his face.

"You're joking."

"Oh, come on! I swear it works," I say, winking.

Cameron shakes his head, a soft chuckle escaping his lips. Then, in two swift strides, he decisively closes the gap between us. His mouth crashes into mine, and the initial shock gives way to a rush of warmth that spreads through my veins. My heart races, my body reacting instinctively. We haven't shared a kiss like this in weeks—just brief, perfunctory pecks along his fingers or the ones he leaves on my cheek. But this kiss? It's something else entirely, the kind that makes your knees weak and your mind blur. His fingers find their way into my hair, his other hand pulling me closer, holding me to him. When he finally pulls back, I'm left breathless, the room seeming to spin slightly.

"What was that for?" I ask, grinning hard.

"Before every game, I stand in my box," he says, dropping his hold on me and stretching his arms wide, legs akimbo. "And I chant, *Be big. Be a fortress. Don't be hasty. Be impenetrable. No ball will touch the back of the net.*"

The sight of him standing there, mimicking my pose, hits me like a punch to the gut. It's all I can do not to burst into laughter. There's something so real, so unapologetically him, in this moment, it makes my chest feel like it's about to burst.

"You're serious?"

"Swear it."

It feels like one of those absurdly cliché moments from a romantic comedy. My mind is screaming, *This is it, we're soulmates!* We're sprawled out like starfish in my living room, and his normally reserved face is lit up with a genuine grin. Everything else blurs into the background, and I want to yell, *I am hopelessly, irreversibly head over heels for you!*

The dim light of the television gives everything a dreamy quality. He reaches for my outstretched hand above my head, and the squeeze feels electric, like a jolt through my veins. Time seems to slow down. I notice the way his eyes crinkle at the corners, the slight blush on his cheeks, and the rise and fall of his chest, as if he's trying to hold on to this moment.

"Thank you, Daphne." The words pop out of his mouth, and he drops his stance, not letting go of my hand. I follow suit. "Thank you."

I shake my head. "I haven't done anything, I promise."

But he pulls me closer until we're just inches apart. His breath mingles with mine as I listen to his heart pounding. His golden eyes meet mine, and for a split second, the world holds its breath.

Cameron's lip quirks up. He rests his forehead on mine, our noses almost touching. His eyes lock onto mine, intense enough to make my heart trip over itself. It's like he's peeking into my soul, untangling every hidden fear and dream.

He runs his fingers through my hair, as if memorizing every strand, trying to remember every single follicle and scent. His chest rises and falls. The moment stretches into a slow dance of touches and whispered breaths. His hand travels to the nape of my neck, sending shivers down my spine.

"You have no idea how much you've done," he whispers.

Chapter 24
Cameron

DECEMBER 18
Hastings Redemption or Rematch? Lyndhurst Keeper Faces Off Against Former Club, Overton, Post-Livestream Scandal!

DECEMBER 18
Is it too late for Lyndhurst to come back this season? Tenth in the table—the lowest they've fallen in a decade.

DECEMBER 18
Keeper Shows Off to the Camera: Shower Stream Resurfaces!!!

TODAY HAS JUST BEEN one bad omen after another.

First, I tripped on the last step of the Lodge on the way to the stadium, and now my ankle feels a bit tight. Next, the wrist strap of my goalkeeper gloves got caught on my bag zipper and ripped, forcing me to wear new ones for the match—something I never do—so now I need to break them in during one of the most important games of the season.

Then, my laces snapped while I was tying my cleats in the locker room.

To top it all off, the first thing I saw on the news this morning was the screenshots from the livestream being recirculated. My body on display for everyone to taunt. For the comments about my dick, my form, my physique to be back in full force. Acid slithers up my throat. Guess nothing can ever be permanently deleted. I'm sure the fans will call out the same remarks I heard during the last two months of last season.

Wanker. Hung Hastings. Drop your kit! Let's see your balls, keeper.

Usually followed up by a hand gesture that really lacks imagination on their part.

All of which was terrible but barely holds a candle to the fact that I'll see my old team. And Charlie.

I haven't seen him since my last Overton game. At least he'll be all the way on the other side of the pitch, nearly a hundred meters away from me.

We have the home advantage. We've run the plays.

All I want is to win this fucking match and get back home to see Daphne. I wish she was here today.

"Does anyone have spare laces?" Okafor calls out into the bustling locker room.

Fuck, I hope that doesn't mean our captain is having an off day too.

Grabbing the third spare pair hanging in my locker, I toss it in his direction without looking over my shoulder.

"Woah," he says with shock. "Thanks, but what's with the aggression?"

A flurry of whispers breaks out behind me before a hand

claps over my shoulder. "We're going to kick Overton's ass today, Hastings," Gustafsson says.

"Yeah," I grunt, burying my head in my locker.

I don't need this right now. *Stay focused. Stay big. Think big, Cam. Win.* I shout into the corners of my mind, but the gripping chains around my chest refuse to loosen.

I envision each play in my mind. I know Overton's weaknesses. Victor favors his left foot; Mikey will try everything to get penalty kicks. Lionel will attempt to foul Okafor and take him out of the game. No, wait—Mikey likes to hog the ball, and Punum is always up for penalty kicks. *Get it fucking together.* I can't be messing up simple facts.

"We got you, man," Tae-woo whispers from the bench next to me. I give him a curt nod.

Okafor leads us through our ritual. I attempt to roar with the team, but my voice turns hoarse. *Not now.* I fix my eyes ahead as we line up, Okafor in front of me and Tae-woo behind. We shuffle into the tunnel. A cold splash of dread washes over me. Out of the corner of my eye, I can feel Charlie's laser beam of attention boring into my face.

"Purple's just not your color, Hastings," Charlie sneers, a venomous edge on every word.

I gulp in a breath. It's sharp and cold, not unlike the ice that crept into our friendship last season. I refuse to acknowledge Charlie's dull gray eyes, devoid of their previous warmth. He looks the same as he did all those months ago, except his jaw is set in a permanent scowl. And now he's in the starting jersey again.

How could he have been my best friend once?

My heart is a frantic drum in my chest. I need to drown out the noise of the world around me. Keep a level head. I have to stay focused.

You got this, Cam. You're a fucking fortress. No ball is getting past you.

"Got yourself a new girl to keep you in the tabloids?" Charlie taunts. "Daphne Quinn, was it? You her new charity case? Fixing up poor Cameron Hastings."

I whirl to face him, scanning his smug face. "What did you say?"

"Break a sweat out there. Heard there's great showers here." Charlie grins like a wolf snarling at the moon and follows his captain onto the field.

My mind reels. Anger boils up inside me. How fucking dare he say anything about Daphne.

"We're walking." Tae-woo's voice pierces through the haze swarming my mind. My feet obey the command, moving as if choreographed.

A surge of anger floods me. The roaring stadium is a blur.

First, Charlie befriended me. Then he violated my trust, trampled over our friendship, and used my privacy as a pawn in his twisted game. He tried to sabotage my career, the very thing I had sacrificed so much for. He was never a friend, just a snake hiding in the tall grass, biding his time until he could strike.

Now he's fucking coming for my girl, my safety, my woman. Absolutely not. He got what he wanted. He's back in the starting lineup.

To hell with him.

The only thing I need to focus on is winning. Saving this game. Putting Lyndhurst first. As the opening ceremony concludes, I unclench my fists, the tension seeping out of me.

"You okay?" Gustafsson asks as we move to our positions on the field.

"Don't let them get to you," Tae-woo adds.

I grumble an affirmative.

FORTY-THREE MINUTES INTO THE GAME, the score is still nil-nil.

We're desperate for a goal.

I'm desperate.

Overton's striker manages to get a shot through our back four. I make the save, but he continues into my box and whispers into my ear as I stand up from the grass, "Enjoying the spotlight, Hastings?"

"Fuck off," I hiss.

"*Be better.*" He mimics Rossi. "You're looking pathetic."

The ref blows his whistle, waving him out of my box.

Fucking worthless. Rossi's voice booms in my mind.

Not now.

I grip the ball tightly, feeling the pressure mounting. I only have six seconds to release it back into open play, but my mind is racing. I glance over at Coach, who's motioning for us to enact the play we've been practicing all week. My heart pounds louder with each tick of the clock.

I survey the field in a frenzy. Mohamed is frantically waving his hand, as he should be. He has a decent opening, but even with Gustafsson engaged with Overton's left winger, he's the closest to Okafor to make the pass. My vision blurs, and my thoughts spin wildly.

Indecision tumbles through me, and time is ticking. The play won't work. I know it. Mohamed isn't fast enough to get through Overton's midfield and hand off the ball to our offense. But no, that can't be right. Maybe I'm overthinking it. Maybe it will work. I shake my head, trying to clear the doubts, but they cling on stubbornly.

Sweat trickles down my face, and my grip on the ball tightens even more. I have to decide, and fast. But every option feels like a guaranteed mistake. My mind screams that I'm setting myself up for a bad play, but I push the thought away. It can't be that bad, can it?

I have to make this call. Now.

We need to win this.

As I prepare to throw, my heart races. Adrenaline surges. My muscles tense. My mind is in fight-or-flight mode, and panic creeps in, but I push through the freeze. Clearing the fog of anxiety, I lock eyes with Mohamed, take a deep breath, and do what needs to be done.

With all my strength, I launch the ball toward Gustafsson, hoping it'll reach him in time.

"Gustafsson!" I shout, my voice echoing across the field. His eyes widen in shock, but before he can react, Overton's forward appears like an apparition and steals the ball swiftly. He outmaneuvers my center-backs and sprints toward me.

A sense of icy dread grips me.

Fuck.

The crowd holds their breath.

I know this guy. He goes right. He always goes right. I squat; every muscle in my body tenses in anticipation of the shot, and I dive. In a cruel twist of fate, at the very last moment, the ball swerves left. It barely grazes the tips of my outstretched gloves before it hurtles into the net behind me.

The sound of it swooshing past me is shattering.

My world comes crashing down.

1-0.

The cheers of Overton's fans feel like a mocking slap. The groans from our side echo my internal turmoil.

Stay big! I scream into my mind.

Each sound is a piercing needle of humiliation stabbing at me. *Pathetic.*

Be impenetrable.

But the sinking feeling of worthlessness threatens to consume me.

The net behind me feels like a taunt. *Break a sweat out there.*

Stay focused.

"Get the Yankee off the field," they chant as the referee blows his whistle, ending the first half.

"What the fuck, Hastings?" Tae-woo jogs across the field. "Omar was wide open."

I shrug him off and storm into the locker room.

"Hastings!" Coach's voice is a sharp command, stopping me dead in my tracks. His hand clamps onto my shoulder as I try to stride past him in the tunnel. "What was that out there?" I can't bring myself to tell him the truth, can't conjure up any justification for having seen a better play. "You're really not going to say anything?" I grunt a response. "Really?" Coach examines my face, searching for something that must not be there. "Fine," he barks and shoves me into the locker room. He swivels toward Matos. "Ivan, are you warmed up?"

"Yes, Coach," he responds.

"Good. Hastings's on the bench for the second half," Coach declares.

The lights of the locker room are piercing. Each bulb is like a spotlight. My teammates' voices grate on my nerves.

"Don't do this," I plead through gritted teeth.

"You don't get to ask for that," Coach snaps, his words slicing through my last shred of hope. "Frankly, Hastings, you don't get to ask for anything. We've done that play a dozen times. Everyone on the pitch was calling it. I can't afford a player who doesn't trust or listen to the team. If I knew what was wrong, maybe I could help. But until then, you're not stepping foot on that pitch."

"Nothing's wrong," I choke out.

"Until you can pull yourself together, you're not playing," Coach continues, his words relentless. "I'm done with this loner act, and so is the team. They've put themselves out there for you, tried to make you feel welcome. This isn't about one bad call or a goal we definitely needed. You let down your teammates. You don't belong on that field until that changes."

He turns his back to me, a clear dismissal. Then he calls Okafor over to strategize.

At Overton, a benching could last weeks. Hell, a whole damn season.

My heart shatters in my chest, words scraping at my throat.

Please. Please let me fix this.

Nothing comes.

I messed up. Tomorrow's headlines are already forming in my mind.

New American Keeper Old News Already?

Did Lyndhurst Manager Sir Millsbury Make A Mistake With The New Keeper?

Is Hastings's New Girl The Reason For The Distraction On The Pitch?

My thoughts spiral. A whirlpool of doubt and fear. I can't breathe. Everything I've worked for is gone. I'm suffocating.

Be fucking better, Hastings. Don't be such a fucking loser. Do you even want to be in the Premier League? Rossi's familiar barks pummel my mind.

My dreams are disintegrating into dust, and it's all my fault.

Halftime passes in a breath before I'm sitting on the bench, watching the team. There's no denying that they have chemistry on the field.

A unit that's played together for years. Cohesive without my isolated presence.

Our captain is relentless with the offense and scores a goal in the first ten minutes, tying us. When the crowd cheers and my teammates revel in the glory, I feel nothing. Afterward, the second half of the game blurs by. Our defense stays tight as Overton attacks again and again.

I can't be there. I can't make this better. I can't help the team. My teammates. I've let them all down.

All my stubborn pride and refusal to trust have led to this utter failure. Getting benched mid-game as a keeper is pathetic.

I've made an effort to bond with them; I've tried. But I'm not capable of being the player I used to be back in LA. I can't tell my teammates what Charlie did, how he hurt me, or how my old coach's words sear my mind, making me question every decision. I can't admit that I acted emotionally when I should've had my head in the game.

I could have forced Lyndhurst into a draw or, worse, a loss. I pushed them away only to lose everything—the chance to play, redeem myself, and win the Premier League.

My heart pounds. My hands are hands clammy, and my legs are tingling as I watch Matos stand slightly off the goal line, eyes sharp and alert, ready to react to any incoming shot. His voice echoes across the field as he directs the defenders, orchestrating their every move.

The center-backs form an impenetrable barrier just in front of him. Gustafsson is locked in a physical duel with Overton's main striker, using every ounce of strength to limit his opponent's movement. Kamara positions himself to intercept any through balls or crosses that might dare venture into their territory.

Okafor lingers near the halfway line, poised like a predator waiting for the right moment to pounce.

On the flank, Tae-woo stays tight and closely marks the opposing wingers. Overton breaks past him and bullets for a chance at another goal. Matos reacts fast, signaling toward Mohamed.

My heart collapses into my gut.

The clock ticks down.

Overton presses forward, their winger attempting a cross into the box. Mohamed intercepts the ball with a decisive tackle. Without hesitation, he launches the ball to a midfielder with a short, sharp pass.

Surveying the field, our midfielder spots Okafor making a run down the right flank. With precision, he delivers a pinpoint pass that finds Okafor's feet. Our captain sprints toward the opposing half and draws the defenders toward him as he tears down the wing. Then, with a flash of brilliance, he sends a low cross into the box.

It's the play we've been practicing for weeks, executed to perfection.

The ball flies past Charlie and into the net.

The final whistle blows, and my team rushes our captain, lifting him high in the air.

This is my rock bottom. I have to get off this bench, face my teammates, and make things right.

But I don't know how.

Chapter 25
Daphne

Lyndhurst Keeper Kicked to the Curb: Midgame Blunder Results in Benching!

December **19**

From Starter to Sidelines: Keeper Cameron Hastings Benched as Team Wins Without Him—Is His Contract at Risk?

GOOSE

Packed for San Francisco?

DAPHNE

I am.

Are you all right? Are you hurt?

I was watching the game and you didn't come back out for the second half.

GOOSE

Meet me at 1 Radnor Terrace.

I'll send a car in 10 mins.

DAPHNE

Okay.

GOOSE

Be careful.

TONIGHT, I'm finally getting a glimpse into Cameron's mysterious Knightsbridge apartment.

Between this and our upcoming California trip, everything feels like it's on the brink of changing. The tangled mess in my chest refuses to untie.

I hope he's okay. While I was watching the Overton game from the confines of my couch, the announcer mentioned that Cameron had made a bad call. But he's had goals scored on him before, so I'm unsure why he'd get benched over it.

No matter what, if he's having a rough day, I'll be his sunshine tonight. I'll cheer him up like he's done for me.

When I arrive, I hit the elevator to the top floor per Cameron's instructions. As expected, entering his penthouse is like stepping into another world, especially compared to his sterile digs at the Lodge. The place radiates warmth. Panoramic views of London's skyline, deep greens and blues in his decor, and a couch that looks so plush it could hug you. The dining room has a gallery wall full of family photos and moody art. Every nook and cranny screams, *This is a life well-lived!*

He doesn't acknowledge me when I step inside.

"You have trinkets!" I say, running a finger over a walnut credenza showcasing sport memorabilia. A keeper's glove in glass, bronzed soccer balls, a photo of young Cameron on a pitch, grinning with a ball under his arm—my heart aches for that kid. I trace a finger over his face, wishing I could see that smile now. When I turn, Cameron's still by the window, his gaze shifting between me and the city lights. His face is tense. Eyes dim. Broad shoulders hunched.

I try again. "It's beautiful here."

"I've never brought anyone here before," he admits in a voice barely above a whisper.

"Ever?"

"Just my family when they visit."

"Then thank you for inviting me." He responds with a subtle nod. His mind is elsewhere. I join him by the window. "Do you want to talk about what happened today?"

Cameron silently shakes his head. I stand beside him and shrink the gap between us until my fingertips brush his. Pinky to pinky. Thumb to thumb. He lets out a deep sigh. I fully take his hand in mine, feeling his strength waver, and pull him into a hug, wrapping my arms around him.

Typically, he's a wall of muscle and power, but right now, he trembles in my embrace. I run one of my hands over his back, the way he likes me to, and whisper soothing words until he finally gives in and leans his weight onto me.

I want to take this away from him. But picking up knitting needles again? Probably not the move. His hard edges mold to my soft ones, his strength leaning on mine. Maybe this is all I can do right now. Let him lean on me. His breaths come in shaky waves, rustling my hair as I press my cheek closer into his chest and listen.

Listen to his heartbeat. His breath. And hold him.

Hold him until my legs ache. Until the soles of my feet burn. Until my shoulders scream for me to stop. Hold him with a silent promise that I'm here to help him pick up the pieces.

"I messed up, Daphne, I really did," he says.

"You had a bad day on the pitch. It's okay, it happens."

"No, not to me. It never does, but that—" Cameron pulls

away from me. His fists clench at his sides. "I got benched, Daphne. At halftime. That never happens to a goalie. That's never happened to me. I'm a laughingstock *again*." It's hard to see the man you care about falling apart at the seams. "Coach thinks I only care about myself. That my plays are selfish, that I'm pushing away the team. I don't want to be, but he doesn't understand."

"Maybe you can help me understand."

His face is the picture of despair, the strong lines of his jaw tightened, his usually golden eyes clouded with regret. "I told you about Charlie."

"Your old friend on the Overton team. Of course. I remember."

"In March…" He looks at me, his eyes carefully searching my face, as if he's afraid of how I might react. "You know how I'm wary of the tabloids or having my life on public display? It's because, at the end of last season, a livestream of me got leaked to the tabloids. A livestream of me in the shower. Charlie was the one who streamed it. He called it a harmless fucking prank."

"What?" My heart quakes against my chest.

"It was taken inside the Overton locker room." His teeth are clenched.

"That's so violating." I rest my hand on his arm, offering him a small comfort. He doesn't retreat.

"You know what was worse? My eldest sister was the first one to see it. She called me in the middle of the night. Can you imagine? My family saw me that way, exposed, stripped down to my bones." His laugh is cold and harsh. "Today, I let that fucking prick get in my head again. Before the game, he tried to rattle me. So did another player on the field. And it worked. I let them get to me when I should've been better. I shouldn't have reacted."

"I don't understand. Why would he do that in the first place?"

"I don't know." He scoffs. "Maybe he was trying to get me off the first string? Jeopardize my contract? Whatever it was, he succeeded. I fled Overton like some pathetic loser who couldn't cut it."

A pain scrapes through my gut at his words. "The last thing you are is a pathetic loser," I say angrily. "Don't say things like that about yourself. You're Cameron fucking Hastings."

"No, I let him get under my skin. After all this time, even after I accepted Lyndhurst's offer, even now that I'm on a better team, I let Charlie get into my head. I'm a fool for not controlling my emotions."

"You're not a fool. Cameron, March was only nine months ago. We can all try to be strong, but this is still the recent past. You can't be hard on yourself."

His eyes linger behind me, never meeting mine before he walks over to the couch. I follow in his wake. "The first match after the livestream, the crowd shouted horrible things at me. About my body, about how I played, about wanting attention. I sucked it up. I kept my head down and put up walls. I played and trained because the only thing I have in my life is football. All I've ever loved is football." His golden eyes turn glassy. "But my team joined in on the ridicule too. Coach Rossi was no fucking help. I felt so alone. Just like today. Just like I've been feeling ever since I joined Lyndhurst."

The revelation hits me hard. The cautious way he was around the media, his aversion to my phone, the distance he keeps from his teammates—it all makes sense now. Cameron wasn't just betrayed by his friend, but by the fans, by his team.

He was isolated.

"Is that why you never came back out after the first half?"

He nods solemnly. "Coach put me on the bench for the rest of the game. Maybe for the rest of the season, because my bad call hurt my teammates. I was selfish, and because of that, I'm going to lose my contract."

I recognize this negative self-talk. He's spiraling, just like I did a few weeks ago. With so much to process at once, how could he not? There's no way that what happened today could cost him his career. I wish there was some way I could show the world that he isn't just an athlete, but a man who was broken and given no outlet to process his trauma. He just needed someone to talk to.

"I—"

"Don't say you're sorry." His voice turns to stone. "Please. I can't hear it from you."

"I wasn't about to. I'm angry, Cameron. I'm seething about the fact that anyone could do what Charlie did to you."

"I shouldn't have let it affect me. I let Charlie worm his way into my thoughts. I messed up. Coach is done with me. The team detests me. After all the effort I've made this season to try and let them in, to try and trust them. Why?" His voice cracks again. "My shot at winning this season is fucking over. Hell, my career in the Premier League is probably over. I'll have to sit here this season watching my team play without me, and then I'll be shipped back to play in the States. I'll lose my shot at competing in other leagues or starting for the World Cup." He sinks deeper into the couch, like a deflated pool toy being discarded after the summer.

"Does the team know everything that happened at Overton?" I interrupt his spiraling thoughts.

"About Charlie?" His head tilts. "I don't know. They all probably read the tabloids. No one ever bothered to clarify. All the rumors suggest I had it leaked for clout."

"*Clout?* You don't need clout." His eyes blink at me, surprised. "Is there anything I can do?"

"Don't pity me."

"I don't," I state firmly. "I don't pity you."

He drops his face into his palms. "Then forgive me for putting you in my mess."

"I don't need you to do that. There's nothing to forgive." I stand, wedging myself in between his knees and wrapping my arms around his head. His earthy musk is tinged with salt.

"I don't know what I was made for if it isn't football. I've been a winner my whole life, and now I'm just—" He believes he's ruined everything, but I know he hasn't. This is his fear speaking. "I don't know how to feel. I don't know how to make this right."

His breath becomes ragged, matching the rhythm of my heart, and his arms gently rub the backs of my thighs. I want to make him forget and give him the peace he deserves.

My mind drifts back to the night we first met. I'm done holding back.

"Look at me," I whisper, my voice barely audible. He tips his chin up. His eyes are clouded with fog. His skin an icy breeze. "Let me take care of you."

"You're too good, Daphne. Too good to get wrapped up in this."

"You could use some good to get wrapped up in." There's a shadow of a smile at the edges of his mouth. "Kiss me."

He obeys and lets out a low hum of relief. Raw, unadulterated. *I got you.* Our tongues move slowly, deliberately, each motion calculated and filled with a shared need that's as desperate as it is comforting. *Let me take this load off.*

He guides me closer. The world fades away. It's as if our hearts are entwined in their own little rhythm, finding solace in each other. *I'm here.* Before something insatiable split between us and is ready to consume me whole. *Yes.*

My mind wants to snap me back to reality. To remind me of all the reasons that sleeping with Cameron could be a mistake. That it could complicate things. That a girl like me could never be with a guy like him. But dancing barefoot on the edge of unknown territory feels so good. *Yes.* A kiss to take away the pain. *I'm never letting go.*

"I need you, Daphne."

"Yes," I coax him, leaning on top of him as he sinks deeper into his sofa. I brush a stray lock of hair away from his forehead. His eyes flutter closed, a soft moan escaping his lips. I let my hand linger, memorizing each perfect imperfection. Color has slowly absorbed back into his cheeks. "You played well today, Cameron," I murmur. "One game doesn't define you."

"Please," he whispers.

I can't wait any longer. I need for us to be closer, to throw all my fears to the side. I trace the contour of his torso before relieving him of his shirt. His touch turns fervent, tugging my sweater off with urgency. My breath hitches, as if I've dived headfirst into a frozen lake. I strip off his trousers, tasting the adrenaline passing between us. The rest of our clothes come off.

"Cameron." I gasp at the sight of his cock, remembering how it felt inside of me.

He groans as I straddle him, my knees pressing into the couch. My hands run over his firm shoulder blades. It's been months of foreplay, months of lying in bed wanting him again, and now he's so close. My core aches.

He places light kisses along my breastbone before looking up at me. The warmth in his eyes holds steady, unwavering, as if silently vowing to always be there. His body radiates heat, begging me to close the distance between our naked bodies. His cock twitches beneath me, pressing against my entrance.

"Come here." He hooks his arm around my waist, attempting to lift me from the couch. I grip the fabric behind us.

"No, let me. I got you." He lowers us back down, and I roll my hips against him, rubbing the wetness pooling in my core up and down his length. I brace my hand on his chest, and he clasps his over mine. "I have you, Cameron."

Tonight, I want to take care of him. I want to watch the concern shadowing his face melt away and to make him forget, for however long, about being benched, about the paparazzi, and about all the people who hurt him.

"You have no idea, sweet girl," he sighs.

This might be the stupidest, most erratic, and most impulsive thing I'll ever do, but I'm tired of denying this need for him any longer.

Chapter 26
Cameron

MY DEFENSES CRUMBLE. Brick by brick, they built the walls I wore as badges of strength and resilience.

Then, she happened.

With Daphne, everything aligns, despite my broken pieces.

She reminds me of a version of myself that I thought was lost —a version that knew how to live and not just bear the days. The old Cam. Her presence mends wounds that I and others deemed beyond repair.

She sees me, not for the football legacy, but for the man I truly am. Even with the parts of myself I'm ashamed of.

Daphne is stunning as she pushes her lavender hair back, quickening her pace as she grinds her hips over me. She's so wet that with one buck of my hips, I could be inside of her.

I rake my gaze along her body, the one I've dreamt about for months. It's even better than I remembered. Soft, dimpled skin. My hands squeeze over her thighs and hips, leaving pink imprints, marking her.

Her rhythm intensifies as she leans forward so her perfect breasts are in my face. I run my tongue along her nipples, and her breathing deepens.

God, she's so fucking perfect.

She reaches behind her back, grabbing the base of my cock, positioning it at her entrance. Bare and raw.

She is so tight, so wet, so warm. I have never been stupid enough to fuck without a condom. But this…there's no coming back from having her like this.

"Wait," I breathe.

"Don't worry." She shakes her head. "I'm on Depo, and, well, you're the last person I've been with," she says through an erratic breath. "A-are you clear?"

My teeth grit together. "Nothing to report." My brain is short-circuiting.

"I need to feel you like this, Cameron." Her eyelashes flutter as she places the tip of my cock inside of her. I watch her body respond, clenching around me. "I want to feel all of you."

I'm a fucking goner.

"Daphne" is all I can manage to say in a ragged breath.

Our eyes lock, and she slides down slowly, tightening around me. Her mouth contorts into an O, and then she drags her teeth over her bottom lip. Her thighs tremble as she takes more than half of me. I don't move yet. Instead, I rub her soft skin, clasping one of her hands in mine. She sets her free hand on my chest and leans forward, rubbing a nipple along my lips again. I oblige, taking it into my mouth. Vanilla intoxicates me. With a final drop, she takes all of me.

"Fuck," I rasp.

"Cameron, you feel so good." Back arching. Hips shaking. We still as she adjusts to me. I pant against her pebbled skin, her neck. "You're so good. My wonderful, strong, incredible man. I've waited for this for so long."

Her words shoot like needles into my chest. I want to believe her. I want to be the man she sees. My control collapses. I grip her hips, letting her find her own pace.

"Me too," I moan into her.

I didn't think anything could be better than our first time, but this time she's with Cameron Hastings, not some pseudonym.

I've memorized the goddess hidden beneath her sweaters, her crooked smile, the way she holds her breath when she messes up a stitch, and how her eyes glow brighter when she looks at me.

She's the stillness in my chaos.

I want more. I want all of her.

She's in my home, in my mind, a burst of color in my gray world.

"Oh god," she says with a half laugh, half cry, just like that night we spent together. My favorite. I feel myself getting harder as she quickens her hips. "I've never felt like this before," she says. "I love it."

I press my lips to her ear. "I've never felt like this before either." Christ. I won't last long like this. "You may have ruined me."

"You could never be ruined."

A sharp ache explodes in my chest at her words.

Her nails dig into my collarbone as she glides over my cock. We're skin against skin. Mine hard and hers soft. I meet each roll of her hips with my own thrusts.

"So good, Cameron. You make me feel so good." She praises me, and I can't get enough. I'm her hound, begging for a treat that will help me forget I'm not broken. That I haven't just put everything I've ever loved at risk. "Yes, yes, yes." Her head falls back.

It's not just about the touch, the taste, the tangled limbs—it's more. We resonate with each other. The girl with the heart on her sleeve. And me, the tin man, yearning for a new heart.

Her pace turns erratic, selfish. She arches and pins her hands back on my knees, letting me see all of her.

"I don't deserve you."

"You always have," she moans and picks up the pace. The coiling need at the base of my spine doubles.

"Daph," I whimper and clasp her hips, feeling her heartbeat around my throbbing length. "Sweet girl, slow down," I beg. "I missed you too fucking much."

She looks up at the ceiling, her breath coming in short bursts. "I missed you."

I pull one of her hands to my lips, kissing each knuckle. "I-I don't want this to end. It feels...overwhelming after so long. Too good. This is too good."

The heat at the base of my spine mocks me. Stamina goes out the window with her. She strips me to my bones.

"I feel that." She smiles. "I feel you getting bigger, harder, because of me."

I chuckle. "All because of you."

Sex has always been a release, a distraction. But never like this. Never filled with so much pleasure, a space where my body hums with a joy I've never felt before.

Addictive.

"Then be selfish, Cameron," she whispers, and I flip her over. "Take me. Make it feel good."

Whatever Daphne thinks, I'm certain that I'm unworthy of the woman in front of me.

At her words, I give in. I grip her tighter, my fingers digging into her skin until it's raw. I take her, moving and groaning, lost in the moment, until time disappears like morning dew. I press my thumb against her clit, circling until her moans guide my pace. She's writhing, screaming my name mixed into a chorus of yeses. Our movements are frantic and desperate. I feel broken, but with her, it's like I'm a shattered vase being pieced back together. She makes me feel whole again.

"Daphne," I rasp.

"Together."

And we collapse.

My consciousness seems to untether from my body, merging

with hers. It's pure bliss. Our bliss. We stay wrapped in each other for a while.

"I made a real mess of you." I kiss her forehead, drape a blanket over her from the back of the couch, and fetch a warm towel and a glass of water. I clean her up with care, then cover her in kisses before connecting my lips with hers.

She yawns, and I follow suit.

The past month has been exhausting for both of us. I pull on my boxers, wrap her in the blanket, and lift her off the couch. "You make me feel like a person," I say.

"And you make me feel like I'm exactly where I need to be."

She's everything I'm not—the only light in my dark world. Maybe one day, when I fix the broken parts of myself, I can be worthy of her love.

Chapter 27
Daphne

December 22
Hastings Rumors Remain Unconfirmed as Premier League Plays Their Last Game Before the New Year

December 22
Cameron Hastings Benched for the Remainder of the Season? Lyndhurst FC: No Comment on His Return

GOOSE

Got any plans for Christmas dinner?

DAPHNE

Movie marathon and knitting :)

Moms are leaving at dawn and Juni is working all day.

GOOSE

Feel like a trip to Mill Valley? We're hosting a dinner.

There will be lots of people here and my family.

It'll be fun.

DAPHNE

!!!!!!!!!!!!!

What should I wear?

What should I bring?

GOOSE

Yourself.

Be ready at 10am.

DAPHNE

Okay. :) <3

"WE'RE happy you're home, sweetheart," Dani says, scooting closer to me on the picnic blanket. We're cliffside in Wilder Ranch State Park.

"It's really nice to be here with you guys." I smile.

Every year, my moms, sister, and I hike the easy trail to watch the whale migration. Some years, it's an endless ocean, but this year we're lucky. Though, despite my favorite golden brome and coastal sage scrub, my heart is still tugging at something that feels like homesickness.

I miss the wacky Wednesday nights with the boys. Planning sessions for the retreat with Rosie at Petal & Plate over flaky pastries. The apartment's leaky faucet—my own mini waterfall. Texting Bea about knitting patterns like we're cracking codes. Lugging my tripod and SLR through Bloomsbury's stately Georgian townhouses to Notting Hill's Victorian terraces to make content.

But mostly, I miss Cameron.

Being with him again felt so different, like we had leveled up in some cosmic game of *us*. It felt right to take care of him. To be close to him.

Every breath, touch, and kiss kept replaying in my mind during the flight, so much so that it took me ages to register that we were on his family's private jet over the Atlantic.

While he dozed off beside me, a much-needed reprieve from the emotionally and physically exhausting day he had, I needed something to keep my hands busy and my mind out of the gutter. That's when I noticed a tiny tear in Cameron's leather jacket. Out came my trusty embroidery kit. My original plan was just to fix it, but after a few inhalations of his jacket's intoxicating scent, I ended up stitching a tiny heart-shaped soccer ball inside his sleeve. A harmless secret, just for me.

Cameron.

I miss his half-smile and his adorable grumpiness. We've been texting nonstop. Erin was right: stress does bring people closer. With London's tabloids finally chilling out—which I know thanks to Bea's updates and my mild snooping—it looks like we'll have a chance to figure out what we are when we get back.

Until then, I'm going to do my best to enjoy being with my family after so many months apart.

"Logged back into your socials yet?" Juni asks, pulling me back out of my mind.

I sigh again, knowing this moment was inevitable. "Not yet. I miss it, though. I'll be back on after the New Year."

"I still can't believe those soccer jerks." Juni scoffs. "If I could, I'd track them down and make them get their blood drawn by novice phlebotomists. Unnecessary pain and bruising for all!"

We all turn to stare at her. "What? I'm sleep-deprived, and that's the worst thing I could think of."

"Dan, remind me not to get my blood drawn by Dr. Quinn when she's mad." Prim laughs.

"Ditto."

Three pairs of eyes zero in on me. Time to rip off the Band-Aid.

"Well, go on then," I say, tipping my nose at them. "Ask what you want to ask."

Prim rubs my shin. "We're just a little worried, Duckie."

"If you want to cancel your retreat—" Dani starts.

That stings. Mom, the steel-armored warrior, suggesting I throw in the towel?

"No! I don't want to let the bullies win. My true community is so excited about the retreat, and so am I."

"Nobody will blame you if you choose to postpone," Prim says gently. "Your safety and mental health come first."

"I know, but I have a plan. I'm going to filter my comments and block the crappy people. It's my space, and I have every right to kick out anyone who doesn't belong there. Plus, I'm seeing my therapist weekly again. Erin is helping me cope." I'm confident I have the tools to navigate this uncharted territory, bumps and all. Figuring out how to return to posting content is scary. But here's the thing—I've already faced down bullies and learned to love myself once.

Juni frowns. "You *can* always come back home, though. Your room is just as you left it."

Annoyance prickles my throat. "I know you all mean well, but it feels like you don't think I can handle this. I've grown so much these past few months, and I don't want you to see me as a helpless teenager anymore. I want to stand on my own two feet. That's the whole point of my Yes Year."

"We're sorry, sweetheart. We miss you, and with the boy and

the bullies, we're just giving you an out if you want one," Prim says.

"I don't," I say firmly. My nerves settle as I stand my ground. "This past month, I've reflected on why I share my life online. It's a way for me to celebrate myself because, for the longest time, outside of you three, I never thought anyone else would— especially after I was bullied." Juni slings her arm over my shoulder, tears already pricking her eyes. I look away, because if she starts crying, we'll all be a mess. I continue. "Wooly Duck gave me the confidence to be me again."

"Duckie." Prim rubs my cheek.

"When the ridiculous news broke, I felt like that little girl again, the one who let words cut her to pieces. But here's the thing, I've learned it takes a heck of a lot of courage to put yourself out there. Sure, it may look like I just share knitting patterns, skeins of yarn, or the coffee I scored on my afternoon stroll, but that's my world. *Mine.* And I want to shout into the digital abyss about my struggles, my journey, and my growth."

"We always knew you were making an impact."

"And if I quit now, those trolls win. They hide behind their screens, trying to make me feel small because their own lives are crumbling. Shrinking myself for people who don't even matter? Nope. Not this time."

"Sweetheart." Prim's voice cracks with a heartfelt sob. All right, cue the waterworks. "You've always been strong, but you're right; now you're running your own show."

A few days away from London has given me the clarity I need to understand my next steps.

I love our family fortress, but even King Arthur had to leave his castle to fight dragons. My dragon is an internet troll, and my magical sword? Knitting needles.

"Honestly, I'm not the only person in the world who has been cyberbullied. I can focus on that during my retreat in March. If it goes well, maybe I'll take my retreats global and spread a message about the importance of compassion and care."

My family stares at me, their mouths open in a mix of excitement and surprise. Juni always knew what her purpose was. As soon as I was born, she was treating me like one of her patients, from bandaging scraped knees to protecting me from harm.

I always thought I needed a *real* job. Sure, knitting was my passion, but was that enough? I wish someone had told me that my life is whatever I make it. That it would take time to find a thing that ignites every cell in my body—combating bullying is that thing. This is me saying yes to myself.

"That sounds incredible! Maybe one in Athens? We've been dying to go there," Dani laughs.

"Or Sydney!" Juni chimes in.

"Let's see how London goes first," I say, feeling lighter.

"We'll support you every step of the way."

We huddle together for a group hug, and for a while, we enjoy the afternoon, spotting giant whale tails splashing in the distance, picking wildflowers, and lying on our backs to watch the clouds. A perfect family afternoon.

Then Juni opens the third Tupperware of snickerdoodles and passes us each one.

"So, about the boy. I still can't believe the odds of you two living in the same building," Dani says.

"Maybe it was fate?" Prim smiles.

"You've always been a hopeless romantic."

"Correction, *hopeful* romantic." Prim nudges Dani.

"Hopeful or hopeless, I hate that Cameron brought all that bad energy into your safe space, Duckie," Juni says.

"It wasn't his fault," I assure them. "I won't lie, those trolls hurt and scared me, but I've had a month to process it. And here's the thing: if I want to make a splash on a global scale, I need to get used to being in the spotlight. Which means I'll have to deal with internet trolls."

"Yes, but Juni's right, we saw some…stuff about him online and—" Prim starts.

"And was everything those girls posted about me true?" I bark, becoming defensive. I want my family to see the man I see, not the one the world sees.

A man who's so much more than some headlines could capture.

It's wild how social media can lift people up on a pedestal one minute and yank the rug out from under them the next.

"But it was *his* fans doing the bullying."

I glare at my sister.

"All your sister is trying to say is that this friend seems to have created a lot of drama in your life." Prim rests her hand on my shoulder.

Why won't they hear me?

"Cameron is someone I care about deeply. He's been helping me with my Yes Year. He was there for me when the article broke. I trust him. Along with all my new friends."

"Do you want to be more than friends?" Dani breaks through their sympathy, clearly sensing that I'm not in the mood for any more coddling.

"Think so. I do like him a lot." A lot. "You guys would too. He's sharp, kind, and his smile—oh, his smile. It could light up an entire city if it ever decided to stay awhile."

"You must like him if you're speaking in rhymes," Juni says.

Prim breaks out into song. "His smile could light up a city!"

"Do wop." Dani joins her, snapping her fingers. "If it could stay awhile!"

"You guys!" I roll over, laughing.

My heart flutters. Cameron's married to football. But maybe, just maybe, there's room for a person in his life too. A person who truly gets him.

"This could be a hopeful romance story after all." Prim smiles.

Chapter 28
Daphne

THE HASTINGS FAMILY Christmas has shot straight to the top of my favorite Yes Year experiences list.

For the past three hours, Cameron's family, family friends, and I have been cozied up on a covered patio at a teak table big enough for his entire football team. The chorus of crickets and crisp, sixty-degree California winter air created a bubble of warmth, flushed cheeks, and full bellies.

I glance around, letting it all sink in. The Hastingses are just as striking and beautiful as Cameron.

Eight faces, eight stories, all with those strong brows, chiseled jaws, golden eyes, and dark brown hair—except for Ezra, the family's delightful plot twist with his dirty blonde locks.

At the head of the table, Leo and Selene Hastings sit, radiating soulmate-level love. They're like Mr. and Mrs. Smith, but with less assassinating and more swooning. No wonder every member of this family is such a knockout.

Cameron's siblings are just as intense as he is—and now I see why. His eldest brother, Alec, is detailing plans to conquer a terrifying Icelandic mountain with his best friend Finn, who's here for dinner too. Selene's making a case for a tracking device, but Alec and Finn's nods scream, *We're totally not doing that.*

"I'm glad you're here," Cameron whispers, his breath warm in my ear. He's wearing the red sweater I knit him, despite his siblings' relentless teasing about it looking like a dry cleaner's worst nightmare. He just grunted and brushed the jabs off.

There's a very obvious pain behind his eyes, even as he's trying his best to keep his spirits up for everyone's sake. In the months we've spent together, I've learned to see all the small signs of his retreat.

The tension in his jaw. The cuticle picking. The crease between his brows. He deserves to feel at ease after what happened at the Overton game. Any kind of relief. I can't imagine how much it's hurting him, and he's not letting it show.

I finish my bite of tiramisu and tilt toward him, nudging the top of my head against his jaw. "Merry Christmas, Goose."

"Merry Christmas, Duck." Under the table, he alternates between toying with the hem of my sweater dress and digging his nails into his fingers.

"I still can't believe you made this," Brooklyn says, admiring the glittering ice skate ornament I crocheted. Cameron's oldest sister looks like she was birthed out of Aphrodite's rock. When I first saw her, I had to do everything I possibly could to keep my jaw from hitting the floor.

"It was really nothing," I say, trying to wave off the praise.

I made ornaments for each of his family members, tokens from their favorite sport. I feel a little bad for not accounting for the extras—Ezra's fiancée Hazel, Finn, and Dante's entire university entourage of six. But no one made me feel awkward about it.

"My girlfriend has this frustratingly charming habit of underestimating how amazing she is." Cameron's arm snugly wraps around me like it's the most natural thing in the world.

Wait, did he just say girlfriend? Did he mean me? My mind fizzes with questions.

"I can see that." Brooklyn raises her wineglass in my direction with a knowing smile. "I'm definitely attaching this to my skate bag."

The conversation flows on, but my brain is stuck on repeat, replaying the moment Cameron casually dropped the girlfriend bomb.

I shoot him a look that's a mix of *What did you just say* and *No, seriously, Cameron, what on earth did you just say*, but he's unaware, now fiddling with his tiny soccer ball instead of noticing my existential crisis.

It's not until I catch Brooklyn's eye that she says, "Thank you for helping our brother."

"What do you mean?" I say, but everyone around the table shares a knowing glance.

"Now that you're here, he's finally softened up."

"I'm not soft," he grumbles in his typical way.

"It's not a bad thing." Dante rolls his eyes.

Leo nods along. "Being in touch with his vulnerable side is what makes a man strong."

"All right." Resigned, Cameron returns to a conversation with his youngest sister, Francesca. All day, I was sure he was starting to come around, but now he seems annoyed. Similar to how I got when my moms and Juni whipped out their protective shields on my behalf.

We really are alike.

Francesca grips her tiny crocheted steering wheel with a mischievous grin, pretending to drive a bread roll across the tablecloth. "Mine's epic, way better than all of yours."

"En garde!" Dante chortles from across the table, brandishing a diminutive knitted fencing sword. His entourage bursts into synchronized laughter. Honestly, Cameron's brother looks so much like Cillian Murphy that my sister would be having a full-on meltdown right now. "Truly, this is a stroke of brilliance. Your creativity deserves nothing less than a crown!"

The rest of the Hastings crew nods in agreement, each clutching their own quirky ornaments. Alec shows off his tiny ice cube, Leo has a miniature laptop, Selene flaunts a basketball, and Ezra proudly displays a wave.

"So, Daphne, Cameron tells us you're an entrepreneur with a heart of gold?" Leo says, making the entire table hush.

I feel my cheeks heat up but manage a confident smile. "You could say that."

Cameron rolls his eyes and sighs. "Daphne's too humble. She was featured in the *Stone Times* for donating to the UCSF hospital, and she's organizing a knitting retreat for mental health."

"Do you have a foundation set up? We always love to support a good cause," Leo insists. "Carlyle, get whatever details you need from Daphne, and we'll make a generous contribution."

My eyes widen; I'm taken aback.

"Well, right now I'm a one-woman show. No foundations just yet." I laugh, feeling a bubbly excitement at the thought of what a family like this could do for an important cause. "However, I plan to fundraise at my retreat and donate to organizations that provide anti-bullying services, education, and support for families and kids."

"That is so kind!" Brooklyn coos. "Trust me, one thing this family knows about is bullies." She frowns and glances at Cameron.

"Can we not bring that up?" he snaps.

"Of course, Cameron." Selene looks at him sympathetically and turns to me. "We are genuinely sorry for what happened in the tabloids last month." She gives me a warm smile. "When Leo and I were first getting to know each other, reporters would camp outside of our homes for a photograph."

Her husband tsks with a smile, shaking his head. "My

favorite headline from those years was: 'Rejected! WNBA All-Star Dumps Tech Billionaire After He Buys Her Team and Pleads for a Date!' Fucking bastards." he laughs.

"You never really forget what they write about you," Selene adds.

"How do you move past it then?"

"Fuck 'em," Frankie chimes in. The heads around the table break into agreeable nods.

"Newspapers are a business. They want profit," Leo explains. "The more chatter they can drum up, the bigger they can make something out of nothing, the more papers they sell. It's as simple as that."

"Don't let yourself get commoditized," Alec adds.

The advice is spot-on.

My life has expanded greatly, and, sure, the bad stuff got bigger too. But now I'm sitting around this table with a bunch of wonderful, supportive people and, most importantly, Cameron by my side.

If Selene and Leo Hastings can build a dreamy life and everyone here can find happiness despite the media circus, I've got a fighting chance too.

I'm going to crank up the volume on my life and embrace every quirky, vulnerable, too-much bit of myself.

"All of you are really inspiring." I beam. "Honestly, I've been thinking about using my platform to take a stand against bullying when we get back to London." After the chat with my moms and Juni, I stayed up all night putting together a list of ways I could integrate resilience into my retreat.

"That is marvelous, sweetheart!" Selene replies with a warm smile. "Whatever support you need from us, please do not hesitate. Carlyle can help set you up with a nonprofit, and we have all the connections under the sun to put you on the map."

Dante slinks both elbows onto the table and tuts his parents. "You're scaring her off. Take it easy, or she'll vanish, and we'll be waiting years before Cameron finds the courage to bring someone else home." The table shakes slightly as Cameron kicks his brother underneath it. "Ouch, Cam, always with the violence!" Dante grins, not missing a beat.

A few seats down, Finn catches my eye and winks, his fingers keeping up a steady drumbeat on the table. "Don't take them too seriously," he says with an easy grin. "They've got a talent for being nosy, but it's just their way of showing love."

Laughter ripples around the table again.

Alec remains unfazed. "We're not nosy, Finn."

"No," Dante chimes in, his smirk growing. "What he meant is we're *noisy.*"

Brooklyn flashes me a wink. "We're inquisitive, maybe a bit too much. But we could definitely use another sister around here."

Sister.

I let myself believe that this won't be my last night in this house.

"Am I not enough?" Frankie quips, her eyes twinkling mischievously. Brooklyn whirls around, and in the process, her wineglass topples off the table. "For someone with two gold medals, you're surprisingly clumsy."

"Why don't we strap you into a pair of skates then?" Brooklyn snaps, rolling her eyes in that exaggerated way she does.

"I'll stick to my wheels."

"I promise, Frankie: you, Hazel, and Dante are all the feminine energy I need." She turns to me, mouthing, *Just kidding,* and I can tell she's just trying to rile up her youngest sister. Moments like this make me wish my sister were here to witness the chaos.

"I'll take that as a compliment," Dante says with a nonchalant shrug, a smirk tugging at his lips.

"You guys are such children." Cameron rolls his eyes.

"Whatever," Frankie says, tossing a truffle at Brooklyn's forehead with terrifying precision—one, two, three times.

Brooklyn sucks her teeth before shouting, "You're dead!" She shoves her chair back and lunges across the table.

Frankie cackles, leaping up and sprinting away, toward the karting track in the distance. "Race you!"

"I'm so sorry, Daphne; my kids are absolute animals," Selene says with a laugh, her eyes twinkling with amusement.

"Trust me, my sister and I are no different. Although, she might not have the same deadly aim," I reply.

Leo shoots me a warm smile. "Well, you'll just have to invite her next year. Your parents, too."

"Thank you, my moms would absolutely love that," I say, feeling a flutter of excitement.

Cameron stands up, extending his hand to me. "I've got a pitch to show you."

"Have fun," Selene calls, winking at me. "But hurry back; I've got a whole album of baby photos."

"Oh, I'd love to see baby Cameron with his little football."

Dante smirks. "That's all you'll see. There aren't many photos of him without one."

"Shut up," Cameron groans, grabbing my hand.

"Bet there are prom photos!" I tease and give him a nudge with my shoulder.

"Cameron never went to prom," Alec says with a casual shrug, as if it's the most ordinary thing in the world.

"Because there was a game the next day." Cameron leans over to explain.

"That's our Cameron," Leo chimes in. "Always preferred the grassy pitch to childhood chaos."

Selene grins. "And when friends came over, he'd plant himself in the goalie box—the loneliest spot on the field. A tiny fortress, guarding the net like it was Narnia." I can almost see it—a pint-sized Cameron, every blocked shot a quiet victory. An introverted kid, just like me. Even now, there's a part of him still connected to that solitary boy, and it tugs at my heartstrings. "We'll tell you all about it when you're back."

"Mom, please don't." Cameron sighs.

"Please do." I giggle.

"All right, that's enough," he says, but with him, it'll never be enough.

Chapter 29
Cameron

DAPHNE and I walk along the stone path behind my family's property, my siblings' laughter fading with each step. The night sky is heavy with stars. A cool breeze sweeps through, and I shrug off my jacket and place it over her shoulders. Then I wrap my arm around her, drawing her close.

My eyes are heavy, and exhaustion weighs on my muscles.

Even when I've managed to sleep this week, it's only been for a few hours before I wake up covered in sweat from yet another incessant nightmare. I slink out of my childhood bedroom and run this path into the woods for hours. But no distance has been enough to keep my brain from replaying my fuckup with Overton.

But since Daphne arrived a few hours ago, I've found a few moments of silence.

I've missed her.

She adjusts the collar of my coat, looking up at me. "Do you think your family liked me?"

"Is that even a question?" I raise a brow at her. "Don't be surprised if you get some adoption papers in the mail."

Seeing her with my family, fitting in naturally, just confirms my feelings for her. She's meant to be by my side.

"They also adore you. When you slipped away to the restroom, Frankie told me that if I hurt you, I'd have to answer to her and Dante."

"They're harmless," I assure her. "Just intense."

She giggles. "I loved them. You seem to be doing a little better than when I last saw you."

If only she knew what was ripping me up inside.

Are you her new charity case? Is she trying to fix weak little Cameron Hastings?

I shake the thought from my mind.

Be present.

"I'm staying focused." I attempt to make my tone light-hearted. "This way." I lead us up the stone stairs to my old stomping grounds. The motion lights flicker on, casting a glow over Daphne's face and illuminating the lush grass. The pitch is serene. Goalposts stand silent, nets swaying in the cool breeze. I glance over at her awestruck expression. "Here is where I first fell in love with football."

I don't tell her that it's a feeling I'd forgotten until her.

"Time me," she says.

"What?"

"Time me! I want to see how long it takes me to run to the goal." Daphne bolts across the field, only to halt a few yards later. "Scratch that. Running is a terrible idea. I don't do running." She huffs, bending over.

"Why do you think I chose to be a goalie?" I approach her.

"Because you're a smart one, Goose." She rights herself, twirling around with her arms splayed out toward the sky. Her sweater dress hugs her legs in a ridiculously mouthwatering way. "In gym class, I was always the kid walking laps and picking flowers. Or I became target practice during dodgeball."

"Your school sounds fucking horrible. If I could, I'd make

those kids my target practice."

"If only we had each other back then to beat up our bullies." She smiles, and I'm glad we have each other now. She follows me to the goalpost, and we lie right below the net. "So," she says, keeping her eyes on the stars above.

"So?"

"Are we going to talk about the fact that you called me your girlfriend at dinner?"

Fuck. A slip of the tongue, as casual as it felt. I had hoped we'd have a proper conversation about it rather than me blurting it out in front of my family like an idiot.

I turn and look at her, really look at her. She has this uncanny knack of seeing straight into the heart of things.

It's everything. Her laughter, her kindness, her just being there. She's created this safe space around me, and for a moment, I want to be vulnerable. A part of me screams that after all my fuckups, I don't deserve to be happy, but tonight I want to be brave. As brave as Daphne was when she announced she was going to kiss me that first night we spent together.

"You have me," I mutter, the words feeling as true as the air I breathe. Like they've always been a part of me, just waiting for the right moment to be spoken. "You can do whatever you want with that, but you have me."

She tips her temple to my shoulder and looks up at me. "You have me too."

"Good."

She tosses her legs over mine, scooting closer to the grass. The comforting weight of her body eases my nerves. "Maybe when we're back in London, we can just…continue to spend time together?"

"I'd like that." I don't want anything to change between us.

"You know, I've fallen in love with my life there the past couple of months. A big part of that is thanks to you."

My pulse elevates at her insinuation. The consequences of

my actions at the Overton game multiply. I could truly lose my spot on the team. All the work I've put in, the fact that I'm in my prime, slipped away because I let Charlie's betrayal get into my head once again.

I want a shot at making things right. I want a real shot at something real with this precious woman beside me.

"Same." My voice is quiet. I'm dying to tell her that I'm crazy about her, that I'm praying to every god I know to get re-signed to Lyndhurst. But I can't, because honestly, I'm waiting for the moment she realizes she's worth more than everything I can try to provide her. So instead, I say, "With the tabloid drama back home, maybe we can just tell the people we're close to that we're dating?"

"That feels right to me."

"And maybe I can spend the night at your place. If you're okay with me waking up at 4:45 every morning?"

"Are you going to be grumpy if my livestreams go past midnight?"

"I'm sure we'll figure it out."

"I like that. Guess that means I need to give you my spare key." She squeezes me close. "Things are going to be different when we get back."

The familiar strum of nerves returns, crashing me out of the little bubble we've built under the safety of the net. "How so?"

"Well, the last few days, being back home, I realized that I'm glad I took a social media detox. I really needed it to clear my head. I gave those bullies way too much power over me, and I don't want to do that anymore," she says, running her hand over my stubble.

"What's your plan, sweet girl?"

"I don't want to be scared of being in the public eye. Sure, the ridiculous tabloids brought in a lot of hate, but the *Stone Times* article about my beanies gave me the boost I needed to start my retreat. So, in a way, the media helped me."

"Can't say I've ever felt the same way," I grunt, uneasiness building in my chest. "But I hear where you're coming from."

Those around me, from Charlie to Mal, have all benefited from the toxic press. Charlie returned to the starting string. Mal got her *Lust Island* spot and the chance to be the victim after my livestream hit the news. Everyone seems to be using the tabloids to their advantage, but I have no interest in that. The last thing those vultures need is more of my blood.

"Your family seems to have a good perspective on the whole media circus. The headlines are impossible to run from, and, like you just saw, I can't run very far." She nudges me, trying to lighten the mood.

"None of them experienced it the way I have."

"You're right. I can't imagine what those weeks after Charlie's cruelty felt like," she says with a trembling lip. For the first time, her understanding feels like pity. Though I'm certain that's just my fear talking. "And honestly, what happened to you and what I experienced last month has made me realize that I want to use my platform to help people stand up to cyberbullying."

Daphne Quinn is a saint.

"Has anyone told you how incredible you are? Strong and determined. I'm so proud of you."

"I like when you say nice things about me." She chuckles.

I hesitate with the next words because they feel monumental. "I don't want to hold you back. I want to support you in every way I can, but I don't think I'm ever going to be ready to return to the limelight after what happened." The last thing I would want is to have my scandal and shame associated with her well-deserved and impactful success. Maybe, in this way, our worlds don't mix well.

"Cameron, if you want to keep a low profile, then I'm fine with that." Her hand finds mine, stopping the picking I didn't even realize I was doing. "Hopefully, when we get back, the only articles that'll get published will be about my initiatives and your football."

She's right. I can ignore the tabloids again. All that matters is getting back in the game and winning the Premier League. I want to be better for my team, and I want to be better for her.

"Speaking of football, I don't know if I'll be able to play for the rest of the season. The last update I got from the club was a text from my agent saying she was talking to Coach, but truthfully, I deserve to sit out." At Overton, Rossi wouldn't have hesitated to pull me for weeks. I know I'm a good keeper. I know I can be one of the best, but even still, his constant criticism has been the voice of doubt inside of me.

"Don't say—"

"No, I do," I say. "I made selfish moves. I let my feelings get in the way of the match, and now my team can't trust me to not be impulsive on the field. If I don't make things right, my career will be over."

"That can't be true."

"It is. My team tried with me, and when I started letting them in, I pushed them all away again. They didn't even look me in the eye during halftime."

"You just need to talk to them. Once they know what happened at Overton and with Charlie, they won't hold it against you."

"That's the problem. I don't know how, or if they'll even care." I sigh, reaching my free hand up and running it over the net above us.

"Don't write them off," she advises, her voice soft but firm. "Your past isn't your identity, not really. It's the steps you take after. That's where you truly find yourself."

I nod. "You're right." At this point, I have nothing to lose— well, except my contract, career, and everything I worked my entire life for. "Can I come to your next knitting circle and try to make amends there?"

"I think that's a good idea. Tamu will be there, and so will your defense."

Okay. That's a good place to start. However, I haven't a clue about the reality TV they watch. "Are you going to be watching *Lust Island*?" I cringe. The thought of seeing my ex-situationship on the screen while I attempt to smooth things over with my teammates sounds like hell.

"No, silly. That show has tragically come to an end. The contestant I was rooting for won, Georgia Woods." She smiles. "We're watching *The Great British Bake Off* now. It's really easy to follow."

"Okay." I sigh. "This is going to be hard for me. I'm not great at sharing my feelings."

"Yeah, and you're not great at apologizing either," she teases.

"Hey!" I drop my hand from twirling her hair and tickle her side.

"I'm kidding! Look, from what I've seen, you're definitely capable of opening up. You can start small, and I'll be there with you. Be honest, and talk from the heart."

What if they use the livestream against me? Or think I'm lying? What if they think I'm weak? "Maybe I could also get them some gifts. You liked the soft serve machine, so—" I stop, my voice faltering. Doubt gnaws at me.

"Wouldn't hurt your case."

I run through the ideas. "A new TV for all of them?"

"Probably needs to be a little more personal than that." She tilts her chin upward, the light illuminating her neck.

"Right."

"Show them that you know who they are. It's not about grand gestures; it's the small stuff that counts. Show them they matter, that you see them, that you care about their friendship."

"Um—well, I've noticed that Tae-woo…" I start.

"Maybe let's start with calling them by their first names,"

Daphne suggests. "They never call each other by their last names."

That's an easy switch. "Jung always has a new pair of sneakers and a ton of designer shit; maybe I could get him a cool pair of kicks?"

"Yes. Perfect!" She nods approvingly. "You know, Sven is really homesick. Maybe get him some treats from Norway that might remind him of home?"

"I can figure out how to import a basket of stuff."

"Make sure to add a few things in there for me." She winks.

In a few minutes, we have the rest of the gifts figured out. I'll talk to Dante and get Omar a VIP membership to the hottest London club. I'll get Ibrahim tickets to a music festival, maybe Tomorrowland. Tamu collects watches, and I have a great guy in London who services my Rolexes and could probably hook me up.

Hopefully, it's enough to convince them that I'm showing up in ways that matter. It could be the start of making things right.

"Thank you, Daphne."

"Of course." She slinks back into the net, lies on the grass, and reaches back to loop the net through her fingers. The smell of dewy grass makes me feel at home. *She* makes me feel at home. "You can really be a total sentimental mush, you know?"

"I don't know about that."

"Well, you finally took me back to the stars," she says.

"I have a lot more to show you."

For months, she's helped me rediscover feelings I thought I'd lost. Happiness. Genuine, unadulterated happiness. Safety, too. Trust. The most basic things—the smack of the ball against my glove, the electric thrill that zips through the locker room after a win, the taste of my morning protein shakes. Even the quiet walks to practice on crisp London mornings all feel better.

Daphne Quinn has painted my world in vibrant colors, and I'll be damned if I let it fade again.

Chapter 30
Cameron

I GENTLY BRUSH the hair away from Daphne's face. Lying on the pillowcases of my childhood bedroom, she breathes deeply, nestling her feet between mine and clinging to my forearm. A freckle beneath her right eye catches my attention. The creases on her forehead, the dimples on her cheeks, her thick lashes, and that full lower lip...Perfect.

This is the first night I've been able to sleep without the tormented nightmares of the Overton game revisiting me. Sleeping next to someone is new territory for me. It's not like those nights of rushed undressing and empty promises—nights that ended with me leaving as soon as I got what I wanted.

I've always played goalkeeper with my emotions—deflecting and blocking, never letting anything get past. I told myself I didn't have the time or energy to deal with other people's feelings, but maybe that's not true. Maybe it's the fact that when I finally let my guard down, it only led to betrayal.

"Cameron?" Her soft murmur nuzzles my chest.

"I'm right here, sweet girl." I press my lips against her temple and pull her closer. "Go back to sleep." Soon her breath deepens again, and I let my head fall back against the pillow.

Chapter 31
Daphne

December 26
Daphne Quinn's Followers Clap Back at Football Fanatics' Cruel Comments!

December 27
Will Cameron Hastings Return for the First Game of the New Year?

"Seriously?" I sputter, my eyes popping out at the Everest-like mountain of packages barricading my apartment door. It looks like a game of Tetris gone horribly wrong. Bright red *Forwarded* stickers are slapped across them. The luggage that Cameron hauled up three flights of stairs looks like feathers in comparison to this cardboard monstrosity looming before us.

Cameron drops our bags on the floor. "This is more than I'm used to carrying up the stairs," he says, an eyebrow cocked.

"Right?" I shake my head. "This resembles a small warehouse." My surprise is palpable. The labels are all addressed to

@wooly.duck. *These are all from my followers?* "We were gone a week!" I exclaim in a hushed whisper.

Together, Cameron and I start the mammoth task of shifting the packages to unearth my front door.

Suddenly, a head pops up in the hallway like a gopher in a field. "*Hallo?*" It's Sven, wrapped in a fluffy baby-blue robe that swallows him whole. "Oh, Daphne, you're back! Thought you were Ibrahim coming home from the Labyrinth concert."

Cameron smiles at Sven, but the moment is as awkward as a sheep trying to knit its own wool. Sven avoids his gaze, and Cameron resumes clearing a path to my apartment. Guess the guys are still upset after the Overton game. I hope the knitting circle helps bind them back together.

"Hey, Sven," I whisper across the hall, aware that most of the building is asleep. "How long have these been here?"

"Mailman dropped them off two days ago," he says, rubbing his eyes. "Your PO box was overflowing, so we hauled it up."

"That's so kind. Thank you!"

"No worries. We'll catch up on Wednesday?"

"See you then."

"Goodnight." He disappears into his apartment, closing the door.

Once we make it inside, my hero works to wrangle the boxes into one corner of my living room. I grab a bright pink package and tear it open.

My eyes well up as I read a letter from a woman in Stockholm. Knitting my Juni sweater has become her therapy, helping her cope with anxiety. Now she's teaching her daughter to knit, turning it into a bonding experience.

I open another letter. A man from New England writes that knitting with his wife helped save their marriage. They didn't just stitch scarves and beanies; they stitched their relationship back together.

Then there's a tiny knitted duck from a college student in

London, who writes that I inspired her to start a campus knitting club. It's now a popular stress-buster and social hub, and it helped land the founder an internship. She even wants to write a college essay about me.

Despite my initial fears of returning home, I'm suddenly swept up in a wave of love so cheesy it could top a pizza. It's easy to forget the impact you're having when you spend most of your day glued to a phone screen.

But this, this is why I want to run this retreat—to forge genuine connections and stretch my reach beyond the pixels and screens.

I hand the notes to Cameron.

He reads them one by one. "They adore you." I'm practically floating on air. "Not surprising, really," he adds with a grin.

"I think this is the most overwhelmed I've felt," I say, half laughing, half crying.

"Does that cry feel as good as an orgasm?" he teases, gently brushing away a tear with his thumb.

"Better," I retort with a snicker.

He laughs along, but there's a mischievous glint in his eyes. "Is that a challenge?"

"You just get off on winning." I roll my eyes playfully.

He shrugs. "Is that so wrong?"

"You're going to spoil me with a private jet *and* an orgasm before bed?"

"Wait until I wake you up early in the morning to go get groceries for the week." He frowns at my empty fridge.

"That's some real dating-level stuff right there." I chuckle.

"Bet your sweet ass it is."

Chapter 32
Daphne

I SLEEPILY WANDER into the living room, the afternoon light streaming into my apartment. Cameron must already be up, because the mountain of boxes and packages that littered my place last night has mysteriously vanished. On my kitchen counter, there's a huge white box with the signature Petal & Plate logo imprinted on the top.

I love having Cameron Hastings in my bed and treating my place as if it were his own.

He's like my own personal radiator at night, letting me tuck my cold feet in between his thighs. I've never felt unsafe in my apartment, but knowing that he was beside me let me drift off easier without my usual cryfest blaring on the television.

With my almond croissant in hand, I slink onto my couch and take three deep breaths before redownloading each of my social apps.

You got this, Daphne.

Before I check the hundreds of notifications, I filter out every negative word ever thrown my way—*weird, stupid, ugly, attention, Lyndhurst.* Luckily, Juni and my moms helped me make the list, shielding me from having to dig through the onslaught of online nonsense.

Authors must feel like this when they handle book reviews—gearing up in shiny armor to collect praise and dodge critiques. It must be tiring watching your work get tossed around in the unpredictable arena of public opinion.

I quickly scan through my email, and a subject line catches my attention.

The Stone Times: Cyberbullying Piece Quote Request

I click into it and read. The *Stone Times* wants me to open up about cyberbullying and how it affected the peaceful place I created online. My heart strums with worry and...excitement. This could be my chance to take the narrative back into my own hands and speak out on the true effects of bullying.

I hesitate. Am I really going to risk having my words spun by the media again? I saw what the tabloids did to Cameron, but I have a chance to handle things differently. For him, speaking out was impossible, and I understand that. But I want to use the opportunity to raise awareness.

With resolve, I type out a reply, agreeing to a written interview where I'll be able to control my own words, and hit send. Then I prepare a post, uploading a selfie of me knitting at my favorite green bench on the Santa Cruz Boardwalk at sunset, and type out:

Hey, my ducks! Guess who's back in London after some precious family time?

The past few weeks have been wild, with some serious hate splashing onto my page. But guess what? We're not handing the bullies the victory flag.

Coming home to an avalanche of your packages and letters made my heart swell bigger than a giant ball of yarn. It reminded me of those childhood days when bullying taught me to stand taller.

Here's the thing: not everyone will be your number one fan, so you might as well adore yourself and scatter kindness like confetti.

Now, hold onto your knitting needles!

The tickets for our Wooly Duck Knitting Retreat are here! We're celebrating our fifth anniversary on March 6th at Petal & Plate in London! Tickets are limited to 50 people, so grab yours before they're gone! Link in bio.

Our Thursday livestreams are back. This week, we'll be crafting a Stop Bullying Beanie. The pattern can be found on my website, and 100% of the proceeds will be donated to The Kindness Coalition, which supports anti-bullying services, education, and support for families and kids.

Let's see how many donations our amazing community can rack up. Get your knit on and spread the love.

Love you all to bits!

#woolyducks #KnittingCommunity #BeYourself #StrongerTogether #AntiBullying

Once I hit post, I'm swept up in a deluge of elation. *Yes.* I'm doing it. Barely ten minutes later, an update pings—every single ticket is gone, snapped up like hot cakes. My phone hums in my hand.

BEA MATOS

just saw your post. congrats on your knitting retreat announcement! xx

DAPHNE

Can't wait to see you there.

BEA MATOS

you are the best daph

coffee catch up after the new year?

DAPHNE

Yes, please.

BEA MATOS

yay kisses!!!!

I made the right choice coming back to London. I have

friends here—a group I would've never found if I hadn't taken a leap of faith. Sure, the future is foggy, but the idea of carving out my own little corner of this city feels just right.

Everything's falling into place.

Chapter 33
Cameron

"THIS WAS A MISTAKE," I mutter, fidgeting on the common room sofa for what feels like the hundredth time. Talking isn't going to make them see me as a teammate again. And friends? Forget it. Coach isn't putting me back in the lineup just because I say a few words.

Since returning to practice, my teammates have been avoiding me. The frost in the locker room has been unbearable, especially after the warmth of family over the holidays. I craved solitude, but Lyndhurst's silence only reminds me of the bleak final weeks at Overton. They barely looked at me when I asked to join their Wednesday night knitting circle with Daphne. Thankfully, Ivan stepped in and convinced them. It feels pathetic to need someone else to fight my battles, but maybe accepting help isn't as terrifying as I thought.

"They said they'll be here, so they'll be here," Daphne reassures me, squeezing my knee. Her words are meant to comfort, but they just heighten my tension. "This is just the first step, and talking to your coach will be easier afterward."

I fumble with the gift bags on the coffee table, my hands trembling. The sound of footsteps makes my heart pound, and I jump like a mouse caught raiding the pantry. I stand, taking a shaky breath.

Jung, Omar, Ibrahim, Sven, and Tamu march into my self-imposed intervention, their expressions unreadable and their gazes averted. The room feels smaller, the walls closing in on me.

I squeak out a greeting, my voice barely above a whisper. "Hey." My wave is as awkward as a bad throw-in, and my forced smile is more like a grimace. It's clear they're not convinced.

"Is Daphne meant to be your shield?" Omar rolls his eyes.

"I—" The words stick in my throat, anxiety swirling inside me. "No. She leads your knitting circle. This is where I want to talk. If you're willing to listen." My heart pounds, and I glance back at Daphne for support. She nods, but it barely boosts my confidence. The group grumbles, hanging back. My hands tremble as I hand out the gift bags. "I got these." Each moment feels like an eternity.

They glance at each other before unwrapping their gifts. Jung gets Nike sneakers that left a dent on my Amex. Omar gets an exclusive club membership. Ibrahim gets Tomorrowland tickets. Tamu gets a new watch, and Sven gets a basket of Norwegian delicacies.

"This is thoughtful, Hastings," Sven says, flipping over a bag of krumkakes.

Jung holds up the sneakers. "Where did you get these? They were a limited run."

"You can't buy our forgiveness," Tamu says, his voice rough as he places the watch back in the bag. "It's all nice and good, but you've let us down on the pitch time and time again. We nearly lost that match with Overton because of you."

His words cut through the air like a knife. My breath comes in shallow, rapid bursts.

I start picking at my cuticles. The sharp sting provides a familiar, albeit painful, distraction from the disappointment etched on my teammates' faces. My vision blurs with tears I refuse to shed. I had hoped the gifts would at least soften their reactions, but now everything feels like it's falling apart.

"I'm sorry for my actions during our last match," I let out in one breath, my voice trembling. "I fucked up the play we'd been practicing. Got in my head. Made a terrible call. If it weren't for you guys stepping up in the second half, Lyndhurst would've lost."

"You made us look terrible," Tamu says. "How could you let us down like that?"

"It's not just about the play," Jung chimes in, his dark eyes turning into cold obsidian. "We helped you avoid the paparazzi, and we invited you to hang with us. But you have no interest in being part of this team."

"Nobody doubts your skill. We all mess up on the field. But we take responsibility and lean on each other," Tamu says. "You're one of the best keepers in the Premier League, but that's not enough. We needed you to be our teammate, not just our goalie."

I halt.

There it is. The truth I've been dodging like a penalty kick. They're not angry about the game; they're disappointed in me.

"I tried."

"You prioritized yourself over us," Sven states, his tall figure looming like a disapproving shadow from across the common room, his jaw firmly set.

They all nod, a silent, unified front against me. Regret hits me hard, a stark reminder of the bridges I've burned. Sweat trickles down my forehead.

"I thought I had things handled."

"We handle things together," Tamu snaps. His usual sunny disposition is nowhere to be found.

My chest tightens—a familiar sensation of failure. Maybe

my prime has already slipped through my fingers. Maybe Rossi was right, and I am insignificant.

I wish I were on the pitch, where at least I know how to respond when they kick balls at me. There's a simplicity in blocking a shot. Doing the job you're meant to do.

But this? This is an entirely different game. Each disappointed glance from my teammates feels like a shot I failed to save. I want redemption. I don't want to let them down. Can I somehow make things right?

"Why don't you all take a seat?" Daphne's voice slices through the tension, warm and soothing as a summer breeze. "There's clearly a lot of hurt feelings to sift through."

The guys stand there like immovable statues. I feel like a complete fool for dragging Daphne into the middle of my personal battlefield. What was I thinking? This isn't her fight, and yet here she is, trying to mediate a mess I created.

"Daphne, it's okay." I shake my head, trying to brush her off.

Of course, she doesn't back down. "You know, back in my group therapy days, we did this thing where we all sat in a circle and just spilled our guts. At first, it was super awkward—like, please-someone-get-me-out-of-here awkward—but once the share stick came to me, it was like this massive weight lifted off my shoulders. Seriously, it was weirdly amazing."

The guys stare at her like she's sprouted three heads.

Sven squints at her. "Share stick?"

Daphne grabs a chunky wooden knitting needle from her basket and waves it like it's a golden ticket. "When you're holding this, it's your turn to talk. Everyone else? Zip it." She hands it to me and pats the couch for everyone to take a seat. They obey her instantly. The wood is cold in my hand. "Be big," she whispers. "You're Cameron fucking Hastings."

And damn it, I want to be.

Daphne's right. It's get big or run home, and I'm not ready to go home.

Not yet.

Opening up about Charlie feels ridiculous. Embarrassing, even. What if they throw it back in my face? What if they think I'm weak or judge me for not handling it better?

But I have to try. It's either swallow my pride or remain an outcast for the season. Or, worse, get dropped from the Premier League.

"I'm sure you all saw the fucking articles back in March, but that's not all…" I start, my voice shaky. I recount Rossi's brutal coaching, the duct-taped silences, and the relentless drills. The nightmares. The isolation. And how Charlie Lewis, my supposed friend, leaked the shower video and whispered hurtful things about Daphne and me on match day. "So, when we played them, I lost my cool. I needed to win to prove I was better despite everything."

The weight of my past loosens slightly. I look up at the team. They're not pitying me. It's genuine concern I see on their faces.

Sven rubs his hands together. "We didn't know it was that bad."

"Figured you guys believed I leaked my own video," I admit.

"What? We never believed that. It's just not something you bring up during practice or in the locker room. But we were idiots for thinking you'd open up if we stayed silent," Tamu says, shaking his head beside me. "It sounds like a terrible excuse now that I say it out loud."

"Does Coach —" Jung begins.

"Remember to ask for the share stick when you are speaking," Daphne chimes in.

"You're right." Jung stern face softens, and he reaches for the knitting needle. I hand it over to him. "Does Coach know what happened?"

"Talked with Matos, but never with Coach. Only my family and the people in this room know," I confess, taking the share stick back from Jung. My hands tremble as I clutch it.

"How did you even survive something like that?"

"I'm just realizing the toll it took on me," I say. Daphne squeezes my leg, but it barely comforts me. "I can't shake Rossi's voice from my head, always telling me I'm a useless keeper. I get nightmares about the damn livestream."

It's terrifying to lay my heart out for them to possibly trample on. The silence that follows is suffocating; each second feels like an eternity.

"That's terrible." Sven takes the stick and frowns. We abide by Daphne's rules, passing it back and forth when we're ready to speak.

"It is," I finally admit, because saying it out loud makes it real. "That's why I get dressed in the shower stalls."

"Coach had Femi arrange for closed stalls before you came," Sven says.

I could cry. They'd been trying to be my family this whole time, and I never noticed. I was too wrapped up in my own head to see the lifelines they were throwing me. The realization hits me like a kick to the gut.

"We should go to the Football Federation, get Rossi and Charlie suspended."

The idea makes me uneasy. Drawing more attention to this— to me—is the last thing I want.

"Maybe," I say, trying to steady my voice. "I want to put this behind me."

"We can talk to Coach," Sven says.

"Opening up to him might help your case," Tamu asserts, wrapping me in a tight hug. The warmth brings a lump to my throat. The rest of the crew piles in, creating a cocoon of support around me. Daphne's in the corner, her eyes glistening.

"Thanks," I manage to say, my voice cracking.

A wave of nostalgia hits me. Back in LA, those guys were like brothers. I miss that. Maybe Lyndhurst could feel like that too.

"I'm next," Daphne declares, snatching the share stick from me. I exhale, relieved she's taking the helm. "Moving to London was terrifying, but you guys made me feel so welcome. With all the recent bullying, I'm grateful for each of you checking in on me. Apart from my sister, I've never had many friends, but now it feels like I've gained a whole crew of brothers. I love you guys."

"We love you too," Sven and Omar chime together, both giving her a casual jostle on the shoulders.

Daphne grabs her current project out of the knitting basket. The guys join in, pulling out their own yarn and needles before sitting back down on the sofa. Weeks after Femi's auction, they're still knitting together. I should've been here. Daphne's eyes lock onto mine, and she hands me a ball of yarn and needles. I take a deep breath, determined to conquer this.

"Anyone else want to share?" she asks, eyes twinkling.

Jung grabs the share stick. "Being an athlete has affected my relationship with food," he admits. "Counting calories, weighing portions, and staying fit during the season is challenging. Sometimes I only have a protein shake for dinner because preparing a meal is overwhelming."

Omar nods. "I understand, mate. It feels like no matter what we do, it's never enough."

Jung's voice wavers. "Sometimes I'm more focused on how I look than on my actual game."

Sven softens. "I used to check my weight obsessively every day."

Daphne listens, eyes filled with compassion. "You guys are under so much pressure to meet these unrealistic standards. It's important to remember that you're more than your bodies. You're incredible athletes and even better people."

Jung takes a deep breath, visibly relieved. "Thanks."

Omar smiles, patting Jung on the back. "Gotta make sure we're there for each other."

"I like to cook." The words slip out of me, surprising everyone, including myself. "I mean—maybe we could eat together a few times a week?"

Tamu, hunched over his knitting project, looks up. "That's the effort we've been missing."

Jung turns red. "I'd appreciate it."

Omar goes next as I struggle with my yarn. "I've got a bad habit of dating guys I know aren't good for me," he admits, nervously picking at his unfinished project. "Deep down, I'm scared they'll see the real me and realize there's nothing there— my whole personality is just football."

Daphne sits beside him. "Omar, there's so much more to you," she reassures him.

Sven and Tamu nod. "Yeah, man."

Daphne continues, "You're always listening. You're funny, kind, and loyal. And you always correctly guess who's going to win the technical challenges on GBBO nights. Don't sell yourself short."

Ibrahim chimes in, "It's not just relationships. Maintaining friendships outside of the team is hard. People don't get why we can't hang out or why we're so exhausted."

"But we understand." Tamu smiles. Omar looks around, relieved.

I think about how lucky we are to have Daphne. She's never made us feel bad about the hours we have to put in.

Ibrahim adds that a specialist confirmed he has partial hearing loss from standing front row at too many concerts without earplugs, and he's concerned it might be affecting his balance on the pitch. Sven shares that his family is pressuring him about getting married and having kids, and that they don't fully understand his dedication to his football career.

But I understand. We all do.

Turns out we're all carrying more than just the weight of the game. What if the rest of the team feels the same way? Maybe even the whole league? Could opening up be our strength? Finding support in each other, like Daphne's been doing for me? If we start doing this, could we become better players? Maybe even improve our chances of winning?

Now that the weight has lifted, I feel ready to start fresh. First, I'll talk to Coach. Then I'll apologize to Ivan for not appreciating his support. I also want to reconnect with my old Los Angeles team and invite them to a game. Even if I'm just warming the bench, it would be great to see them again and introduce them to my new teammates.

"Thanks for doing this, Cameron," Tamu says. "So, are you coming out with us for New Year's tomorrow?"

I look at Daphne, whose grin is wider than the Cheshire cat's.

"As long as it's not karaoke," I grumble.

"It's in a private room again," Sven says, tilting his head at me. "We can even queue your song."

"What's your song?" Daphne asks.

I glare at the guys, and in unison they sing, "Wake me up inside—"

Chapter 34
Cameron

I LOAD the last plate into the dishwasher and glance over at Daphne. She's curled up on the couch, engrossed in *Gilmore Girls*, knitting a new blanket. The empty bowl of soft serve I made her sits on the coffee table next to a lit candle. I've looked forward to this all day.

After I apologized and opened up to Coach and Ivan last week, they were understanding. But I'm still on the bench. Coach told me I needed to show him I've changed. I agreed. I've been pushing myself harder at practice. It sucks sitting out and watching my team win without me. Ivan has been unstoppable these last two matches—he could play the rest of the season.

I don't know who I am without football. Ivan's in his forties and still a force; that could be me. Perhaps the fear of being in my prime stemmed more from Rossi's incessant taunting. I still have plenty of time left in my career if I can turn this season around.

I've been trying to bond with my teammates. At my suggestion, Ivan and I started weight training with the rest of the team. After practice, we sometimes meet at the arcade next door and play *Mortal Kombat II*. It's nice because we don't have to talk;

for a while, I can just lose myself in the game, yelling at the screen and keeping my mind busy.

It's the same when I'm around Daphne—a peace for my relentless thoughts about not being enough.

As I grab a dish towel to dry my hands, I notice a tangled pile of yarn bunched up on a chair near her recording window. She usually has projects scattered around the apartment, but this one has been sitting untouched for over a week.

"What's going on with this?" I ask, pointing to the yarn.

She glances at the pile and then back at me. "Oh, that's been officially named Project Time-Out."

"Explain." I tilt my head, prompting her to continue.

The wrinkle above her nose appears as she hikes up onto her knees. "Something about that particular yarn has caused a fuss. I've been spending more time trying to untangle it than actually knitting. So, it's in time-out until I decide if I want to salvage it or scrap it."

"That won't do." It's a perfect opportunity. Something to keep my mind quiet.

"You're spot on, Goose. I will not be doing it!" She plops back down on her couch as I pick up the half-knitted sweater and inspect it. It's a new stitch I haven't seen before.

"What if I helped untangle it for you?"

"It's your funeral."

"I don't mind." I sit next to her, yellow yarn in hand, and she tosses the blanket over both of our laps. "When I was younger, I used to replace the netting on my goal post. Sometimes the new nets would come tangled, and I'd spend hours making sure it was perfect before putting it in. I liked the ritual of it."

"Well, when you put it like that, I'd be a fool to deny you the privilege of untangling my yarn," Daphne says with a playful smile. A loose strand of hair falls from her messy bun, and she blows it out of the way. I thought she already took her makeup off for the night, but her cheeks seem to have some sort of lumi-nescent powder on them.

I kiss her cheek, and she shimmies her shoulders deeper into her pink couch. Fucking adorable. I start unlooping the yarn from the wooden knitting needles. It's soothing.

"How are you feeling about your retreat after tickets sold out?" I ask.

"Excited, nervous, overwhelmed, over the moon," she admits. "I still need to finalize all the workshops, but luckily I got all the finances sorted out this week." She nods to herself, her needles clicking faster, matching the pace of the rain pelting the windows. "Since I already had established connections with brands, it was easy to get sponsors. They'll be mentioned online and in my vlogs during the weekend, so it pays for itself. My favorite yarn company, Knitty Gritty, sent over three hundred skeins of yarn in every color. Erin hooked me up with some mental health professionals who each only charged for their time. I only had to use up a little of my savings. Practically the whole weekend is covered between the ticket sales and sponsor-ships. But I'm still so nervous."

There is a confidence in her voice that is extremely sexy.

"About what?"

"Honestly, my welcome speech. I haven't spoken in front of a crowd like that before. Oh, actually, maybe I'm more scared of the Q&A session?" She huffs. "I'm worried my brain is going to short-circuit."

"You can practice on me," I suggest, unlooping another knot but accidentally tightening another. I grab a loose wooden needle from the counter and hold it like a microphone. A flash of discomfort zips through me, but I push it away. "Daphne Quinn," I mimic an announcer voice, "many influencers don't make it in this competitive field. How did you get your big break?"

She laughs, straightening her back and placing her hand over mine on the knitting needle. "Well, I'm glad you asked, Mr.

Featherington. It didn't happen overnight. It took a lot of trial and error, finding my voice, and connecting with my audience." She looks around, trying to find her next words. "When I was in fashion school, I had a teacher who encouraged me to post a pattern online. In the first week, I received over three hundred sales. It was the first time I thought that this could be something. I went to school knowing I loved fashion but not exactly what 'real' job I wanted to do. I never thought this was an option. Toward the end of college, I started posting videos for fun to teach some of my classmates' new stitches, and those videos gained traction. I got a few yarn kits for free. I began testing patterns for people, and it kind of just snowballed from there. I started sharing my projects and personal stories. It resonated with people."

"I wish I could be there to see you talk about this."

"I know, but it's okay." She strokes her thumb along the back of my hand.

I inhale a deep breath, leaning toward her. I relinquish my knitting-needle microphone to her and rub my hand along the top side of her bare thigh, chuckling as I glance at her shirt of the night. In big block letters, it says, *Wooly Temptress*, with a sheep lying—too provocatively for an animal—on a bed and proudly holding a pair of shears. The sheep is freshly shaven with a fur blanket draped over herself.

I chuckle, picking back up the tangled mess of yarn and starting again. "Do you remember your first sponsorship?"

"You're too good at the announcer voice." She continues her project, thinking for a second. "I was sitting with my sister when I got the email." Her mouth breaks into a toothy smile. "It was for SkillLearn, a video-tutorial-based website. Not only did they pay me three thousand dollars to mention them in a livestream, but they also asked me to make a Knitting Class for Beginners that still brings me a little bit of money every month."

"Really impressive, Duck." From my dad, I know how much

perseverance someone has to have to grit their teeth and get through the highs and lows of owning their own business.

"Thank you. Obviously, everything with the bullying has really sucked, but this month I got my highest check yet from my YouTube streams. Each hateful comment actually made me money, though I'd trade the money for my mental health any day." She finishes her row and flips her project.

I cringe, feeling guilty. "You always see the positive in things."

"For a long time, I felt like I was just knitting silly little patterns, but now it feels like I have a purpose. It's easy to forget how much I know, because I've been doing it for close to five years. Talking to brands and making videos is second nature to me at this point. At first, I never felt like it was a real job, but one day I brought in more money than Juni made in a month—and she's a doctor. We're lucky, you know."

"Agreed." I've never had to worry about money. My parents always gave us everything we wanted, and then at eighteen, when I went to go play for LA, my first contract was for six figures.

"Every day I wake up so grateful. I don't pay rent here, so I donate a lot of it. Most people need it more than me." She says it so plainly, so freely, like she's not trying to impress me. Like it's who she really is. A goddamn saint.

"You're so kind." I untie a section of knots; the end is in sight.

"So are you." She bumps her foot on my leg.

My chest constricts. I can't quite believe her. "So, Daphne Quinn, last question. How do you feel about Cameron Hastings?"

"I like him. Like, *like* him." She scoots closer to me.

"I like, *like* you too," I say and finish untangling the remainder of the yarn before setting it beside her. I rub my hand over her ankle. "Do you like this too?" I ask.

"Yes." She smirks. The last couple nights I've spent over here have been like this. A little game, seeing how long we can hold off without giving in. Since we got back from California, my appetite for her has been insatiable.

"And this." I turn toward her, moving back on the couch so I can kiss her ankle and that damn chain that drives me wild.

"I'm still a little sore from ice skating yesterday." She giggles. I took her to a private rink for our recent Yes Year activity. She was terrible, but it was okay because that meant she had to hold onto me the entire time.

"What if I had a way of making you feel a little better?" I kiss up her calf.

Daphne sets down her blanket and picks up Project Time-Out, inspecting the tangle-free mess. "But you just untangled my yarn; I was going to start working on my project," she says innocently.

"Well, don't let me stop you."

She picks up her needles and yarn, her eyes sparkling with a mischievous glint. Daphne's needles click rhythmically. I can't resist as I work my lips up her legs, each kiss drawing a soft sigh from her. "Oh."

This is about to become a very fun game.

"How's the knitting?"

"No problem at all, don't even know what you're talking about."

"Not distracted?"

She bats her head side to side. The pink tinge in her cheeks is obvious. "Nope."

The corner of my lip lifts in a smirk. If that's how she wants to play it. "What if I grab your rose-shaped vibrator? Are you going to be able to keep working?"

Daphne's flirty expression drops, and her cheeks burn red. Her needles stop clicking. "How do you know about that?"

She left it out on her nightstand after one of our make-out

sessions on the couch got very hot and heavy first thing in the morning. I found it that night, after I got back from practice.

I lean in closer, my breath warm against her ear. "Is it in your nightstand?" I whisper, my hand trailing up her thigh. Her breath hitches. Sliding my hand up her leg, I watch as her body responds to my touch.

She nods. "In the drawer."

"Let's see if you can keep your focus then," I murmur, my lips finding the sensitive skin just below her ear. She shivers, her body arching toward me. I pull away from her, fetch the rose-shaped vibrator out of her nightstand drawer, and quickly wash it in the sink. When I return to the living room, I find Daphne's anticipatory gaze tracking my every move, her knitting needles working overtime.

"Ready to play?" I ask.

A fire burns in her eyes, and she slides back in her seat. "I'm not going to get in the way of you making me feel better, now am I?"

"Good girl." I leave the battery-powered friend on the coffee table for the time being and begin unraveling my woman.

I kneel before her, my hands tracing the curves of her legs. My fingers glide slowly, savoring every inch of her silky skin. My lips follow the path of my hands, leaving a trail of soft, lingering kisses.

Her breathing quickens, and her knitting needles quiet down. "Are you getting distracted?"

"Not a chance." She sighs, betraying her arousal as I continue my worship.

My hands move higher, caressing her thighs. With excruciating slowness, I slide off her pajama shorts and panties, exposing her to my hungry gaze. I drink in the sight of her, the evidence of her desire making my pulse race.

"You're already getting worked up, aren't you?" I tease, my voice thick with lust.

She attempts to play coy. "I'm trying to knit," she says, her voice shaky as she tries to focus on her task and not the fire I'm stoking within her.

A flush spreads across her cheeks. It won't be long before she surrenders completely.

A chuckle escapes me. "That shirt is doing inexplicable things to me," I murmur. "It's so adorably sexy."

"You like it?"

"Like, *like* all of them." With a satisfied smile, my hands continue their worship, exploring, caressing, loving every part of her. I kiss around her thighs, making her even wetter and more turned on. Despite this, she tries to keep knitting, her determination both amusing and arousing.

She looks down at me with a playful glint in her eyes. "I thought you were going to try and distract me," she teases.

"And make you feel good."

"It has five different modes," she whispers.

"Let's see what they do to you."

"Please," she begs, igniting something primal within me.

I flick on the first mode, a steady pulsing, and kiss her deeply. She tries to focus on her hands, but her breath catches as I bring the vibrator closer to her legs. She whimpers and sighs, her body responding instantly. I hover the toy just above her clit, teasing her with the anticipation.

"God, you're so beautiful," I say, my voice filled with adoration. "But you know you're not going to be able to stay focused on that knitting, right?"

She bites her lip, determined. "Watch me," she challenges.

I move the toy across her clit for a second, then pull it away. Her hips buck involuntarily.

"Having trouble focusing?" I tease, sliding the toy through her, adjusting the pressure and circling it. Her moans are music to my ears. My cock is so fucking hard. A mixture of pleasure and pain.

"Cameron," she scolds.

I press warm, wet kisses along her thigh and twist the toy, switching to the second mode. This one comes in short bursts, like a jackhammer.

Daphne sighs heavily. "Maybe I'm not going to make it."

"Oh, you will," I assure her, my voice a low growl. "You're a winner; you can do it."

She rolls her eyes at me, but the defiance is mixed with lust. "You think so?" A hint of a smirk plays on her lips as her fingers run over the yarn.

"I know so. You're incredible. You always rise to the occasion." Her body arches. "I love how you're so wet for me," I whisper, my lips brushing against her skin. I trail my mouth up her thigh, licking and nipping while never letting up the rhythm of my fingers. "I could watch you torture yourself like this all night."

She bites her lip, trying to maintain her composure. "I'm... I'm almost done with this row."

"Are you now?" I say, my voice dripping with playful sarcasm. "Let's see how long you can keep it up."

Her eyes flutter shut as she tries to concentrate, but her knitting becomes more erratic. The pleasure is too good, too intense. "Please, I need to finish," she begs, but her voice lacks conviction.

I switch to a third mode, the vibrations coming and going in gentle waves. It seems to relax her. I'm on my knees in her living room, watching her come undone. Her cheeks flush, her breath comes in short, desperate gasps, and her hands falter over the yarn.

"Just a little more," I coax, slipping a finger inside of her, working slowly in and out, feeling her warmth envelop me. I can barely contain myself as I watch her unravel before me. Every soft gasp, every tremble of her body drives me wild. My desire for her is overwhelming, a constant thrum in my veins, but I hold back, wanting to savor this moment, to make it perfect for her.

She whimpers, "I can't...I can't do it."

"Yes, you can," I murmur, my eyes locked on her face, watching every delicious expression as she falls apart.

"More," she demands, her voice dripping with need.

I switch to the fourth mode, something between a steady rumble and a high speed. I hold her gaze, slipping in another finger, and then kiss her deeply.

"You're perfect, you know that? I love watching you come. I love getting you there," I whisper against her lips.

Her knitting needles clatter to the floor as she finally gives in, her body arching, her moans filling the room. Her body responds to every touch, every word.

"You're going to come so hard for me," I tell her. "I can feel it; you're right on the edge."

Her moans grow louder, her hips bucking against my hand. "Yes, yes, please," she gasps, her voice a desperate plea. "Don't stop."

"I won't," I promise, feeling a surge of power as I slow down the speed of the vibrator, teasing her mercilessly. "But I want you to hold on just a little longer. I want to savor this." I press the vibrator harder against her clit, then pull back, switching to my fingers as I trace delicate circles around her sensitive spot. The heat at the base of my spine only multiplies with every passing second, making it incredibly difficult to maintain control.

"Oh god, please," she begs, her tone a mixture of frustration and desire. "Cameron."

I lean in close, my lips brushing against her ear. "You're doing so well," I whisper, my fingers moving faster now, then slower again, keeping her teetering on the edge. "I want to hear you say my name, tell me how good it feels."

"Please, Cameron, it feels so good, please," she moans.

I switch to my mouth, my tongue flicking against her clit, my fingers not breaking pace inside of her as she gets louder and louder.

"Fuck, I love the way you beg, sweet girl," I murmur against her skin and suck. "I love how responsive you are, how your body reacts to my touch." She tightens around me, the same way she did the night we first met. "Just a little more, you're almost there."

I can sense her frustration building, the need for release overwhelming her. I grab the vibrator and increase the speed again, my fingers and the toy working together as I kiss up her thighs. "I love watching you like this, so desperate and needy." I growl, my voice low and intense.

Her hips buck against me, her body trembling. "Yes, yes, oh god, yes!" she cries out.

I push her right to the edge, then pull back, slowing down just enough to keep her from tipping over. "You're doing so good," I praise.

"Please," she whimpers, her body writhing beneath me. "I can't take it; please let me come."

I smile, knowing I have her exactly where I want her. "All right, let go," I command, my voice a low growl. "Come for me, show me how good I make you feel."

And she does, her body convulsing, a cry of pure pleasure escaping her lips. Her eyes lock onto mine. "That's it." Her body collapses against the couch. I hold her close, my fingers still gently stroking her, prolonging her pleasure. "You're incredible," I whisper, kissing her forehead.

Her eyes flutter open. "That was so fun. Even if I didn't get to finish my knitting project, and the yarn is all tangled again."

I laugh and reply, "You're still a winner, tangled yarn or not."

She grins mischievously as I get up from the couch. I grab a towel and gently clean her up, then fetch a glass of water and a piece of her favorite chocolate. "Here you go," I say.

"Thank you," she says, her eyes filled with gratitude as she takes a sip and nibbles on the chocolate.

When she's done, she slides off the couch and gets down onto the floor. "Now let's see if you can stay focused on untangling this yarn again," she challenges, handing me the mess we made of her project. "Because I'm going to make it very difficult for you," she adds, a playful glint in her eyes.

I can't help but let out a groan, running a hand through my hair. "You know, this is really unfair," I mutter, trying to mask the smirk tugging at my lips. "I have no control around you."

She looks up at me, her eyes sparkling with mischief. "Life's not fair, grumpy," she teases. Her voice softens as her fingers deftly unbuckle my belt and pull down my jeans. "But I promise, it'll be worth it."

"All right, you win," I concede. "But just know, you're making it very hard to focus."

She grins, her eyes locking onto mine. "Good," she whispers. Her breath is warm against my skin. "That's exactly what I was hoping for."

And with that, our night is far from over.

Chapter 35
Cameron

Influencer Daphne Quinn Knits a New Narrative on Cyberbullying Awareness

"Hastings!" Coach yells, stopping me on my way out of the locker room. "Come into my office for a second."

"Yeah. I'll see you guys in the parking lot," I call out to my defensive line.

"Don't keep him for too long; he challenged me to a *Mortal Kombat* battle." Omar tilts his head, pointing to me.

"It'll be the quickest fifty pounds you ever lost." I scoff before following Coach to his office. "Hey," I say, sitting in the chair opposite his desk.

"That new play you collaborated on with Sven in practice today is exactly what Ivan and I have been looking for." Coach shoots me a toothy smile. "Great job utilizing his strengths."

I can only nod. "Trying to work with the team."

We came up with the play last week by rewatching the Parkside City match together. As much as I've fucking hated sitting on the bench, at least now I can watch tapes and be objective about my teammates instead of mentally rewinding each of my fuckups.

Today, we executed a new play together. Tamu pushed forward, with Omar and Ibrahim closing in. He flashed his left pinky upward—the signal we made up. Jung got into position, and Sven readied for backup. Following my lead, Sven intercepted the ball with a header, sending it to Jung, who navigated it to midfield.

Another good practice in the books.

"You've shown good initiative over the last two weeks. Team says you've been warming up with them, figuratively and literally." He laughs. "How do you think it's going?" He stares at me, tapping his fingers over his desk.

My insides twist. I'm realizing that this guy is just genuinely nice, however much his constant grin freaks me out.

I suck in a breath, knowing my two-word answers and grunts won't cut it anymore. "Good. Being benched reminded me what I have to lose—not just my place on this team, but my love for the game."

Coach stands, leans over his desk, and clasps his hand on my shoulder. "There it is. The Hastings spark I glimpsed when you played in LA. That's how I know you're ready to start against Riverton tomorrow."

I clench my fist. *Fuck yeah.* "I won't let the club down." I stand to shake his hand, but then he gives me a cocky grin and holds up his other arm like he wants to hug me.

Oh, what the hell?

I hug my coach for the first time since that last championship game in LA. "I'm proud of you, Cameron."

"Thanks for giving me another shot," I say, pulling away.

Overton has climbed the table. Last year's champions, Parkside City, are falling behind. Right now, we're sitting in the seventh spot. There are twenty games left this season. If we win at least sixteen of those, there's a chance—the smallest chance— we could snag the championship. Every match from here on will be a battle, and Lyndhurst needs to bring our A-game for every. Single. One.

For the first time this season, I can feel the cold metal of the trophy in my hands. Hear the shouts in the stadium, the roar of fans pouring onto the pitch like a damn flood. The purple and white confetti raining from the sky.

One hundred and thirty-four days.

We can still win.

I leave Coach's office, pull out my phone, and open the neglected text chain with my Los Angeles team.

CAMERON

> How do you guys feel about coming to the final Lyndhurst match in May?

#8 DYNAMO DIEGO RIVERA

> FUCK YEAH!

#4 OCTO OLLIE BENNETT

> Can't wait 2 fucking celebrate when ur holding that trophy bro

CAMERON

> Let me know who can make it. I'll organize your tickets.

Leaving the stadium, I'm immediately overwhelmed by flashing lights.

"Hastings, when do you think you'll be back on the field again?" a voice shouts.

Fucking hell. I throw my hand up in front of my face, propelling myself into the media circus. Microphones and cameras line my path. The reporters stick to me like gnats.

"Is this the end of your legacy?"

"How do you feel about the anniversary of your livestream next month?"

My nerves explode, and the high I felt moments ago crashes. It's like being caught in an earthquake, each flash and question jolting me. For the past month, I've been tormenting myself, each moment of peace overshadowed by intrusive thoughts that scream that no matter how hard I try to fix things, I'll just end up losing it all again. The reporters' voices amplify my fears a hundredfold.

"No comment," I say, inhaling deep breaths.

"How are you handling being benched?"

"Are you going to throw in the towel at your prime?"

"What toll is this taking on your personal life?"

My heart races faster. I shield my face with my jacket, trying to block them out.

"Give him some space!" a familiar voice shouts.

Another one follows. "Back off!"

Jung, Omar, and Sven surround me, ushering me to my car.

"Meet you there," Sven says, closing my door and yelling at the media to back up. I'm mad I didn't give these men a chance sooner.

TEN MINUTES LATER, I enter the arcade next door to the Lion's Lodge. The sounds of clinking coins fill the old, musty place. Most of the team is already here. Pitchers of beer and pint glasses clutter the large wooden table in the center of the place.

"Those knobheads never stop. Had to sprint to my car. Didn't have time to warn you," Ivan says, approaching me and clapping me on the back. "You all right?"

I nod, and my words stick in my throat like they always do when the spotlight burns too brightly. "Yeah," I assure him.

"Spoke to Coach today. Glad you're starting tomorrow."

"Not mad that you're sitting out?" I scan Ivan's face, and a whisper of panic brushes down my neck.

"No, my knee's been giving me hell." He waves his hand at me, looking genuinely relieved. "I'm glad to see you're fitting in with the team. Knew you'd come around."

For once, it doesn't sound patronizing. It's nice to know someone had faith in me. "Had to sort out my priorities."

"Good," he says. Then he pauses as if he's holding back something important.

I scan the arcade, spotting Omar over at *Mortal Kombat* already. "Are we good?" I ask.

"Have you thought more about reporting Rossi to the Football Federation?" Ivan prods. "If not him, you've got solid evidence against Charlie."

I grit my teeth, recoiling. Going public with the livestream business is a nonstarter. One accusation leads to another. If there's a case against Charlie, the media will be all over me even more.

"Not worth it."

"I get that coming forward isn't easy," he says, his tone serious. "But it's important to make sure that kind of misconduct doesn't happen again."

Maybe he's right, but I don't want to be a martyr. The claims will be dismissed as exaggerated, and I'll be left alone to deal with the fallout. I can't handle the possibility of reliving that nightmare.

"I hear you," I mutter, shrugging like I couldn't care less, even though my insides are twisting. "But I'm not gonna be the poster boy for this. The game's brutal, and the media's worse. I have other people to think about." Daphne's been out there, making waves about cyberbullying and gaining traction for her retreat. The last thing she needs is to be dragged back into my mess.

Ivan looks unimpressed. "Whatever happens, we've got your back."

"Hastings, let's go!" Omar shouts, shaking a cup full of coins at me, offering me an escape from this conversation.

"Thanks, Ivan. Appreciate it," I say, walking off.

Life is finally improving. My team and I are getting along, things with Daphne are amazing, and I have a shot at winning the trophy again. I don't want to jeopardize all of that. Let the midfielders and strikers chase the glory. As the goalkeeper, my job is to keep the ball out of the net and focus. That's where I'll stay, right where things make sense.

"Ready to lose some money?" I sidle up next to Omar, who's already loading *Mortal Kombat II* with coins, his grin radiating an overconfidence that's disgustingly infectious.

"You wish." He nudges my shoulder.

At least for the length of this tournament against Omar, my brain will be quiet.

The game starts with its nostalgic intro, the music blasting louder than a heavy metal concert. The roster of fighters appears in all their pixelated glory: Sub-Zero, Scorpion, Raiden, and more. I pick Johnny Cage with his signature sunglasses, and the battle begins.

Thirty minutes later, I'm ahead by two wins. Omar's not one to give up easily, though. He picks Liu Kang, determined to make a comeback. The arcade around us is a cacophony of flashing lights and electronic beeps, the smell of popcorn and soda filling the air, reminding me of her.

"Come on, Johnny, don't fail me now," I mutter, fingers flying over the buttons.

Omar grunts, his eyes never leaving the screen. "I'm going to beat you this time."

Our characters clash, trading blows and special moves. The tension rises as our health bars dwindle.

Finally, with a well-timed shadow kick, I land the final blow. "Yes!" I shout, throwing my hands up in victory.

Omar laughs, shaking his head. "Go again!"

"You enjoy losing, don't you?"

"I'm Scorpion this time." He feeds more coins into the machine. As the game loads, I sip my seltzer, but an unexpected, sickly sweetness floods my mouth. Instead of swallowing, I perform an involuntary, over-the-top spit take, sending the liquid cascading down my black tee.

"What the hell?" I mutter, glaring daggers at Omar.

"Oi! That was my cosmo twist."

"What was the twist?" I ask, horror creeping into my voice.

"No vodka, extra syrup."

I gag, shaking my head. "I'm texting Daphne to bring me a change of clothes."

Knowing she's likely prepping for her livestream in a few hours, I quickly type out a message.

CAMERON

> Any chance you can please bring one of my t-shirts down to the arcade?

DUCK

Arcade!? Yes. I'll be down in a minute.

Thank God.

Moments later, Daphne bursts through the doors.

"Who's ready to rumble?" Her voice booms across the dimly lit, neon-hued arcade, shattering my concentration on the fight. She skips over, wearing that thigh-length sweater that makes her look like a pair of perfect legs wrapped in knitted yarn. She's carrying a flower-print crochet bag. A sense of calm overcomes me.

The team erupts in cheers at her arrival. "Daphne! Daphne! Daphne!"

Her hair glows and twirls as she does a dramatic spin and bows before making her way to me. My heart beats rapidly in my chest, a mix of adrenaline from the game and the excitement of seeing her.

"I'm gonna kick your ass," Omar challenges.

Well, I'm not about to lose in front of my girl.

"You wish," I mutter, refocusing on the screen.

"Come on, guys, let's see some action!" Daphne shouts. Her enthusiasm is infectious as she stands next to me, her presence a bright spot amid the sensory overload. My thumbs work in overdrive as Johnny Cage trades brutal blows with Scorpion.

"Finish him!" echoes in the background.

"I got the goods," she whispers conspiratorially into my ear. The smell of vanilla fills my senses, distracting me.

"Thanks," I say, leaning over to kiss her—and losing the game in the process.

"Fatality!" screams the game as Scorpion delivers the final blow to Johnny Cage. Everyone around us yells and cheers, but all I can focus on is her. Worth it.

"You're such a sap." Omar cackles, slapping my back. I shoot him a glare.

"Shut up, Omar. Let's go again. Load it up."

As Omar shoves more coins into the machine, I yank off my tee and grab the shirt Daphne brought me without looking. When I pull it on, the room erupts into laughter. I glance at Daphne and see her doubled over, barely holding back her giggles.

"Nice shirt, man! Where'd you get it, the Big Balls Emporium?" Ibrahim calls out.

"Hey, does that come in my size?" Sven yells.

What now?

I look down at the tee, which reads, *I Like Big Balls and I Cannot Lie* in yarn letters, with a skein right in the middle.

"Are you serious?" I scold as I attempt to keep a straight face.

"It was all I could find on such short notice!" she says, failing to suppress the dimples forming in her cheeks.

I roll my eyes, a smirk tugging at the corner of my mouth. I lean down toward her, and her hot breath hits my neck. I've been practically living at her place and have a dresser drawer full of clothes there.

"I'm pretty sure I had a couple more shirts at your place."

She flashes her innocent Bambie eyes. "Guess they were in the laundry."

"I dry-clean them," I counter, narrowing my eyes.

"Who dry-cleans T-shirts?" She scrunches her nose, leaning her body into the corner of the arcade machine. I love being this close to her with people around.

"They come out extra crispy that way," I say, pretending to be defensive but failing miserably.

"My particular man." She giggles and tiptoes up to kiss me before running her hand over the wording across my chest. "I think it looks adorable on you."

"Of course you do," I grumble.

She bites her bottom lip, tilting her head in a ridiculously adorable way. "You're just pretending to be mad, but I can see right through the fact that you've been dying to borrow one of these."

"Like you've been dying to borrow my earring?"

"Aye aye, captain!"

I cup my hand around her lower back and growl into her ear, "Don't think you're getting away with this. I'll make you pay for it later."

She presses her body into mine. "Is that a promise?"

"Absolutely," I murmur, letting my hand slide down to her waist. "Just wait until we're alone. I'll make sure you lose track of every stitch."

"Again?" She shivers, her breath catching. "I look forward to it."

I pull her in for another kiss, the arcade fading away as I lose myself in her. "That was for good luck."

"You don't need it," she whispers, her eyes sparkling with anticipation.

"You two are disgustingly cute." Omar is propped up on his elbow on the other side of the machine, staring at us. Sven's head bobbles between us with a smile on his face. "Now I can see why you bought a scarf from the Femi auction for ten thousand pounds."

"What?" Daphne gasps loudly. "You never told me that."

I never mentioned the scarf to her because of what happened with the paparazzi the next day. I keep it tucked away in my closet. Supporting her and the team in any way I could felt like the least I could do at the time.

"It's cold out. Needed to keep my neck warm." I shrug. Her face lights up, and a wave of happiness washes over me. I love seeing her happy. Then I turn to Omar. "All right, let's do this," I say, cracking my knuckles and taking my position.

Daphne stands beside me and claps. "Get 'em, Goose!"

I dive into the game, my focus sharper than ever. I've learned that winning is lackluster in comparison to proving to Daphne that I'm worth rooting for. The arcade buzzes around us, but all I hear is her voice.

Chapter 36
Daphne

Cameron Hastings Back on the Field After Benching in Critical Overton Match

"Fuck yes!" I roar, leaping off the plush leather couch at Bea and Ivan's home in the Champion's Triangle. Getting here was quite the trek from my apartment. Cameron practically twisted my arm to borrow his car to ensure my safe journey. My chest feels like a shaken soda can about to burst as I watch Cameron block another goal. He's on fire on his first day back.

"That's it, Hastings!" Bea shouts, and the rest of the glamorous WAGs join our cheers. Our faces are canvases of purple and white stripes. These women are incredible—running businesses, parenting full-time, sometimes both. It's inspiring and comforting to be around people who understand the quirks of my job.

Victoria, Ben's wife, idly stirs her Lyndhurst Martini—a regular martini sprinkled with dried beet powder to give it a vibrant purple hue. She's perched on a stool as one of her toddlers teeters at her feet. "That holiday rest did the whole team good. They've been untouchable for the past four matches."

"Or perhaps it was the lack of rest." Bea playfully nudges my ribs. Heat rises to my cheeks. "Wait, don't sit there." Like Cameron diving for the ball moments ago, Bea lunges and blocks Maya—one of the players' kids—from sinking into the leather chaise. "Nobody sits there on game days, okay, sweetie? It's bad luck."

A chuckle bubbles up from me. No one beats football fans when it comes to superstitions.

"Give 'em hell, Tamu!" I whoop. Between the rain and his speed, our striker is a blur of motion, the enemy defense line nothing more than a temporary roadblock. The room collectively holds its breath, every gaze riveted to the screen.

Then, Tamu shoots…and he scores! Applause erupts through the living room like a sudden downpour. He just secured another win for Lyndhurst.

I never thought I'd be a sports girl, but I love being here, cheering on a man I'm head over heels for. That intense but ridiculously hot stare as he claps his gloved hands together, sweat trickling down his face and mud splattered across his uniform.

"Daphne," Bea says, sliding into the seat beside me. "I'm so excited for your retreat, my love. Our financial manager wrote a very generous check to support The Kindness Coalition."

"I appreciate you so much. They've been doing amazing work." My heart warms at our community rallying behind my cause. "I was thrilled to highlight them in the *Stone Times* piece on cyberbullying."

In the recent article, I emphasized how cyberbullying leads to emotional distress, anxiety, and depression.

"I adored that article!" Amelia, a successful news anchor married to one of the team's starting midfielders, says next to us. "Before Daniel transferred to Lyndhurst, I was under constant public scrutiny. From my fashion choices to my career, I was pigeonholed as just a footballer's wife instead of a businesswoman."

"Remember what happened to Rebekah after the Wagatha Christie scandal?" Victoria chimes in.

They all shudder at the memory. Tabloid wounds run deep, but I think about Bea's words from when we first met. *At least we have each other.* Spreading empathy, fostering positivity, and supporting each other is crucial. We all play a role in creating a kinder internet, and I'm empowered to carry that message forward.

"When Nero and I holidayed in Aruba and I dared to wear a bikini four months after giving birth, the hounds made it seem like I was cheating on my husband. When we returned, all my collaboration offers were to promote weight loss gummies or bedroom toys." Emily, a budding fashion influencer and Nero's childhood sweetheart, laughs.

"Did you accept any of them?" Bea asks, eyebrow raised, glass midair.

"Only the bedroom toys. I like my momma curves as they are, but who doesn't want to spice up the bedroom? Nero loves our well-stocked bedside drawer."

"Nero, huh?" Bea says cheekily, setting off a chain reaction of giggles.

"A French boutique sent us some new beads," Emily whispers conspiratorially. "Let's just say he's in for a treat after tonight's win."

"I'm going to need more details on that. Anything with the word *beads* in it sounds like something I would enjoy," I chuckle.

"What you need is the guide they sent me on tantric massages." Emily winks. "I'll send it over to you right now."

"Yes, please!" The sex with Cameron has been amazing, but adding a few Yes Year activities—sex edition—seems fun. I blush, remembering how Cameron used the rose-shaped vibrator from my nightstand last week. With my anxiety meds, it's easier for me to *get there* with a little extra help.

My phone pings, like he knew I was thinking of him.

GOOSE

Are you still at Bea's?

DAPHNE

Yes!

GOOSE

See you soon. x

It feels like time is flying by since we returned from California three weeks ago. Cameron has joined us for the last two weeks of *The Great British Bake Off*, even taking bets with the guys on who will win this season, We've been ice skating and have gone to winter pop-up markets. He's spent the night every night except for his away games.

Bit by bit, I've been sneaking cozy touches into his place: potholders in the kitchen and a throw blanket on his lone chair. Even his bed is gradually turning into a nest of my knitted creations.

But my real pièce de résistance? The tiny designs I've been quietly embroidering into his things. It started with the small heart in his leather jacket sleeve and has grown to secret flowers in his training shorts, a sheep on his socks, and a redwood tree inside his pillowcase. The jersey he has on today even has a hidden duck and goose stitched into the hem.

A small game I'm playing, waiting to see how long it'll take for him to notice.

Now he's with the team and on his way to the Matoses' house. It's our first big, public activity as two people who are dating. It's been so nice being open about our relationship in front of the people close to us. It feels like we're on the right track to build something extraordinary together outside of this bubble.

Another chime comes from my phone—this time an email. I tap into it and nearly pass out reading the subject.

GEORGIAWOODS@VIGGLE.COM, pr@lustisland.com

Collaboration Opportunity: Knitting X Lust Island Initiative

Hi Daphne,

I'm Georgia Woods, fresh off my Lust Island win. First off, I'm obsessed with your page and your Juni Sweater pattern—seriously, I can't stop knitting it! Your recent article about cyberbullying in the Stone Times tugged at my heartstrings. Most of the contestants coming off Lust Island received tons of hate online, and as the show goes on, it's becoming a bigger and bigger issue.

So next season, I'm teaming up with Lust Island's PR crew to create a handcrafted wardrobe for the contestants to wear on the show and your article inspired me to raise awareness about the impact of cyberbullying. We'll also be helping contestants build resilience for life after the villa.

I think you'd be perfect for this collaboration with me. I see that you have a knitting retreat coming up in March. I'd love to come and meet you in person.

I'm super excited about the possibility of working together.

Looking forward to hearing from you!

Live, laugh, lust,

Georgia

HOLY FREAKIN' bananas!

Yes.

Yes.

Yes!

A million times yes.

This is the kind of stuff a Yes Year is made of. I nearly screech in my seat, my eyes going blurry with excitement as I hammer out a response.

DAPHNE@WOOLYDUCK.COM
RE: Collaboration Opportunity: Knitting X Lust Island Initiative
Georgia,
I absolutely loved you on Lust Island! I am in. Send over any and all details, my knitting needles are at your service. Attached is a ticket to my event. I'd love to do an intro call to chat about your initial ideas—feel free to send over your availability.
Knit Regards,
Daphne Quinn
@wooly.duck

MY HEART POUNDS in my chest. The reply comes in instantly. *Eek!*

PR@LUSTISLAND.COM, georgiawoods@viggle.com
RE: RE: Collaboration Opportunity: Knitting X Lust Island Initiative
Daphne and Georgia, we're thrilled! Use this link to schedule a kickoff call, and let's get started.
Got a text,
Lust Island PR Team

I PICK the earliest slot available, two weeks from now, and read the message one more time, searing the feeling into my mind.

The Georgia Woods, the *Lust Island* star with the brightest pink hair and the sweetest heart, wants to collaborate with me.

Breathe, Daphne. Just breathe. You're freaking out.

When I finally glance up, the entire team files into Bea's house one by one, and Cameron appears behind them. He's got this beautiful, wide, and absolutely unusual smile stretching across his face. It's like he's a supernova.

Around his neck is the purple scarf I knitted for Femi's auction. I can't believe he brought it with him without telling me. My heart tightens with emotion. He played it cool, even after I questioned him about it at the arcade.

I can't wait to tell him my news. But as I jump up, my stomach twists. I don't want to make today about me. I quickly shoot a text to my sister and moms about the news, so at least I have someone to celebrate with for now.

I sidle up to him. "Hey, big man, that save—" Cameron sweeps me right into his chest and plants a knee-wobbling kiss on me.

Whoops and whistles erupt from the room. When we finally break apart, my lungs are desperately fighting to catch a breath. Oh wow. He really does take my breath away—literally and figuratively.

I glance around, cheeks blazing, and realize everyone is staring at us with goofy grins plastered on their faces.

"Hi," he whispers against my lips, completely ignoring our very entertained audience.

"Hi. You were amazing out there."

"I loved knowing that you were watching. Gave me an extra kick in my ass to push harder," he says, giving me an illegal, panty-dropping wink that makes me melt like butter on a warm skillet. "How was your day, sweet girl?"

"Had a blast celebrating the Lions' win and, uh—" Who am I kidding, I can never keep a secret. "And I was going to wait to tell you because I don't want to overshadow your win today, but I just got an offer for an amazing collab deal, to design clothes for a show and team up with them on anti-bullying initiatives," I say, trying to sound casual. "No big deal."

"What?" His eyes light up, and he rubs his thumb across my cheek.

"It's nothing. I really don't want to distract from your win today."

"Please," Cameron says in that delicious stern voice of his. "I love celebrating you as much as I love winning."

I gulp. "I'm lucky to have you, Goose."

"It's me who's lucky. Now, tell me more."

I hesitate. "It's for *Lust Island*." I scan his face. His jaw tenses, but he waits for me to continue. "Apparently, Georgia Woods, who knits and crochets too, read my article in the *Stone Times* and wants to collaborate for next season."

"That's fucking great, Daphne," he says, looking genuinely thrilled.

"Really? I was nervous to tell you because I know you don't like the show."

"It's not like you're ditching me to go on *Lust Island*." He shrugs, but there's a strange, fleeting emotion on his face—a ghostly shadow I haven't seen in months. It comes and goes so quickly, I'm sure I imagined it. He must be exhausted after giving it his all out there.

"I could never be a bombshell."

"Because you'd be too good for every guy there." He kisses the top of my head. "We have to celebrate."

His hand tightens on my waist, and I know if we weren't in a room full of people, he'd be ripping this little knitted number right off me and we'd be celebrating both of our big wins today.

I trace a line over his leather jacket and rise on my toes to whisper in his ear. "Maybe that can wait until tonight." I giggle, my voice light and teasing.

"I love where your head's at." He gives my butt a playful pat. "But I was thinking of something bigger. A trip."

"A trip?" I squeal, my excitement barely contained.

"I have a weekend off in three weeks, my last one until May. How do you feel about a quick getaway to see the northern lights?"

I practically bounce into the air, feeling a giddy thrill bubbling up inside me. "Are you serious?"

"Absolutely. Finland is only a three-hour flight away," he says nonchalantly, as if a spontaneous trip to see the northern lights is the most natural thing in the world.

"No way!" My mind races with excitement. "Oh my god, there's a yarn store in Helsinki that I absolutely love. I've ordered wool from them a bunch of times. I'd love to visit! It'd be amazing to see it in person. And I could test out some samples for that collaboration with Georgia. Oh, and I heard there's an overnight train—imagine that!"

He smiles warmly. "Anything you want, my sweet girl."

Just then, Sven and Omar crash onto the scene like a pack of overexcited golden retrievers, clapping Cameron on the back and showering him with congratulations for today's save. "Man of the match!" they shout, raising their drinks high in a toast.

"Couldn't have done it without you all," he says, pulling me into their hug and flashing that proud smile that makes me weak in the knees.

Our cozy cuddle session disintegrates as the guys untangle themselves. But they don't leave, clearly baffled by this rare, mushy side of Cameron that I've come to adore. They stare at him like he's some sort of interactive art piece, waiting for him to make the next move.

"What's this about a trip?" Omar nudges his arm.

I glance at Cameron, and he nods. "Cameron's taking me to Finland to see the northern lights."

Sven chimes in, "You have to stay at Octola."

"Don't ruin the surprise," Cameron grumbles with an amused smile.

I have no idea where or what Octola is, but knowing these guys' knack for the finer things in life, it's bound to be something extraordinary.

Can this day get any better?

My heart feels like it'll pop open. "Wait, you already booked it? What if I didn't say yes?"

"Worth the risk."

I chuckle. "Since when did you become a high-stakes gambler?"

"I only bet when I know the odds are in my favor," he retorts with a playful wink, running his hand along my back, stopping at the base of my spine. "And trust me, I always come out on top where you're concerned." Every hair on my body stands at attention.

"Oh really?" I arch an eyebrow, a smirk creeping onto my lips. "And what if I had other plans?"

He leans in, his breath tickling my ear. "Then I'd just have to convince you otherwise."

"All right, cocky." I giggle. "I guess Finland it is."

Sven claps Cameron on the back, shattering our suddenly hundred-degree flirting session in front of his teammates. "Man, you two are gonna have an awesome time. Just promise to bring me back some Dumles. They're these little chocolate candies you'll absolutely love."

"You had me sold at chocolate," I say, grinning. "We'll even throw in a few selfies with the northern lights for good measure."

Cameron smirks and lowers his voice to another spine-tingling octave. "And maybe a few other surprises, too."

"Oh, now you're really talking. I can't wait."

"Me neither," he murmurs, his voice low and full of promise. "It's going to be unforgettable."

Omar erupts into a hearty laugh. "Look at Mr. Romance over here! Who knew our Hastings had it in him?"

Cameron just rolls his eyes. "Go ahead, laugh."

"Such a sap," Sven says. "Just make sure you don't get a soggy bottom on your trip. We wouldn't want to disappoint Paul Hollywood."

"Trust me, Cameron's going to get all the star bakes while you're all stuck here with soggy bottoms and underbaked biscuits."

"Will I?"

It's adorable that he's finally getting the references now that he's been joining us for *The Great British Bake Off*. He's terrible at guessing the winners of the challenges—he always cheers for the underdog—but it's endearing that he's trying.

The room continues to hum with celebration, the noise level climbing to rock concert decibels as more teammates filter into the house.

Ivan and Bea saunter over to us, drinks in hand, and I feel a surge of admiration and a smidgen of hope. The more I get to know them, the more I yearn for Cameron and me to have something like what they have. Their love is pure, even if it's tangled up in football superstitions and the occasional tabloid headline. They've been together for what feels like eons, and they still look at each other like they're discovering new stars in the sky. It's the same way my moms look at each other and the way Cameron's parents did. I want that. I really, really do.

"Enjoy celebrating tonight." Ivan flashes me a grin. "He's earned it after today's performance."

If Cameron Hastings could blush, I swear this would be the perfect moment for him to turn a rosy shade of pink.

"Oh, don't you worry," I reply with a wink so exaggerated it could rival the cheesiest slice of cheddar. "We'll be celebrating a lot!"

"Surely whatever you have planned will be *bead-yond* amazing," Bea adds, batting her lashes in a mock-serious way.

I snort, which makes Cameron glance between us, utterly perplexed.

"What's so funny?" he asks.

"Oh, nothing!" I say, trying to sound as casual as possible. I'm not sure if either of us is ready for bead play...yet.

We join his teammates, who are now cozily gathered in a circle on Bea's couch.

We plop down among them, and the team dives into the game's nitty-gritty. Each play and strategy is recounted with such enthusiasm, it's as if they're reliving it all over again. For the first time in what feels like forever, Cameron looks completely at ease. The room is alive with energy. Kids dart around, jokes zip through the air, and laughter bubbles up like a shaken soda.

Cameron wraps an arm around my shoulders, pulling me closer to him on the couch. His warm body feels like a home for mine as we laugh together.

"I like seeing you this happy," he whispers, his eyes twinkling with that heart-melting sweetness.

"Happiness looks good on you too."

"It's easy when you're around."

I lean in, feeling like the luckiest girl ever. Surrounded by my new friends, this night feels like a perfect slice of happiness, one I'm certain will last forever.

Chapter 37
Cameron

February **4**
Lyndhurst FC Soars to Top 5 Amid Recent
Winning Streak—Is This the Turnaround They've
Been Waiting For?

February **6**
Are the Dating Rumors True? Cameron Hast-
ings Spotted at Helsinki-Vantaa Airport With
Influencer Daphne Quinn

After practice on Friday, I picked up Daphne, and we headed
to the airport for our flight to Finland. With the family jet
unavailable, we settled for first class. Daphne ordered every
snack and knitted the whole flight, while I struggled to stay
awake, exhausted from the week's workouts.

The cold hit us hard when we landed. Daphne, in her yellow
puffer coat, brown boots, and pink beanie, looked adorably

radiant against the snow. Her excitement was contagious as we made our way to the town car I hired.

I can't help but feel excited to share another Yes Year adventure with her.

"You know, you sort of look like a duck right now," I say, trying to keep my grin in check.

"Juni said the same thing when I bought this puffer for our family trip to Alaska a few years ago. But you're one to talk." She squeezes my hand tighter in the back seat of the car and laughs, a sound that always manages to thaw the icy parts of me.

"Hey, my girl made these." I run my gloved hand over my scarf and beanie, both painstakingly knitted by Daphne.

"*My girl.*" She scrunches her nose, smiling. "I still can't believe you convinced the yarn store to stay open for us. I feel kind of bad." Her gaze shifts to the outside, taking in the snowy landscape as it whizzes by. I keep my eyes on the road ahead, fighting off the creeping motion sickness.

I wanted to keep what I'd planned a surprise, but she hates surprises, so I ended up sending her an itinerary for the weekend.

"It's only an hour, and they were happy to help." I shrug, not mentioning that I had to shell out five-thousand euros to the shop owner to make it worth their while. *Who knew knitting was so expensive?*

"I can't wait. It's so cool here. I'm excited to see all the snow during the day." She leans her cheek against the window, eyes wide with wonder.

Twenty minutes later, we pull up to Villainen Metsä, a sprawling shop nestled in downtown Helsinki.

The lights are dim as we walk in, with wooden shelves packed with colorful yarns, sorted by color and type. Large tables in the center hold knitting needles, baskets of yarn, and other supplies. A small fire crackles in the background, with oversized chairs.

"*Tervetuloa.*" An older gentleman greets us with a nod.

"*Hei*," I mutter, trying to sound appreciative. "My name is Cameron Hastings; I believe we spoke earlier."

"Ah yes!"

"Thanks for staying open."

"*Kiitos*," Daphne chimes in, her smile radiant. We've tried to learn a few Finnish words this week, mostly during quiet moments when she braids her hair before bed. The gentleman nods again. "*Ei kestä*." He retreats behind the register, picks up an almost-finished cardigan, and resumes his knitting.

"Maybe that will be you someday," Daphne says, nudging me in the ribs as I grab a wooden basket. She wanders around the store, her eyes wide with excitement.

I scoff. "That looks like it involves purling, so not likely." My knitting progress has been embarrassingly slow. Untangling her yarn is about the extent of my skills right now.

"By the end of this year, you'll be making sweaters. Mark my words." She trails her fingers over the yarn, her voice full of conviction.

I roll my eyes, a reluctant smile tugging at the corners of my lips. "We'll see about that. I'd be happy if I could manage a potholder that looks more like a square and less like a parallelogram," I say, moving toward a shelf lined with vibrant yarns.

"A parallelo-what?" Daphne laughs, spinning around to face me. "You aced math, didn't you?"

"Had to keep my grades up to stay on the team. Finn helped tutor me; he's been friends with Alec since I was born," I reply, picking up a skein of blue yarn, savoring its softness.

"Juni tutored me in everything," she says, picking up some red yarn and rubbing it on the back of her hand. "She's brilliant."

"Knitting involves a lot of counting," I mention.

"Counting and geometry are worlds apart," she counters. "Feel how soft this is." She rubs the yarn over my hand before tossing the ball into the basket. Her fingers brush against mine, and I can't ignore the jolt of electricity that zips through me.

"And here I thought you liked challenging things." I wink, and she scrunches her nose. My phone pings. I silence it. "That's my alarm. We've got about thirty minutes before we need to get back to the town car and catch the train."

She laughs. "You're such an airport dad." I'm not entirely sure what that means, but if it makes her happy, I'll wear the title. She said the same thing when my alarm went off for our boarding time, and the way her eyes lit up was worth any confusion on my part. "All right, that's plenty of time. Now that we're here, I wish I'd left more space in my suitcase," she says, handing me six more skeins of the red yarn.

"I left some room in mine for you," I offer, trailing her around the store.

"Surprised it's not filled with your hair products." She shrugs and resumes her browsing.

"I don't have *that* many hair products," I grumble.

"Four containers at my place! That's a lot of pomade. And I still don't get it—you put it on and then you get all sweaty anyway."

"It works better with sweat," I say, a smirk playing on my lips.

"Keep telling yourself that." She reaches up and threads her fingers through my hair, messing it up. I grunt but can't help the smile tugging at my mouth as she laughs, turning back to the yarn and handing each ball to me. "Whoa," she says suddenly, pausing. "I just got déjà vu. Or maybe it's just my brain remembering our last trip to Morrisons. You holding the grocery basket, letting me throw things in."

Our Sunday night ritual—stocking up for the week. I used to get my groceries delivered, but she loves the store, loves picking out new snacks, even though my list never changes.

"It's because I like walking behind you," I murmur,

squeezing her butt. She playfully slaps my chest, her eyes sparkling.

"That reminds me, can you make that butternut squash soup this week? And get the sourdough from the shop around the corner? That was so good."

I've been trying to figure out dinners that both Daphne and I will enjoy; squashes have been a hit.

I lean in, my lips brushing her ear. "Only if you promise to taste it…off my fingers."

"Taste soup? Off of your fingers?" She snorts.

"Sounded sexier in my head."

A blush creeps up her neck. "I'll try anything once."

She adds a few more yarn balls to the basket as we plan our meals for the week. I can't take my eyes off her. Her movements, deliberate and graceful, stir something deep inside me. The way she carefully selects each ball of yarn, her fingers lingering on the soft textures, mesmerizes me.

She suddenly stops, counting the balls in the basket. "Wait… it's like I blacked out for a second. I can't possibly buy all this yarn. I don't need them! Even though they're so pretty."

"They're on me."

"Seriously?"

"This weekend's my treat."

"Thanks, Goose." Her smile widens.

"You're welcome. How much can each yarn ball cost, a hundred bucks?"

"Fifty?" She laughs. "The priciest one here is probably thirty euros, and that's for local wool."

I definitely got played by the shop owner when arranging this private shopping trip. "Go wild. I can ask them to ship a box back, if you want."

When the basket is overflowing, we head to the checkout. I spent more on yarn than I did on those damn vanilla candles, but her smile makes it worth every penny. Seeing her happiness as she moves around the store, knowing I can provide for her, makes my heart race.

As we leave, I pull her close, my voice low and rough. "You know, seeing you like this does things to me."

She looks up, her eyes sparkling. "Oh? What kind of things?"

I lean in closer. "The kind that makes me want to keep you smiling, any way I can."

———

WINTER MAKES the days short and the nights endless in Finland. The overnight train we took arrived in Lapland early this morning, and today was our only full day here before we head home tomorrow. The sun barely made an appearance before disappearing again. During twilight, we strapped on our snowshoes and ventured into the forest. Daphne's nose and cheeks turned an adorable shade of pink, catching our guide's eye and securing us an intimate meet and greet with the sled dogs.

By afternoon, we were lounging in the spa, soaking in the hot spring baths. We dared each other to plunge into the icy lake. She jumped in first, her squeal echoing off the frigid water. I couldn't back down, not with her eyes on me.

Dinner was a five-course Finnish feast. Daphne ordered every dessert: Runeberg torte, pulla, and lingonberry pie. We lingered over strong black tea, determined to catch the northern lights. Last night on the train, the sky was too cloudy and I was far too motion sick to look out the window.

Now we're back in our igloo room, trying to kill time. The glass ceiling arches overhead, offering a clear view of the sky. But nothing's going as planned.

"Cameron, you're down fifteen, and it's the last sixty seconds of the game. It's not happening," Daphne says, her body laid back on the white hotel bedding.

It's 2:00 a.m. and there are no northern lights, and now I

can't get her off. I roll my shoulders back, wiping the sweat off my brow. *Come on, Cameron.*

What am I doing wrong?

"Let's try something else then," I suggest. I've touched, licked, kissed, bit, pulled, and fucked her pretty cunt, but I can't manage to get her to finish. This is outside my realm of experience.

Daphne giggles, tucking her hand between the space of my jaw and her thigh and pulling my gaze up to hers. I pull myself out of the heaven between her thighs and sit up. Is she no longer comfortable with me? We've been fooling around for the last half hour. Everything started as usual—hot and heavy and fucking perfect. But I immediately noticed something was off with Daphne.

"What you're doing feels great, but it's my anxiety meds, and we had a long day," she assures me, wrapping her fingers in mine. "Fluoxetine sometimes just shuts off my libido. A stupid side effect."

I frown. There has to be something I can do to make her feel good. To take care of her the way she does for me. "I typically have enough tools in my toolbox."

"This isn't about your tool or your toolbox, which we both know have never failed me before. This just happens. Even when I'm alone."

"Can you explain it to me?"

"I'll do my best." She sits up on the bed and hesitates for a few moments, seemingly turning over the words in her head. "It's like every part of my mental and emotional state wants you to shred me to pieces." She laughs awkwardly. "I'm in the most romantic place in the world with the most gorgeous man—and you're wearing that mouthwatering hoop earring—but it's out of our hands."

I hear her, I really do, but I can't help but feel like I've lost when I'm meant to be her winner.

"Stupid side effects."

"Tell me about it." She playfully rolls her eyes.

I am so glad we're here. Neither of us has seen the northern lights, and it felt like the perfect thing to add to her Yes Year experiences list. However, now my big romantic gesture is feeling like a failure. Well, more accurately, I am.

"All right." I resign, put on my boxer briefs, and help Daphne get dressed, covering her forehead in kisses. The last thing I want to do is admit to her how insufficient I'm feeling right now. It's like I've let her down in some crucial way. I want to make her feel good, not just physically, but emotionally. I want her to know she's cherished, desired, and seen. "Is there anything I can do for you? To make you feel good right now?"

"We're literally in an igloo in Finland. The snow is falling, and there are miles of stars in the sky. All I really want is to feel close to you."

I kiss her hand. "I do too, sweet girl." I want to be the man who makes her feel appreciated. "How about we cuddle and watch a movie?" I offer.

"Absolutely," she says. There's a small twinkle in her eyes of something more. "And maybe you can give me a massage?"

"You'd like that?"

"Um, yes." She giggles. "I still want to be touched by you. You know, without the pressure of it needing to end somewhere."

"Sounds perfect to me. Get comfortable. I'll throw on a movie and grab some lotion."

"Now that's five-star service."

I grab the remote, flicking through the channels. "On a scale of *Up* to *Past Lives,* what level of tears are we thinking?"

"That may be the sexiest question you've ever asked me."

I chuckle. "Fuck yeah, crying movies."

"All right, now I know you're flirting with me." Daphne playfully tosses a pillow my way. I catch it and set it on the bed.

"I'm always flirting with you."

Her cheeks blush. "Then turn on *Before Sunrise* and put those hands to work."

"Yes, ma'am." I rent the movie, walk over to the bathroom sink, and pick up the vanilla-scented cream she uses, the one that always drives me wild.

My heart pounds when I return and see her lying on her stomach, waiting for me. Her cheek is pressed to her palms, and she gives me a smile. The starlight from our panoramic windows dances across her beautiful body.

I'm so lucky. I take a deep breath, feeling the heat of anticipation course through my veins.

I approach her slowly, the scent of vanilla filling my senses as I squeeze the lotion into my hands and rub my palms together to warm it. The sound of the movie hums in the background. She tugs up her shirt, revealing her bare back. My fingers tremble as they make contact, the smoothness of her skin sending a jolt of electricity through me.

She lets out a soft sigh. "Oh, that's nice."

"Relax and let me take care of you."

A small spark ignites in my chest.

I begin at her shoulders, my hands firm yet gentle as they work the tension from her muscles. She melts under my touch, her body softening with every motion. My fingers trace the lines of her spine, moving with purpose and care, as if I'm doing my pregame ritual.

"You're so beautiful, Daphne," I whisper. "This gorgeous hair, long legs, your beautiful body...every part of you is perfect."

She grins, a twinkle in her eye. "I like hearing that. It makes me feel good."

"Does it now?" I ask, raising an eyebrow.

She tilts her head ever so slightly, her eyes locking onto mine. "Yes, Mr. Grunts-instead-of-using-his-words."

A laugh escapes my lips as I give her a playful pat on the butt. "I guess I save my words for you."

"And I cherish every single one."

Her reaction gives me a hesitant boost of confidence to open up. If there was ever a right moment to tell her how Daphne makes my heart race, it's now. My hands move across her skin, tentative yet deliberate. "I want to take care of every part of you," I murmur. "I like showing you just how much you mean to me." She exhales, pressing into my touch. "When I kiss you, it's like I'm somewhere else. Feeling you under my lips, tasting the faint salt of your sweat. It…it makes me feel alive."

"As alive as when you're glaring at everyone from the goalpost?"

"Better," I respond without hesitation, surprising even myself. My hand moves slowly down to her lower back, tracing the curve of her hips as I continue the massage. I press a gentle kiss to her shoulder, my voice softening. "I can't get enough of these legs," I admit, my lips brushing against her ear. "The first time I saw you in that long, colorful sweater, you knocked the wind out of me."

"I wasn't just a sweater with legs, was I?" she teases.

"You were so much more," I reply, grinning. "Especially with all those seams you showed me."

She laughs a sound that makes my heart do a little flip. "We definitely didn't admire my mattress stitch on that rainbow sweater nearly enough."

I smirk, my tone dripping with mock seriousness. "Shame on us. Guess we'll have to admire what's on the mattress now."

In the background, *Before Sunrise* plays softly, the TV casts a warm, golden glow around our cozy little haven. The atmosphere is just right, and I let myself relax, savoring the moment.

"You're getting all mushy on me now."

"Don't get used to it. This is a one-time deal," I grumble, but the smile on my face gives me away.

"Oh, sure." She laughs, playfully rolling her eyes. "I believe that."

I try to ignore the warm feeling spreading in my chest. "You're right, I like spoiling you too much."

"You really do."

"You are my sunshine, Daphne," I say, my voice gruff but sincere. I move down her legs, onto her thighs and calves. I pause, taking a moment to admire her. This feels right. "You are precious to me," I murmur, massaging her feet as she giggles. I kiss each toe, earning more laughter. "From the tips of your toes to the crown of your head. Every part of you is special to me."

"You went into the wrong career with football when your hands can be put to such good use," she jokes as I finish the massage and gently pull her pajama shirt down, smoothing out the wrinkles on her shorts. "Honestly, if you keep this up, I might just marry you."

"Promises, promises," I mutter, putting socks on her feet, making sure she's comfortable and warm.

We cuddle up in bed, her head resting on my chest. I turn up the movie, and we lie there, enjoying each other's company.

After the movie ends, she sniffles. "It gets me every time."

I chuckle, wiping a stray tear off my cheek. "Me too."

She grins, snuggling closer. Her eyes drag up to mine before they float up to the panoramic windows above us. "Oh my god, they're here." She points upward. I follow her gaze and see the aurora borealis, ribbons of neon greens and pinks undulating across the night sky.

But honestly, the real show is Daphne. I watch her watching it, her pupils wide with wonder. This is my favorite view—her face lit up by the celestial light show.

"What?" she asks me, catching my gaze with a smile.

"Nothing. Just you," I say, wrapping my arm around her. "Come here."

We lie back, moving under the blankets, and she rests her

head on my chest. Her lavender hair cascades over both of us, and I can't help but think how perfect this moment is.

Our future has become so vivid in my mind—waking up next to Daphne, her knitting projects littering the bedside table. She spends her mornings creating patterns, planning retreats, or designing a wardrobe. I've won the Premier League and am training for the World Cup.

Our weekends are a blur of laughter and love.

Down the road, I'm coaching our kids' football games. Daphne is on the sidelines, needles clicking, knitting tiny scarves and hats to keep them warm. Maybe we'll get a dog, though deep down we're both cat people. Maybe one of each.

My nerves fizzle because I don't want anything to change. I want everything to stay as it is. This fragile, beautiful thing we've built—it scares me how much I need it.

How much I need her, and how much I want to prove to her I deserve her.

Chapter 38
Cameron

DUCK

cucumber emoji

CAMERON

Hungry?

For a salad?

Are you okay?

DUCK

Nooooooooooooooooooo silly! Im with the grls!
Did u forget alredy?

I told you last weekend when we were in teh
iggglooooo

the WAGgiees *dog emoji*

Where is my sober salad king!!!!!!!

CAMERON

How many cucumbers deep are you?

DUCK

I only have taste for one particular cucumber
and hes not hre :(((((

And a taste 4 martinis *martini emoji*

You caut me it's 5 martinis!!!!!

I**T'S PAST MIDNIGHT**, and I can't sleep without her. Tonight, her friends took her out for a night on the town, and she deserves it. She's been so busy wrapping up her final preparations for her retreat.

I sit up in bed and call her, just to make sure she's safe. She answers on the first ring.

"Caaaaaaameron," she slurs. "What a strong name that is, you know that?"

"I suppose it is."

"It's my favorite name. Cameron Hastings. Daphne Quinn Hastings." My heart lurches. I like hearing our names together. "Gosh, it has such a good mouth feel, but not as good as how your mouth feels." She bursts out laughing, a little hiccup escaping her lips. Daphne is absolutely plastered.

"Sounds like you're having fun, Daphne Quinn Hastings."

"So much," she drawls. "Soooo much. I love being with you, you know? And your forearms—nicest in the world. Has anyone told you that?"

"Not recently, no." I chuckle. "But I'm glad you think so."

"Think I do. I do-do-wop-a-doo you. I like you, Cam-a-doodle-dooooo," she croons, breaking into a ridiculous beatbox that syncs with the bass thumping in the background.

"I like you too."

"So much. Even when you're an absolute grouch. But you're my grouch, my little—I should say big, very big"—she hiccups—"Scrooge man who always gives me little presents and the best hugs. Ugh, Cameron, you give the best hugs, and you make me come, and your nose has that little bend in it that I just think is so sexy, Cameron. You are so sexy!"

She's never been drunk around me, but it's absolutely adorable.

"So are you, Daphne. Are you inside?" I ask.

"There's just something about you, you know? Like, your laugh. It's like if a puppy could giggle. And your eyes! They're like little pools of melted chocolate I want to slather all over my tongue. Have I ever told you that?"

"Once or twice." I reposition my head on my pillow, picturing her slathering chocolate all over her body. Now that is a sweet thing I wouldn't mind devouring.

"And you know what else? I always feel like I'm in this bubble of safety with you. Like if a pack of wild animals showed up, you'd take them down." She howls. "And even though your knitting skills are…questionable, it's adorable that you're giving it a shot. Oh, and it kind of turns me on when you get all teary at movies. Oops, did I just say that out loud?"

"I'm starting to get the picture," I say, trying to keep my laughter in check.

"And don't even get me started on how you look in a tux. Seriously. James Bond, who? Cameron Bond is more like it. You're just…you're just so awesome. Do you think I could knit an entire suit for *Lust Island*? I'm going to ask Georgia."

"Maybe wait to text her until the morning?" I suggest.

"Right, right, right. Always with the good ideas!"

Daphne had her first meeting with Georgia and the *Lust Island* team two weeks ago, and since then she's been on a roll with ideas for wardrobe. She's already started knitting to prepare for the premiere, which is the same week as the championship matches in May.

There's a commotion on the other end of the line. Her voice fades in and out. "Are you sure you're okay?"

"Yeah, just telling Bea here how amazing you are!" Her voice darts off the line. "No, seriously, you won't believe my man's hair, it's so soft. I could just run my fingers through it forever."

Oh boy, she's really gone. But I love her calling me her man. "Did you just—"

"Also, he has the most gorgeous you-know-what..."

"Daphne," I say more sternly.

Bea whoops and cheers, then grabs the phone. "Cameron, you better get your big cock-a-doodle-do over here before I steal your girlfriend."

"Yes! Yes! Yes!" Daphne chants.

"We should get drinks into you more often," I tease.

"You think so? I did break my heel, so maybe not this many drinks." She giggles.

"I'm coming to get you," I say, already tugging on my leather jacket and grabbing my keys.

"Yay! I can get you onto the dance floor. The girls taught me a move that I promise I didn't whip out on anyone," she purrs, mischief lacing her words.

Jealousy flares. "What move?"

"It involves a lot of shaking. I promise you'll love it."

"You'll love it!" Bea chimes in.

"I'm on my way," I say.

"Bring your forearms!" she commands, and I can practically hear the wink in her voice.

"Text me your location."

I drive through the empty London streets. When I arrive, the club-thumping bass reverberates through my car. Neon lights cast a glow on the bustling street, with a line of eager partygoers snaking around the building. I slip the doorman a couple of bills and push through the crowd, my mind blurred by flashing lights and writhing bodies.

Then I see Daphne. On the dance floor, her lavender hair shimmers like a halo under the lights. Every curve of her body is accentuated by her tiny knitted dress, a vision that makes my fists curl with raw desire. When she spots me, her face lights up, and she runs over, almost tripping on her broken heel. Her eyes sparkle with excitement as she reaches me, breathing in happy bursts. "Cameron! You came." She hugs me, placing a sloppy kiss on my cheek. She smells like a vodka distillery. "Come dance with me!" she insists, pulling me onto the crowded dance floor.

"I don't know…" I have practice in a few hours. But then she looks up at me with half-lidded eyes, and I'm a goner. She spins around, twirling and stumbling. She hooks her arms around my neck and leans in close, and before I can process it, her teeth clasp my earring, tugging and pulling.

My dick responds immediately, aching for me to take her home. Fucking hell.

"What was that?" I yell over the music.

"You got to lick my anklet; it's only fair." She opens her mouth and blinks her eyes in what I can only assume was an attempt at a wink.

"What'd you think?"

"Loved it!" Daphne purrs, sliding her hand up my inner thigh until her fingers brush against me through my sweats. "Guess you loved it too."

I pull her closer, find the curve of her ass, and squeeze hard. She gasps. Her eyes smolder with that familiar passion, making my heart race. "You're impossible, you know that?"

"And you love it," she says, sticking her tongue out.

I wrap my lips around that devious little tongue and give it a loud suck. "Yeah, I guess I do." She giggles in my arms, body swaying to the music. "Remember when you said you loved my forearms?" I say into her ear.

"Mm-hmm," she hums.

"Well, I love your everything," I say. Now is not the time to tell her what I've been slowly coming to terms with—that I love her. But I do.

I'm certain of it.

I love Daphne Quinn.

Her eyes are soft with affection. "Even when I'm a drunken mess?"

"Especially when you're a drunken mess," I reply, kissing her forehead. "You're my drunken mess."

"Let's stay like this forever."

"Forever sounds perfect." I hold her close as we sway to the music, lost in our own little world.

Chapter 39
Daphne

FEBRUARY 11

Lyndhurst FC's Cameron Hastings Seen at a Club with Influencer Daphne Quinn

IT'S SUNDAY NIGHT. The front door clicks open, which means Cameron just got back from his away game. I sit on the floor of the bedroom, braiding my hair in front of the floor-length mirror.

"Hey, sweet girl," he says, dropping his stuff by the door and lying down on the bed.

I smile. "Sven's header in your box was one for the books today."

"Wasn't it? Glad he had my back during that penalty kick." He stretches and rolls over to my side of the bed, noticing a crimson-red book on my nightstand. Oh crap!

"*Naughty Knots*?" He reads the title and reaches for it. "What's this?"

"Wait!" I bolt up, lunging across the room and yanking the pages out of his hand. "I thought it was a knitting book..." The book disappears behind my back. My blue knitted nightgown is working overtime, trying to mask the spine.

His brow quirks up with curiosity. "And?"

I blush. "I was sorely mistaken."

"Interesting." He props his head up with his palm, smirking. "Let me see it, Daphne," he says sternly.

Flush spreads across my chest and collarbones. "No."

He reaches around me, attempting to grab it, but I leap back.

A spark lights up in his eyes. That was totally the wrong move. He loves it when I toy with him. Cameron stands, towering over me. Shrinking beneath his gaze, I toss on my most innocent look and flutter my eyelashes up toward him.

"Enough. Hand it over."

"Fine, but just know that the cover is misleading." I show him the glossy cover, where there's a hand bound with rope around each finger. He takes it and flips through the pages. My insides turn and twist with excitement as he takes in the very saucy images in front of him.

"This is a book on bondage."

Be big, Daphne. I flick my eyes toward the ground, nod, and inhale before looking back up with a newfound confidence.

"Well, I ended up looking through it, and it seemed really interesting," I say in a flirty tone. "Figured it could be a fun Yes Year activity for us."

Oh my god, am I out of my comfort zone. My nerves are on edge, but I try to stay confident and own it.

"Well, we do have plenty of yarn." He tilts his chin to the wooden basket brimming with various yarns in the corner of her room. The air between us is heavy with anticipation and a touch of thrill.

"Pick a color, Cameron."

"Pick the knot, you naughty girl." He winks, returning the book to me and slowly meandering to the yarn.

"Eek! Okay, I'm actually totally excited." I sit cross-legged on the edge of my bed, flipping to a page that I dog-eared when the book arrived in the mail yesterday. What can I say? I was intrigued by all the knots and handiwork. Maybe it's the knitter in me.

"You've already done your homework?"

"Took me over an hour to find the position I wanted to try first," I admit, running my hand over the page. "Grab one of the three yarns on top—they're the best for…bondage."

"I think it's sexy that you planned this for us." He grabs the yarn in a blue-green shade that closely matches my eyes. My pulse escalates.

"Think you can manage this?" I flip the book around, showing him the instructions for a chest harness.

"I'm always up for learning new techniques," he replies, a wicked grin playing on his lips.

I sit on the bed, my heart pounding in a heady mix of anticipation and nervous excitement, as both Cameron and I read the instructions for the harness. And by *read*, I mean stare at Cameron's abs, which are looking extra taut tonight. I gulp, letting my fingers trace the soft, thick yarn in my lap. He splays a palm against my thigh, the weight possessive and reassuring. My throat feels hot as his hand climbs up my torso and his fingers wander across my skin.

"I'll start with two loops of the yarn, wrapping them around your chest from front to back."

"Should I take off my nightgown?" I ask, my pulse quickening at the mere thought of what we're about to do.

"Whatever you're comfortable with," he assures me. With that, I remove my dress in one smooth motion, tossing it to the floor. He inhales, taking in my nude body, then leans forward and whispers in my ear, "You are so gorgeous." His breath is tinged with peppermint, feeling icy along my skin. Goose bumps prickle my entire body. "Let's pick a safe word," he says as he hovers over my collarbone.

"A safe word?" I gulp, arching my back, aching for him to touch me. "My goodness, how kinky are these knots?"

"So eager for me to touch you." He chuckles in a deep tone. "Pick a word."

I meet his darkened gaze, thinking for a second. "Um —stop?"

He laughs. "Okay, so if you say *stop,* we'll stop."

"Good with me."

With that, he begins. His hands move deftly, looping the yarn around my chest with surprising expertise, given how terrible his knitting skills usually are. Cameron's touch is warm and firm, sending a ripple of shivers coursing down my spine.

"I like this," I say as he ties the first knot, snugly but not restraining, on the base of my back.

"Spread these open for me, please." He nudges my knees, and I do as he says. He flushes as he crosses the yarn over the top of my breast and uses his free hand to run along my core. "So wet already, Daph."

I blush and glance down at his boxer briefs. "Seems like we're both enjoying this."

"I really am. Although I hope I'm doing it right." He chuckles sardonically. "The aim is to create a box-like shape with the rope as I pull your arms back."

Our laughter doesn't feel awkward. It's the kind of comfort I imagine you can only have after spending years with someone.

"I think you're doing great," I say. I'll never be able to look at yarn again without thinking about this moment. Cameron's forearms flex, a vein popping as he pulls my wrists back and gets behind me. He places kisses along my shoulder blades as he secures my arm back.

"There," he says. I can almost sense the satisfied smile on his face. "Fuck, Daph, I am going to take such good care of you like this."

My heart flutters at the promise. "What's the next step in the instructions?"

His fingers pause momentarily as he glances at the pages in front of him. "It says to make sure the loops are snug but not too tight. How does it feel?"

"Good," I assure him, my voice barely more than a whisper. Cameron's fingers keep their steady pace, the loops of yarn growing steadily across my breasts as he licks, bites, and pulls on each of my hardened nipples. Each pass of his hands brings a wave of warmth, the sensation of the yarn against my skin a gentle reminder of the trust and connection between us.

Cameron evens out the yarn, his fingers tracing my body through the soft wool. Each touch is electric, the yarn soft and yielding beneath his fingers. His knuckles brush against me, a jolt of electricity that has me biting my lip to keep from gasping.

"Fucking perfect." Once he's done, he steps back, his gaze intense as it sweeps over me. "You okay?" he asks, his voice low and filled with desire.

"Yes," I whisper, the word barely audible as my heart pounds against the confines of the yarn.

"Remember, say stop, and we're done."

"I don't have any interest in stopping any time soon," I say, smiling and thankful for the reminder.

"Good."

He kisses me deeply, wrapping his hand around the base of my skull. I moan as he splits my lips with his tongue. I feel alive with him, like every nerve is on fire. The bind cinches against my wrists. I want to reach for him, touch him like I normally do, but I can't.

He's so far away, yet so close. The kiss breaks, and a devilish grin plays on his lips. I want him to map that smile across my body and pull me apart.

"Now, claim me."

"Where do you want me to claim you?"

"Anywhere," I manage to say. "I don't want to think."

"Could start at these pretty lips." He takes his thumb and swipes it along my bottom lip. "Open up." I oblige, and he swipes against the wetness on my tongue. "Though, if I'm filling up this pretty mouth, I won't get to see you smile for me. And we can't have that, can we?"

I whimper, straining against my bonds, craving any form of contact. "No."

His breath is hot against my check. I need him. "Maybe I'll skip taking my time and take you right here." He presses two fingers against my entrance, making me gasp. "Or maybe…" Cameron grabs me and easily flips me onto my knees, my face collapsing into the mattress. He gently brushes the hair out of my face. "I'll keep you here, bound and needing." His fingers trace my cheekbone, leaving a trail of fire in their wake. "All night." The suggestion sends a thrill of panic through me. "No, I don't have that kind of control even if I tried."

"More," I say the moment he pulls away.

"More what, Daphne?"

I stay quiet as my heart slams louder and louder into my chest, then whisper, "Just more. Of you. Of anything."

From the corner of my eye, I see him lower his boxers, his ample size revealing itself between us. I anticipate him plunging directly into me, but he withholds that gratification. Instead, he drags the firm tip across me, and he moans. My thoughts go haywire. He continues his game, applying pressure to my core but never providing the satisfaction of his fullness. It's maddening. "Cameron," I beg. But he doesn't stop, his gaze focused on where he's grazing me. A deeper desire stirs within me, an urge beneath the tension of the restraints, and I yearn for more, arching my back until just his tip begins to fill me.

A guttural sound escapes him.

"My sweet, needy girl." He laughs. "Already becoming so impatient."

"I am," I admit.

He runs a palm over my ties. "This still feel good? The book said it could get a little exhausting."

"So good." He starts to caress me with his fingers now, and I'm nearly thrashing on the bed with need when he begins playing, stroking and circling my clit. "That feels amazing, Cameron." The wet sound of his fingers along me and my heavy breaths echo in the room. "Feels so right."

With each word, he picks up pace, as if taking on the challenge of getting me there. It's not going to take long.

"Cameron." My voice is strained.

"I know, Daphne." He says it like a soothing promise. "Give it to me, okay?"

My body shamelessly obeys and lets go, trying to reach the overwhelming need for release that's blistering my head. I force my face into the mattress as an animalistic groan crawls out of me, my heart pounding so loudly in my ears I can't tell where I am.

"That was one." He smiles, gently patting my behind as I collapse onto my side.

My eyes widen. "One?"

He sits me on the edge of the bed and props pillows behind me so that I'm sitting with my legs hanging off the mattress. He gives my damp forehead a kiss and gets on his knees in front of me.

"Now, another," he says.

"I don't think that I can."

"You can and you will. I'll get you ready."

He doesn't wait for me to protest as he pulls open my knees, and the familiar feel of his scruff glides along the inside of my thighs before his hot breath gently kisses me. My lungs and heart stop working as a shiver shoots through my spine, and I toss my head back.

"Fuck," I groan. Cameron chuckles between my legs. He's

enjoying this, isn't he? This is payback for the damn fucking push-ups. Next thing I know, he's going to start making me count these orgasms off one by one.

I close my eyes as I moan and breathe in a wave of sensations while Cameron's mouth possessively takes me. He reaches up to trace his fingers over the harness while his tongue caresses my clit. I start to grind my hips against my will. Clearly, I was more ready than I thought I was.

"I love this," I groan. "Love it, love it, love it."

His hands spread my thighs wider, and one of his fingers teases my entrance. The soft push and pull splinters my mind. He breaks for a moment, his voice traveling up to my ears. "Look at me, sweetheart. Look at how I worship this sweet, pretty cunt."

My mouth drops open, and I do exactly as he commands. He continues his pace, relentlessly bringing me back to the edge until my walls are tightening around his fingers again. I tense and tense and tense, the yarn burning my chest. Suddenly, my mind is blank, and I collapse again, at his mercy. His arms collect me into his chest, pressing my damp skin close to his warmth. So close. So right. He kisses me and wipes the hair out of my eyes. His lips are on my cheeks, my neck, my ear with a soft bite. When I manage to regain any sort of breath, the animal that's taken over Cameron's body growls in my ear. "That's two."

I muster up the laziest protest my sore body can manage. "Absolutely not."

"You know what to say when you want to be done," he reminds me.

And for some sick, twisted reason, I don't say stop. The challenge seems all too exciting to refuse. I even manage to taunt, "You really think you can break your personal best? More than two orgasms in one night?"

A fire blazes in his eyes. "There she is. My favorite brat." He chuckles, and his tenderness disappears.

Cameron drops me onto the bed on my side and stretches one of my legs out. As he settles behind me, his hands take my other leg and wrap it around his waist.

No teasing this time, not even a warning as he thrusts himself inside of me. "Fuck, you're so hard," I gasp with disbelief. "Oh my god? This is impaling territory all over again."

He lets out a laugh. "You're going to take all of it like a good girl, aren't you?"

I am. "If you don't break me with that thing first."

"I'll put you back together," he promises. My heart soars. With that, he begins to take me slowly, deliciously.

Each stroke is attentive, as it always is when we're together. He listens to my breathing, watches me with that hawk-eyed gaze. I don't know if that's just what happens when you're fucking an athlete or if Cameron's that in tune with me, but he just knows what he's doing when he's with me. Through every groan, I tell him that.

He knows every touch that feels right. Knows every limit. Knows what lines he can cross.

This is what love feels like, I'm sure. A constant risk of being on the brink but knowing you can risk it all and be okay.

When both of his hands grip my skin and his thrusts get longer, deeper, his hips slapping against me, I know he's trying to control himself, but I can tell he's on the edge.

"Too good, Daphne, always too fucking good," he whimpers.

"Don't stop," I say and start to meet his every thrust, forcing him as deep into me as I can. I groan, grunt, and toss around beneath him until the assailing need starts to unhinge again, louder and bigger than the other two. I tighten around him until that familiar look of shock hits his face. I feel that first pulse as he releases into me, his climax shuddering through him. I keep rocking against him until my own follows. My heartbeat pounds in every pulse point across my skin.

Cameron drags his warm, comforting weight off of me. He starts by gently untying each knot, careful not to abruptly pull on any of the ropes. He carries out this process slowly and methodically, somehow even gentler than when he started. Once the ropes are removed, he checks for any areas that may have been affected by circulation issues and uses his fingers to massage those spots before sealing them with a kiss.

"One sec, okay?" he whispers in my ear, and I collapse against the pillow. He returns with one of the electrolyte drinks he keeps in my fridge and a bowl of sour gummy colas. Oh gosh. If I thought I was head over heels before, I definitely am now. "Here, fuel up."

As I nosh on my candies and down the cool liquid, he drapes me in one of my throws and cuddles in beside me.

"How do you feel?"

"Like I'm not even inside of my body."

"Good or bad?"

"Good," I promise. "What was your favorite part?"

"Honestly, the same as it always is: hearing you tell me how much you like what I'm doing."

It's gotta be that athletes have a praise kink. I blush. "Communication is important." I snicker.

"Having you tied up while you ran your mouth didn't hurt," he admits and gives my temple a kiss.

"I'm sure."

"What about you? Favorite part? Something different for next time?"

I curl up into his chest. "I never thought I'd say this, but giving up control to you...it was oddly satisfying. Like I stumbled upon a brand-new flavor of freedom sundae, with a cherry of trust on top."

"Very sweet analogy there, Duck." He laughs. "I'm glad you had fun."

I bite my lip. "And, you know, doing a role reversal could be fun. I mean, wouldn't it be intriguing for me to wear the bossy pants for a change? And for you to, you know, experience the whole surrender thingy?"

"Bossy pants for a change?" He lifts a brow at me.

I feign innocence. "Yes."

"Giving up having to think and make decisions may be a nice change."

I give him a kiss. "Well, we do have plenty of yarn."

Chapter 40
Daphne

You've got this, Daphne. You're smart, brave, and charming. This weekend will be epic, I tell my reflection in the mirror of the bathroom at Petal & Plate. I adjust a stray hair one final time, then strike a ridiculous starfish pose for good measure. A laugh escapes me, shaking off the remnants of my nervous energy. With a deep breath, I head out to deliver my opening remarks and kick off my retreat, feeling a surge of confidence.

People begin casting on their beanies for local hospital patients, and I inhale a deep breath. Young Daphne would be proud.

"Thank you everyone for coming! I'm Daphne Quinn, the mastermind behind Wooly Duck." My nerves cartwheel around my body as I look out at the packed room of fifty women, memorizing each of their faces. "This year, I embarked on a Yes Year. Basically, I signed myself up for a roller coaster of anxiety, trying scary new things, making friends, and generally grabbing life by the—excuse my language—balls," I add, earning a chuckle from the crowd.

"People always said I was too much—too loud, too enthusiastic, too different. I was the outcast who got shoved into lockers and had her gym clothes stolen. So I hid my real self, trying to fit into their mold." I pause, seeing nods and understanding eyes. "In my quest to be normal, I suffocated who I was. Anxiety took over, making me question every move." I shrug with a laugh. "Then I found knitting and a fluoxetine prescription. Knitting became my refuge, transforming my anxiety into something beautiful. It gave me the courage to embrace who I truly am." The room pulses with silent nods and glistening eyes. The soft clicking of knitting needles whispers back to me. "Knitting and this community taught me something invaluable. Being too much isn't a flaw; it's a testament to life," I say, my voice trembling with emotion. "This year, I learned that being brave enough to fail, resilient enough to feel, and audacious enough to live with your heart leading the way is something special. Your *too much* is just too vibrant for someone else's *too little*."

My heart swells. "So, thank you all for helping me stretch the boundaries of my world this year. Thank you for letting my *too much* weave into yours. And let's enjoy the weekend."

The room bursts into applause as I step away from the mic, and suddenly I'm engulfed by a swarm of new friends. I thought I'd be terrified for my first in-person meet and greet, but as soon as the first person walks up to me, my nerves fade away. It feels like being surrounded by a hive of incredibly supportive, yarn-loving bees. Their excitement is contagious, and I feel like the queen bee in this cozy hive. My cheeks ache from smiling, but I wouldn't trade this moment for anything.

Petal & Plate is decorated perfectly—exposed brick walls adorned with lush, trailing plants and twinkling fairy lights. Wooden shelves display colorful skeins of yarn and cozy knitted blankets, adding warmth to the space. After our kickoff session, we do icebreakers, the room buzzing with laughter and conversation. The vibes are immaculate, and Rosie's almond croissants disappeared within the hour—I may have had three. Bea showed up, ensuring I took a water and food break mid-morning. My sister and moms joined over video call for Miranda Lambright's chat about wool production.

A reporter from the *Stone Times* stopped by to cover the event.

As people break for lunch and I'm binding off my third beanie, I hear, "Daphne Quinn!"

I turn and spot Georgia Woods walking through Petal & Plate in a crochet sweater dress that hugs all her curves. Her pink hair is thrown up in a perfectly imperfect messy bun. After a month of video calls designing outfits together, she is even more gorgeous in person. I'm so awestruck, I might just faint. "It's so nice to meet you in person!" she says, hugging me.

"Oh my god, you smell so good," I blurt out, laughing. "I mean, hi, thank you for coming."

"And you smell like a vanilla bean cupcake. We gotta swap perfume links." She shoots me a cheeky smile. "Congrats on your event. This place is a stunner."

How is this my freaking life? "You flatter me! I had so much fun working on the strawberry skirt pattern you designed last week. Whoever ends up with it may have to sleep with one eye open."

We have about ten designs finalized for the show, but we need about fifty more before the start of the season in two months.

"Tell me about it. I made it on my season, but it disappeared before I even had a chance to wear it. I swear, one of the girls put it in their suitcase."

"They did not! Well, come this way, I'll help you get settled in," I say, leading her up the stairs while people finish up their lunch. Georgia agreed to co-lead a breakout session with me today about cyberbullying and the importance of fostering kindness and empathy online. Our first official *Lust Island* initiative together!

"I was thinking about your comment last week, about how

we can start documenting our collaboration. We should totally take a picture today. Do some fun hinting on the socials, right?" she asks.

"Let's do it," I respond, my words bubbling over with giddy excitement.

We get set up, strategically laying out our yarn and needles, and snap a photo near the table Cameron and I sat at when he first brought me here.

Our session is a success. Georgia opens up about being bullied after winning last season. She shares how anonymous trolls flooded her social media with cruel comments, mocking her appearance and questioning her talent, which led her to take a month away from all platforms to regain her mental health. Her story, so similar to my own, resonates deeply.

Others join in, sharing their experiences. Sarah, a twenty-year-old who flew out from New York, recounts how a jealous coworker spread lies about her at the office, making her dread going to work every day. Ursula, a university student, speaks about classmates creating a fake profile to harass her online, leaving her feeling isolated and scared to attend school.

It becomes clear that everyone has encountered someone who has tried to tear them down. By the end of the session, there isn't a dry eye in sight.

The rest of the day whizzes by in a blur of yarn and laughter. Cocktail hour is a riot. I feel like I've found a community that's more like family. If I could bottle up the support and enthusiasm in that room, I'd be a billionaire.

I leave Petal & Plate with cheeks aching from a daylong grin and a heart so full it might burst. One thing's for sure—even though there's one more day left, I can confidently say this won't be my last retreat.

My fingers throb with fatigue, and exhaustion seeps in as I ride the elevator up to Cameron's apartment. He insisted I stay here instead of taking a taxi home in the middle of the night. I turn on the lights and look up, and there he is.

I shake my head in disbelief. There's no way he's here. But then his flat expression blooms into a warm smile as he sees me. My Cameron. In his kit. Clutching a bouquet of flowers like a kid with a winning lottery ticket.

"What are you doing here?" I squeak out, practically launching myself into his arms. He wraps me in a bear hug. "You have a game tomorrow morning," I remind him. "You're supposed to be three hours away and resting, mister!"

"I know." He draws me closer and inhales deeply. "I came right after training, and I have to drive back, but I needed to see you on your big day. And do this." He kisses me, leaving me stunned. My knees go wobbly. My insides soften like a fire-roasted marshmallow as his warmth envelops me.

His eyes twinkle with admiration as he leans in, his lips brushing gently against my forehead, then my lips again.

"I'm so happy to see you," I murmur, burying my face into his chest.

"How'd it go?" he whispers, his breath tickling my hair. "How do you feel?"

"Probably as good as you're going to feel when you win your big game tomorrow."

"Good." His arms tighten around me. "Daph, I—" He falters, his heart thumping like crazy against his chest. I what? I'm happy to be here? I forgot something in my apartment and had to come back and get it? "I'm super proud of you, and, uh…" His face scrunches up. "I do have to get back soon. I'm so sorry. Coach didn't love that I'm not riding with the team to the match. If he finds out I broke curfew, I might end up on the bench again."

He risked that much for me? A shaky smile spreads across my face at the realization. "How long do I have you for?"

He glances at the clock on the television. "Thirty minutes."

My heart does a little flip-flop, a mix of gratitude and longing. "Well, what should we do?"

"Can we just lie down together? I missed sleeping next to you last night."

"Not a second to waste, then," I whisper.

We shuffle to the bedroom and collapse onto the bed in a heap, Cameron pulling me into his arms. I nestle against his chest, feeling the steady, reassuring rhythm of his heartbeat. My exhaustion melts away as he holds me, his presence a balm for my frazzled soul. We lie there in blissful silence, the world outside fading into oblivion, leaving just the two of us in this cocoon of cozy intimacy.

I trace little doodles on his chest, my fingers moving in sync with his breaths. "You really drove all the way here just to see me for a minute?"

He tilts my chin up, his eyes locking onto mine with that heart-melting gaze of his. "No distance is too far for a glimpse of you," he replies, pressing a tender kiss to my forehead.

We fall into a comfortable silence, our bodies entwined. For thirty precious minutes, it's just us. No worries, no obligations, just the simple joy of being together.

My heart takes flight, and I'm pretty sure I'm unequivocally, undeniably, up-in-the-air in love with Cameron Hastings.

Chapter 41
Cameron

Lyndhurst FC Blaze to Victory: Oakwood United Win Marks Tenth Straight!

CAMERON

Stopped by the complex. Forgot Jung's gift.

See you soon.

DUCK

Okay! xo

Hurry though, or you'll miss the flash mob dance Bea and I just choreographed.

CAMERON

And miss you shaking that pretty ass around?

Wouldn't dare.

DUCK

Especially since I wore the low-back sweater dress that didn't block properly.

Dangerously short.

CAMERON

Killing me.

DUCK

Might need your big, strong hands to block
any unwanted flashes. ;)

CAMERON

Good time to remind everyone on the team
that I can throw a fucking punch.

DUCK

Why is that doing it for me?

In all seriousness, no violence.

CAMERON

In all non-seriousness?

DUCK

I'll save the move where I raise my hands in
the air for when you're here.

See you soon. xxxxx

CAMERON

x

I flick on the lights in Daphne's apartment, which has felt more and more like home to me over the past two months. The soft glow illuminates the fresh bouquet of flowers, a framed photo of Daphne and me snowshoeing in Finland, and a half-eaten box of pastries on the kitchen counter. My eyes land on the purple gift bag meant for Jung when my phone vibrates again.

I'm half expecting a sneak peek of my girl's dance routine or a snapshot of her in that sexy sweater dress. But instead, it's a message from an unknown number.

UNKNOWN NUMBER

rumors goin around ur tryin to get me
suspended.......

well i got smthn to say about u

Article From The Stone Times - The Talk of The
Town Section

How the fuck did Charlie get this number?

I still haven't pressed charges with the Football Federation.
Even though I detest causing a scene, I went out of my way to
gather evidence and secure the footage. We've got a video of
him recording me inside the Overton locker rooms, and the security guard's ready to give a statement. If I pushed it, I could
make a case. But the truth is, I don't want to go up against Charlie. The thought of it makes my chest ache, like there's a weight I
can't shake off.

I take a breath. I should ignore the message and head to
Ivan's for Jung's birthday, but curiosity gnaws at me, and I click
the link.

MARCH 10

Daphne Quinn's Charitable Heart Saves Lyndhurst FC Keeper, Cameron Hastings

*Cameron Hastings hasn't just had a rough start at Lyndhurst FC
this Premier League season; he's had a disastrous year. After the
humiliating nude livestream he himself leaked last March and a
forced benching mid-season, he's been desperately trying to get his
act together. Thankfully, Lyndhurst FC has been on a tear as of late.
We can't help but question how much of that has to do with the
keeper's skillset.*

*The footballer was linked to knitting influencer Daphne Quinn
nearly five months ago. Rumors had died down, but the pair have
recently been sighted clubbing around London and at an airport in
Finland.*

*So who is this woman mending Cameron Hastings's heart? Is
she the reason for his sudden form? And, most of all, what happens*

to Lyndhurst when she inevitably leaves him?

She's not just about yarn and needles. Here she is pictured at UCSF Medical Center in San Francisco after donating over one thousand beanies! In November, she spearheaded an auction for Lyndhurst's beloved groundskeeper, and she hosted a fabulous mental health awareness knitting retreat last weekend, raising a whopping fifty thousand pounds for an anti-cyberbullying charity.

Hastings's former teammate, Charlie Lewis, stated in an interview yesterday that Hastings has always been "a troubled, broken man" who likes the media to see him as a victim.

The public can't help but question if the keeper's recent success is due to his new fling breathing life back into his game. Can her charitable heart continue to help him turn over a new leaf? As the last two months of the season unfold, all eyes will be glued to this compelling duo.

NEXT TO THE article is a photograph of Daphne's beaming face beside a blurred screenshot of me in the shower from last year's fucking livestream.

Hundreds of thousands of people are devouring this article.

My vision starts to swim. Every one of my deepest fears is laid bare. *Daphne Quinn, too good for Cameron Hastings. The catalyst for his sudden turnaround.*

What *will* happen to me if she leaves?

My fingers clench around the phone, the device practically groaning under the strain. I read the article again and again and again until the words start to echo in my mind.

This is the truth, isn't it? Beneath this relationship lies a broken man. What was I thinking letting Daphne treat me like I wasn't? How could I ever pretend I'm not?

I knew, deep down, that being with me would only tarnish her image. Future headlines play out in my mind: *Cameron Hastings Flounders as Another Influencer Leaves Him. Cameron*

Hastings Surrenders Another Girlfriend. Each imaginary article feels like a dagger to my heart.

I'm a complete fool for ever thinking I deserved her. For believing our relationship had a chance. Everyone sees me for what I am—broken. My heart twists in anguish, a vise tightening around my chest. What if every moment we shared was built on me being someone I'm not? Daphne deserves the world, and all I've ever brought anyone is darkness. A trail of failures that shadows my every step.

I try to read the article again, but I can barely make it past the first few lines.

"Fuckkkkk!" The word rips from my throat.

I wasn't strong enough to keep the paparazzi from ruining my life.

Couldn't put an end to their tabloid nonsense after all this time.

I hate that I can't be the person Daphne deserves.

I hate…me.

The truth I've been dodging all year has been staring me in the face. The livestream, that mess at Overton, Charlie's betrayal, even Mal Kelly's absurd press parade—each one chiseled away at me, reshaped who I am.

I'm not the old Cam, no matter how desperately I wish I could be when I'm with Daphne. That Cam, the one who'd have truly earned the right to be with her, is long gone.

The room feels like it's closing in on me. The walls seem to tilt, and I collapse onto the couch, clutching my head in an attempt to quiet the storm of thoughts. But they only grow louder, more insistent.

Pathetic, Hastings. Rossi's voice is now my own, bouncing around my skull with unrelenting force.

Time becomes meaningless—minutes, hours, who knows—until the front door creaks open.

"Cameron?" Daphne's voice calls out. *No.* She can't see me like this.

"I thought you were at Bea's?" I spring up from the couch, my voice harsher than intended.

"I hopped in the car the moment I saw the article." She takes a cautious step back, concern etched on her face. "Are you okay?"

"I need to leave," I mumble, my voice barely audible. I avoid her eyes as I head for the door. I can't face her right now. I'm not strong enough to figure this out.

"Wait. That story was awful," she says, her hand reaching out to touch my arm. I flinch away. "None of it is true. You know that, right? The reporters are just doing their job. It's how they make a living."

I take a deep breath, trying to keep the anger swelling in my chest from spilling over onto the one person who's always been there for me. "Daphne." My chest tightens. "I—I'm sorry, but I can't do this."

This is the only way. The only way to keep her safe from my mess.

"Yeah, those reporters are absolute jerks!" Sourness churns in my gut. She takes two small steps forward, approaching me like I'm a stray cat.

I look away, unsure if I can say what needs to be said. "You don't understand." My fingers pick at my bleeding cuticles.

At first, I thought she was just a distraction. A beautiful, maddening, way-too-good-for-me distraction. But Daphne's become something else entirely—a mirror that reflects the man I'm not. A man who would worship and adore a woman like her. Who would succeed on his own two feet. Who wouldn't have his shame attached to her accomplishments. Who wouldn't need to save his relationship with his own team. Who wouldn't need her to praise him into usefulness on the pitch.

She shouldn't have to carry the weight of my burdens.

Daphne deserves someone whole, someone who isn't a work in progress.

"You deserve someone who isn't a project, Daphne."

"Everyone's a project, aren't they?" she murmurs, her thumb brushing away a tear I didn't even realize had fallen. Her eyes are glassy and filled with a sorrow that cuts me deeper than any words ever could. I hate that I'm the one causing her pain again, but I should've never let it get to this point.

"You're not listening," I say, my voice rough. "I can't be the man you need."

"What does that even mean?"

"This whole year, all I've brought into your life is chaos. The tabloids, the hateful comments. You had to step away from what mattered to you because of me." The words are a bitter pill I can't seem to swallow. She's too good, too kind, too perfect. "I can't keep asking you to clean up my messes. I can't rely on you to be the only source of happiness in my life. Because you do make me happy, Daphne. So incredibly happy. You've brought color and joy into my world, but without you, I don't even know who I am. And I can't do that to you. I need—" The words feel like shards of glass in my throat. "I need to figure things out on my own. I need to fix myself."

"Hey, wait a minute! Don't I get a vote here? Isn't it up to me if I want you, flaws and all, even if you think you need a major renovation?" She tries to sound stern, but her voice wobbles.

I take a step back, my eyes tracing every detail of her face. "I've messed up with you once before. Twice, if you count me leaving after that first night. I can't start something real with you until I'm a man you can be proud of."

"What does that mean for us?"

"We're done."

"Can't we talk about this?"

My heart clenches painfully. "I can't say something I'll regret."

I turn away, my feet heavy. Each step feels like I'm abandoning the only anchor I've ever had. She's the only one who's ever made me feel like I have a place in this world, and yet here I am, walking away from the best thing that's ever happened to me. But somewhere deep inside, I hope that one day I will be the partner she deserves.

Chapter 42
Cameron

DAPHNE'S GONE.

Because of me.

I've been holed up in my apartment the past two nights, too afraid of being around her, of seeing her face, of wishing I could take back everything I said and beg for another chance.

Which turned out to be pointless, because when I went to practice today, Sven and Omar asked me why Daphne left. She texted them this morning, saying she was heading back to California. She said she loved London and wanted to stay, but she left because of what I did to us.

I never wanted this to happen, but maybe if we're five thousand miles apart, I can't ruin her life any more than I already have. Maybe it's for the best. I can finally learn to stand on my own. The reminder of how lonely I felt when I was trying to do just that floats to my mind. I shudder at the thought and force my attention back on the road.

Rain pounds the windshield of my Stradale as I speed between Royal Albert and Royal Victoria Docks, engine roaring, wipers struggling with the downpour. My grip on the black leather steering wheel burns my palm.

Cameron Pathetic Hastings.

How could I have ignored my own fucking unresolved issues for so long? I did the right thing by walking away from her.

The thought doesn't feel convincing, but I'm certain it's true.

The radio crackles to life, a familiar melody cutting through the static as the streets blur past.

You'll never be good enough. Be better.

The ghostly piano melody for "Bring Me to Life" sends chills down my spine before it's drowned out by the crash of guitar riffs, the thunder of drums, and the scream of strings.

Save me from the nothing I've become.

I slam my hand on the dash as the car skids on a slick patch of water in the road. "You've got to be fucking kidding me."

Adrenaline spikes, ramming my heart against my ribs. I'm pushing too hard, driving too fast, but I can't slow down. It's like speed could somehow outpace the memories, outrun the regret.

But they're always there, she's always there, in the rearview mirror, no matter how fast I go.

The radio volume climbs as my speed picks up. Damn it. I relax my neck and flex my fingers, seeking control. Then I latch on to the lyrics.

"Wake me up inside!" I yell along with the tune. My teammates were right. I'm just like a fucking moody teenager. My hands beat a relentless rhythm on the steering wheel.

I glance at the center console and spot a strand of purple hair, a stark contrast against the dark interior. She's everywhere. I swipe at the strand, feeling its silkiness between my fingers.

The hollow ache inside me cracks open. My nose tingles, my eyes sting.

In a futile attempt to hold back the onslaught of emotion, I slam my palm against my face. Too late. One more flaw she discovered in me, turning me into some pathetic, weeping bastard.

Outside, the rain intensifies, the roads becoming rivers. I should ease off the accelerator, but I don't give a damn.

Whatever the future holds, I've earned it. The failure, the loss, the gaping void where she once fit perfectly.

What if this was a mistake? What if, in losing her, there won't be any saving me?

I ARRIVE at the Lion's Lodge with barely a gallon of gas left. The rain is still relentless as I run upstairs and hover in front of her door. The last place I saw her.

Fucking hell. At least there's no temptation to knock, knowing she's far away from here.

I unlock my apartment, yank my jacket off, and toss the leather onto the couch. As I do, something on the inside sleeve catches my eye.

Curious, I run my fingertips over a small black heart embroidered into the leather. How did I not notice this before? It's a tiny, intricate detail, almost like a secret message sewn into the fabric.

Daphne.

Heartache grips me as I bundle up my jacket in my fist. I look up and spot the kitchen counter, cluttered with the checkered coasters and potholders she knitted for me. My gaze drifts over to the stack of blankets piled next to the couch, each one a reminder of her warmth and care.

I can't breathe. I dash to my bedroom, and mocking me from my bed is the tiny football she gifted me at Christmas. It's too hot in here. I pull off my sweater and go to the closet, searching for a new shirt. Wedged between my clothes and kits is the red sweater she knitted. My vision blurs as I tear through my things, finding her everywhere—hearts stitched into sleeves, the scarf I bought at Femi's auction, black and charcoal sweaters.

I drop to the floor, clutching the red sweater.

I rake my hands through my hair, realizing I wrecked the best thing in my life because of my stupid fears. She always treated me with kindness and patience, and I repaid her by walking out on her without ever admitting how broken I truly am. I relied on her to be the sun in every single day of my life. Even with my teammates helping me rediscover myself, I haven't been able to silence the voices gnawing at my mind. The brief moments of peace I got were because she was near.

The voices in my head are telling me I'm pathetic. Shouting at me about the things I don't deserve.

Daphne doesn't need a person who's haunted by the ghosts of his past, who hasn't been able to move forward. And besides, how can I achieve greatness on the pitch when I can barely breathe in my own apartment?

I kept my mouth shut while tabloids spread nonsense. I let Rossi relentlessly tell me I'm worthless instead of standing up for myself. I let Charlie get away with hurting me because I was too afraid of letting him have that power over me. The years at Overton and the livestream leak have been eating at me, poisoning the best thing in my life. I could've taken control of the story, reported it to the Football Federation. Instead, I acted like a coward.

I ran from her like a coward.

My mistakes pile up like a bad car wreck. Every moment I chose silence over courage, every time I forewent being soft to fake being tough.

I have to make myself right, like I promised. Not just for the game I've dedicated my life to, but to ever have a chance at getting Daphne back. I have to prove to her that I can be who she needs me to be.

I want to be the man I deserve to be.

Now that I'm alone, the weight of my actions hits me like a freight train.

I need help. Serious help. Someone to talk to. My past trauma can't keep holding me back. Even if Daphne and I are done, I owe it to myself to stop prioritizing saves on the field and start saving myself.

It's time for me to find a bottom I can bounce off of.

Cameron Underdog Hastings.

Now that feels like something very familiar.

> CAMERON
>
> Hey.

Do you have a therapist you can recommend? I know you did a lot of research for yours.

BROOKLYN

Of course, I have just the one!!

Are you alright?

Jenny Therapist Contact

> CAMERON
>
> Trying to be.

BROOKLYN

:(Okay

I'm on a plane heading to a meet but I'll call you after!!

What's going on?

> CAMERON
>
> Broke it off with Daphne.

BROOKLYN

What?!??? Why?

> CAMERON
>
> Need to get better.

BROOKLYN

Cam...

We'll chat more tonight. I'm proud of you for reaching out. This is a big step and I'm here for you!!!!

CAMERON

Shouldn't have kept you at arms length for this long.

Sorry.

BROOKLYN

I get it. We all do <3

Everything will be alright...I'm sure of it.

CAMERON

Thanks.

Chapter 43
Cameron

Lyndhurst FC's Winning Streak Has Ended
with Another Draw Against Northwood City

SWEAT SEARS my face as I pummel the treadmill's speed button.

My body revolts, every muscle screaming for mercy, lungs clawing for air like a drowning man. Sleep has become a stranger these past three weeks, and nothing is helping. Each evening blends into the next, a never-ending cycle of regret and longing.

It's not just the physical exhaustion beating me down; it's the heartache. I see her in my dreams and feel her absence in every corner of my life. I miss her so much.

Every step on this treadmill feels like a step away from the life I could have had with her.

Jenny, the therapist I started seeing three weeks ago—on Brooklyn's recommendation—has made me expose the uncomfortable by discussing personal and painful experiences. We began with my move to the UK and how I started to sever ties with my family and LA team shortly after. Begrudgingly, I've been logging in twice a week for our virtual sessions.

Daphne always emphasized the importance of a support system, and she was right. Talking to someone with no preconceived opinions about me has been helpful.

Therapy has been revealing, though uncomfortable. The symptoms I'm experiencing—insomnia, hypervigilance, and emotional numbness—are consistent with Complex PTSD. Hearing that was tough, but it made sense. The nightmares, constant dread, and inability to connect with others are deeper wounds, not just stress. Jenny has been guiding me to confront these feelings rather than bury them. It's a slow process, but each session feels like peeling back layers of scar tissue. Finally putting a name to what I'm experiencing brings a strange sort of comfort. It means there's a path to recovery, even if it's a long one. I feel like I'm walking two steps forward and one step back every day. *There's no progression without regression*, Jenny always reminds me.

It's exhausting.

A long, lonely road.

"Cameron." A voice slices through the relentless rhythm pounding in my ears. My vision flickers, but I'm unyielding, forcing the speed, demanding more from my drained body. *I can be better.* "Cameron!" Ivan's shout stabs through the fog.

My head shakes in refusal. With an exasperated sigh, he yanks the treadmill's cord from its socket. The belt grinds to a jarring halt, and I rip off my headphones.

"What?" I bark, my breaths jagged. The Lyndhurst gym reverberates with my outburst, filled only with the defensive line and our captain. All of their eyes are trained on me.

"You were going so hard, you were going to hurt yourself," Ivan declares, handing me a towel.

I glance at my heart rate monitor. 185 bpm. *Fuck.* "My mind's elsewhere."

"We noticed," Sven says with a frown.

"We've got nine matches left," Tamu reminds me. "We can't afford another draw. Not when Lyndhurst has a shot at victory for the first time in ten years."

"I know." The memory of that draw-deciding goal is still fresh. The sting of the ball on my gloves, the sinking feeling as it sailed past. The echo of my mistake is a constant reminder of what I've lost.

Jung tries to ease the tension. "You wanna talk about it?"

They're trying to help, but their words just scrape over my raw wounds.

Noise. All of it is noise. A dull roar in the back of my mind.

All I see is purple. Everywhere. In our uniforms, in our stadium seats, anytime I close my eyes.

I can't bring myself to reach out to her. Every time I think about it, I freeze, mulling over the right words, trying to ensure I won't bolt again. Do I even deserve her forgiveness? I keep my back turned, masking my face. They can't see how much this is tearing me apart.

"I'm in a bad place," I admit.

My defense line flanks me, and I collapse onto the nearby bench.

"What's going on?" Tamu asks.

My stomach twists. I feel broken in front of them, but they're all I got. Besides my family, they're the ones who've been with me through everything. "I fucked it up with Daphne."

"She's in love with you. Don't be a muppet," Omar says.

"Whatever happened can be fixed," Jung suggests.

Right here, in front of my team, I feel myself unravel. My face sinks into my hands, the weight of everything pressing down as I struggle to keep it together.

"The man she thought she had was not one I could be." I let the words escape from my mouth. "I've been working on myself and trying to make things right, but I'm scared it won't be enough. Some part of me is afraid that I don't deserve her."

Ivan sits beside me. "Cameron, I've been married a long time, and to this day I am still trying to reach my wife's level. If you feel like you don't deserve Daphne, you have to work that out for yourself. That's what's blocking you both from being happy."

"Everything that happened at Overton. Rossi's…abuse. What Charlie did. I hadn't realized how much it broke me. It shattered any sense of self I had. It destroyed me. And instead of fixing it, instead of being a man and working on things with her, I pushed Daphne away."

"There are many ways to be a man," Ivan says, his voice steady and firm.

It's hard to drown out the months of negative thoughts that have been on repeat in my head. It's not easy to just flip a switch and believe I'm enough.

Tamu is the first to break the silence. "There's this idea that men have to be tough, that showing emotion is a sign of weakness." His tone is serious but soft. "It's what makes us bottle things up and have heart attacks at forty instead of ever asking for help. It's what made you think you had to deal with what happened at Overton on your own."

Ivan nods. "We've all been there. Feeling like we have to be invincible, that we can't show vulnerability. But that's bullshit. Being a man isn't about being tough all the time. It's about being honest and being able to admit when you're hurt and when you need help."

"You've been through hell, Cameron. No one expects you to handle it alone. You said it yourself—you've been broken. But that doesn't make you less of a man. It just makes you human," Sven says. I look up at my friends.

"Daphne loved the person you are. Whatever you did, certainly there's a path back." Jung pats my shoulder.

"She's already given me my second chance. She may not want anything to do with me after the way I left things." Guilt and shame tug at each of my nerves. "I don't know if I can make things right," I admit.

"We never leave a lion behind, remember?"

Omar bumps his sneakers against mine. "You don't have to do it alone."

"You'll find your way to being the man you want to be." Ivan nods. "You know, speaking out about things like this is important. Especially in sports. It's something Daphne would have pushed for. Just a thought, but maybe it's something to consider."

I nod, taking in their words.

"I think I'm ready to press charges against Charlie," I admit, my voice steadier than I feel.

It's the next step.

Ivan's eyebrows lift, a flicker of surprise breaking his usual gruff demeanor. "Really?" he asks, a hint of something—pride, maybe?—in his voice. I nod again. "I happen to know someone at the Football Federation," he says, his tone softening. "They can help speed things up. With the footage of him recording you and the security guard's testimony, it should be a straightforward case."

"Fuck yeah," Omar says.

My heart thrums wildly in my chest.

No more running away.

No more letting fear dictate my life.

The livestream has gnawed at the edges of my sanity for a year. It's time for justice to be served. Not just for me, but for anyone this might happen to in the future.

My mind flashes with the headlines that will surely be published after I come forward, but I push them aside. I can't keep letting them have this power over me. It's the reason I lost

Daphne. I have to seize control, even if it's daunting. There's no other way I can start to heal, to rebuild.

If there's a way forward, then there's also a way toward Daphne. She deserves someone who can face the tabloids. Someone with courage and integrity, not like the coward I've been. I need to stop letting my fears and trauma steal my life from me. I need to be brave. For her and for us.

"And, most importantly, if I want to get my girl back," I say. "I'll need your help."

This isn't just about me anymore; it's about her knowing I will fight for our future. I still have a shot at becoming the man she thought I was.

I'll win her back.

Chapter 44
Daphne

A<small>PRIL</small> 13

At Daphne Quinn's Insistence, *Lust Island* Agrees to Donate 1% of Season's Profits to The Kindness Coalition Ahead of New Season's Wardrobe Collab

DAPHNE@WOOLYDUCK.COM

Subject: Patterns for Review

Georgia and Lust Island Team,

Thanks again for your decision to contribute to The Kindness Coalition. We're really making a change! Attaching some of my concept designs for this coming season. I kept the patterns very easy—I promise a squad of football players could do it. Let me know what you think!

GEORGIAWOODS@VIGGLE.COM, pr@lustisland.com

Subject: GW's Favorites and Bikinis!

Miss girl, you are blowing me away! Mugged Off Miniskirt—

screeching. Let's do the Casa Amor Cover-Up in three shades.
Love that it could fit a range of body types.

Attaching what I was thinking for the bikinis, let me know. Still
workshopping names, don't think the Bully Bikini has the right
intentions.

DAPHNE@WOOLYDUCK.COM
Subject: Color Palette Galore
What about the Band Together Bikini? Lust Island team, this
one's up to you. Here's a first pass on color palettes. Thinking we
could include some golden thread through these oranges and pinks?

PR@LUSTISLAND, georgiawoods@viggle.com
Subject: Approval Granted, Production Is Starting!
Ladies, you are blowing us away. These designs, patterns, and
colors are just what we need for this season. Would love to have
some finals to sign off on by the end of the month so we can get
them into production. Appreciate the quick turnaround.

DAPHNE@WOOLYDUCK.COM
Subject: Final Touches
Amazing. I'm wrapping up location scouting for my next retreat
and will get the finals to you by the end of the month. So excited for
the season premiere next month!

FOR THE PAST MONTH, this tiny bungalow, just a ten-minute walk
from the Santa Cruz Boardwalk, has been my home. It's a far cry
from the comfort of my place back in London, but it's mine.
Yarn, patterns, and *Lust Island* color palettes are spread across

every available surface. Nearby, my little window nook is set up for hosting livestreams. In the corner, there's a stack of agendas for my upcoming San Francisco knitting retreat at a yarn store in Presidio Heights, happening at the beginning of May—this one was much quicker to plan. I used a lot of the same sponsors from my first retreat, and the yarn store is allowing me to host for free in exchange for promotion.

Sure, my bedsheets no longer have the scent of grass on them. And, sure, there isn't a teeming amount of men's hair pomade on my sink or glass containers of meal-prepped veggies in the fridge. My Saturdays are quieter now—I watch Premier League matches on the rattan couch without Bea's banter in the background. But we FaceTime once a week, and she spills all the team gossip—even updates on Cameron, which always make my heart ache.

But here I am, not living on pause.

I slip on my jelly Mary Janes, throw my crochet bag over my shoulder, and head out the door. I've been making it a goal to get out at least once a day—whether it's walking on the beach, dinner with my moms, or driving up to the city each week for a milkshake at the St. Claridge with Juni. I stick around for an hour every time, partly hoping Cameron will walk in and sit in my booth again.

I sigh, locking my door.

Time to face the day, one stitch at a time.

Spring is doing its thing in Santa Cruz, with poppies popping up on every corner like they own the place. The morning air is crisp on the short walk to the boardwalk. I hang a left, heading to my favorite bench. The heat is picking up, and I can't fake it—I miss London's gloom. I miss my friends' faces. The life I pieced together, bit by bit.

I kick off my shoes, sink my toes into the sand, and watch the morning sun battle the fog. The sea lions bark near the pier, and seagulls screech above me. The salty air twists my hair, and my mind drifts to his hands tangling in my waves.

Even with the persistent ache in my heart, I know that giving the situation space was the right choice.

The day after Cameron ended things with us, I caught the first flight from Heathrow to San Francisco. I couldn't stick around. I didn't want to make it hard on the guys, didn't want to have to avoid Cameron in the hallway or feel the constant weight of what could've been hanging over us.

I wouldn't have been able to give him the space he needed or deal with my heartache if I were across the hall from him.

However much I wanted to stick by his side—to help him figure things out, to convince him that he never needed to change —it wouldn't be right. That's not my place.

It's not my job to fix the boy with the sad eyes. It's not my job to fix anyone.

I won't trade my peace for his turmoil.

Time is supposed to heal, but some days it feels like the clock is ticking agonizingly slow. How could he feel he was beneath me? I thought we loved helping each other. Growing together. What did he think he was going to regret saying before he walked out on us?

The thought twists my stomach in knots. I know he has deep scars, but I was there for him. I loved him without wanting to fix him. I just wanted to stand by him.

If he saw himself as someone undeserving of the love we shared, there's only so much I could do to try and convince him otherwise.

After everything that's happened—pulling myself together, moving past the storm of bullies, and finding my voice again—I won't dim my light to make him or any man feel better about themselves. It's a hard truth, but the love I want would never make me think I had to sacrifice my own glow.

I understand his pain, and I genuinely hope he finds a way to heal. I wish only the best for him. He was my first love—I would never wish for anything else. But I know my worth and my boundaries, and I can't be the one to hold him together while he works through what happened to him. I have to protect myself. Even if it means stepping back and letting go.

But I miss him.

I miss the promise of the life I thought we'd bumble through together.

But he was more into self-preservation than us-preservation.

Maybe, somewhere down the road, that's something we can both be thankful for.

The tears slip out unbidden. My first real heartbreak—the worst item on the Yes Year list. They say there's a first time for everything—whoever *they* are could've added *and it's going to suck a lot*. My hands itch to reach for my phone, to tell him that, to tell him anything. To hear the deep sound of his voice one more time. But I resist.

If Cameron needs space, then I won't force my way back into his life.

I sit on my favorite green bench—the same bench I saw that elderly man knitting on when I was at one of the lowest points of my life. This bench has seen it all—my tears, my dreams, a few panic attacks here and there.

With a deep breath, I pull out my needles and yarn.

You're going to be just fine. You're going to be big, larger than life.

Be big, Daphne fucking Quinn.

APRIL 19

Lyndhurst FC Back on Track with Third Win in a Row—Can They Keep It Up the Rest of the Season?

BEA MATOS

Are you seeing this???

DAPHNE

No, what's going on!!!

BEA MATOS

Turn on the game!

Without thinking, I toss the pattern for the Bind Together Bikini to the side and fumble toward the living room. The game is already playing on my TV. My mouth drops open in disbelief as I witness the entire Lyndhurst team march onto the field, their torsos draped in knitwear. My fingers scramble for the remote, cranking up the volume.

"This is…strange," the announcer begins, confusion tingling his voice. "Apparently the sweaters are meant to convey a message? I'm sorry, what's that last word?"

"Wait, is that a certain expletive?" his co-host chimes in.

Duck.

"No, Richard, I believe that says *duck*."

"Wonder if that has anything to do with Hastings's ex, the knitting sensation Daphne Quinn, also known as Wooly Duck online."

Hearing my name on TV sends me into overdrive as the cameraman zooms in on the team.

The sweaters are a complete disaster. They look like they were attacked by a pack of yarn-hungry moths. Some resemble half-knitted vests, others have streams of yarn trailing to the grass like colorful wedding trains. There are players who've resorted to scrawling words across their chests in what can only be described as chicken-scratch handwriting, while others have decided to stick letters onto their shirts with duct tape. My star pupil, Sven, stands out from the crowd, proudly wearing a sweater with a neatly stitched S.

Cameron, in the midst of the lineup, sports a D on his chest.

As the camera pans over the team, he locks eyes with the lens, as if he knows I'm here, glued to the screen, dissecting each brief peek of him on the television.

My traitorous heart flutter-kicks in my chest.

It's been five weeks of silence. Yet staring right at me over an international broadcast is a knitted apology—*I am sorry, Duck.*

I'm speechless.

Of course, I hoped he'd reach out, but this is massive. He's making a statement even though he knows the tabloids will go wild over this.

For the next ninety minutes, I stare at the TV screen, wondering if the sweaters will make another appearance.

Cameron asked his team to help him apologize to me.

For what? For letting us end? For pushing me away?

My brain feels like a bingo cage.

The game ends with Lyndhurst snagging another victory, three to zero. I leap off the couch and make the three-step journey to my kitchen, scavenging for any comfort snacks. I rummage through the cabinets, snatching a bag of sour colas and some frozen grapes—Cameron's idea of a perfect combo, which I now begrudgingly crave.

"In his first interview since his transfer last year, Lyndhurst keeper Cameron Hastings will be answering questions today." A voice from the TV pipes up. I spin around, eyes wide, and rush for the television.

Cameron fills the screen. He's at the postgame press conference, blinking under harsh lights and flashing cameras. Microphones are thrust in his direction. I can practically feel the tension from here. I swear my anxiety has anxiety right now.

"Cameron, congrats on the clean sheet and another win! To get right into it, are you leaving Lyndhurst?" a reporter from the front row bellows.

I take a deep breath, steeling myself for the answer.

"No, I'm not leaving Lyndhurst," Cameron declares, his kit still clinging damp to his skin. Hair slicked back over his head. "I want to talk about something important today." His voice holds a gravity I haven't heard before. "Last season was rough for me. As everyone knows, Charlie Lewis from my old team was suspended for unethical and harmful conduct after he publicly streamed me taking a shower at Overton Stadium."

Cameron pauses, allowing the weight of his words to settle. "But I'm not the only player who's been harmed by what many of us view as harmless pranks and just jokes. Over the past few weeks, I've learned that many players in the league are in the shadows of shame cast by toxic masculinity. It's despicable that we've allowed so many men to suffer in silence, believing they had to endure it alone. Which is why I'm speaking up. I hope that others find the courage to step forward too. I'm certain that the online circus will come for me for saying this, but you aren't alone. This culture has been festering for decades. Too many people suffer quietly, thinking they have to tough it out on their own."

My heart is doing an impromptu drum solo in my chest. What in the name of all things wooly is happening? Is Cameron seriously opening up about this now?

Reporters' questions come in waves, but Cameron continues, ignoring them. "I'm a professional football player, and I go to therapy. There's this idea that footballers need to be tough all the time, on and off the pitch. That the only emotions we're allowed are anger, pride, and joy. I bought into that for a long time.

But it wasn't until I joined Lyndhurst, was welcomed in by my teammates—my brothers, my blood—and met someone who showed me real compassion that I realized how wrong I was. The truly strong ones? They're the people who embrace every feeling, who aren't afraid to use their platform to talk about them."

My ears ring as I attempt to process what he's saying.

He pauses, adjusting the microphone before continuing, "If you've ever rooted for Lyndhurst on the field, now's the time to show your support off it too. And if you've taken it upon yourself to cast stones and leave hateful comments online for anyone associated with our team, we open our arms to you, especially."

I clutch my blanket tighter around me, half expecting him to call out my name next.

A vein in Cameron's forearm twitches as he runs a hand through the scruff peppering his jaw. I'm proud of him. He's facing the beast he's been trying to escape.

"Which is why my teammates and I are proud to announce a new foundation, Birds of a Feather, focusing on the mental health of all Premier League players."

My eyes blink rapidly, my mouth dropping open. He's starting a charity for mental health?

Birds of a Feather.

Duck and Goose.

Our nicknames for each other.

The room suddenly fills with the chatter of reporters. He points to one. "Tiara with the *Stone Times*. You had a question?"

"What exactly is the function of this charity?"

"We're going to advocate for every team in the league—hell, beyond the league—to hire a full-time therapist on staff," he says surely. "My own experience with therapy has helped me deal with all sorts of feelings I didn't even realize I was wrestling with. Because of my own hurt, I pushed away someone who was close to me, and I've been working endlessly to repair the ache I've been living with for months." Oh my goodness, he's talking about me. "Every single one of us—the players, the staff, our coaches, our management—we're all fighting battles inside. We deserve to play the game as mentally fit as we can be."

There's a lump in my throat, a traffic jam of emotions looking for an exit. The man I love is not just saying he's changed; he's actively proving it to the world.

His words echo in the empty chamber of my chest, stirring up a bittersweet kind of ache.

"Does this have anything to do with Daphne Quinn?"

"Is that who the sweater apology was for?"

"No more comments at this time." He strolls off the stage.

I'm left here, gaping at the screen. There's this whirlwind of emotions inside me, like I swallowed a snow globe.

Do we still have a shot?

And is it enough? Can it stitch up the gaping hole he left in my heart when he walked away from us?

> DAPHNE
>
> Can we talk?

GOOSE

Yes. In person.

Santa Cruz on May 13th?

Want to be there sooner, but we have back to back matches and practices.

My pulse skyrockets at the thought of seeing him again.

> DAPHNE
>
> May 13th works.

GOOSE

Green bench, 5pm?

> DAPHNE
>
> My bench?

GOOSE

Yes.

> DAPHNE
>
> See you then.

I rack my brain, trying to remember if I mentioned my bench

to him. Regardless, he's coming. That gives me nineteen days to figure out what I'm going to do.

I miss him.

But he walked out of my life without much of an explanation. I understand he was hurt, but I need to know that he won't run every time there is a rough patch.

He's actually trying to heal, though. I mean, announcing to everyone that he's battling mental health issues and launching a foundation? Those are pretty big moves. Maybe that's what he needed to do to feel like he was enough?

After all of this, I owe him—and myself—a chance to hear him out.

Chapter 45
Daphne

MAY 1

Lyndhurst FC's Birds of a Feather Foundation Raises a Groundbreaking £2.5 Million One Week After Inception

MAY 3

More FC Players Speak Out About Mental Health

MAY 5

Cameron Hastings Files Charges Against Charlie Lewis, Leading to Shocking Suspension Right Before Lyndhurst and Overton Final!

MAY 11

Daphne Quinn Hosts Second Knitting Retreat

in San Francisco, Donating Half the Revenue
to The Kindness Coalition

AT THE END of the pier, a man sits alone on my green bench. His back is to me, but there's something achingly familiar about the way his shoulders hunch and the lazy waves in his hair. The setting sun splashes the sky with pinks and purples, casting a golden glow around him. The sound of waves crashing and seals barking does nothing to calm the milkshake of excitement and fear bubbling inside me.

Be big. You've got this.

The boardwalk planks groan under my hesitant steps, each creak matching my jittery nerves. Kids' laughter fizzes like soda, and tourists snap photos. None of that matters—my world has zoomed in on just him. Cameron must sense me; he turns, his eyes locking onto mine with an intensity that sends a delicious shiver down my spine. Then he's up, and suddenly it's like the universe is holding its breath.

He's wearing the red sweater I knitted for him, paired with his usual dark jeans and sneakers. His small, adorable smile is infuriatingly disarming, especially considering the serious conversation we need to have. There's an undeniable confidence in his stride as he walks toward me.

Something's different, but I can't put my finger on what.

Suddenly, my tongue feels like it's been replaced with a sandbag, and my throat tightens. All the words I carefully rehearsed over the past nineteen days vanish into thin air.

He stops just inches away. He opens his mouth, hesitates, and then says, "I love you."

"Oh." Of all the things he could have said, I never expected those three words. My eyes blink rapidly, my brain scrambling to process his declaration.

"Sorry, that's not how I planned to do that."

"Cameron—"

Another step forward, and I can barely catch my breath. "I put so much pressure on myself this season. I wanted to win so badly, both for me and to prove to everyone I wasn't broken. But as the season went on, I realized the only time I was happy, the only time I could forget about everything holding me back, was when I was with you. Even being in the box didn't bring me the joy it used to. So when I wasn't with you, it felt like I was drowning and—" His eyes meet mine, and they're filled with a sincerity that makes my heart do a little dance. "I didn't want you to be my life raft, Daphne. I didn't want to need saving."

"I don't think you need saving."

"I know that now. But after what happened with Rossi, Charlie, heck, even women I dated, I just kept avoiding it, hoping it would disappear." He winces, looking at the waves. "After the livestream scandal, a woman I was seeing went public, claiming to be my suffering girlfriend. She plastered private photos of me online and even announced she was going on *Lust Island* because I was too broken for her. The media ate it up."

I furrow my brows, trying to piece together what Jung had mentioned all those months ago about Mal Kelly being Cameron's ex. It must be her he's talking about.

"That's really terrible," I murmur, my heart aching for him.

"I felt like everyone had their lives together except me. But now I finally feel in control again. I know walking out on you was wrong, but I've been working on myself, going to therapy. I started the foundation. You inspired that."

Cameron Hastings, the guy who used to hide his feelings behind a tough exterior and monosyllabic grunts, is actually opening up.

"I saw the press conference."

"I was hoping you would."

I pause, a small smile quaking at the corner of my lips. "Your stockinette has definitely improved."

His golden eyes dance with laughter. "Sven is not as patient of a teacher as you."

"You boys did all right." I fumble with the bag on my shoulder. There's so much I want to ask, so much I want to say, but my mind is a whirlwind. "So, you're in therapy?"

"For over a month now. Apparently, I've been showing clear signs of C-PTSD, and it's not all that rare for men to deal with," he says, frowning. The thought of him enduring this alone twists my heart. "The team and I have been reaching out to players who might be struggling with their mental health, offering support. I didn't realize how many of us were silently suffering and how normalized it had become."

"Why?"

"Because it's what you would do. It's the right thing." He pauses, searching my face. "Daphne, I love you. I've never loved anything as much as I love you. Not even the game. You should've heard that from me sooner. I never should've asked you to lay low, suggested you step back from your platforms when that first rumor about us broke. I never should've tried to dim your light just because I was living in the shadows."

Tears spill from my eyes, and I can't hold them in. So much of him is still the same—the crease in his brow, the scruff on his face, that messily styled hair. But it feels like I'm meeting a part of him I never knew existed.

"Cameron, I never wanted to spend my time chipping away at your walls, only for them to spring back up again."

He inches closer to me. The sky envelops him in a vibrant cocoon, painting him in the hues of a setting sun.

"You're right," he murmurs, his voice barely audible over the gentle crash of the waves. "The real apology I owe you is for leaving without an explanation. I couldn't admit any of this to myself. I was too afraid, too ashamed, too embarrassed to say the words out loud, to admit that I was hurt. I had no right to avoid discussing it with you. I shouldn't have ended our last conversation the way I did."

Tears fall from my eyes. These past two months, I've thrown myself into being the best version of me. But his absence has been like a bad song stuck on repeat. The ache of what we could have been has lingered. Despite it all, I still dreamed of a life together, even when he needed to prioritize himself.

I still want us to have a chance. Could we?

"It really hurt when you walked out on me, on us," I say, my voice steady but soft. "I understand why you had to do it. Trust me, of all people, I get it. I know how hard trauma and pain can be, and I'm genuinely glad you're finding your way back. But you didn't let me choose whether or not I deserved you. You didn't give me the chance to understand. In a relationship, two people get to make that choice, and I didn't need you to protect me from yourself."

"I was foolish to try and protect you."

My heart twists. "I thought we could get through anything, and these past two months without you...well, they've been dreadful, Cameron. I love my life in London. I love my friends. I love...I love you. And if we're going to try again, I need to know we can face things together and that you won't leave me when you're scared."

"I never want to leave you again."

His words strike a chord deep within me. Despite everything, I can't deny the love that still lingers, the hope that we can make it work.

The salty breeze tugs at my hair, and my heart races—not just for Cameron, but for the hidden burdens he's been carrying. Change is hard, but if my Yes Year has shown me anything, it's that the ache of disappointment is a small price for the growth it brings, even when it hurts. I want to be with Cameron, and that's the choice I'm making.

"Do you mean that?" I ask, my voice wobbling like a poorly

balanced Jenga tower, a cocktail of hope and fear swirling in my chest. If his changes are real, maybe, just maybe, we have a chance.

"I do," he says, flashing me a smile that's all sincerity. "I'll do a thousand push-ups to prove it, and I'll untangle a million balls of yarn if it means you'll forgive me." He chuckles, and it's this warm, genuine sound that makes my heart do an embarrassing little flip inside my chest. "I'll show you every day, Daphne, that I'm on the right path now. No more bottling up my emotions. I feel like I can finally be the man I want to be."

"You're just saying that because you like it when I force you to do push-ups and untangle my yarn," I tease, feeling a tiny bubble of joy pop inside me.

"*Love* it. Almost as much as I love you," he says, his eyes soft and sincere.

"I love you too," I whisper, tears of relief pricking at the corners of my eyes. "I just need your word, because you've always had mine."

"You have it. You have me. Always," he says, his voice ringing with conviction.

We kiss, and it's like a thousand tiny fireworks explode in the most delightful way. The Santa Cruz Boardwalk hums around us, the laughter from the roller coasters and the salty ocean air blending into a perfect symphony.

My trusty green bench, the one that's been a silent witness to all my dramatic monologues and tear-filled moments, now gets to see this burst of happiness.

His lips are soft and warm, moving with a tenderness that makes my heart do an actual gymnastics routine. I feel the promise of new beginnings and the comforting realization that maybe we're finally on the right path.

"I want to go back home," I murmur, pulling back just enough to look into his eyes.

"I want that too," he replies, his gaze steady and full of affection.

"I can't yet, though. There's stuff going on here that I need to wrap up," I say, a twinge of regret in my voice. "And *Lust Island* is flying me out for the premiere next week. But I can come to your final game," I explain, feeling this weird mix of excitement and responsibility. "We can press play on us then."

"I'd love that," he says, his eyes sparkling with appreciation. He takes my hands in his, giving them a gentle squeeze. "I'm sorry, Daphne Quinn. For everything."

His apology, sincere and heartfelt, dissolves the last of my defenses. I pull him close, feeling our hearts sync up like a perfectly choreographed dance number. "You've really leveled up your apology game." I giggle.

"Does that mean you forgive me?" he asks.

"I do," I say, unable to hide my smile.

"Then there's one last thing I need to do." He grabs my hand, and I can feel my cheeks heating up. "Duck, will you be my girlfriend?"

"For real?"

"For real."

"Well, in that case, of course, I'll be your girlfriend."

I kiss him hard. I kiss him like I'm trying to make up for every second we spent apart, every second we weren't together. The warmth in my chest fills me with joy and hope, like I've just discovered the meaning of life in a really soft cardigan.

"Now, how about we ride a roller coaster?" he asks, grinning like he's just invented fun.

"What?" I laugh, shaking my head. "Who are you, and what have you done with Cameron?"

"I mean it! Let's go have some fun. It's what we do best, remember?" he says. "Say yes."

"All right, but if I scream, you owe me ice cream," I declare, trying to sound stern but failing miserably. "And if we're giving this a shot, then everything is one giant yes, okay? One giant Yes Life."

"A Yes Life. Deal."

"Deal. Now let's go find the craziest roller coaster out there." And with that, we're off, laughing like kids who just discovered their parents' candy stash.

Maybe second chances are just chances, and maybe we all take steps forward and back, but we can't be big all the time. If Cameron's learning that it's okay to be small, then I can rely on him to be any size with me, and I can be any size with him.

Chapter 46
Cameron

MAY 22

Lust Island Premieres Tonight, Featuring Daphne Quinn and Georgia Woods's Anti-Bullying Knitting Initiative

MAY 28

Mateo Rossi Faces Pressure to "Reevaluate His Tactics" or Step Down, as Told by Inside Sources

I'M SITTING on the bench in the guest locker room at Overton Stadium, lacing up my cleats. Never had I imagined when I returned to this place, after all that's happened, that I'd feel so differently than the last time I was here.

It's been a month since I last heard the echoing voices of my old coach and Charlie. The nightmares still come, sprout up without resolve, but I don't feel so afraid anymore. I'm no longer waiting for the other shoe to drop, no longer expecting the worst.

After the press conference, more and more players have come forth about misconduct or spoken out about the importance of prioritizing mental health, both on the field and for fans at home. Like Daphne, I've been trying to be outspoken about what I experienced, and it's helped more than the year I spent hiding. Reporters have been requesting comments and quotes on the Birds of a Feather Foundation. Thankfully, my agent has been a rockstar at fielding them and only scheduling interviews with papers that matter, not those itching for a spell of gossip they can sensationalize.

Still, I know my name's been lighting up the media circuit now that Charlie's suspension is in place. But I've never cared less about what they have to say.

Over a year ago, I let myself believe that being strong meant being silent. My teammates and Daphne taught me the opposite. Now, I get to share that with others. I get to show my LA team, who are here watching the game, and my family the person I've become. The man I'm proud of.

From being battered to competing in the final game of the Premier League season.

The familiar chaos of pregame rituals buzzes around me—taping ankles, adjusting jerseys, muttering last-minute prayers. I tape my knuckles one hand at a time, the black tape tight but comforting. Left first, then right. Then I put on my gloves, feeling the familiar grip, and slather them in Vaseline, making them slick but resilient, a final touch to complete my personal rite. My heart hammers against my chest like it's trying to escape, each beat syncing with the team's collective bustle.

I glance around at my teammates.

My new family. My friends.

We've poured everything into this season—the bad and the good. I let them see my entire heart, all of me, and they've done the same tenfold, never looking back.

Every single one of us has bled, sweated, and cried for a shot at the Premier League title. Since we were little, with a dream and a football, this has been a goal of ours. Of any player. I'll get to carry the legacy of this game with me forever—my name memorialized alongside my teammates.

Lyndhurst FC has always been the underdog, never quite breaking through to the top two, but today feels different. Today, we're brothers, bound by trust.

I force myself to stay present, joining the huddle of teammates bumping shoulders. Coach is gearing up for one of his *you got this* speeches, but my mind keeps drifting to Daphne. As we stand in a tight huddle, Coach surprises us with a simple, "Boys, you go out there and you fucking win."

We glance at each other, sharing knowing smiles. We're ready to give it our all.

"Hastings, send us out?" Tamu nods, dropping his hand in the center.

I slap my glove over his, and every single one of my teammates piles their palms on mine.

"Let's fucking roar. Three, two, one," I shout. "Lyndhurst!"

The locker room erupts in beastly roars as we roll out and onto the pitch. My heart swells with pride, soaking in the magnitude of the moment. We exchange quick hugs and slap each other's asses. The air is thick with anticipation and the smell of sweaty socks.

"Let's do this!" someone yells, and we all echo the sentiment with another determined roar.

I'm a fucking lion. A Lyndhurst Lion. And I'm going to do my team proud.

This is what we dreamed of as kids, kicking around tattered balls in empty fields. Now, under the blinding stadium lights, that dream is within our grasp. As we take our positions, I methodically tap the top left corner of the goal, then the top right, and finally look up at the stands. My eyes search the crowd until they find the familiar lavender hair—just as she said.

Daphne's here, watching the final game of the Premier League. A warmth spreads through me, though I keep my expression neutral. I lift my hand and form a small heart shape with my fingers, and she mirrors the gesture from the directors box. *I'm going to give this everything I've got,* I promise her and myself, before turning my attention back to the field.

This is it. The endgame. Lyndhurst FC versus Overton.

My past and my present.

THE MATCH TEETERS on the precipice of the final grueling stretch of overtime. The roar of the crowd at Overton Stadium blisters my eardrums. Our fans have been relentless. The thunderous vibrations of their cheering pulse under my cleats.

We can win this.

We're neck and neck with Overton, squaring off for the winning points and championship title.

My legs burn. My muscles are scorched from so many dives.

The game's final six minutes are imminent. We're up 2-1.

The tension is thick. Overton's attackers are a force to be reckoned with, ruthless and unyielding in their pursuit of victory. They've been on our side of the field, desperately seeking an opportunity.

A familiar weight of responsibility settles on my shoulders. The fate of the game is going to be determined by me and my defensive line—Sven, Omar, Ibrahim, and Jung. They've been an impenetrable wall of resistance against Overton's fierce onslaught.

Sven has been shadowing Overton's star striker, an echo to his every move. Omar is intercepting passes with an uncanny sense of anticipation. Ibrahim is our bulwark in the center, while Jung, the fleetest of us all, is thwarting any attempts down the flanks.

My heart nearly collapses when Overton sees an opening.

Their winger launches a cross, a perfect arc soaring across the stadium's night sky. I track it like a hawk. *Be big.* Time seems to slow. *Be impenetrable.* I watch the trajectory of the ball. I can predict where it will land. I spring into action, my heart pounding against my ribs, every muscle in my body coiled and ready.

"Right! Right!" I yell, my voice echoing into the defense line.

Omar darts at my command, cutting off the striker's direct route to the goal as he turns into a human barricade.

Stay focused.

At the same time, Sven bodychecks Overton's center-forward, disrupting his run.

No ball is getting past us.

Meanwhile, Ibrahim and Jung are forming a barrier in front of the net.

We're not going to let the ball touch the net.

The ball hurtles toward the goal like a meteor on a collision course.

I suck in a deep breath, momentarily shutting out the noise of the crowd, the shouts of my teammates, the pounding of my heart. *Focus.*

My eyes track the spinning sphere of leather in the sky.

I fucking got it.

I launch myself at the ball. The world blurs around the edges. There's a moment of weightlessness, of suspension, as I stretch out my gloved hand.

And then, a rush of sheer relief as my fingers connect with the rough surface of the ball and I slam it back into my chest.

I got it.

I land heavily on the ground, the ball clutched safely in my hands. I look up at the scoreboard, my heartbeat hammering in my ears.

We've done it. We've held them off.

We did it.

Lyndhurst FC is the winner of the Premier League for the second time in its history.

The moment the final whistle screeches, the stadium erupts. Our fans roar louder than lions as they pour from the stands, their faces painted in our team colors. Tears are flowing from even the most stoic among them.

My teammates are on me in seconds, faces shining with sweat and pure glee. In a blink, I'm weightless, suspended in a moment of absolute victory as they launch me into the air above them. I'm in the eye of a storm of celebration. The pulse in my veins sloshes in my ears. Fans flood the field. Purple and white confetti bursts from the sky like stars raining down on me, and my head spins.

Then I see her.

Daphne.

A flash of lavender right in the middle of this chaotic celebration. Next to her, Bea bolts to the left, probably spotting Ivan. Our eyes lock. The crowd continues pulsating around us, growing larger and larger, but she's the only thing I can focus on. She fights her way through the sea of ecstatic fans to reach me.

Time seems to stretch out, and the world fades away until it's just Daphne and this pull between us. Until it's my girl running toward me. My number on her back.

When she finally reaches me, my teammates drop me back onto the field, and I yank her into my arms. Relief and joy surge through me. She fits against me like she was made for me.

"I'm so happy to see you," I yell.

"Me too." Her body vibrates, probably from the echoes of our victory. The team yells around us. Her cheeks are flushed, brighter than the stadium lights. And her eyes—those eyes that outshine any star—meet mine. I hoist her up, her laughter ringing in my ears. This laugh is the sweetest victory chant.

"I love you!" I shout. "I love you, Daphne Quinn. I love you, I love you—I am so down bad with love for you."

"I love you too." She presses her forehead against mine, her palms cupping my jaw.

"I never want to go a single day without you in my life."

She shakes her head. "I'm proud of you, Cameron, for finding the courage to grow."

"For me and for us. There was never another option." I can't believe that I almost lost her. That thought shakes me more than any opponent on the field ever could. I'll never make that mistake again. "You and me, Duck?"

She nods. "Yes, yes, yes." Her words are like a chant in my ears.

Having her here with me, in my arms, makes me feel like I can take on the world. It feels right; it feels like home. This victory isn't just for me or my team. It's for her, for making me stronger, for making me better. For helping me find myself.

A reporter thrusts a camera in our faces. The flash is blinding, an unwanted guest in this intimate moment. But instead of recoiling, I make a choice. A choice I should've made a long fucking time ago.

"Daphne," I mutter, my voice barely a whisper among the ruckus.

She glances up, those wide eyes full of questions.

"Yes?" she manages, her voice a shaky melody amid the uproar.

I lean in, taking her face in my hands. "I'm going to kiss you."

"No one's ever announced it like that before, Goose." Her laughter rings in my ears as our lips finally meet.

This kiss shouts the endless tomorrows we're going to have. The life we will create together. It feels like the end of a long, grueling marathon. It tastes of the sweat of the game, the whispered doubts we stomped into the ground, the sweetness of her tongue. Raucous noise, my teammates, the blinding lights…they just fade into oblivion.

All that's left is the feel of her lips against mine and the synchrony of our racing hearts.

"Too much?" I mumble against her lips, all too aware of the flashing cameras. Frankly, I couldn't care less. I want the whole world to know that Daphne Quinn has me.

"Not nearly enough." She laughs.

"Good."

Forget the trophy. This right here, my two feet on solid ground, her in my arms, is the real victory. Everything I fought for and won.

Epilogue
Daphne

Six Months Later

Today is moving day!

Since I moved back to London in May, after Lyndhurst won the championship, Cameron and I have flourished like wildflowers on Miracle-Gro. We decided to stay in London because it's the city where we fell in love, our circle of friends is here, and his contract with Lyndhurst got renewed. It feels like we never took time apart. We tried to keep our separate apartments at the Lion's Lodge, but it was pointless—he never seemed to leave my bed, except on weekends when he was off blocking goals at away matches or when I was traveling through the UK for my knitting retreats, hitting a new town every month with my yarn and needles!

I steal a glance at the driver's seat, where Cameron's grinning like he just pulled off a last-second save in a World Cup final. We're pulling into the parking lot of his—scratch that —*our* apartment, and he's rocking the navy sweater I gave him this morning for his birthday. Nestled in my lap is a surprise birthday cake, and he's completely clueless. He thinks I popped into Petal & Plate to snag some moving-day pastries, which I was very easily able to convince him were a thing. Little does he know, the surprise I have planned is going to be one for the books.

Cameron is happier now.

I am, too.

The gloomy Eeyore cloud that used to hover over him has evaporated; he's going to therapy, actively engaging with his friends, and giving back at the foundation. Charlie Lewis was permanently barred from the Premier League after the investigation, and Cameron's old coach, Mateo Rossi, was pressured into retiring. Despite wishing more justice would've been served, I'm so glad that he's never going to coach another team ever again.

So is Cameron.

His smiles are real now, practically permanent, and I'm obsessed.

"I have to say, you look ridiculously handsome in that color," I remark, placing my hand on his thigh and leaning over to plant a quick kiss on his cheek.

"Is it bringing out my cool winter tones?" he retorts with a sarcastic grin, cupping the back of my head and pulling me in for a real kiss. No matter how many times we find ourselves in this exact situation, I always crave more.

Last week, for our Monday date night, I decided to spice things up and take us to get our color palettes analyzed. Picture this: Cameron, all banged up from his match over the weekend, sitting in a chic studio surrounded by swatches of every conceivable hue. The stylist, Stella—an eccentric woman in oversized glasses—draped different colored fabrics over his shoulders, declaring with utmost seriousness, *These cool tones will make your big brown eyes pop!* He just grunted and nodded along. I couldn't stop laughing.

We still keep our weekly date night tradition alive, a relic from my Yes Year that's now *our* Yes Life. Maybe one day we'll exhaust our list of new activities, but until then, I fully intend to savor every cozy night we spend together. My favorite is ordering takeout from a new restaurant and watching a movie that will undoubtedly make Cameron cry. So far, the tearjerkers include *Coco*, *Marley & Me*, and *Suzume*.

When I'm not orchestrating my retreats or working on new collaborations—which have skyrocketed after this season of *Lust Island*; other shows want exclusive Wooly Duck projects and celebrities want to use my patterns for fundraising—I've invested back into my business. This includes hiring a personal assistant to manage comments, plan retreats, and book guest speakers to discuss the importance of mental health.

After *Lust Island* ended, Georgia and I had an inbox full of collaboration requests. I nearly fainted when we got asked to work on a new book-to-movie adaptation for *Secrets, Sex, and Sunflowers* by Lily Rodin, coming out early next year. I'm also running monthly knitting retreats at Petal & Plate, training people worldwide to host their own retreats, and have been a guest speaker on anxiety relief hobbies in Lisbon, Athens, and Oslo.

Talk about leveling up!

"What do you think?" I say, leaning back and unbuckling my seatbelt with a dramatic flourish. "By the end of the year, I'll be rocking a fuchsia sweater. It's totally on your color palette."

He rolls his eyes, smirking. "I'll wear one if you're the one taking it off."

I laugh. "Can I get that in writing?" I ask as he steps out of the car.

I hop out too, the crisp autumn breeze sending a delightful shiver down my spine.

"I still can't believe you didn't let me hire movers," Cameron grumbles, yanking my suitcase from his car's trunk, which is so tiny it barely fits a single item.

"Are you serious? You saw how pumped the guys were about

helping us move." Sven and Omar practically fell over themselves to get a sneak peek of Cameron's apartment. They'll be here soon with the moving truck—Omar borrowed one from his family, and, miraculously, it fit all my stuff. But I'm still stashing some things at my place at the Lion's Lodge for our Wednesday night reality TV marathons.

"If anyone gets hurt, Coach will have our heads, especially since we're on a winning streak," Cameron says, though his tone is more amused than worried. He wheels my suitcase toward the elevator, and I trot along after him.

"Then you better pitch in, birthday boy." I give his shoulder a playful nudge, and he grins as he hits the button for the penthouse suite.

"Before everyone gets here, I have a surprise for you," he says.

"But it's *your* birthday!" I tilt my head, one eyebrow raised.

"And my favorite thing to do is spoil you," he replies with a grin.

I laugh. "Well, who am I to deny you what you want on your birthday?" I give him a cheeky smile.

We stroll through our apartment. The sun is out, but the clouds are doing their best to stage a coup. He stops at the door of his second bedroom, which he's been using as a gym.

"Go on," he says, motioning me forward.

Curious, I push open the door and step into…an entirely different room. Custom-made cabinets line the walls, a cozy window nook looks out over the sprawling London skyline, and the walls are a soft, dreamy purple.

There's my tripod facing a clean wall with fairy lights dangling down it. Baskets for my yarn. A giant corkboard with sparkling pins in it.

I turn to him, wide-eyed. "When did you have time to do all this?"

"I know a guy," he says, leaning casually against the doorframe like he didn't just orchestrate an HGTV-level transformation overnight. "Do you like it?"

My heart thuds against my rib cage. "You made a whole room for me? But where are you going to work out? Your biceps have their own zip code!"

He chuckles. "I think they'll survive. I've been liking working out at Lyndhurst Stadium with the guys. Besides, I thought you'd get more use out of it. I left space for your boucle chair, and your pink couch can go here. Now you can use this room to work on meetings and collaborations and to film all your YouTube videos."

I blink. Cameron giving me a whole room is like a unicorn offering free rides—it's magical and a bit unbelievable. This is next-level.

I wrap my hands around his waist. "I love it. Are you sure it's not too much estrogen too fast?"

"Duck, how many times do I have to tell you that this is *our* home? I love your stuff."

"Even the sparkly pink things?"

"Especially those."

My cheeks flush. "Well, I wish the couch was already here so I could thank you properly."

"Hello, we are here!" Sven's voice booms from the living room.

I roll my eyes and laugh. "Guess that'll have to wait. Time to get this party started!"

"Party?" Cameron tilts his head, a puzzled puppy dog look on his face.

"Yes, party! Moving heavy furniture is the new rave, didn't you know?" I wink at him before darting out to greet Sven. "All right, muscle man, let's get this show on the road!"

"Hey, guys!"

"Thank goodness, no narrow stairwells this time." Omar chuckles, lugging my pink couch with Sven right behind him.

The rest of the crew is juggling my boxes and the big surprise that Cameron insists he won't like, but I know he will. They start to filter in with balloons in tow and grins plastered on their faces.

"Happy birthday!" they shout in unison.

Cameron gives me a side-eye. "What did I—"

"It's not a birthday party!" I insist.

His grumpy, gorgeous face doesn't buy it for a second.

"It's a housewarming party," Tamu explains with a mischievous wink, signaling the guys to help.

"We're right behind you!" Bea announces as she strides into the apartment, Ivan and the offensive team trailing behind her.

"I thought you said you were going to keep it small," Cameron mutters, his grumpy demeanor only slightly softened by the sight of so many people.

"What can I say? There are a lot of people who want to celebrate you—I mean, us moving in together! Duh!" I chirp, my sunny disposition trying to melt his perpetual frown.

"Hi, Bea!" I squeal, skipping away from Cameron to hug her. After Ivan retired at the end of last season, they've both been knee-deep in organizing the first-ever Birds of a Feather auction, aimed at supporting young athletes in sports leagues. The plan is to have professionals talk to the kids about mental health, helping them understand that their worth isn't tied to their performance in sports.

More people pour in, and soon the table is laden with presents. Cameron's laughing, surrounded by his teammates, who've surprised him with a full-sized *Mortal Kombat II* arcade game. But my real surprise is just around the corner.

"Brother!" Dante calls out, stepping into our not-quite-lived-in-yet apartment.

Cameron's head whips around so fast, I half expect him to pull a muscle. I practically bounce on my tiptoes, beaming like I just won the lottery.

"You invited my siblings?" Cameron's tough-guy façade cracks as he pulls Dante into a hug.

"Sure did!" I chirp, my smile bright enough to power a small city.

"Brooklyn and Alec should be right behind me," Dante adds, patting Cameron on the back.

Seizing the brief opportunity, I dash to the kitchen. There it is: the gluten-free, no-sugar, no-frosting cake Rosie made. On top is a fruit-carved goose kicking a soccer ball. It's ridiculous. It's perfect.

Cameron catches sight of me.

"Happy birthday, Goose," I say. The room starts to sing, and Cameron's grumpiness melts, replaced by a smile that could rival the sun.

I remember lying in bed on my twenty-sixth birthday, at the start of my Yes Year, dreaming about all the ways my life could change. Volunteering more, maybe skydiving, making a friend or two, even finding a boyfriend. Fast forward a year and a half, and here I am, moving in with my first and only love.

Acknowledgments

After writing our first series together, starting out with fresh, new characters was daunting, but Cameron and Daphne's story made it easy. These two made us remember why writing truly fills our hearts in a way nothing else can.

We write love stories that are meant to make you feel alive again. What does that mean? To us, it means handling the toughest, scariest moments of our lives, moments filled with anxiety, stress, burnout, heartache, and grief, with a little bit of humor and love. Because life is weird that way. It can break you in half and then knit you back together.

It's the little things that breathe life back into us, like sending a text message to your friend only to find out she's sending the exact same one back to you and laughing about how you share one brain cell. It's venting for hours about what we learn in therapy and how it relates to our reality TV addiction. It's the love notes our partners leave and the water they bring to us when we haven't left our keyboards for over an hour. It's the bit of sunshine on a cloudy day and a sprinkle of rain to break up the thick humidity.

We always hope our stories do what they're intended to do—make you feel less alone with the pain you carry. We hope they make you feel seen in any struggles you face and give you an opportunity to laugh at something goofy, odd, and fun. Because fiction, at its heart, is both a lesson and an escape. We hope you walk away with a smidge of both after reading *Close Knit*.

Daphne's openness about her mental health and her positive

outlook on life is something we deeply admire and strive to emulate. She teaches us to love ourselves out loud and without apology. Every day, Daphne shows up with her best self, being loud, silly, and childlike because that's what brings her joy. While we may not all thrive on candy and sass, we can all aspire to Daphne's fortitude and bravery, to viewing our past not just as something to overcome but as a stepping stone for evolution.

Cameron's journey with C-PTSD is deeply personal, and stepping into his mind was challenging at times. When we decided to write about a family with intense personalities and significant accomplishments, we had to consider how each thought and situation would be handled. Each moment of self-worth can be called into question by the smallest thing, and the only thing every athlete needs to keep going is grit and a ton of self-esteem—which our lovely goalkeeper learns to cultivate. We often expect things from people, whether knowingly or subconsciously, and the expectation for someone to have it all figured out comes naturally to us. Writing Cameron's story, with its deep pain of toxic masculinity and the constant need to appear strong, is personal to us, as it is to many people in our lives who struggle with vulnerability. We hope to have handled it with the care and love it deserves.

If you are struggling with your mental health, know that you are not alone and that you are so loved. We hope that you found comfort in these pages.

This story is also for everyone who has spent years dreaming about football players. There's something incredibly scrumptious about a man who not only looks great on the field but is also open about his feelings.

No part of this book would be possible without our lovely team behind us.

Caroline A., we absolutely adore you and appreciate your patience and desire to make our stories the best they can be. Your input is always invaluable. You challenge us to become better writers, and for that we are tremendously thankful.

Caroline K., we truly appreciate the meticulousness and thoughtfulness you provide to our novels. We cannot stress enough how thankful we are to have you on our team.

Thank you to our proofreader, Christine Yates. Our beta team: Nicole McCrane, Isabella F., Jos, Kejsi, Logan, Sophia Welch, and Brooke. Your feedback is unmatched. You never fail to make us laugh at your comments, and you provide the best ideas. You all deserve a Premier League football player equipped with a hoop earring to spoil you with his credit card and buy you endless books and treats.

For the Stone Romantics on Patreon, we love you more than words can describe.

To our lovely readers, whether this is your first dive into our world or you're back for the seventh adventure, we can't thank you enough for being here. Each post, share, video, and purchase means the world to us. We started as two corporate gals with a big dream, and because of you that dream is now our everyday reality. Your love for our stories and steadfast support let us chase our passion daily. From the bottom of our hearts, thank you!

And finally, to our partners, who give us space to play and heal our inner children, who refill our coffee mugs, and who will stay up all night listening to us talk about our imaginary friends. We love you. #betweenthemeats for life.

Playlist

"Lose Control (Strings Version)" by Teddy Swims
"Did I Make You Up?" by half•alive
"New Person, Same Old Mistakes" by Tame Impala
"Bring Me to Life" by Evanescence
"we can't be friends (wait for your love)" by Ariana Grande
"Loud Places" by Jamie xx, Romy
"Alors on danse (Radio Edit)" by Stromae
"Sunlight" by Hozier
"The Alchemy" by Taylor Swift
"Just Fine (Alternate Version)" by Desiree Dawson
"Dispose of Me" by Omar Apollo
"The Winner Takes It All (Unplugged)" by Natalie Madigan
"Cold Little Heart (Radio Edit)" by Michael Kiwanuka
"Seven Nation Army" by The White Stripes
"A Troubled Mind" by Noah Kahan
"Birds of a Feather" by Billie Eilish

.

About the Authors

Kels & Denise are authors, best friends, and the definition of the found family trope. The pair bonded over their love for romance and turned all their late-night chats into writing together. Their enjoyment for storytelling morphed into writing impactful love stories. While Kels travels the world with her high-school-sweetheart husband, Denise is making her way through every restaurant with her boyfriend.

Stay in touch!
@authorkelsdenisestone
kelsdenisestone.com

Join our newsletter *The Sticky Note*
kelsdenisestone.com/the-sticky-note
Join our Patreon for exclusive content

Also By Kels & Denise Stone
Perks & Benefits Series:

Water Under the Bridge
Workplace Romance

Our Scorching Summer
Friends to Lovers Romance

On Cloud Nine
Fake Dating Romance

Falling for Meadow
Small Town Romance

Printed in Great Britain
by Amazon

49207351Π00243